ROTHACKE
Rothacker, Jordan A.
And wind will wash away.

AND WIND
WILL WASH AWAY

AND WIND WILL WASH AWAY

A NOVEL BY JORDAN A. ROTHACKER

Deeds Publishing | Athens

Published by Deeds Publishing in Athens, GA
www.deedspublishing.com

Printed in The United States of America

Cover art by Matt King and Mark Babcock. Text layout by Mark Babcock.

Library of Congress Cataloging-in-Publications data is available upon request.

ISBN 978-1-944193-26-3

Books are available in quantity for promotional or premium use. For information,
email info@deedspublishing.com.

First Edition, 2016

10 9 8 7 6 5 4 3 2 1

Dedicated with love to Jessica Erin
and
in memory of Caroline Daniel Ramsey (1982-2015)
and
Thomas Edward Polk II (1940-2014)

AUTHOR'S PREFACE

The world has always been and will always be a pulsing fire, flaring up accordingly and dying down accordingly, with the cycling of the eternal world breath.   —Heraclitus

Dear Reader,

The theme of this work is wind, so I have called upon a muse of wind. As a muse and theme, wind contains the futile passions, the blustery sufferings, and all active, invisible, ephemera. Dante punished the lustful—those who subject reason to desire—with whipping crosswinds in his second ring of Inferno, but the range of all his sinners could justifiably suffer this lex talionis, as could most of us. Wind is the doom of reason in an illusory world, a world constructed and maintained by desire. And is it not Hobbes who reminds us that curiosity is lust of the mind?

You are about to behold Jonathan Wind and his adventures into mystery. This work was composed between 2002 and 2005 and all of the action there within takes place over a short amount of time in autumn of 2003. Jonathan Wind's time of adventure was one of blustery rhetoric and much suffering around the world. With the ascendancy of the Internet, the ubiquity of the mobile phone with increasing "smarts," and an American presidency defined by creative war aims, the time in which we encounter our protagonist was a time of great winds and windy pursuits.

The ancient Israelites referred both to wind and the breath of their god as *ruach*. For the Greeks, *pneuma* was at once breath and soul. *Spiritus* served the same function for the Romans, and the Rome-centered Christians found their god, their soul, and their wind in that same spiritus. Eventually, the concept fractured in the west into oh so many words, winds, passions, sufferings, songs of soul, and daily gods.

I can only promise that I did my best at trying to capture myriad winds in the pages of this book, but my net has many holes. My humble tale has no moral other than to heed one's elders, for chaos is older than order and nature older than man.

Ave atque vale!
Jordan A. Rothacker

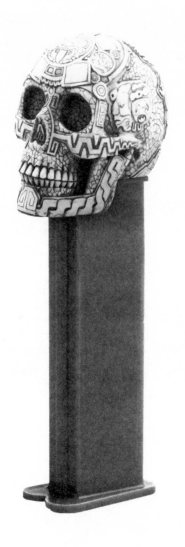

I. EOS

Let the stars of the dawn be dark; let it hope for light, but have none; may it not see the eyelids of the morning—because it did not shut the doors on my mother's womb, and hide trouble from my eyes. —Job 3:9-10

"DON'T TRY TO UNDERSTAND ME, BABY, I'M THE WIND," HE SAID, BUT that old line, a line from a television show they both enjoyed, a line he often delivered to make her laugh, now just made her cry even more. He felt like an asshole, but that didn't stop him from walking out on her and out of her apartment. It was a sleepless night and he was tired of fighting. He needed to get out of there. If he couldn't end the fight, at least he could finally end the night.

Aurora, as the fiery dawn is called by some, kissed Jonathan Wind good morning from polished tips of his black shoes to the crown of his golden head, her lipless lights laying a warm caress to the black pants and white shirt of his uniform and the beige barn-jacket employed to conceal his sidearm and shield. Out in the bright coolness of the morning he sighed deeply and noticed for a brief moment a tiny place within him that wanted to cry, but he grit his teeth and rolled his head clockwise and back, releasing tension with crackling noises.

He slid his left hand into his pants pocket and shook out where his boxers were bunched and sticky with the slow drying residue of last evening's one high point. He was grateful for Aurora, her colors peach and rose bleeding out slowly behind the dark building, half the sky lessening in blackness to blue.

His girlfriend had picked him up from the station last night to go back to her place and now he looked out across the parking lot at nothing to carry him away. Trudging forward, he crossed the parking lot, head down, and out through the complex's brick gates, turning towards the Circle K station at the corner. Soft wet blades of grass, standing and reaching easterly, in their own dawn-worship, were crushed down by Wind's black soles, spilling their dew about his leather, as he made his way up a hill off the sidewalk to the gas station.

The pay phones faced out to the gas pumps just past the front. When Jonathan Wind reached the second phone, he leaned within its walls and breathed out a thin cloud from deep inside his lungs to watch Aurora's lights tear through it. With his left hand he dug into his pocket and produced a small, mixed grouping of change, laying a dime and quarter onto the top of the telephone. Repositioning himself, he eased his right hand into the low pocket of his barn jacket, gripping the body of a Pez dispenser and allowing his thumb to slide across the smooth surface of its head. Mechanically, he brought it to his mouth, his thoughts only as far away as last night, and tipped the plastic Dwight Eisenhower head back before popping its cartridge into his mouth. The yellow brick of candy dissolved on his tongue, and when the taste and smell of artificial lemon released, it flooded him with a kaleidoscopic montage of unfocused childhood memories spun out of its similarities to the smell of lemon Pledge.

He was drawn to a clear scene from his tenth year, a scene in which he cried alone. The taste of tears and smell of Pledge welled up inside his mind. The young Jonathan had not yet cried over the death of his father, even after three years; he was always strict in his coordination of emotions. They were living in their first Atlanta apartment. Besides the tears, it was an ordinary memory, like any other night since his mother had to go to work and he was left with the care of his sister, Astrid. He had walked her home from Kinder Care on his way from school. They watched television and ate macaroni and cheese and hot-dogs before he put the three year old to bed. Before he tucked himself in, young Jonathan would clean the kitchen, doing the dishes of his dinner, taking out the trash, and generally tidy the small apartment, making a particular effort to dust and polish the few wood surfaces. Since his mother worked a two-to-ten shift, unless there was over-time, at the US Postal Facility, he always tried to be asleep by the time she got home; the boy, as prideful as his mother, he did not want to see her tired and sad. And so she would have no worries awaiting her at home, he cleaned. Like all the other nights back then, that night he pretended to sleep when she came up to kiss him. Maybe she knew he was awake, but it was his young understanding that this was easier for both of them. She touched his hair gently, and said she loved him, and that she was sorry, and then she sighed with her whole body and went downstairs. Through the floor he could hear her cleaning. He could picture her then, a prematurely aged angel, working beneath the shadow of her bent back in low light. Betrayed and sobbing, young Jonathan, with his little wind, beat his small fists against his pillow. He was too young to understand what martyring was and her slaving was taken as a rejection of his love-offering: the care of his sister and the home. It seemed his efforts were not good enough. She worked all day, could she not let him give her repose? The rejection made him

3

feel very alone and powerless. He could not save her; she would not let him. He had given her his only power and only offering, a child's desire to please his mother, and yet she wouldn't accept it out of her own similar compulsion to please. He felt that she denied him, that her love negated his. It was the first time he felt that he must leave her, that one day he must run away from her home, from this city, from this state. Through a process that stirred multifarious smells of Mr. Clean, Murphy's Oil Soap, Lysol Spray, and Pledge, the smell that now remained was that of chemical lemon as his mother polished the wooden furniture that he had polished only hours before, covering his small efforts with her own.

Coming back to the sticky lemon Pez candy residue now on his tongue he tried to push away thoughts of his mother. In their place were thoughts of his girlfriend, Monica, a woman frighteningly similar to his mother, whose home he had just left. He had walked directly to this pay phone with intention and would stand for no further delay, yet in a moment of reflexive weakness, his right hand went back into his jacket pocket and gripped the Pez shaft with thumb on Ike's smooth head. With his free hand he trickled the quarter and dime into the change slot, positioned the phone on his shoulder and dialed the ten digits to an apartment of another woman across town. Removing the Pez dispenser, and waiting for the first ring, he chided himself for his deceit. Between the first and second ring he flicked the plastic Ike-head up and down and thought quickly of how calling his mistress, Flora, was a knee-jerk reaction to a fight with Monica. By the fourth ring, the flicking resounded loudly and he just wanted his thoughts to be gone and her voice to calm him. After the fifth ring the other line answered and he heard a man's voice slowly and cautiously say hello before he slammed down the receiver and smashed the bald head of the Pez dispenser into the shiny metal front of the pay phone.

Jonathan Wind sighed deeply, with more anger than frustration, and paced in a little circle towards the trashcan at the yellow curb and back to the phone, crunching on the shattered remains of a once well-cast plastic likeness of Dwight Eisenhower and broken yellow bricks of lemon Pez. It was too early in the morning for that to be a client, unless someone spent the whole night with Flora, so it was either a wealthy client or it was an actual romantic date, thought Jonathan Wind. He was not jealous of her clients. He made a great effort to understand her and her work and trusted her more than he trusted most people, but it hurt him to need her and there be someone else with her, answering her phone. He did not think it was actually a date; for in matters of the heart he believed her to be faithful to only him, which he knew to be strange, since he was faithful to her in no outward way; his heart, like his time, always fractured. He had been seeing her secretly for just over five months, since right before his twenty-seventh birthday, when he first questioned her as a witness to a suicide. The jumper who took a seven-story fall landed not fifty feet from her as she passed. Finding her visibly shaken, the kind and thoughtful Detective Sergeant Wind took her to a neighboring diner where he could comfortably question her. Her eyes were beautiful and sparkled with tears, and after being with her for just a few minutes he wanted to kiss each one away. He lowered his eyes from hers, down her long red hair past her shoulders, until they fell upon her freck-led breasts and the necklace that hung between them. To change the subject, he complimented her and asked her about the necklace. The stone at its center was moonstone and silver legs wrapped around its bottom, silver arms around its sides, silver breasts rested on top and a silver rapturous woman's face within long hair covered the top loop a silver chain ran through. She smiled a sly and seductive smile at the compliment and wiping her eyes she told him it was the Goddess. He not only took her statement, but also her number, and soon she became his secret life, a shadow world fit thinly in between, underneath, and around the demands of both his full-time job and full-time girlfriend.

However, this morning Detective Sergeant Jonathan Wind would not wallow longer in his thoughts, memories, or worry. They were gone, jarred from him, a disrupted channel, with the summoning ring of his mobile phone. From the east whipped a rustling morning breeze, so he turned to the shelter of the payphone to answer the call. Night had been rolling into morning so gently beneath constant distraction that now morning was very much here; and with no rest his day was about to begin, a new day with the same clothes and the same dirt on the back of his neck.

"Wind, where are you? Your car's at the station. We've got a call," his partner said, urgent, loud, and quick to the point.

"I'm in a phone booth," said Detective Sergeant Wind trying to be playful.

"But I called your mobile, why are you at a phone booth if your mobile is working?"

"What's the call? Are you coming to get me? I'm in Vinings at the Circle K station by Monica's apartment," said Wind, blowing around his partner's question. Flora was a secret he kept to himself, though he suspected that his partner must have his own suspicions.

"Yeah, I'm coming for you already. I thought you would be there. I called your place. Where else could you be? I'm close and just getting coffee now. Do you need anything else?"

"Thanks. Yeah. Some Pez actually, if you don't mind."

"Alright, I'll be there in ten and tell you all about it after we get some coffee into you." They didn't even say good-bye.

Jonathan Wind stepped out of the shade and leaned back on a trashcan. Above his head, Aurora stretched and arched far across the sky to color the west, supple like a body, like a bough. Her wide tendrils from the east of peaches and fading purples tickled and reached through light atmospheric pressure and the greater she became the less she was. This dawn-time is hers and it vanishes the more she gives of herself. To some this phenomenon is a goddess and not a half-hour ago she awoke through the mists of night and threw wide her crimson doors. At the threshold, she stood with braided tresses, a floral embroidered robe, passing from her rosy fingers the golden reigns of fiery steeds to the golden-boy in her diamond chariot. As it surged east, with soundless galloping, cracking the surface of the dewy horizon, she lingered to watch her brazen charge erupt and proceed, no longer needing her; like the winds and stars she bore before, and that she will bear forever again. From her, the earth warms for all men, but in her light Jonathan Wind slumped within himself, oblivious to the energy surging around him.

He was trying to clear his mind, in preparation for work, but it felt impossible. He had complicated his mind with distractions of Monica's eyes at his back as he walked away, her smells still on him everywhere, and the way she grabbed tighter throughout the night as he pulled away; the struggle of words and needs. And then Flora: his comfort, his secret retreat from a dirty day, his confessor. Why did a man answer her phone?

He concentrated on breathing, exhaling only as much as he had inhaled, attempting to relax without falling too close to sleep, but after a quick isolated pinch of pain from the back of his scalp he jumped up and swiveled on his heels. When he was all the way around, he was looking into the pink eyes of a little man standing on the trashcan. Backlit by the raging dawn, he looked like a little angel with demon eyes. His short hair was white along with his shirt and pants and the total lack of color allowed the lights to flow, not just around him, but through him. Wind squinted while he rubbed the back of his head and resisted the urge to grab his sidearm. The little person stood there on the far edge of the trashcan holding a three-inch dark hair between two fingers of his pale hand. He beckoned with his empty hand for Wind to lean in closer and then whispered in a soft voice of indiscernible accent.

"A long-unwonted shudder over me falls, the woe of human lot lays hold on me. Here then she dwells, within these humid walls, and her crime was a fond fantasy. You hesitate to go to her? You fear again to see her near? On! Your faltering brings death lingering here! Goethe said it once before and you must bear it ever more."

"Wind," called his partner, as the squad car pulled up behind him.

Wind turned to see his partner but when he swiveled back to the trashcan no one was there. His partner, honked and shouted again. As he walked to the car, he shot back a glance and heard a rustle and a giggle coming from within the trashcan.

"Did you see that?" he asked as he opened the door and slid into the car, taking a cup of hot coffee from his partner's hand.

"Did I see what?" said his partner already driving away, not giving the question any time.

"Did you see an albino midget dressed in all white standing on the trashcan and quoting Goethe?" Wind asked point blank.

"No," his partner laughed. "I didn't see an albino midget quoting

8

Goethe, but that's where that German idealist shit belongs anyway, in the trash. No, that I didn't see," he said, still laughing. "Now cut that shit out and drink your coffee, you're gonna need it, you look like shit. Rough night? You look like you haven't even slept. Have you?"

"Not really, no," said Detective Sergeant Jonathan Wind, sliding back into his element and sipping from the tall hot coffee. "I'm feeling better already, though. Tell me where we're going, but first, did you pick up any Pez?"

"Yeah, here, all they had was Golda Meir. I wish they had a Joan of Arc, considering where we're going."

2. HOLOCAUST

...and he shall take up the ashes to which the fire has reduced
the burnt offering on the altar and place them beside the altar.
Then he shall take off his vestments and put on other garments
and carry the ashes out to a clean place outside the camp. The
fire on the altar will be kept burning; it will not go out.

—Leviticus 6:10-12

NORMALLY, WALKING TOWARDS THE ENTRANCE OF A CRIME SCENE
made him feel like a boxer on his way to the ring, a silent warrior under bright lights, passing under yellow tape like ring-ropes, adrenaline
rushing, a hint of fear; focused, regardless of circumstance, pomp, and
whatever awaited him in the ring. After a few years he had hardened
to the gore, the smells, the human at its worst. In homicide, he was
never called for a beautiful corpse. Each physical result of murder is
repellent in its own way as all living things are beautiful in their own
ways. But this time he was walking down a familiar hall and everything
was different, it had been different since they pulled up to the building.

The entrance to the apartment lay at the end of the hall. An officer stood at the open door, on the foreground of the tape, holding
a clipboard. This hall had never seemed so long before, so long and

so narrow, he thought to his inner self, a place that also felt more distant and smaller than normal; but he glided down the hall, on energy not his own, looking straight ahead and hearing nothing. His partner was right behind him to the left, keeping the same pace, but Detective Sergeant Wind felt totally alone, allowing the look from the oncoming officer and the conversation around him to slide off his slick hard shell. He felt nothing and numbed his mind to match his facade, aware only of his heart, tearing belligerently within his chest cavity, viciously beating and foaming, a delirious rabid dog on a tether.

On the autopilot of training and muscle memory, he signed the clipboarded logbook held by the officer guarding the crime scene and passed beneath the tape, taking in the broken chain-lock, and the unscathed deadbolt and standard lock, to stand up in the room. The room was still dark with red curtains filtering thin morning light, as through a thick sieve, casting a crimson glow over everything. He knew where everything was, where everything should be, but still he scanned, flitting his eyes, stretching his vision to the corners, the peripheral rods sensitive to low light as he drifted through the living room, the small kitchen to his right, towards the bedroom where the other men stood. His partner had passed him in the living room and stood with the others talking quietly and gesturing.

Within the deep dark redness of the room, a room he used to regard as a sanctuary, he was engulfed by a burnt, putrid odor, which moved his anxiety evenly down from his heart to his gut to tighten and bubble as if his stomach was gasping for air and retching into itself. The Captain of the Homicide Division stood in a broken circle at the end of the bed with Wind's partner, a pale young officer Wind knew only by sight, and a short dark-haired man wearing black pants and a white shirt bearing the badge and patches of the Atlanta Fire

Department. Behind them vines and flowers were wrapped around the iron bedposts. Wind stopped just within the doorway and closed the broken circle, careful of not going too far, watching where the gestures and eyes of the others fell on the floor before him. He stretched his eyes with subtle and short turns of the neck to look farther into the room, adjusting to the choking gloom while trying to remain calm. The crime scene photographer slowly moved past him farther into the room.

"Now that y'all are here and the photographer is moving on, we'll cast some light on this scene and see what we can find," said Don Faulkner, their tall and narrow Captain with thinning gray hair. He re-covered his mouth and sharp nose with a handkerchief and raised a flashlight.

The pale young officer went to the window, noticeably tired and nauseated, and parted the heavy red velvet curtains, before the Captain could even snap a reprimand, spilling hopeful beams of light over his white gloves and the velvet folds into the room, innocent of what they were to illuminate. The surgical-masked photographer was carefully shooting the space around them, moving on guarded toe, in an awkward dance like a marionette, and the forensic crime scene unit from the Georgia Bureau of Investigation was spreading out on all sides already processing beyond the room. Amid his shifting thoughts and the movement around him, Detective Wind was focused on the patch of floor within the loose circle. When the followspot of morning light angled down through the dust and the quickly thinning air, he could just make clear the scene of human remains. There was no visual corollary between what he saw and what he knew to be human.

In the car on the way here, Wind interrupted his partner, Detective Sergeant Ledbetter, when he tried to brief him beyond only the most general details of this call. He said that an officer responded to a call from a landlord complaining of smoke, a strange smell, and a moisture stain spreading on his ceiling coming from his tenant's apartment above. The officer arrived on the scene and found the possible burnt remains of a human body in the apartment. Wind asked not to hear any more, he wanted to take it all in, fresh on the scene, with no preconceived notions or influence. This was not abnormal. Wind usually sought to allow the *being* of the crime, the truth of the scene, to reveal itself purely to him as an initial step in investigation. He had to find a place of unconcealment from which to ask questions, like Heidegger courting Aletheia, he once explained. Detective Ledbetter originally thought it sounded pretty ridiculous and pretentious, but Wind was a good detective and got results. He grew to respect his partner and realized there was no pretension, the ridiculousness was just who he was. After the basic facts, they made small talk all the way to Buckhead.

Now, in the new light, his eyes adjusted and through sooty gloom and an abyss of gray dust, Wind found a small, low, dense mound of ash with small bone fragments and unburned teeth jutting out of the top. He couldn't look away. Squinting in the sun, and holding his breath loosely so to control its path through the nose, he just stared. But everyone was working on their breathing too and staring. The mound was sticky in some parts, as if the burned, moist matter had yet to dry or cool, and its wide lightning-bolt zigzag shape was lined on the floor by a thin, yellow liquid. Strips of ash were flaking, like gray petals, in the movement of the air, and indentations along the mound suggested limb-bone and rib-bone shapes. Speckled black and gray chunks of unburned bones seemed to shine like mushrooms in dirt, their singed gristle falling away back into the fold of the greater mass to reveal more gray bone. Wind concentrated, examining only what he saw and only the most technical assessment of what he thought of what he saw, and only then, as he became the role he had trained himself to play, did he speak.

"So, Officer Curtis broke the chain-lock on the door when he arrived on the scene?" He exhaled hard and thin between his teeth, reestablishing the objective for everyone stunned by the sight, concentrating on their footing, and their breath. His desire to cry was third in line, right behind his fear of giving in to feeling, and his always-primary desire to understand.

"Why yes, actually, good eye, Detective." He coughed. "If y'all were here ten minutes earlier, you would have heard it the first time, but let's have Officer Curtis give us his full report again so you two can be caught up to speed. First, y'all don't know Inspector Brennen, do you?"

The partners exchanged greetings with the Fire Inspector, shaking hands.

"You can call me Aaron. It's very nice to meet you both. Officer, go ahead."

The young patrol officer gained back a little color as he gave them his report of how things led up to this point. He was slow and careful, thinking before he spoke and only stammering in an effort to make what came out of his mouth exactly what he had said ten minutes before to the Captain. He had been driving down West Paces Ferry at seven-ten on his patrol when he had received a call from dispatch. The call said that the landlord of this house here on Valley Road reported smoke and a disturbance from the apartment above him. A fire engine was alerted and the officer proceeded to the scene. The officer arrived at the scene at seven-fifteen, before the fire engine, since he was just a mile away, and found the landlord. The landlord told him the tenant, a young woman named Flora Ross came in late last night around two and went up to her apartment. He could hear her through the floor as he was falling asleep. At about four-thirty in the morning he heard her fire alarm go off and ring for about fifteen minutes and then stop. Since it stopped, he thought nothing of it and went back to sleep. At seven he woke up and immediately smelled something smoky and saw a sticky yellow substance on the ceiling of his bedroom, which is directly beneath her bedroom. He went straight up to the apartment with his cordless telephone and knocked on the door to no answer. He then called her to no answer before dialing 911. When the officer arrived at the apartment, the landlord unlocked both locks on the door, and the officer broke in the chain. He made his way slowly and cautiously, remembering his crime scene procedure, and found what he believed to be the remains in the bedroom. At this point, he radioed back to dispatch and gave a description of what he saw stating that it was a homicide before moving to secure the scene.

Captain Faulkner thanked the officer and proceeded to relate that when he was informed of the perplexing nature of the crime, he left immediately, bringing the Fire Inspector with him, seeking interdepartmental cooperation and hoping to liaise personally between the two departments on whatever the situation might be.

"Since Officer Curtis was able to contain the scene before any firemen entered, things are still pretty neat here. Well, except for the chain-lock and the curtains, but from here it doesn't seem there are any signs of forced entry on the window over there so maybe Officer Curtis didn't do so bad. I am sure they will mostly find smoke and soot on the curtains. We're all breathing it in now. But let's see what they can turn up," said the Captain.

The crime scene investigators were at the curtains while he spoke and some were dusting the windows and windowsill. People moved around the room, slowly and carefully like somber, dutiful acolytes, the flash from the cameras audible over all the slight methodical movements.

"Oh, and Officer Curtis also answered the phone," Captain Faulkner sighed. "It rang at seven fifty-one and he answered it and said hello. Whoever it was didn't say anything and hung up. The caller ID reads the time and number and I already called the number in to have it checked out."

Wind remained quiet at his work, observing the mound with slight shifts of his eyes, and bleeding out drawings of what he saw with a roller-ball pen onto a page of his notepad. His contour drawings took what was before him further away from human but retained the essence of how the tissue and muscle and bone burned, breaking down into a complex yet unified mass. When no one had more questions for the young awkward officer, Captain Faulkner sent him out. The four of them stood with a lighter posture and a freer ability to speak now that the rookie and his nervousness had left them.

"Man, that looks like something Biblical, like an act of God, freaking *Force Majeure*. Just see how only the carpet is burned to the point of that yellow fluid and nothing else. Inspector Brennen, Aaron, have you ever seen anything like this before? What's your take?" asked Detective Ledbetter.

"Well, I have never actually seen anything like this before, in person. It is fascinating the way the body seems to have burned so thoroughly as if from the inside out, leaving only the thickest parts of the bones and the teeth in solid form."

He crouched low, his face close to the mound. He pointed to some bones and teeth and mumbled to himself as the photographer snapped at the mound a couple more pictures. As he bent back up, his speech was now clearly directed to the others, and his dark eyes sat deeper beneath his brow.

"If this is the woman, the tenant, Flora Ross, then she most likely burned very quickly at a very great temperature and if she were alive when it happened it would have been very painful. I will be able to understand more when I read the medical examiner's report. The fluid is very curious, most likely fat, and the burn patterns on the bones can tell us a lot, as can the ash. Clothing burns differently from flesh so we can see what she was wearing and how that affected her combustibility. So far, I cannot see any trace of clothing. As far as fire goes, this scene is extremely contained. The fire centered only on this location where the body was and damaged nothing but the floor just around the remains. The closed door and windows allowed little oxygen into the room. Whatever the fire began from, it burned itself out on the body and died unable to feed off the body or any more oxygen. It was just so controlled and isolated, only on the body. It's very unique."

"Are you saying that this might not be an accidental death?" Wind's partner asked before Wind could, both scanning the room, starting slowly to loosen the structure of the circle around the remains, wanting to listen, yet eager to begin their own searches. Detective Wind especially was torn in his need to learn all that he could from the Inspector and also to survey everything that was Flora's first, knowing he could understand what had been disturbed better than any of the others.

"The front door was locked from the inside with three separate locks and all of the windows are locked also from the inside. The landlord downstairs says it sounded like she was alone when she came in. Apparently, he hears pretty well what goes on with her up here and his bedroom is directly beneath hers. But at this point we haven't ruled the possibility of anything out." Captain Faulkner made eye contact with both Wind and his partner while he spoke, making sure they recorded all that he said while their anxious gazes drifted over the room.

"Yes, I can't be sure of anything yet, either." Inspector Brennen leaned down low again and sifted gently in the remains with his white latex-gloved finger, pushing the ash with care like it was gold dust. "The human body is difficult to incinerate to such a degree. In the cremation process temperatures get up to 1,300 degrees Fahrenheit, but that is a controlled environment. In here, a fire of that temperature would have set the room ablaze. Still, to get a human body to such powder, such calcine dust, in this room, with this much oxygen, and possibly some clothing would take a temperature close to that, yet amazingly enough, whatever fire did that damaged nothing else in the room. In our lab tests, we will look for traces of accelerants that might have been used. It's very strange though. There is no trace of the fire damaging anything else beyond where it seems the body crumpled, not even the dust-ruffle or comforter are singed, only darkened by the smoke, and they are only about a foot and a half from where the yellow fluid stopped spreading."

"I am glad you are so fascinated, but what are you saying, that she spontaneously combusted?" asked Wind's partner, Detective Sergeant Ledbetter, as Wind was transfixed by the latex fingers moving like a rake in the sand of a Zen rock garden.

"Well, we do have a record of mysterious fire investigations that have never been solved to any great satisfaction. The term spontaneous human combustion is really a misnomer since no fire is ever spontaneous. There is always a cause, a spark. What characterizes many of the mysterious ones that people often apply the phrase to is that the fire seems to begin from inside the body and doesn't spread much farther than the body. The study of such fires is for us like studying abnormal psychology for the average therapist. It is mostly for hobbyists, geeks."

"Great, but the bodies burn from the inside out? That sounds supernatural, like God smiting people in the Bible, punishing someone for their sins, or for questioning him. How is that supposed to happen today, in Atlanta in 2003, you know, in modern times, without all the angry God stuff?" asked Detective Ledbetter.

"Well, in the strangest of cases, no one is sure exactly. Most often the person is a smoker and a consumer of alcohol, usually a woman since they have a higher percentage of body fat than men." The faces of all three men directed expressions equally inquisitive and skeptical towards the squatting, sifting Inspector. "The FBI conducted tests on this subject in the 1950s and came up with the 'Wick Theory,' which reasons that the body in these cases will burn like an inside-out candle. Alcohol is usually involved to make the body fat more flammable and work as a general accelerant. After the initial spark from a cigarette or some other source, the clothing will burn like a wick with the body fat as the wax, this includes fatty bone marrow, and then the body will burn, or melt, from the inside out. The burning only stops when the wick of clothing is gone or the fat is all burned up. Typically, there is a yellow fluid of unburned body fat around the body since it takes longer to burn than clothing. The torso with the stomach and breasts, along with fatty thighs and brain matter burn the fastest, and often in these strange cases the outer extremities like feet and hands are left as untouched as their surroundings. I have never even heard of a case this thorough, or well, whatever happened here."

"There is an ashtray, a box of matches, and a cigarette pack—Capri's I believe—on the nightstand, so she was a smoker. There are all those candles and some incense. They seem undamaged," said Captain Faulkner, the closer of the detectives to that side of the bed. "I am sure as y'all Detectives investigate you will find out more about Miss Ross's character. Do you have some reasoning Aaron, why those matches over there didn't ignite?"

"Well, it is pretty strange, but so much is strange here. All these candles should be melted and those candles at least singed. The fire must have raged intensely for just a brief time and smothered itself. My guess right now would be that it probably only lasted during the fire alarm that the landlord heard at four-thirty, if not for less time. Fires burn in an upward cone, but there is no significant burning on the ceiling. There is just the same smoke damage that is everywhere. With the door and windows locked, I would just suspect suicide or natural causes, but it would be very difficult for someone to do this to themselves, especially without leaving a trace. So self-immolation is very unlikely. The wiring would need to be checked, but there is the possibility of an arc shooting out of a nearby socket, maybe even that one, and catching her clothing. It would be very unlikely for an electrical arc to burn this hot without spreading any farther. Other than the teeth and some thick bone, the body is pretty much cremated. The appearance is so neat, so precise and thorough, it appears almost intentional, ritualistic. Whatever did this didn't seem to burn anything else except the floor right beneath the remains, as if that was its intention, as if it was only meant to burn her. Of course that is only supposition." His sifting had turned to digging and his efforts showed the scorched wood floor beneath the carpet. In one of his purposeful scoops he pulled up a loose handful of powder and shook it slowly until all the gray dust fell away from his latex palm revealing a silver chain with a silver shape around a white stone.

"What is that?" asked Captain Faulkner.

"It looks like a necklace of a woman embracing a crystal, like quartz, or maybe moonstone. It appears totally unaffected by the fire. It is cool, like the rest of the dust, but it isn't even tarnished by the fire, like silver should be. It says on the back here sterling silver. Maybe it was dropped here after the fire, but that would suppose a second person was here and possible homicide," said Inspector Brennen, assuredly taking the lead in this investigation, secure with his knowledge and experience.

As the Inspector showed the necklace to Detective Ledbetter while they were putting it into a small plastic bag, Captain Faulkner's mobile phone rang out. He answered it and Wind's eyes followed his lips as he mouthed what he heard back to himself. When he closed the phone, he told them the phone call that Officer Curtis answered came from a payphone in Vinings outside of a gas station. Already Detective Ledbetter had found it odd that Detective Wind was not sketching the necklace, and now he watched his partner with sad suspicion. Before he could say anything Wind spoke.

"I am going to look around, unless there is something else that Inspector Brennen notices at this time."

"No, if I discover anything else I will tell you. I'm just going to take samples of everything. Go right ahead, Detective."

And that was it. Wind's partner watched as Wind moved towards the right side of the bed, observing the night table with its candles, incense, and slim lamp with dark red shade, passing the door to the bathroom and stopping at the dresser, making a passable effort to sketch. At the dresser, he made himself look at all of her things. He could tell nothing was different from the last time he was here. It had been just over a week, the weekend before last, since he had stood in this very place, a place where he would linger for a moment before entering her bathroom to urinate or wash his face and he would let his eyes and sometimes his fingertips survey the texture of the breasts or the buttocks on the statuettes lining her dresser. Now he wondered if any of his fingerprints lingered on the Venus of Willendorf's wide bare breasts or on Kali's smooth round buttocks. His prints must be all over the room, but so must many men's. In the week and three days since last he visited enough men must have passed through here that his are buried deep or cleaned away. He scanned widely and thoroughly, knowing what had been moved and to what degree. On the whole, the dresser was undisturbed, the jewelry box sat within its established location made clear by soot lines, as did Kali; the Venus of Willendorf, a thin marble pious Virgin Mary; an aged silver-handled mirror; a wooden hand ringed by tree veins and painted green vines and white daisies, reaching upward with Flora's various rings on the fingers, along with hair elastics; a silver bowl containing a half-burned bundle of sage smudge-wrap; and a multi-colored glass vase three-quarters full of matches from various Atlanta and out of town restaurants. In the bottom right corner of the mirror was a postcard of an exceptionably vulvic Georgia O'Keefe floral cross-section that he brought her from the Museum of Modern Art when he visited friends in New York City over the summer. Above the postcard was a staged picture of Flora in a sheer silk wrap like a Grecian goddess under a marble arch, a gold band around her forehead, from a photo shoot that she did for her website. In the bottom left corner of the mirror was a photograph of her in full vinyl dominatrix costume from last New Year's Eve at The Chamber. Above, was stuck a business card

23

for Tia Maite's Psychic Readings, a woman whom Wind knew to be a sort of therapist or guiding counselor for Flora at a regular weekly appointment.

Detective Wind could hear the other officers moving about the room behind him and by some passing remark he inferred that one of them discovered Flora's sex toys and paraphernalia stored within both of her night tables. He looked up to see himself in the mirror as he had done so many times before but instead of seeing Flora behind him staring back from the bed glowing in her sex, he found a room busy with men, men touching what was once hers, poking, prodding, and breaking the peace that she created for her space, stirring up more of the haze that was left of her body, like death pollen.

He quickly lowered his eyes and went into the bathroom. He scanned with brevity and confidence. This was not out of character for his methods; he often scanned in many short sweeps, allowing things to catch his eyes when there was nothing specific he was searching for. Here it was far easier than normal; everything was where it was a week ago. A pink-nippled mermaid with a bright green tail and pale porcelain skin sat on the back of the toilet combing her long red hair. On the sink edge stood a porcelain Botticelli's Venus and at her feet in a seashell, the soap looked new as it always did since a maid service came weekly. Cleanliness being an important part of a serene home with a near continuous flow of male clients, Flora often cleaned between the maid's visits. The rest of the sink area was clear and shiny. He looked through and around the curtain and gave the shower a once-over before leaving the bathroom. So far, he could find no sign of another person other than Flora having been in the apartment, but that was also the way she kept things. His work as a detective was an exciting challenge for her cleanliness and sense of order, and she was obsessively tactful in her ability to cover any traces of any other man when he visited. Her meticulousness was consistent and ritualistic in its own way and he was always impressed by her devotion. Outside the range of the soot he could find no dust.

Detective Ledbetter watched his partner with concern and followed him over to the left side of the bed where he now stood before a bookcase. The tall, thin, brown-skinned detective, only two inches taller than his equally slim, but pale partner, squatted down and exchanged slight smiles with Wind before joining him to look around. On each of the three shelves of the low bookcase there were knick-knacks and statuettes on display. On top was a portable stereo, a small CD rack, and two framed pictures, one of Flora and a female friend, and another of a black-mouthed Aztec Goddess. Detective Ledbetter drew from the top bookshelf a tall slim volume of live action photographs of Kama Sutra positions. He flipped through it and then put it away. He then moved a bronze statuette of Hans Christian Andersen's Little Mermaid seated on a rock and went to the next book entitled *The Ultimate Kiss: A Guide to Oral Sex* and pulled it out just enough to see its cover before sliding it back in. He slowly moved his fingers against each book on that row, acknowledging them as he read their titles, drawing from the shelf the ones that caught his eye. Detective Wind moved from the right to the left towards him with matching, studied movements. The two of them hovered there on the balls of their feet over the cream carpet, careful not to fall back against the bed covered in a lavender comforter with a pattern of violet vines and oval leaves, round buds and bursting dendrobium orchids. The mass of pillows at the head of the bed followed the same theme as the comforter, but in reverse, the background in violet with the vines, leaves, buds, and orchids in lavender.

Detective Wind could hear that the other detectives searching about on the far side of the bed had looked under it to find Flora's storage of extra clothes, costumes, and sheets as well as her box of photos. The photos included her modeling for her website and advertisements, her art photography from ex-boyfriends as well as pictures from her childhood and personal life. He knew there were no pictures of him and her together in there. In the short time that they had been seeing each other, the few pictures she had of him, all Polaroids, were hidden in a book on her shelf. Calmly, he was being careful to get to that book before his partner. They both ran their fingers across three shelves of books including: *Aphrodite: A Memoir of the Senses* and *Eva Luna* by Isabel Allende; *Drawing Down the Moon* by Margot Adler; *The Great Cosmic Mother* by Monica Sjoo; Nabokov's *Lolita*; Plath's *The Bell Jar* and *Ariel*; Dumas's *Camille*; *Tess of the D'Urbervilles* and *Jude the Obscure* by Thomas Hardy; Edith Hamilton's *Mythology*; Tolstoy's *Russian Fairy Tales and Fables*; Ovid's *Metamorphosis*; Frida Kahlo's journals and a book of her paintings; the erotic illustrations of Aubrey Beardsley; *The I-Ching*; *The Astrological Almanac*; *Sun Signs: Gemini* and *Sun Signs: Taurus*; *ESO: Extended Sexual Orgasm for Women*; a printed manual of Tantric practices; Anton LaVey's *Satanic Bible*; *The Holy Bible*; *Woman* by China Hamilton; De Sade's *Justine*; the collected poems of Oscar Wilde; the collected poems of Edna St. Vincent Millay; Salinger's *Franny and Zooey*; Marquez's *One Hundred Years of Solitude*, a large volume of Native American myths and legends; a dictionary of dream symbols; Freud's *Interpretation of Dreams*; *The Portable Viking Reader: Jung*; *Man and His Symbols* by Carl Jung; *The Sacred Prostitute* by Nancy Qualls-Corbett; the collected poems of Emily Dickinson; *Whores for Gloria* by William T. Vollmann;

Mitchell's *Gone With the Wind*; Grimm's fairy tales; *Skinny Legs and All* and *Jitterbug Perfume* by Tom Robbins; the collected prints and poems of William Blake; a tall, thin book of Gustav Klimt paintings; the catalog of Judy Chicago's "The Dinner Party"; *Tituba of Salem Village* by Ann Petry; *Mists of Avalon* by Bradley; *The Vampire Lestat* by Ann Rice; *Spy in the House of Love* and *Henry and June* by Anais Nin; Kate Chopin's *The Awakening*; Margret Atwood's *Surfacing* and *The Handmaid's Tale*; a collection of Man Ray's photographs; *Beloved* by Toni Morrison; an illustrated copy of *The Perfumed Garden of the Cheikh Nefaoui*; *The Seducer's Diary* by Søren Kierkegaard and *Blessings of the Blood: A Book of Menstrual Rituals for Women*. It was a collection that laid her more bare before them than any photographs could.

As his white latex fingers were closing in on the laden text, Wind moved a small white statuette of Rodin's *The Eternal Idol* and pulled out the copy of *The Perfumed Garden*. He flipped through it slowly as his partner watched, moving to another book on his own. Wind went to put it back and moved to the next. He slid out Kierkegaard's *The Seducer's Diary* and slowly drew it up to peruse, biding his time. As Captain Faulkner called from the other room to say that he was about to examine the contents of the victim's purse and ask if the other detectives would like to join him, Detective Wind had his chance. His partner had turned his head just long enough and Wind flipped the pages and let the Polaroids fall into his right hand, which he then slid into his right coat pocket behind the Golda Meir Pez dispenser. His partner turned back to the shelf as Wind replaced *The Seducer's Diary* to where he had pulled it from, the place where Flora put it after he gave it to her in an effort to explain what he once felt about love, and what she helped him to understand again.

The detectives both rose and went into the other room divided up with couches, stereo, and television on one half and a computer desk and breakfast table on the other half. The computer and its desk were being dusted for prints while Captain Faulkner stood at the table holding a deep handbag with bright full-color images of Ganesha in lotus position on both sides and a trim of fluffy black faux fur lining the seams. Detective Ledbetter had assumed responsibility for evidence collection and prepared a cellophane bindle for each of the items that his superior drew from the purse. Eye-liner, mascara, lipstick, a compact, ChapStick, two tampons, a pink panty-liner, a key ring with a heart-shaped Tiffany's key chain, a silver mobile phone, a black vinyl folding wallet sealed with a snap, a planner that matched the wallet, and sunglasses in a black case were all emptied from the bag and sealed except for the wallet and planner, which the detectives flipped through. Wind took notes in his notepad on what was in the wallet as everyone else spoke about her driver's license picture and how different it looked from the pictures in the bedroom.

They opened the planner and turned the pages towards the current week and confirmed their suspicions about Flora's profession along the way. Men's names filled each week, usually one per daily column, with details of or directions to each appointment's location. Wind knew any mention of him in the planner would be under the name Jon and might be detailed with a small heart and he was grateful for the ordinariness of his own name and the fact most people just called him Wind. There were no entries or appointments for the prior day and only one for Saturday night: the name "Frank" followed by the word "in" on the eight o'clock line. For Monday, the 29th of September, they found only one appointment scheduled. It was on the twelve noon line and read plainly, "Reading @ Tia Maite's."

"Y'all should find out what or who Tia Maite's is, and let them know that Miss Ross won't be making her appointment," said Captain Faulkner.

"She's a psychic, she has a parlor off Buford Highway on Buford Drive," responded Wind.

"How did you know that?" asked his partner suspiciously.

"The business card is on the mirror in the bedroom."

"Alright, that is great, Wind, be sure to get that number, maybe y'all can make a time to talk to the psychic when you tell her why Miss Ross won't be making her appointment. Whenever the medical examiner gets here, we should know a little more about what is going on here. Until then, how about we go over everything again, alright?"

Detective Wind moved as if he was dispersing into the bedroom, but returned instantly, flashing the card and a keen look at his partner who knowingly nodded and cleared his throat.

"Actually, Sir, it might work out for us to keep Miss Ross's appointment, we might be able to learn something about the victim from her psychic." He had been flipping through the planner as he spoke and noticed an appointment the week before and checked to find another the week before that. "It appears she has a regular appointment with this woman. Wind and I will go after we hear what the medical examiner has to say." And with that he looked back at his partner, giving a slight nod as if he had done him a favor, making an effort not to smile or reveal his growing suspicions.

3. SERPENTS WITH WINGS

The ocean boiled; towering waves beat upon all promonto-
ries of the coast; the ground quaked; Hades, lord of the dead
trembled; and even Zeus himself, for a time, was unstrung.
But when he had summoned again his strength, gripping his
terrific weapon, the great hero sprang from his mountain and,
hurling the bolt, set fire to all those flashing, bellowing, roar-
ing, baying hissing heads. The monster crashed to earth, and
the earth-goddess Gaea groaned beneath her child.

          —Joseph Campbell, *Occidental Mythology*

TURNING ONTO BUFORD HIGHWAY, THEY ENTERED DEKALB COUNTY
and the neighborhood of North Druid Hills, technically outside of
their jurisdiction, though still an integral part of Metropolitan Atlanta.
This roadway leads northeast, wide and industrialized, tapering gradually as it moves up through Dekalb and the counties of Gwinnett and
Hall, through the towns and neighborhoods of Clairmont, Chamblee,
Doraville, Norcross, Duluth, Suwanee, Sugar Hill, and Buford where
its skin sloughs and it is born again under another name. As other
roadways of Atlanta twist and bend to their environment in random,
serpentine ways, Buford Highway remains virtually straight and unwa-

vering, being crossed all the while by major and minor roadways, the mightiest of which is Highway 285, a shaky Ouroborus that establishes Atlanta's great perimeter for routing traffic, making some residents inside and others out, and, as local legend has it, confusing any returning Sherman's advance.

Within the perimeter they slowed, looking for their turn, two miles before the encompassing ring, in an area occasionally and back-handedly called Chambodia on occasion, a play on the name Chamblee with a slight at the Southeast Asian population. But this area is no Little Phnom Penh, nor is it a Little Saigon as the hot pink and white sign above a strip mall of mostly Vietnamese shops declares, for just down the street is a Mexican restaurant and a Peruvian one is less than a mile away. On this highway lay the largest and most diverse concentration of ethnic-owned establishments in the southeast, non-isolationist immigrants working together or at least beside each other while still retaining identity and community. Sliding up or down Buford Highway is a dissection of Atlanta's immigrant population of various Asian and Latin American countries, which instead of segregated ethno-clustering, is a writhing mass of peoples and communities distinct yet unified in commercial purpose.

Inside the car, they only spoke to read out the street names, looking for their turn before they could see the sign. They were across from the Vietnamese Center strip mall at a lane of small white houses reborn as professional offices, on the double dead-ended Buford Drive, set parallel to and a little back from the highway and surrounded by evergreens and elms still lush this late in the season. It was an isolated strip more quiet and subtle than the preceding, opposing, and anteceding neon monstrosities of multi-ethnic commerce. Parking in the meager lot, not much more than a driveway, they could read the words,

"Tia Maite's Psychic Readings" on the white marquee with smaller print stating the ability to service customers in Spanish as well as accept payment in Visa, Master Card, and American Express. Chimes rang as they entered, metal on metal, clanging against the door, until the broken notes dissolved into the crosscurrent of white noise from the dehumidifier in the foyer's right corner and the central-air vent in the upper left ceiling. The small room was laden with icons, Aztec gods and goddesses, pictures of the Virgin of Guadalupe, and glass candle holders painted with pious saints in action, spattering color against the wood paneled walls dating back to the mid 1970's. As a foyer, the room's shape suggested that the two men venture towards either the less inviting and less assuming closed door to their left or the swaying beaded doorway at the room's other end above which hung a Mexican flag. An eagle devoured a snake, flanked by fertility and blood, marking the place where a wayward people were destined to found their kingdom away from home. As they were about to spread the plastic beads hanging from the doorless doorframe a woman called out to them.

"Buenos días, please come in gentlemen," invited a deep and heavy voice, thick with Mexican accent and intonation.

"Good afternoon. I am Detective Sergeant Jonathan Wind, with the Atlanta Police Department Homicide Division," he said as they entered.

"And I am Detective Sergeant Cedric Ledbetter, but you can call me Sonny."

Detective Wind cultivated his silence during an investigation, when questioning witnesses or interacting with the public in any way. Excessive verbiage, that he feared complicated interpersonal relationships, was also kept in check on the job; he concentrated on listening deeply and postponing his rationalizations and his desire to fix things. It was Sonny's role to be the outgoing one, with charm and the nickname to pull it off.

"Cómo estás, gentlemen, detectives? Come, sit, siéntate. Yes, right there, Detective Wind, *Sonny*," she said as she pointed to the two chairs on the other side of her table, saying his name with a nod and a smile, drawing out the two syllables to show her respect for the courtesy and easy intimacy.

"I am Tia Maite, what can I do for you today?" Behind the table, she sat erect on a wide bench seat draped in a traditional Mexican blanket, as if it were a throne or nest. Her face was large, flat, and austere with high cheekbones and forehead, the color of coffee with a teaspoon of cream, a severe nose and a tender mouth, tight with age lines at the corners, like the corners of her dark full eyes. Her hair, almost fully gray, revealing moments of darker depths, was pulled back tight as one braid coiled into a wide bun on the back of her head. Below, the three hundred pounds of her massive body was all but draped in the yellow and red blanket except where it was parted with the protrusion of her breasts, their upper pillowy terrain soft and brown like her face, and where it was lost below the table. Both men found her large reserved presence intriguing and sensual.

"We are here on business, Ma'am, with some questions," said Sonny as they sat.

"Well, you must be quick. I have a twelve o'clock appointment. She is already late... something is wrong."

"Actually, that is why we are here."

"Oh, pobrecita, ichpochotli, pobrecita...," she whispered to herself as a visible crack of emotion ran through her cool stone face. With a sort of Old World dignity, she held back her tears as her eyes went glossy. She drew an embroidered handkerchief from her lap beneath the table and dabbed at her eyes amid sniffles. "Pardon me, gentlemen, just a moment," she said to them and whispered pobrecita, ichpochotli, to herself as she sighed and looked away to dab at her eyes and nose more, her breasts heaving and falling like the living earth.

"Alright gentlemen, please tell me what has happened," she said with forced composure.

"We are not quite sure what has happened as of yet. We have found what we believe to be her remains, but this is just the beginning of the investigation. We cannot tell you any more about an ongoing investigation." Detective Wind spoke now, hoping to make her more comfortable.

"Then what can I do for you?"

"In her planner Miss Ross has an appointment with you listed for every Monday at noon for the last few months. If this is accurate we would imagine that you knew her pretty well and that maybe you could tell us about Miss Ross, give us some insight," said Wind.

"Well yes, I knew her well, she was a very sweet girl, pobrecita. I liked her, that is why I gave her one of my best appointment of the week."

"What do you mean, one of your best appointments?" asked Sonny.

"My first appointment of the week on Monday is one of my freshest times, since it is after my constitutional, as is my Thursday twelve noon appointment. They are when I am most sensitive and open, when my energy flows most freely, when I am a pure vessel to take in the excess and waste that can plague my customers and I can weed through the filth and noise and see clearly."

"What is this constitutional, ma'am, that you do twice a week that makes you so... sensitive?" asked Sonny.

"I am sorry Detectives, but a lady does not speak of such things to gentlemen."

Detective Wind knew of what she spoke. Flora had told him about her visits to Tia Maite. With great detail Flora would relate, while they lay in bed, reaching the highest levels of intimacy through talking, how Tia Maite provided more than a therapist ever could, since she was a spiritual counselor, and not only gave advice but tried to create a harmony between Flora's individual fate and the fate of the universe. She would point out to Wind how her week flowed with ease in the direction that Tia Maite advised and how it reached stagnation when she did not heed her warnings. He would listen, accepting her beliefs in this as he accepted her beliefs in everything, as valid for her as anything worth believing in is for anybody. And even though in his own consumption of knowledge he found little room for beliefs, he loved her will to believe, even her deductive ability to believe, where even her belief had a system and a method. Flora could reject the whole pharmaceutical industry as a greedy corporate sham, yet take the random beauty of a tarot reading as a truth of the universe. Divination was one of the many unconventional sciences she took very seriously, as she took Tia Maite very seriously. Amazed and amused by her character, she described Tia Maite to him in almost exact measure from what he could now discern: her size, her manner, and even the intricate tattoo of Quetzalcoatl detailed on her wide back that he had yet to see. He wondered if in Tia Maite, Flora had found some of the maternal guidance she had lacked since her own mother's early passing. Her visits to Tia Maite took on a religious form and dedication, as did many of Flora's habits. Each week she would relate some tale or amusing fact about Tia Maite to Wind, whether a profound mystical story from her childhood in Mexico or some funny thing Tia Maite said about catching one of her grandsons doing cocaine. It was on one of these occasions of amusing or profound trivia that Flora told Wind about Tia Maite's constitutionals.

Tia Maite did not defecate. Flora had gone into great detail about her psychic's process of waste removal and how it related to her insight and foresight. The name constitutional was employed since the process was a rest and reinvigoration for all four of Tia Maite's bodies: physical, emotional, mental, and spiritual. During the course of the day Tia Maite could hunker her massive frame down to hover over any toilet and urinate as needed. But, it was only for an hour during those two predetermined days of the week, at eight in the morning, that the spiritual adviser would go to a specialist for colon hydrotherapy or as it is more commonly known, a high colonic. It was there that she let herself go, prone and relaxed she allowed the opaque plastic snake to enter her dark pucker, all but lost in folds of flesh, and take away all the filth that she had built up over the last few days. Down the hose with the ten to fifteen gallons of temperature-controlled filtered water and solid human waste went the sorrow of the housewife, the misguided aspirations of the young sweetheart, the dreams of lottery fortune for the day-laborer, the spiritual searching of the escort, and whatever else was vented to the counselor in exchange for the promise of symbolic guidance. After, she would float out the door with a glow, a sheen, and a freshness as if she had a new skin, ready for her first appointment and the subsequent days of bearing the burden of the lust and filth and desire and sadness and sticky glee that she takes away from her customers in helping them relate to their own fate.

"Pardon me, ma'am. Back to Miss Ross. Did she seem worried or scared or was she acting at all out of the ordinary when you saw her last week?"

"She was excited. But she is, was, always excited when she visited me. Her visits here were *her* constitutionals. She was always excited to see what the cards said. She said that my words soothed her, but she was always excited, just full of life, always with great energy. Even though she knew how to be calm, outwardly, very poised, seductive even, she was always very much alive inside."

"She didn't express any fears on that last visit? Or was she involved with anyone or any groups that could possibly be dangerous, anything ritualistic or cultish?"

"With men she was always in control, she was very smart and skilled in such matters. There were many men, but Flora had no trouble with them, to them she was like a goddess or at times even like me, an adviser. There was one man over whom she had no control, but I would not say that their relationship was any more dangerous than any secret love can be." She smiled at them both in turn and Wind thought he saw a tear come to her eye when she looked at him. "Though she has passed, he has not, so of this I should not speak. His secret is still secure even if she is set free. As for groups, she was young, just an ichpochotli. Oh, pobrecita. So young and curious. Yes, there were groups, there were many groups, sometimes it seemed almost as many as the men. She took what she needed from each one and moved on, or sometimes they took what they needed from her and they moved on; in both cases just like the men. She was on a journey that only she understood. Sometimes I understood. I would catch a glimpse. But only her heart fully understood. I would read the cards as they came up and I would see what she saw. I would see what she knew at those times although it was what she didn't know that she knew. You see"—and here she relaxed a little with her breasts resting upon her middle as her shoulders lowered—"gentleman, there is a whole spiritual world within this world, within this city, that she walked freely through, that you gentlemen do not even know of. What you might call *cultish*, she knew as normal and spiritual and found no more dangerous than anything else in this world."

"Again, ma'am, you will have to pardon me. I don't mean to judge anyone's practices. We are just trying to learn more about Miss Ross's life so maybe we can understand what happened to her. The circumstances of her death are awfully strange and possibly look religious in nature. Can you give us the name of the most recent group she was involved with?" Sonny's manners allowed for great ease in questioning.

"That I cannot do."

"Cannot or will not, ma'am? Anything you know can help our investigation," he snapped courteously back at her.

"Those are not matters I can talk about, *Sonny*. You detectives will have to find them the same way that she did, on her path. I understand that you gentlemen have a job to do, but so do I. What I see and what I know about a life are for that life only. What my clients tell me I contain only so long as it is bearable and then all those words are taken away with everything else during my constitutionals. These *groups* are all around you, people meeting to worship, to love, to gain enlightenment. They are under your nose at all times and you do not even know it."

"Can you tell us anything about the reading you did for Miss Ross on her last visit?" Detective Wind spoke and Tia Maite's eyes turned on him suddenly, her shoulders rearing back up high and broad and tight, like a cobra.

"I can tell you the cards and what they often mean, but not specifically what they meant for her. That day, I saw fire. It was nothing new, nothing out of the ordinary for Flora. I drew the card The Tower, in the upright position. Fire and destruction it can mean. Positively it can mean sudden change, or blessings in disguise. That is what it was most often for her. She received many blessings in disguise. I did not draw the card Death, if that is what you are asking, which is most often a sign of rebirth, not actual death. With Flora, it was often The Lovers, since she was a creature of love and a Gemini; and The Tower. Many cards reoccurred in her readings, it was their positions that changed from week to week. The strange card of the reading, rare for Flora was Judgment. It can mean, in the positive position, new opportunities, rebirth, or even absolution, a chance for cleansing and purity, the washing away of guilt. It too corresponds to the element of fire."

"But you are not shocked by her death?" asked Wind.

"I am greatly saddened by it, but shocked, no. It is the risk we all run. Maybe she ran a higher risk. She lived well and it is usually the more that you live, the more death has to come for. It is not my place to question the gods. Life and death is theirs to decide, for us it is only how. Flora knew this too; she was a natural spirit. Whatever her fate, I am sure she embraced it."

"Can I ask you some questions about yourself?" Detective Wind proceeded.

"It would be a shame to waste one of my best appointments. I will answer your questions if I can give one of you a reading. Free of charge, since it is the least I can do for young Flora." She turned to look at Sonny and lowered her head inquiringly.

"I am sorry, ma'am. But I tell my mother everything and in turn she tells all to the First Baptist Congregation of Stone Mountain and they probably wouldn't let her live down her son having his fortune read, even on police business."

"And how about you, Detective?" Her slightly bowed head tilted towards Detective Wind and she smiled and raised her left eyebrow. She reached out with her right hand for his as if she expected it would be his fortune she would read all along.

"Of course. Whatever you see fit." He allowed her to take his right hand in hers and turn it palm-up where she held it with both hands. His eyes followed his hand and as she bent her head down to look closely at his palm, they fell reflexively upon her breasts that hove out of her dark dress, large and alluring. In her left palm his hand lay, as her right traced along its lines and contours. She gently blew on it. With her right hand she drew the shorter of the two decks of cards from the corner of her table and placed it on his palm with her hand resting on top. Finally, she moved the deck to the free space on the table in front of her and slid his hand back to him.

"Alright, Detective, ask your questions."

"For a moment there I thought you were going to read my palm."

"I do read palms, but I prefer the tarot cards. I was just looking at your palm and getting your energy onto the cards. Anything can be read. In ancient Babylon and Mesopotamia, where what I do was once a respected science and art, readings were done on the internal organs of an animal or human, the living offering made the reading more sacred. Or readings were done in far simpler ways, by casting lots or pouring oil into water or smoke from a censor. Or even by watching the fickle and unstable movements of wind. Finding meaning in things that now people think are meaningless. I stick to palms and stars, but mostly tarot cards. They are older than anyone imagines but of course not as old as the stars. That is why I treat the cards and stars together."

As Tia Maite was pulling the first card from the deck, Detective

Wind asked her where she was from. She laid down The Hierophant card in the upright position for her view.

"I was born in Chilchotla in the Puebla State of central Mexico, in the Sierra Madre Mountains. The Hierophant card. You are a Taurus, are you not, Detective?"

"Yes, I am. You can see that in the card?" He had begun to take notes on a small spiral topped notepad, as did Sonny.

"Among other things about you, yes. You believe in old laws, even beyond the badge that you wear. You believe in systems, causes and effects, right and wrong, science, order, traditional values, even though life doesn't always hold up to those values … or maybe you don't. But there is a negative aspect, possibly right now you are having a crisis of faith. You worry that you might not have all the answers. But you always do have all the answers. You are a stranger to confusion. You are wise, your friends know that," she smiled at Sonny, "but you must remember that the disorder you fear is the other side to the order you embrace."

"Okay, I will try to remember that. How long have you been in the country, when did you arrive? And, I beg your pardon, but what is your age presently?"

"I arrived in the United States in 1980. This year I celebrate my 60th birthday and mourn the years that have escaped me. I came directly to Atlanta from Mexico, to help with the children of my son who had already settled here after first living in Texas. I will draw two cards for the two questions you have just asked and will draw a third for the question I answered that you were sure to ask. Ah, The High Priestess, The Empress reversed, and The Lovers. That is quite the combination, all women. All of the women in the deck. There are other feminine cards, but this is very interesting. These are a contrast to you, to how you were represented, The Hierophant, a loner. There is chaos in women that is beyond your sense of order, justice, and law. You need consistency and all these women are always changing. You want to protect them, control them, but they slip from your grasp. The High Priestess, she is important. She is the sacred woman, the eternal woman, the woman we all seek. So maybe here she just represents Flora. It is she you are investigating, yes? And in investigating we could say it is her you seek, but maybe it is someone else, someone else who needs you, someone else you seek and need to save and do not even realize. We shall see," she smiled evenly. "And The Empress reversed is a dominant woman. I see no ring so it must be your girlfriend. You have a girlfriend, no? Yes, this must represent her. You have conflict with her. She wants things from you that you are not ready to give, yet maybe you give more in word than deed? In this way she controls you emotionally. Maybe she is very protective, jealous? Maybe with reason?"

She looked at him and saw the face he used back at the crime scene in Flora's apartment. He did not answer and his mask told her nothing. She felt fear and she assumed that what she felt belonged to him.

"For the third card to be The Lovers adds a fullness to the presence of the other two feminine cards. If The High Priestess in positive position represents Flora, the woman you seek, and The Empress in negative position represents your girlfriend, then The Lovers, the sign of the Gemini, as Flora was, gives you two choices to balance these. It says that you have a conflict with your heart and your head. That you need to make the choice between love and duty. Maybe your girlfriend is your love and is pulling you in one direction and your police work, this investigation, is duty and it is pulling you in another direction.

Or maybe somehow your relationship with your girlfriend is a duty to you and you have some other love that is the conflict. Overall I see this card to be positive in this spread, in the worst case maybe your heart will lead your head. Hopefully you will find your positive High Priestess and be free of the negative Empress. It looks like you have a great deal of women to take care of, maybe more than you know, maybe you work too much, Detective, investigating out there, but missing what is right before your eyes, what has always been there." She smiled and raised her left eyebrow, tipping her head slightly as if to ask his approval for all that she said.

"How often have you been back to visit Mexico since you moved to Atlanta?" Detective Wind spoke with calm and efficiency. When his words came out, even after such a silence, there was no clearing of his throat, no stammer, no clues, nothing to read, just efficiency.

"I have not been back once. This is my home now. That is how my people are, when we move we bring not only our family, but our history with us. With that we also bring our gods and our loves with us and sometimes we find things in the new home that can become just as much a part of us as what we brought. One day when we move on it will all go with us. When the Aztecs found Teotihuacan, they knew it was a sacred place, but it was abandoned. It was there that they believed that gods were born. Soon it was their place and the gods they found there became theirs too. Atlanta is my home; I have brought all that I need with me. I have no reason to return to where I have already been."

"Alright, thank you, one last question, Tia Maite. Do you know any albino midgets?" He looked her in the eyes and let the corners of his mouth toy with the notion of a smile.

"Detective Wind, I have a great many friends and acquaintances and clients of all different shapes and sizes and colors. But, as I have said before, of them I cannot speak. I am sure there are legal means in your investigation that could force me to speak of things that I deem private, but I hope it will not come to that. I do not believe that the private things from my own life or the lives of those who confide in me can help you understand what happened to Flora. If I did I would most surely tell you. I am sorry if you do not understand this. For that last question allow me one more card." Her right hand drew from the top of the short stack and laterally turned the card, revealing before her The Moon in its upright position. "The Moon. That is fortunate. Or it has the possibility for a fortunate result. This card is known to appear to a reader at times of confusion. It warns of lies and deception or that things are not what they seem. The Moon says that if you are on a path, you must stay true to the path and follow where the light of the moon illuminates. It too is a feminine card, Detective. The Moon is always changing, but on a cycle, like women, like life, like the universe. The cycle of the universe is just too big for us to see all of and understand. It seems chaotic and does not fit your rational systems. The chaos is the feminine and you must learn to trust in it, trust in her." And then she was quiet as she gauged the attention levels of the men before her.

The two detectives both stood from their seats, Detective Wind an instant before his partner, who was watching and waiting for his move. Sonny smiled at Tia Maite, they said goodbye and shook hands, and he placed his card on the desk in front of her. Detective Wind enacted the same gesture and before they turned towards the hanging beads of dull multi-colored plastic, they told her that if she thought of anything that might help them to give them a call, Sonny finishing the sentence that Wind began.

"Detectives. Could you tell me how she died? Please?"

"We found what we believe to be her remains. She was burned beyond recognition," Detective Wind said over his shoulder not wishing to pursue the details any further.

"Ay Dios mío en cielos, pobrecita, just an ichpochotli, so young, so sweet. Well... it is the season, as they say...pobrecita."

"What do you mean, 'it is the season'?" asked Detective Wind, turning over his right shoulder, his dark brow tight and pinched.

"It is an expression, no? What I meant was that it was a fitting time for such things. Not a whole season but the Trecena is fitting. In the Aztec calendar." And she pointed behind her to a four-foot square print tacked to the wood-paneled wall, circles within circles, each with four compass-like points, little flaming altars around the outer ring, green plants and ornate patterns working inward to a ring of animal faces and plants, to an innermost ring with what could only be gods, some snarling, some laughing, to a center circle filled by a dark face with red, sharp eyes and a wagging tongue.

"Please explain. I know only very little about the Aztec calendar. What is a Trecena?" Both he and Sonny had turned fully around and stood waiting ready once again to listen.

"Well, the Aztec calendar has three systems that turn together. There is one called the Xiuhpohualli, the calendar of our solar year, which has 365 days in eighteen months of twenty days and five unlucky days. One god will preside over each of these. We are in Acatl, there are only three other gods that rotate the ruling of the year. Within this there are two wheels that rotate together the Tonalpohualli and the Tracena. The Tonalpohualli turns for each day with a god presiding while the Tracena is the Aztec week, thirteen days long with its own separate god presiding. Each god is individually represented by a symbol." She spoke from memory, at once studied and hereditary.

"And what god is presiding over this Tracena?"

"Today is the last day of the week Ollin, which is the symbol of movement, and is ruled by the goddess Tlazolteotl, goddess of cotton and weaving, sex and lust, she is literally the eater of sins, filth; she is terrifying and loving. This Tracena was a time of purification, of taking stock. The rainbow serpent floats enshrouded in smoke and shadow in this time and the earth shakes and its tremors create mysteries and twists of fate."

"Who is the god or goddess of today?" asked Detective Wind almost barking.

"The symbol of the day is Atl, water, and it is ruled by the god, Xiuhtecuhtli, God of Years and the ancient and primal God of Fire. Today is a day of battle and of purification through struggle. It is a day of holy war, where we fight conflicts of the self, often internal conflicts."

"You did not think to tell us about any of this, knowing that we are on an investigation of official police business?" He spoke standing stiffly, allowing his partner the note-taking, which he did in his small spiral pad.

"I do not give more information to people than they ask for, than they are ready to handle and understand. That can be most detrimental in what I do. I give people what they ask for, no more, no less. And I let them make of it what they wish," she said composed and straightforward.

"Did Miss Ross ever consult the Aztec calendar?"

"At times it was brought up in her readings. I do not know, Detective, what she did in her own time, but here it was a common complement to the cards and the Zoroastrian stars."

47

"What were the symbol and presiding god for yesterday, if you wouldn't mind indulging us further?" he asked with the same stern tone.

"Yesterday was the day Tochtli, the rabbit, looked over by Mayahuel, the Goddess of Fertility and the maguey cactus. It was a day when one is supposed to give of oneself to something greater. A day of devotion and self-sacrifice, self-transcendence. It was a day to feel the waxing of the New Moon that we just began on the 25th." She paused for a moment and her silence was an invitation to listen more closely.

"And before you ask, I will tell you that tomorrow begins the Tracena Itzcuintli, the dog, ruled over by Xipe Totec, god of shedding and the releasing of seeds. This next week will be one of further devotion and self-sacrifice. It is a time of duality between the pain of shedding illusions and the enjoyment of creating illusions. We cling to what we understand but that must be sacrificed for what is true. That is what this next week tells us. They are thirteen good days for paying tribute to the dead, but days unfit for holding too tightly to the living. Tomorrow the Tracena also begins with the day of the dog Itzcuintli, ruled over by Mictlantecuhtli, God of Death, and guide of the dead, the link to the spirit world for the living. It is a day for remembrance and being trustworthy of those who are trusting. So remember your dead, Detectives, I will. And be careful. Follow the guidance of the moon. If you can walk in its path, you can walk in trust that the gods are watching out for you. Good day. Ane, adios, y vaya con dios," she closed, dismissing them.

They both smiled and nodded in farewell and in an instant they had passed through the dehumidified room of glowing religious kitsch and streaming sage incense into the heat of the high midday. When they got the car, Sonny put the windows down before the air-conditioning kicked in and steered the vehicle into a left turn out onto Buford Highway, southeast towards the Atlanta Police jurisdiction of Fulton County and their midtown station. High above the metal roof, the sun throbbed and pulsed, burning in a fierce rage against the autumnal coolness taking hold six days after the Fall Equinox. Tomorrow morning would see a denser dew than today and this evening's chill would cause home air-conditioners to be turned off and windows opened. Nature will be welcomed into the homes of men in her milder form, with humidity abated, dried out by this midday sun and the cleansing of a dusk breeze. Three miles behind them sat the entrance to the cycle of I-285 where infinite cars roll endlessly off and on, tramping with their wheels, beating down her hot grooves. All of the serpentine streets seethed in the heat as they twisted off and away from the straight line on which they drove. Some people believe that within the Earth an actual dragon relaxes and contracts, sleeping and dreaming, stretching occasionally in her death-born freedom. Some others believe in a world serpent wrapped around the atmosphere which also contracts and relaxes, and whose death signals a catastrophic end and fresh new beginning. After encountering Tia Maite, the very roads on which they drove were affecting Wind's mind.

"Man, that was very creepy. That woman's whole presence just creeped me out. Then all the talking about things that we wouldn't understand being rational men and then doing the tarot card reading for you and giving you that guidance about Monica and your duty. She did get your sign right, though. And then with all the Aztec calendar crap, man, that was all weirder than we are used to, or at least I am used to," said Sonny, elbowing with his last words.

"Definitely," said Detective Wind smiling distractedly at his partner's exuberance.

49

"And you with the question about the albino midget. I thought you were kidding this morning. I guess not. Were you thinking this situation is just weird enough that it must have something to do with the weird morning you had? I think that fits into Ockham's Razor, the least crazy explanation is usually the most likely. We did that in logic at Morehouse. You're not the only one who's read philosophy." He elbowed again.

"I was taking the chance at that possibility." But Wind's answer was solemn and his eyes continued to float out of the window at the green neon Vietnamese characters, twisting abstractions that he could read as pictures from his own life and experience, but what he knew to be alien symbols of a system just outside his knowledge.

Sonny stole glances from the road, stopping at the red light intersection of Clairmont Road, and observed his partner.

"Hey, uhm, Wind. If there is anything wrong, you can talk to me, you know. Remember, I'm a detective too. I notice things."

"Thank you. I know you do. I am just very tired and this is a very strange investigation and there is a lot going on in my head. Don't worry about me."

"Okay. My head is swimming in Mexican words, I can relate. And I can't seem to get that smell out of my nose, it is like it is deep in the back, like it is lodged in the center of my head, no longer just a smell, but a crystallized memory."

"What smell?"

"The smell of the apartment, that burnt meat smell, but worse than meat because you know it was a person. I feel like I need a shower, like I need to wash it away, to scrub down to a new me. I'm sure you feel it too, and man, I bet you need a shower after your night and then to have to deal with all of this, and that smell."

50

Wind muttered something affirmative and smiled dryly at his partner before returning his gaze beyond the window glass to La Buford rolling by in all its familiar alien splendor from within the air-conditioned safety.

4. THE ALTAR OF OSIRIS

I listen to the wind, to the wind of my soul. Where I end up,
well I think, only God really knows.
—"The Wind," Yusuf Islam
(formerly Cat Stevens, formerly Stephen Demetre Georgiou)

"AMERICA HIDES AN OLD EVIL. IT'S TRUE. IT LIES BENEATH THE SUR-
face, older than we can imagine. It was here before the settlers and before even the Indians, who blindly crossed that land bridge. It affected
the settlers in their cruelty to the natives as it affected the natives in
their cruelty to each other. Man came late to these lands, and what
awaited him but horrors; the horrors of a land where the great horrible
lizards once stamped and warred, where mastodons and saber-toothed
tigers, now trapped in the tar out in California, posed a great mamma-
lian threat and before all of them is the oldest evil of all, the hidden
torrent of raw chaotic nature in its oldest least stable form. This evil
is part of America's age and though the word evil denotes a morality,
America's ancient evil is as non-moral as Nature itself. The mountains
just north of us were once greater and taller than the wise Himala-
yas, they were once the greatest formidable range of mountains in the
world and beyond wise they were primordial. The Appalachians were

worn down over hundreds of thousands of years and have succumbed to the natural movements that once thrust them through the earth's soft crust in the first place. Once shining, heaven-reaching peaks towering over the Earth's dawn, the Appalachian range was worn down by sliding ice sheets and by sun and rain, and the combination brought evergreen trees of pine and slippery elms reaching deep with hungry roots halting the erosion of time and tempest, but sealing their fate. When was the last time you were up at the mounds, Jon?"

The question retrieved Wind from the lost terrain beyond his isolated gaze. He was used to Lao like this, puffing at a chain of cigarettes, pacing about his computer room, sitting on a folded leg to ash, tapping the white paper finger into a cup and then rising again, pacing, only halting his speech to breathe, only breathing to inhale the smoke. He did not think, nor did he hope, that there would be need or room to respond, but the direct question pulled him back into the situation.

"What mounds, what are you talking about?"

"The Etowah Indian mounds, up in Etowah, near Cartersville, at the foot of the Appalachians." His dark eyes in their dark pits swirled, and his wild, prematurely graying hair blending with the cloud of smoke he moved about in, but his smile through the haze sweetened the condescension with which Lao always spoke.

"It must have been third grade, doing Georgia state history, Eli Whitney and the cotton-gin and all that shit. We took field trips around the city and some farther and I remember one of them was to the Etowah Indian mounds." Wind responded, still and slumped in a swivel chair looking up at his friend through red and watery eyes. The smoke was an irritation to his eyes but he had been rubbing them before he arrived.

"I must have gone on one of those too, maybe." A pause in Lao's kinetic force drew Wind's attention, baiting him. "But anyway, I went back recently and I walked around in the rain for a little while while Tammy took pictures and I tried to position myself so the land and its history could reveal itself to me."

"So what did the land tell you?" Wind rose and ran his moist hands through his dark hair and stretched his neck. The room was hot, cluttered, and smoky, and a general collection of filth held dominion over everything: the three operable computers on the long desk, the ancient monitor cast on its side by the closet, the boots and boxes coming out of the closet, the bookshelf with an orderly display of programming and philosophy. Normally, Wind thought this filth to be the filth of genius, but now he was annoyed by what he felt to be too much cold intellectualism, which he could find at his own empty home if that was what he wanted. Here Jon, not Detective Wind, was taking a break and sought Lao for the friendship they had shared for most of their lives and Lao was just being himself, upholding his end of their dialectic. Anxious, Wind did not know how to broach the subject; he paced in a small, agitated circle and leaned against the wall by the door. The smoke, a common characteristic of visits with Lao, took on a darker significance today and with each of his friend's exhalations he felt like this investigation was taunting him and that she was gone forever and there was nothing he could do about it; and his heart moved faster.

Lao Benjoseph did not notice Wind's tension and sorrow and if he did, it did not stop him from answering. Wind sat back down to listen and watch.

"The land told me nothing, it just laid itself there before me exactly how we find it and I knew that was the key. That we who are new here don't respect or acknowledge what is before us, particularly the gods of those who lived here prior to our arrival. The Romans knew to do that. They added the gods of the people they conquered to their Pantheon, gods like Mithras who they just loved. They formed like a warrior cult to him in Rome even though he was some bull-headed deity they found in Persia, and before that Mithras came from farther east... I need to check where. See, that's why it's up to us to seek out the gods who ruled this land before we brought our own. The mound-builders of Etowah were part of a group now referred to as the Southern Cult. This was a part of the Mississippian culture that ruled from around Illinois down to Florida and from Arkansas to the Atlantic, around the Carolinas, for the first five hundred years of the last millennium. It was all most recently theirs before the white man. These different tribes are classified by their common maize-based economy, units of measure, astronomical system, and most importantly a very complex bestiary of god-like figures. Copper plates found in Etowah match other artifacts found at other sites around the south. These mound builders shared a common belief in a vicious birdman-like deity symbolically carrying a severed head or being served a body part on a plate by some woman figure. They had beaks, wings, talons and," he gestured for each appendage, elongating an invisible nose and hooking his fingers and swiping, "often were represented with insects, like butterflies, moths, and spiders, around them, and other body parts like horns and wings, but always man and beast together. Oh, and large vertical weeping eyes." He paused and chuckled a little, working himself up amidst multiple clouds of smoke like those from passing trains. The chuckling cooled him a little and allowed him to breathe.

"The weeping eyes are pretty vaginal, huh?" he asked smiling, instigating.

"I see you have done your homework," said Wind, stalling the subject, but unable to hold back a smirk at the passion he loved and expected from Lao.

"Actually it's all from the brochures I picked up in their information center..." and his words were broken by giggles, erratic and choked, with slight snorts through his nose, little beads of spittle breaking over his lips onto his shaggy black and gray beard. He showed them to his friend, glossy paper folds dense in facts and pictures of copper plates, mounds, and broken shards. He giggled erratic and forced, like a child, and seemingly on cue Tammy called up from downstairs like a mother.

"David, I'm making some coffee, do you or Jonny want some?" She still called him David when she addressed him directly. Legally, his name became Lao Benjoseph when he turned twenty-one, when Wind was away at NYU, and now, almost a decade later, he was Lao to everyone but Tammy, his wife and most intimate companion. To hear him called David stirred in Wind a sense of nostalgia for his teenage years when David Cohen was like a mentor or big brother to him and he remembered the letter he received that day in New York spreading the news. It read simply "A good name is better than precious ointment; and the day of death than the day of one's birth—Lao Benjoseph" and he understood with the reference to Ecclesiastes that that was it. His friend had died and been reborn anew.

Tammy Benjoseph acquired her surname soon after this time when she married Lao, shedding her father's name, Cummings, and her Southern Baptist upbringing in a service distinct to the mutual love between her and Lao. A self-proclaimed prophet of all and no faiths, Lao Benjoseph delighted with his bride in perusing the yellow pages for a church to preside over their nuptials. The Church of Osiris was the fateful ministry. Wind took time off during his second to last semester and flew down to be the best man in their wedding. At the Ramada Plaza Hotel, amid the twisting chaos of concrete overpasses known as Spaghetti Junction, the service and reception were prepared. Both families, divided, faced the stage where the bride and groom, thronged by best man and maid of honor, faced out with the wedding party behind them. The wedding party was four bridesmaids and four groomsmen, each paired up as couples and representing the four elements, fire, wind, earth, and water. Priest and Priestess of Osiris approached and anointed the third eyes of bride and groom, ushering in readings from each couple of the wedding party to invoke their respective element. Wind watched the faces in the audience, the intellectual, Jewish, Cohen family to his left, aware of the Church of Osiris, and the Cummings family to his right, Southern Baptists who were told by Tammy that this was a Jewish wedding. Wind remembers enjoying the confused yet accepting looks during the anointing of the third eyes, as if they were nodding and thinking "So that's how the Jews do it."

Since both men had answered affirmatively, Tammy entered the room with two mugs of coffee. They both took it black and she knew that, a good wife and friend. She put her hand on Wind's shoulder as she gave him the mug and smiled down at him in the swivel chair, a smile with a look that seemed to ask if he was alright, but she said nothing and just smiled more sweetly, walking away, out of the room and back downstairs.

"I should go back to work," Wind said, choking down his second gulp of hot coffee. It burned and he held tight his teeth against the pain.

"Alright," said Lao, looking at his brochures and lighting another cigarette.

Wind stood up to go. Lao sipped his coffee and quickly drew the cigarette back to his mouth as the mug slowly made its descent back down to the table next to a computer keyboard. His movements were quick and erratic, but the butt lingered firmly between his lips showing the sucking pull to be as need-based as physically reflexive. Wind picked up his own mug, finished, and put it back down next to the third keyboard in line on the table. Wind saw Lao's eyes, locked away in no direction, and he stood there watching his friend think. He knew that the words that were soon to come out of Lao's mouth were going to be more fact-based intellectual ramblings or post-witty quips, but for the moment he set his frustration and inexpressible pain aside and savored the rare silence with his friend. Always moving in small ways, as if many physical tics were countering and offsetting each other, Lao leaned and tapped his ash over the burnt, sooty cup next to his coffee mug. He brimmed beneath the surface, like the America he spoke of, uncontrollable and always ready to come alive.

"Oo, Oo, Jon, have I told you about set theory? I have been reading a lot about it recently—and by recently I mean for the last few hours before you showed up—and it fits perfectly with what I have been talking about, what I understood from the mounds, cultural groupings and responsibility..." and he was off again, like a beast from a slumber, like magma through a fissure. Wind was about to speak, he needed to talk to his friend, but life goes on alongside death and Lao knew nothing of Flora. To begin to tell him about this secret segment of a life at this time when it had, instead of ending, become a new passion, in the truth of the suffering and devotion that the word "passion" entails, seemed to be too great an ordeal. The burden of his relationship with Flora and the turn it had now taken was his to bear alone. Still, he wished he could tell Lao about the albino midget, ask him what he thought of Goethe, convey the freakish horror of Flora's death, the psychic, her tattoo, her reading, her insight into his life, and the accuracy of the Aztec calendar, but these incidents all seemed to be connected, even if he saw the connection only in their randomness. To talk about one aspect of his day would easily lead to speaking of another and so easily did his words get away from him, so many facts, so much learning, so much need to do good. Wind had used so much self-control so far this day that he had come to Lao's to rest, and now he was done listening and could wallow no more.

"Lao, I really have to go back to work. I have a lot of work to do today, you know, cop stuff." He interrupted a further demonstration of how set theory can help sort out the many layers of gods that have reigned upon this land and how to pay tribute to all to some degree. His friend understood, dropping that tangent of speech and thought to rise and put his cigarette out.

"Alright. Let's get together again soon. I can tell you more about set theory. And you know I like to hear about what you are working on, when you can tell me."

The two men hugged in the doorway of the computer room. As Lao's soft body pushed against his friend's lithe frame their smells intermingled, and as they squeezed the different smoke traces on both of them rose up together. It was only through the dissonant chord the two distinct smells made together in contrast to the accustomed cigarette smoke that Lao picked up the burnt scent on his friend. He didn't say anything, he knew Wind was on the job, but for a small moment he began to worry about his friend and his friend's work.

In the living room at the bottom of the stairs, Wind found Tammy on the couch with a magazine, amidst the general disarray of their home. Lao remained in the computer room.

"Oh, Jonny, are you going back to work?"

"Yeah. Why isn't Lao at work today, anyway? He never mentioned it and I never thought to ask. I even came over without thinking about it, without thinking what time it was." He raised his eyebrows and blinked hard in an effort to clear his vision from so much smoke only to notice a burning cigarette resting in the stone ashtray in front of Tammy.

"Oh. Well. He did go in. For a little while. In the morning. I had to drive him downtown for a meeting. He has been going to a lot of meetings recently. He gets so lost if I don't drive him. He can make it to work and back and that's it. But not downtown. And then he gets the rest of the day off. He is doing so well. They love him. Any meeting about new software he has to be at." She spoke with these rests, mind thinking with mouth speaking, always careful of what she said, always sensitive. She knew she didn't have the words that Lao did so she was careful and precise with what she had. Often it seemed that she was Lao's liaison to the grounded physical world.

"Oh, I should show you the pictures I took when we went to the Indian mounds a couple of weeks ago. I heard David going on about it to you. Us going up there. I gotta be quick though, the phone could ring any minute. And then it's back to work for me." She laughed and got up to push through a stack of manila envelopes on the far side of the ashy glass coffee table. Wind hovered, floating, polite and waiting. If the telephone rang it would be because she had called and signed in already. An automated voice would brightly announce the fetish within the first two seconds—feet, stockings, Asian, lesbian, wanting to pee on/be peed on, role playing, anal only, domination, public sex, voyeur, large breasts, small feet—and then the tone would change and she would be talking to a customer. At $3.95 a minute, she had to make it worthwhile and draw it out so that all the parties were happy; she only pocketed eighteen dollars an hour. It was a part-time job that gave extra support to her and Lao when her other part-time job of freelance photography did not, in paying for their habits, be they chemical, sexual, or spiritual.

"Here we go. Just look at this. This one I am pretty proud of myself for. It's the biggest mound there was. And this one is Lao at the top of that one," Tammy said.

The first picture, an upward shot in black and white, showed a wide flat mound of grassy earth towering above the point of view like a truncated pyramid with the setting sun behind it, light radiating in overexposed sheets past its crest and sides. The outlining grass, dark and fuzzy in the dying light, was like little prickly hairs on a great head of earth, roused out of a quick nap, never truly still. The second picture was exactly the same as the first, except the dying light fanning across the mound's flat crest was broken by the erect-pillar presence of Lao Benjoseph, mugging for the camera, his left arm out with the hand on his hip and the right hand holding a cigarette in his mouth, smoke visible in a steady stream heavenward. The thought of corpulent, chain-smoking Lao walking the many wooden steps to the top of the mound was barely conceivable to Wind, and he just let the image of Lao rising like a tree out of the earth on the mound's top remain in his mind. The rest of the photographs were more of the same over intervals of time till the last was practically black with slight beams of light stabbing out in the corners of where the mound reached out of the ground.

"And this is funny. They had this sign as you walk out of the visitor's center before you get to the mounds and there was another smaller one at the top of the biggest mound that said the same thing." She showed him a photograph of a large wood sign staked in the ground reading *Any Religious Or Spiritual Activity Performed In Any Manner Is Not Permitted At Mound Area Special First Amendment Right Area Provided With Permit See Manager.*

"David made me take a picture of it. I just think it is sad that that was what these things were made for and now they can't be used for that, ya know? David has got it into his head that we should get divorced so we can get married again at the top of the biggest mound. That would show them. Not that they would give us a permit. We could sneak it. I guess. Just show up like tourists. Tourists all dressed up, and just go on up and do it all sneaky-like. The pictures of him up there would make good invites."

"Well you know I'd be there, as long as I can be best man again."

"Good. You were so sweet the first time. I know David loves you. You are one of the few people he respects. Even if you did become a cop. He gives you shit about it all the time, but he really is cool with it. He likes that you think you are doing good and he believes it. I think he kind of envies you in a way, the stuff you get to see mostly, the gore and depravity. He couldn't handle a job like that, he'd giggle too much. He can be such an ass."

"Well, thank you, Tammy," he said and lowered his eyes. He was visibly awkward with the intimate path the conversation has taken. She had made him smile and the happiness in feeling the care that others had for him made him feel very conscious of somehow letting Flora go, that he was actually losing her. He put his jacket on and stretched, reaching out in the cloudy haze ubiquitous in the Benjoseph home, a movement that was an almost theatrical hint towards making an exit. He told Tammy he had to go back to work and she said okay and that her work could ring for her any minute. They walked to the front door

63

and stopped and she put the pictures down on the glass coffee table, freeing her hands, and hugged him. Wind hugged back for a moment, a moment just shy of letting himself go. It was in resisting the desire to sink, to fall into her embrace, relaxing his spine, head on her shoulder, like actually falling down to sleep, that he made the great disciplined effort of girding up his loins and readying himself for his duty and mission. He pulled away and moved to the door. Opening it and looking back he saw Tammy smile, his friend's wife, understanding, yet ignorant of what was going on, and he just smiled back quickly at her, big and controlled, and turned out the door.

Outside, Wind had only to make it around the block to go to work. With as much as he had on his mind, he still liked being able to have this time to walk out of doors and let the city speak more intimately to him. So much time he spent in the car for work, to see Monica in Vinings, to see Flora in Buckhead, to occasionally visit his mother out in Marietta, that he seized the opportunities to be able to walk the mile from home to work or to Lao's, enjoying the feeling of being back in college, back in New York, a city bare to your senses. Like all Atlantans, his car was an essential appendage, his means of accessing a city comprised of swirling river-like patterns of highways, expressways, avenues, streets, roads, boulevards, routes, drives, places, ways, paths, courts, runs, lanes, points, and trails. The road in Atlanta can change its name within the course of a mile while its direction has not veered or merged in any way; or it could lead to cross street upon cross street bearing the same name with the only slight variation in the roadway type.

Following the order of the road, turning left out of the duplex down Morgan Street to a left turn on Glen Iris Drive, he walked towards North Avenue. The sun falling low in the sky sent its light eastward with the denser movement of traffic as the westward cars trickled and spouted in ebbs and flows across their three lanes of the broad roadway. Outside, the heat of the day lingered in such a way that just the short walk was not bearable for Wind with his jacket on. The Benjoseph home was a distinct and self-sustained microcosm, and by contrast the span and busyness of the street and the wide Atlanta sky, so clear and bright across this concrete valley between the hill at the left and the old railroad bridge on the right, made him feel outwardly small and ineffectual. Walking backwards slowly east and waiting to ford the rolling streams of traffic, his gaze shifted back and forth from gauging the current to marking his destination on the other side. Like some giant post-modern temple to urban renewal, it loomed there, tall and wide: City Hall East. From 1927 to 1989 it was the largest Sears Roebuck and Company catalog clearinghouse for the southeastern United States, a symbol of production and progress, perfectly situated in a city that centered itself in the world of transport and commerce, a city once named Terminus as it was the mouth from which every rail-river of the Southeastern United States poured into and out of. Now since 1991, in this deep dip in the road, it stood as a fortress nestled tight, supporting within its blackened, brown brick walls the Atlanta Police Department, the Atlanta Fire Department, and several municipal offices where once products were made, stored, sold, and shipped. The most visibly new touch to the building's exterior was the tall blue sign by the parking lot that displayed in bold, red lettering CITY HALL EAST above the city's proud seal and symbol, a phoenix rising gloriously from its own burnt demise, just like Atlanta rose to its present glory from the ashes of the Civil War. It was in this same spirit that City Hall expanded into an eastern annex from the remains of a Sears Roebuck clearinghouse.

Enabled by the stagnant flow of cars caused by a truck making a cautiously slow right turn into the Masquerade, Wind waded out into the road. On the other side, he looked back quickly across North Avenue, the truck within the Masquerade gates, and the traffic moving as usual as if he never passed and never disrupted its eternal flow. He didn't even think to question his relevance to something as natural and inevitable as the tides of traffic and quickened his pace into a light jog, eager to get inside, to finish his workday and feed his pain with purpose.

5. MEMORY OF HER

The Great Mother in Her many aspects... call Her what you
may—has been with us from the beginning and awaits us now.
She is the beauty of the green earth, the life-giving waters, the
consuming fire, the radiating moon, and the fiery sun.
—Barbara Mor and Monica Sjoo, *The Great Cosmic Mother*

WITHIN THE DARK APARTMENT, THE OLD UTILITY LIGHTS FROM THE
open-ended courtyard showed bright, but no people congregated or
passed under their orange glow, the facing windows of the two other buildings drawn yet lit. On Highland Avenue only the occasional
passers-by made their way, mostly residents of the neighborhood, as
Monday was the slowest night for the local bars and restaurants, while
most other nights the street was filled with noisy drunken multitudes
in erratic rhythms and sizes. Shoes ticked against the wooden stairs,
faint then louder, all the way up until the front door opened into the
apartment and Jonathan Wind entered with a small pile of mail. With
his left elbow he flicked on the living room light, opening the room to
his view and replacing the image of the courtyard beyond the window
with reflective glare.

It was all a worn routine that he followed: he put the mail on the
kitchen table next to his laptop computer. Next he unbuttoned the

top two buttons from his shirt, laid his sidearm on the table, walked past the table into the kitchen area, opened the refrigerator, and drew out a bottle of beer. Then he walked back over to the table and placed the bottle down next to the mail and instantly removed from the pile all fliers and catalogs and put them into their own pile. Proceeding to sort the original pile, he put all bills into their own new pile and left only a postcard and an envelope from the NYU Department of Alumni Relations before lifting the beer and taking a quick reflexive pull off the bottle; but tonight the routine ended here. An urgent Wind ran to the kitchen sink with a dribble of beer running down his chin and spit out all that he had pulled. From the cabinet he got a glass and filled it half way with tap water, which he then swished in his mouth and spit out into the sink with the last traces of the beer.

Wind moved back into the living room and picked up the pile of trash mail and the bottle of beer. In the kitchen he opened the cabinet beneath the sink and placed the trash mail in bin along with the beer bottle after he emptied it out. He filled the glass again and drank it down and repeated the action a third time. He hoped to flush from his system whatever traces of alcohol were in that one pull of beer. When he tasted that single sip, a fear had shot through him, a fear that this normal action of drinking a beer upon his return from work would lead tonight to drinking a second and then maybe a third and his senses would be dulled and his thoughts would not be as keen and he would be defenseless from his fears and he would let go and fall very far away. He needed to stay sharp. He could not relax. His work had come home with him and he was still on duty.

Returning again to the living room, he rebuttoned the two open buttons of his white uniform shirt. In August of 2000, the Atlanta Police Department began an effort to increase the public visibility of the police force by requiring detectives, except for undercover officers in narcotics, vice, and fugitive squads, to wear uniforms. Some believed the effort was to make a thinning force look larger to the public while others insisted that it created a greater unity between all of the officers. Many detectives complained at first but Wind was newly of detective rank and what he wore in that position was a superficial concern. It was now his armor, his crest and cape, and though he could function without it, it was part of his job and gave him comfort in his role and his ability to play that role all the way.

Back at the table, he dismissed the bills, relegated to their own stack on the other side of the table, and pushed aside the NYU letter to be dealt with in some utopian future when he could care about things that were not matters of life and death. But the postcard he lifted to read, its personal nature inferring some sense of immediacy. On the glossy side was pictured a huge cruise ship on clear blue waters nearing the port of a generic, palm tree-lined coast with white sands, reading at the top it read in bold red letters: *Wish You Were Here!* On the back, the return address was that of his mother's home in Marietta. She began the correspondence *My Big Wonderful Detective*, and proceeded to tell him that she had just set sail with her new boyfriend who suddenly swept her off on an eighteen-day cruise around the Caribbean from Miami to the tip of Belize and back. The card had been postmarked in Miami three days ago. He was not shocked. She had settled back into dating when he went away to school and only recently had a new boyfriend wealthy enough to give her the things that she dreamed of after his father died and she was left raising both him and his sister. On the postcard, his mother mentioned that she tried to call him before she left but he wasn't home and she supposed he was at Monica's but she didn't want to bother them so she didn't call. She had a strange sense of propriety or territoriality about his relationship, constantly not wanting to interfere, but telling him not to take relationships too seriously at his age. She was in a very flippant stage of her life and did not seem to take anything too seriously, which made her hard for him to relate to. He also supposed that she was jealous of Monica taking him away from her, but he had been long gone. He had been gone in his heart and his head before he physically left for school in New York. He wanted to be free from the crushing yoke of her love and the intense responsibility he felt both to her and to his sister, to be both the husband and the father they needed as well as a son and brother.

The last sentence of the dark, bubbly script on the postcard's back read *And Jonathan, please check in on your sister I am worried about her*, followed by some words of extreme maternal adoration and the final: *Your Mother*. He had spoken to his mother once early last week but had not seen her in over a month. She always said she missed him but never seemed to make the effort out of her suburban life to visit him in the city, and he dreaded driving up to Marietta, where it was strip mall after strip mall, if he didn't have to; Monica's apartment in Vinings was far enough to travel regularly. But if his mother was mentioning his sister during her Caribbean cruise and she was actually worried, then there must be something going on. Astrid, his sister, was the troubled problem child to counterbalance his legalism and ardent sense of duty. Analytical Wind was ever aware of all of his own flaws and failings, which he kept hidden deep within his labyrinthine heart and his secret life, but poor Astrid wore hers like a crown.

Only six months old in 1983 when their father, Nathan Wind, succumbed to a brain aneurysm in his sleep, his wife waking to find her husband unable to wake, Astrid never knew her father. She grew up knowing a mother who tried to be both mother and father and a brother who also tried to be a father. She wanted no part in the well-meant efforts of either, and from a premature age she sought for that father, that missing maleness, in older boys masquerading as men. Wind left for college when she was ten and over the four years he was gone their mother began dating, and Astrid too started to seek greater freedom. Her reckless boisterousness, once written off as the energy of youth, soon became the fuel behind a rapid maturation characterized by extreme curiosity and coquettishness. After graduation, Wind moved back to Atlanta into his own place and his mother would call him to check in on his sister when she was at work and she feared Astrid had skipped school. One afternoon after such a call, in the fall of 1997, Wind visited his mother's house in Sandy Springs to find his sister home and on the living room couch with an older boy on top of and within her. Shocked and enraged, Wind threw the naked boy to the carpet and kicked him until he whimpered while his sister screamed in protest from the couch without covering herself. They both forgave each other soon after this, but Astrid learned to conceal more of her life from both her mother and brother.

Along with signs of a free and promiscuous attitude towards sexual conduct developing at the age of fourteen, Astrid also showed signs of a depressive chemical imbalance exhibited by efforts to self-medicate herself with alcohol and other drugs increasingly more at hand. In middle school, she found herself among the students who had already discovered cigarette smoking and how to get a quick buzz from inhaling fumes from the brush end of permanent markers, rubber cement, spray paint, Scotch Guard, white out, or any other school supplies with such warning labels as *Use in a Ventilated Place*. Upon entrance to Riverwood High School, alcohol and marijuana became

71

easy for her to obtain, both staples of a balanced public school education. With blonde hair, a pretty face with pouty lips and big blue eyes, and a physical shape that matured earlier than her innocent smile and twinkling baby blues, she rarely had to pay for such inebriations. High school boys, lured by her beauty and façade of confident worldliness, and older men, lured by her fertile life-force and her epitomizing of the image of sexualized youth, were all at her beck and call, giving her and her friends rides, buying them beer, scoring them bags of marijuana and other drugs as needed. The days of sharing a bottle of Boones Farm strawberry wine between a few friends at a slumber party and watching R-rated movies after the supervising parents went to sleep quickly gave way to sneaking out in the middle of the night and rolling joints behind Waffle House to dropping acid on a school day in Little Five Points and not coming home for a couple of nights. Of only few stories like these—which were either so regular in occurrence as to have odds against Astrid's complete concealment or that resulted in incident—did her mother and brother know.

She was sparkling and cool, distant, like the heavenly body for which she was named. She was also a shooting star, always on the go and always comfortable wherever she was, taking advantage of her mother's newfound romances to avoid almost all but the most basic responsibilities at home and enabled by her brother's presence on the police force to feel like the law didn't apply to her. In light of her blazing charm and fair-haired beauty, she was able to coast through the tribulations of daily life and schoolwork, showing up a couple of nights a week to wait tables at Zappoli's in Sandy Springs as her secondary source of money after her mother's allowance and making enough appearances in school for important tests, which she passed with ease. She was eighteen when she graduated and in not such a far place from where she began at fourteen, except with many loves and drugs about which to reminisce. When last Wind had seen her, before summer began, she was living in an apartment on Roswell Road on the North Springs border of Sandy Springs with a couple of friends and taking the occasional class at Georgia Perimeter Community College. He found her happy, as she always was, and a degree of stoned, as she always was.

This way of Astrid's both mother and brother were used to, but now his mother was worried and that worried Wind. Though he tried to always be there for Astrid, he was often too late. He walked over to his couch a few steps away from the table and sat leaning forward with his hands on his knees, rubbing. The fifteen-inch screen television on top of a VCR/DVD player looked across the small room at him from its place on a low shelf against the wall. Videotapes and DVDs were on the same unit that held the television and VCR/DVD player, which was flanked by two very full bookshelves two levels high. On top of the shelf to the television's right were forty-five carefully lined up Pez dispensers with an unoccupied space in the front where once stood the President Eisenhower dispenser, and where eventually will stand the Golda Meir dispenser, awkwardly between Jack Kerouac and Marlon Brando of the 1950s section until he rearranges the order and she winds up in the miscellaneous 20th century world leader section near Charles de Gaulle and Nelson Mandela. Above his only kitsch collection, and least practical obsession, hung the only framed pictures in his apartment, a print of Raphael's angels in a gold frame given by Monica to watch over him in a home designed very far outside the tenets of her faith, and a poster of Basil Rathbone as Sherlock Holmes smoking a pipe, contributed by the Benjosephs and his friend Jack Thoth in jocular celebration of his appointment to the position of detective. The rest of the apartment was books. The wall to his left, which was mostly window, supported two short, full bookshelves and the wall behind him held two large shelves packed tight with books from floor to ceiling. Low bookcases went around the corner by the front door down the hall to the bedroom and the bathroom. The bedroom was sparse: two lamped nightstands around the bed, each stacked with books, a dresser, neatly filled with clothes, and a closet serving as a refuge for stacks of old newspapers and magazines beneath well-hung slacks and shirts.

Wind breathed nervously as he dried his sweaty hands against the knee of his pants. He could handle this tension, this anxiety so close to panic; it made him feel like he was truly alive and ready for anything. He exhaled deeply and lay back against the couch, putting his drying hands into his short hair. As intended on some level, the exhalation cleared his mind and he jumped up and went for his hanging jacket. From its right outside pocket he drew the Polaroids and the Pez dispenser and moved to sit back down after putting Golda Meir in her temporary resting place. There were five pictures, so he organized the first two on his left leg, the last two on his right and he held the middle one in his hand. With the way the squares fell, what he held was them kissing. It was snapped one-handed, the camera held above their faces in her right hand and it showed two pale faces pressed into one, with one half of short dark hair and stubble and the other a mass of auburn and pink. Their eyes were closed and he could remember the day it was taken.

It was Friday, August 8th, and Monica wasn't even out of town. He had grown bold and quite confident in the divisions of his life and time. Monica was having dinner with some friends and he told her he was going to read and go to sleep early to be rested for Saturday when they were to go to her parents' house for a barbecue. It was that easy. He was able to sacrifice a night of sleep and fake his way sleeplessly through a family event with the Kildaras, making blue-collar small talk with her father, owner and proprietor of Kildara Contracting, in exchange for his time with Flora. He had made up all the things to say, which usually entailed being called to a crime scene as an excuse for not answering either of his phones or not being home if she stopped by. Then off he went to Buckhead, to Flora's apartment, to the shelter of their secret.

That night she took her Polaroid camera out for the first and only time. They were already naked, already cycling between spent and renewed. She told him she needed something for herself when he wasn't there, something more than memories. The top picture on his left knee was of him bare before her on the bed, which she took from standing above. It hurt to see how he pretended to be annoyed with her at the time. He playfully fought the camera away from her and from prone view snapped the second picture up at her, capturing nakedness and a smile. The pictures were in order, and next he pulled her down to him where they put arms beneath pillows and held each other and kissed so she could capture it. She held the camera as he moved back within her, arching his body and allowing her to wrap her long legs around the small of his back before he went up on his knees, pulling her off the bed, except for her head and shoulders. Within the small white frame of the photograph near his right knee was the image she made from this angle. It was him, with a look of serious concentration as he supported her weight down his thighs and from within her vagina, their mutual pubic darknesses mixing as one united place, his chest taut and contracted. Flexing to continue and renew his grip, he bent down deeper inside of her and took the camera from her before pulling back as they were for the previous picture, only now he directed the camera at her. He dropped the shutter and caught her at a gasp for a moment unaware, her arms up behind her head, her chest stretched back to the point of breastlessness with only her dark nipples surviving, and her eyes rolled back to the right while her front teeth escaped with her breath through her gently parting lips. Now the only physical trace of that moment lay on his right thigh.

So Detective Wind began another stage of his investigation while sitting there on the couch and then standing to pace, tracing his fingers down the spines of dustless books. The answers were usually in there, everything was usually in there, in black and white, with index and footnotes and sources. Now he was a source, his lived experience was necessary for the deeper examination of information and the drawing of connections. He began scanning through memories like they were photos or video clips, for clues, off-hand remarks, or other telling signs that could provide further insight into the Flora he knew and the life that she led without him.

He tried to search contextually. Her death had the air of ritual or purpose and Sonny described it as religious, seeing something terrible or terrific in it. Everything that Tia Maite said only complicated what he knew of Flora's associations and deepened the darkness of the mystery of her pursuits. The first time they were together it was so comfortable they shared so much. They slowed down time in an effort to make eternity from one night, since that might be all they had. It was not long after they met, the next weekend, May 30th, a week after Flora's birthday, a day shy of two weeks after Wind's birthday, when Monica was in Houston at a pharmaceuticals convention for her work at St. John's Hospital. Their first lovemaking was passionate and messy and fast, but it was in the lulls between the crescendos that their true union would occur. They would lie naked, spent and sticky, and she would talk and he wouldn't even think, just listen. He didn't use his words to navigate or manipulate. He didn't use them to cast up the image he meant to show. He would lay naked and silent and allow her the innocence of her flowing words, in course flowery and matter of fact. He would drink from her words, from the great stream of their ramble. They rolled over him, and the taste was familiar and dream-like.

That first night, she fell from riding upon him and lay down along his side, her head on his chest, and removed the condom. Down his chest her head gradually slid to rest on his abdomen and she gently handled his moist, limp penis, recovering gradually within her finger-tips. It stood as she explored with her eyes and fingertips. The head, the shaft, the scar, the dense fine hairs, the testicles relaxing in the cool openness present after her body had moved away, but now tight-ening to the new stimulation.

She held the pale pillar heavenward before her and began to nar-rate to him what she saw. He lay, with no words, lost in the curl of her body alongside him, listening. She described a blood vessel visible through the skin of the shaft, in the shape of a tree, a thin pink tree leaning, as on a slope with a bough of branches, spread and reaching. He knew the mark of which she spoke. She narrated on about how the tree is positioned divinely upon his manhood, and his root chakra, the Kundalini serpent. It is the Bodhi tree that the Buddha sat be-neath to meditate and attain awakening, and now she too was be-neath such a tree. It is the Tree of Life and Death that the Kabbalah sought and the shaft behind it is the flaming sword left by Archangel Michael to bar the gate from the fallen, though she said she could bring down the sword and would again soon. It is the Oak of Mamre, under which Abraham made his home and where God came to tell him his destiny and she spoke of this being a fitting place for her to find her destiny. It is the Aztec Tamoanchan tree, the great synthesis of the four cosmic trees. It is Yggdrasil, the World Tree, and upon it, the nine worlds of the universe resided, where she wanted to live and play and rejoice in death or many little deaths. Or maybe it is Daphne, imprisoned in his sex, the woman he desires that he cannot obtain, his love, his truth, his destiny. And with that she said that she must set her free and be her avatar and she enclosed the whole hard mass within her mouth.

She pivoted around over his head without losing contact and positioned herself to squat on his chest where he dragged his fingers through her hair and down her back while her mouth worked. Before his eyes was a bright lavender hyacinth tattooed around the root of her spine, its green stem leading down into the cleavage of her small buttocks. The perennial hypnotized him as he lost himself in her losing herself to please him. She bent farther over, taking him in deeper, and he followed the stem to its end at her dark hairless rectum. He knew that just a bit farther he would see the center of the world, the gates of life, the yawning gap of creation, the channel of eternal return, the tear in the fabric of time, and the intensity he felt, the biological need for release subsided and he smiled and laughed out loud just a little as he playfully rolled her off of him to kiss her. There was a moment of fear, of vulnerability, but then she laughed too and her blue eyes glowed and they kissed and laughed together.

When his turn came, she welcomed him openly to explore her body. It was five feet and eleven inches long, an inch shorter than his and thin its whole length. In their play, he kissed the long length of her as she had done to him, and he delighted in the contrasts her body presented to Monica's. Flora's breasts were a slight A-cup, little more than a dollop off her chest when she stood, their whole tiny mass directed to the perky point of their nipples with hardly any room for areolas. Monica stood only five feet and three inches with long dark curly hair and her bosom was as full as her buttocks, both accentuated by a narrow waist. Flora had none of these curves and his fingers could rake down her ribby torso, but she could curl and get small and they could slide around each other, relatively equal in size and shape. They positioned and repositioned and played and recorded and used what they knew and soon he had learned to please her as she had pleased him.

As their sexual play would build toward its peaks, she would continue to narrate the myths of the world where she found them in their coupling. She had moved on top of him, face to face, and he gave all control to her, to her expression. He was inside her, and in his mouth was her tongue, the man in the woman, the woman in the man. Removing her tongue to speak she told him that like this they closed a circuit of energy, they created a center. She wrapped her long legs over and under his and back on top so that their feet crossed and her ankles lay on top. Coiled, she said their legs made the double helix of DNA, but it was so much more than that. Her left leg and his right leg made Nu-Wa, the first female god, and Fu Xi, the divine monarch, of ancient China, entwined as the double serpent, attaining their cosmic union. Her right leg and his left leg were ancient Sumeria's Ki, goddess of earth, and An, god of the heavens, also entwined as the double serpent, attaining their cosmic union. Chest to chest, they were joined like Kalachakra and his consort Vishvamata, normally in standing position, and with only one mere set of arms a piece to wrap around each other. They were Shakti and Shiva, twin aspects of the same being and she was trying to push them together into one, beyond any sense of self, beyond selfhood, a rejoining of souls until they were one complete entity of masculine and feminine in balance. Maybe they could achieve the state of the divine androgyne, like Nommo, the Mother-Father of the Dogon tribe, the first living being created by Amma, the creator of the universe.

He, such a great collector and cataloger of information, was so impressed by her stores of knowledge. Though it was mainly religious, sexual, or spiritual, it was a dense and thorough body of knowledge. He loved to just listen, and that night it felt great letting her talk, setting the precedent for their dynamic. He would ask questions and only succinctly answer those she asked while she carried on. The sexual dynamic was also set on their first night, where words and gasps were blended into a rolling cycle of contract and relax, with mutual giving without taking, which seemed to pull from an infinite source of energy and desire.

The constant sexual passion and lovemaking between Wind and Flora was in great contrast to his relationship with Monica. Wind had never had sexual intercourse with Monica; she was committed to maintaining her virginity until marriage. When they first started dating, three years ago, he told her he would respect her commitment. This did not stop them from sexually gratifying each other, but special tactics had to be employed, often in a safe, rigid, and mechanical format. At first it was exciting and made him feel like a teenager again, the vigorous foreplay and fumbling towards oral sex, mutual masturbation, or grinding. Wind was her third serious boyfriend, after a couple of failed long relationships and Monica was already a skilled simulatrix by the time they had gotten together. She owned her own lubrication and employed numerous techniques such as straddling him and rubbing her parted sex up and down the length of his penis or lying beneath him she could clench his penis in between her thighs where his strokes within the enveloping pseudo-vagina could stimulate her clitoris. For this second tactic, she kept her pubic hair neat and trimmed to allow greater sensitivity and ease of movement. All of her tricks lead to messy climaxes for him and their sheets, but mutual orgasms for their coupledom. Of course, there was far more of this in the beginning months of their relations and for more than two years now they had fallen into an organized routine with great intervals between dalliances. The initial charm he saw in the ingenuity behind the acts of simulation and the passion that comprised the awkward genital rubbings slowly wore off as Wind realized in this relationship, to be loyal to Monica meant being loyal to the two commitments she embodied, fidelity and chastity. This meant that unless he married her or deceived her, he would never again feel his penis within the heavenly warmth of a moist vagina; a feeling he had never before realize meant so very much to him. For the first year, he rationalized with her. He would ask what was so wrong with a penis inside if his fingers and tongue made their way in there. She used tampons. She didn't even have a hymen any more. As a retort it was easy for her to tell him that he was not Catholic, he believed in nothing but knowledge so he would never understand. Wise Wind knew it was useless trying to convince her and he really didn't even want to. He respected her faith, as technical and spiritless as he found it. He did not want to be the person to make her reject what she had held firm for so long. Her virginity was a mystery for him. For a while, he even subtly tried to get her into the idea of anal sex, telling her he had heard that some cultures practiced it as a way of enjoying intercourse while still saving the hymen for wedding night. She barely made the effort to roll her eyes at these attempts. Soon he just gave up and let the drive for sexual excitement and exploration inside him retreat. He was following her lead, and watched as she grew colder as time wore on, the sexual excitement of newness gone with an efficient routine of mutual orgasm in a rare and timely manner left in its place. He had forgotten that sex, love, and passion could all come together in an event of total surrender, that is, until he met Flora.

At the various superseding occasions of their meetings, stolen out of his real life and scheduled around the paying clients in hers, Flora revealed her childhood to him along with the rest of her life. With it came the pain of her mother's death when she was only eleven, before her first period, and her alienation from her aged father. To escape the memory of the deceased they moved from Cleveland, Ohio to Georgia, and settled in Roswell. Her father never had any time for culturing and was very concerned with making money, so her mother's few books became hers and along with them came a deep passion. She aimed to live creatively and as differently from her father as possible, so she painted herself a Goth and embraced it with all its trappings: accessorizing with fishnet, black lace, gloves; piercings of ear cartilage, nose, tongue, and nipples; blacking her hair; paling her skin; listening to The Cure, Bauhaus, Swans, Dead Can Dance, Siouxsie and the Banshees, My Bloody Valentine, Type-O Negative, Nine Inch Nails, and Sisters of Mercy among others.

She moved out at eighteen to live with a friend and started taking classes part-time at Georgia State University downtown. She worked as a temp, finding her own way, confused at what to study, how to make money, nothing exactly satisfying her interests. By day she removed her obvious piercings, tied up her raven hair, and substituted her black lipstick for her blood red; playing at dress-up with skirts and stockings and silk tops with lace trims. In classes, she devoured psychology and religion courses with sides of English literature and woman's studies, but the academic sphere made her restless and she did not want to do anything with those interests that others wanted her to. Her conversion and calling revealed itself to her during her weekly ritual of getting the Creative Loafing newspaper from the box on the corner and running through the classifieds, where she spotted an ad to *Be a Goddess for a Day, Possible Apprenticeship with a Sensual Massage Therapist, Call Goddess Ashtoreth*. That was how she met Goddess Ashtoreth, who trained her in the art of sensual massage and mentored her like an older sister, and her life was never the same. At the end of her apprenticeship, Ashtoreth included Flora on her website, handsofthegoddess.com, along with her other Goddesses, where she was known as Goddess Chloris, the Greek version of her name. With Ashtoreth's influence and her new confidence, Flora shed the gothic idiom and dyed her hair to a rich auburn, a compromise between the orange it was in her childhood and the walnut it had grown into in her teen years. Massage work allowed her to stop temping and get her own apartment where she could have in-call clients over for very private sessions. She began to understand a real sense of purpose as she felt the energy work through her clients, felt how her hands could heal emotional pains in others, as well as bring genitals to release and pleasure through orgasm. After a few months, as she read more and listened to the wisdom of Ashtoreth, she discovered that her calling was to further explore a direction of sacred prostitution, as she understood it. Ashtoreth let her go with her blessing when Flora branched out as an escort. It was clear that she could do greater good and receive greater pay. In that twilight world of society, she found an autonomous zone where she was free, careful and free. Ashtoreth's years of experience provided a model of precaution, and prepared the neophyte for legal matters and matters of personal safety.

In the three years since she moved into her own place, Flora truly came into her own. Along with finding her own niche in the industry of sex work, she diligently began to explore her own practice of spirituality. She went to temples and covens and meetings of all sorts where she sought to find a personal connection to the Eternal Goddess in all Her aspects, free of dogma, and along with other fellow seekers to whom she could relate. Her restless spirit could not acknowledge any restrictions on her faith and so she was open to many methods. She sought a connection to a deity in a reflective form; she sought the goddess within. When Wind had met her, she was involved with a goddess "reading group," as she called it, which seemed more like a non-Wiccan coven, or cult, to him. In this group, she had many acquaintances; some were also sex workers, this much he knew. Though she did not convey many specifics about the group, parts of this association trickled into their shared life. There was one night in late June when they had found some time together—he thought it had must have been the Friday of the 27th—when he noticed something different about her. As they lay naked and cuddled he trailed his fingertips down her long form and found sharp stubble all about her pubic area, an area that had been totally smooth and hairless all the time he had known her so far. She told him she was growing it all back out, she would still shave her legs and armpits, but she was allowing her womanhood to return to its natural form. There was a split happening in her reading group over the issue of pubic hair shaving and she was following the direction that conveyed what she thought of as the purer message. This was all that he knew about her group affiliation, for it was all that she told him. He was not about to push for more from her

and he saw no reason to worry at the time. She always spoke and acted with thought and confidence. She said she wasn't taking any clients
that weekend because she didn't want anyone to get bothered by the
prickliness, but she assumed he wouldn't mind. He didn't mind; he
just let his fingers play over the tiny spikes. As time passed and they
met in their way, he watched the slow growth of the whole area until
long, fine dark hairs covered her pubic mound and ran down along
her outer labia and surrounded the brown, pinched skin of her rectum.
The base of the hyacinth stem was no longer visible in the thicket, but
he made a game of searching for it.

Their time together was limited in planning, but felt limitless in
the moment. Internally, their nights ran on and he was lost in her. In
his recollections, he sought to find them both. In losing her he worried that he was losing part of himself, for with her went his sense of
perspective. Now, in looking for her, he sought for meaning and the
perspective it would hopefully give. He had the limited information
he learned from her and he had the feelings they had felt together, but
he did not know how any of those factored in relation to her death.
Thinking of her death and the way she died was a prime example of
this gap in his understanding. He knew the result, but he did not
know the how or the why, and this limitation caused him consterna-
tion. How little did he really know her that she could die or be killed
in such a way? The idea of a suicide made her more distant and shad-
owy, as did the thought of some dark ritual gone too far. In looking at
his memories, he found no answers only a deep well of questions. His
proximity to her life did not make it any smaller under observation,
and contrarily he found in it so much he would like to explore. At
least he had an edge on any other detective on this case. This was his
to solve, and he was confident that he could find something out by

entering himself within the basic framework of the life that she had conveyed to him.

There was one close friend, Sutra Diamante, whom Flora mentioned regularly. He could speak to her, along with her old roommate, Iliya Chernovsky. He could speak to Ashtoreth. She and Flora were still in close contact. In regards to the reading groups, Flora would get secretive, a trait that she did not normally express with him. She said that what occurred in the meetings and rituals stayed in the meetings and rituals, and that silence about these experiences preserved their power and sanctity. He was sure Ashtoreth knew something about these groups and might even have been involved in one of them. Secrecy or no, he would implore these women to help him, not only because it was the law, but because he was doing it for Flora. He would bring meaning to Flora's death, and if there were any people responsible for it besides herself, he would bring them to light also.

So, as he sat there on the couch in his living room, kneading his eyes, he knew what he must expose to understand her death. Within those secret rituals where she spent her nights when not with him or a client, must be the answers to what happened to her, he thought. She may have even been at one her last night alive. With a plan of action in mind, his thoughts of her became more fragile and he quickly tried to wrap them around her flickering form. In her, he found his anima, his shadow, his companion and partner, but it was a relation born in deceit and existed outside of the truth of his life that he had created. This justified her presence as shadow, for their relationship carried with it its own darkness. The thought that he was not the last man to be with her enraged one part of him and saddened another. The part it enraged was one that was insecure of his importance in her life, his exclusivity to some extent. The part that it saddened was one that understood that her life was as splintered as his. It had been over a week since he saw her and touched her and heard her voice, and he was trying to gently rub against the memory of each sensation with the fear that he could wear them away if he held them too tight or rubbed too hard. In his mind he reached out for her shimmering spectral form. Her thinness tightened to a further extreme around her bones and her pale skin blanched to opaque, as she floated in a mixed imagery of sheets, deep crimson satin sheets to floral lavender cotton, its orchids bursting independent of the cloth, budding and blooming in a rapid cycle. She shook her head, but he could not see her face, her hair hanging in cover, and with the motion from her shaking it waved and scaled through wild shades of red. He reached out, but could not touch her and just beyond his fingertips her hair burst into flame. She shook her head and the flames licked and whipped and she was screaming and trying to fight off the flames, but then she was all flames and so were the sheets and there was nothing but fire.

It was with the ringing of the telephone that Wind awoke to find that he had fallen asleep. He jolted up from the couch and made it to the table in two rings where he hastily banged the plastic receiver off its cradle. He said "Detective Jonathan Wind here," trying to sound awake and in control. His jaw was sore from clenching in his sleep and he thought he could taste the enamel dust from grinding his teeth. Through the receiver, the lifting fog of sleep, and his beating heart he could hear a woman's voice. It was Monica and she asked him if he was asleep to which he said no. She said she could tell that he was and then went on to tell him how sorry she was about last night. She shouldn't try to pressure him into marriage if he wasn't ready. He breathed heavily, and she asked if he had a hard day at work, to which he replied, yes. She asked if something bad happened, a death, and he answered, yes, again. He listened to the care and concern in her voice as she apologized again and said she was sorry for his day. She said that she loved him and in that foggy moment when he said, "I love you, too," he meant it with all of his heart, though he was not saying it to her.

6. BELOBOG

"You see my fwiend," he said, "when we do not love—we sleep; we are children of dust. But fall in love and you are a god, pure as on the first day of cweation..."   —Count Leo Tolstoy, *War and Peace*

WITHIN THE DARKNESS OF THE NIGHT, WIND HAD FINALLY RETURNED to sleep. It was *the sleep*. It housed *the dream*. The dream from his childhood. The one where he was a child again. In the dream, it seemed that he was about five; an age before the dream began. Two years before the death of his father, five was an age that knew no end, it saw none, there was no end in sight. No horizon broke his child's gaze and each new day rolled sunnily into one newer. Skies blue and lawns green cast his world in aquamarine, as he ran and played in between. Every day was play, every day was summer, and the winter ground was play of a different color. He was an innocent prince, great in the world, held high by a good king and queen. As crown prince, he had no true want, for anything that was not his would be one day and this contentment lay in trust that the firmaments were strong, the sun was warm, and the crown was incontestable. Even the secret murky darkness that raged occasionally, carefully behind his parents' bedroom door could not threaten the gentle breeze that seemed to glide him through the five-year old valley of his youth.

The dream came after five was done and gone. With the dawning of consciousness and the ideas of sin and loss came nostalgia. At seven, he dreamed of five. There were no dreams at six, or none that he could remember. It was an age that had no taste, no flavor for his buds of memory. The tide of five broke over six and seven snatched back across it. He had the memory of childhood joy and the memory of remembering it, but he did not know what came between the memory and remembering. So high and flat and shining was the plateau on which five existed, that the tumbling slope of six could not register in comparison. Seven evened back out, and his life began, as he knew it now, with his father's death. The dream was of what he had before.

In the dream, he is in a theater at a play, as his family often attended when he was young in Athens. The action is set with a forest scene and a great cardboard tree in the center of the background, two-dimensional sets painted with browns and greens in weak sweeps as if done with a marker. He rubs the smooth surface of a hard-boiled egg with his thumb in his hand—his mother frequently provided them as traveling snacks—in anxious expectation. Out comes a knight, shining and proud, but then he is old and could be Don Quixote and his sword, long and glinting, catches fire and then flops and dangles and becomes a snake. The old knight is shocked and then sad and startled again as the snake hisses. Young Jon shouts and laughs, in the pitch of a child with a spitting, giddy giggle, and throws the egg at the snake now at the base of the tree. The egg shatters, as if it is raw, and the tree erupts and grows. Everyone in the theater stands to watch, and he is scared. Then he is in an outside place alone and the tree towers tall and the world is like a cartoon meadow with only the tree at the center. Its branches are long, thick, and inhabitable, like the ones in the movie of Swiss Family Robinson. As the tree grows, the sky lifts up with it, separating from the ground with a noise like they were stuck together. The ground is hard like the shell of a turtle, but the sky is soft. There is a thundering noise, and across the branches stamp the hooves of four goats as they go running by. Little Wind thinks he can see one of them fall, but it is only rain; it is raining cats and dogs. He runs among the animals falling from the sky playfully, dogs and cats and a squirrel and a couple of swans. Across the sky spans a giant rainbow bridge and he can hear others running and laughing on it. Suddenly, Wind is in a hotel room with his parents. Then his mother is gone and he goes to his father. It is not his father, but his grandfather, who died before he was born and whom he never met. The old man strokes the boy's hair and gives him a very small book that Wind clutches in his left hand very tightly. He's worried he'll lose it, so he won't open his hand to look at it, but he is so excited to have it. A young boy his age comes in and tells him they have to leave, they must go to New York. But he is already sitting and packing by wrapping a yellow toy fire truck from a stack on his right under a table in small blankets he is taking from a pile on his left. Wind folds the long toys in the blanket with only his right hand, the left still clutching. The rhythm of folding is bliss, the prospect of travel is exciting, and the tiny book from his grandfather in his left hand that he is scared to open and look at because it might blow away, is keeping him in control. Some nights he opens his hand and there is nothing there and everything is black and he wakes scared. This morning he woke clutching tight his hand and clenching his jaw, tense and angry.

Detective Sergeant Jonathan Wind took a bite of his black olive and potato burrito and in biting felt a line of tension run through his sore jaw. He put down the burrito and rubbed at the sides of his face with his empty left hand, remembering, in a flash, everything he dreamed. Detective Sergeant Cedric "Sonny" Ledbetter continued to speak.

"Yeah, I love this place. The food is great. You ever come here at night? What am I saying? I bet you love this place, when you do get out, when you get your nose out of some book. Look it's great, they have tall boys of Pabst Blue Ribbon and Schlitz for only two bucks. Where else can you find cheap beer like that and such good food?" He smiled. "Also it's nice to go somewhere where we aren't gonna run into other cops. I don't think they could relax around here. The boys can be so cliquey."

"I heard Faulkner say that he and Harris were going to Manny's Tavern for lunch today."

"That is so like them. That place is all right though. Good burgers."

They sat on the porch of El Myr, on Euclid Avenue in Little Five Points. The sun was high and the chill of the morning had all but abated. It was the first cool week of the coming autumn, as it eased in slowly out of the usual southern Indian summer. At the end of the past weekend, a clear division was drawn during the darkness of Sunday night. While for a brief moment a fire raged, over thirteen times the human body temperature, in the small confines of Flora Ross's apartment, outside a frost was ever so gingerly sprinkled on the city of Atlanta and environs. The humidity that gave the summers the distinction of suffocating thickness, drawing out the body's much needed fluids until moisture permeated everything living and non, had been cut by more than half. The wind that came down the avenue and fluttered the napkins in their laps was more cooling and cheery than the bitter one that sat at the table before Detective Ledbetter.

"That is some wind, Wind," he said, but to no smile from his partner. "It is the beginning of the windy season here, the fall can get so gusty. It's still nice in the sun. And the wind can cut the damn humidity. I've never been to Chicago, but as the Windy City, I'd like to check that out. It can get so gusty here sometimes, I'd like to see something to rival it."

"Actually, Chicago is the sixteenth windiest city in the country," Wind could not resist himself, and put his burrito down. He felt too serious for small talk and maybe expounding in his way could take his mind away. "There is a little debate about how it got its nickname. The most common story is about the bidding war between New York and Chicago for the contract to host the 1893 World's Fair. The bidding was pretty crazy, since the fair was to commemorate 400 years since Columbus's discovery. Chicago was tired of being the 'Second City' in relation to New York and talked a lot of talk to try to win the bid. An editor of some New York paper, as the story goes, referred to Chicago as a 'windy city' and said it wouldn't be able to back it up if it did win. There is some speculation that the name was actually created in Chicago over a decade earlier as a tourist ploy and to emphasize the breeze that comes off the lake, but even if it was used then it wasn't popularized until it was in reference to bullshitting."

"Well, what do you know about that? Hum. Well, if that is the case behind the nickname, then this city could take it from them. It is always the season for bullshit here. Bullshit, and lots of craziness that makes no sense. This whole town is swept up in something. It's all image, all trying to make something where it wasn't already, or trying to make things into what they are not. The white people, rich and poor, are waiting for the south to rise again, though it never will. The black people are starting a hip-hop revolution where the Dirty South will rival the East and West Coast rivalries for bling content. And then, damn, so many other races all mixed in all over this city, that how could any one group think it's theirs. It is a melting pot for the world. Lots of people who seem to be living for illusions, or things that look so strange from the outside. I guess it means something to them, though. Don't get me wrong, I am all for faith, I believe in God, I love Jesus, and I do so out of choice after seeing other options. But it's like that woman yesterday, Tia Maite. Man, she was a character. Someone too weird to be real that she just has to be real."

Wind nodded as his partner rambled on, casually and expressively, and finished his burrito, sipping at his coffee, mixing the dissonant tastes in his mouth. Sonny took a quick sip from his iced tea and continued.

"That woman creeped me out. But she was so sincere, she really believed in everything that she was talking about, what she was saying. There is just so much of that windy bullshit from so many people. So many rich white kids trying to look like they are gang-bangers, and in turn ghetto kids trying to steal the American Dream without working for it. People can be whatever they want to be and they don't seem to ever stop wanting, or ever want anything substantial. So many folk who seem so lost. But not Tia Maite, fortuneteller extraordinaire, I bet she really does see herself as a seer from ancient Babylon doing that same thing, predicting the fate of the world, or like some Aztec priestess. She is perfect for this town, the New South. I had never even heard of the Aztec calendar. Man, am I glad she did your cards and not mine. I was serious about my mother, you know how she is like. She gets so narrow-minded with her church that she won't stand for anything occult-like. She'd have the congregation praying for my soul, while they're already praying for my safety. I am sure you imagined that that went on. I bet my mom even has them praying for you and the rest of the force. All this stuff you don't know about, people out there praying for you, and you don't even know. Tia Maite alluded to worlds within ours that we don't know about and I believe her. So much goes on behind closed doors and there are so many closed doors in this town, with fake, polite façades."

"Exactly, but it is our job to kick open those doors, to throw light into places of darkness. However dark they might be."

"Yeah, like yesterday, at Miss Ross's apartment. It was exactly that. Like a dank cave that we threw light into. Well actually not we, it was that fucking rook, Curtis. He really threw the light into that place, if you know what I mean. What a fool. But inside, it was like a New Age swinger's paradise with naked goddesses and sex books and candles everywhere. That place gave me the same strange feeling that the fortuneteller's shop did. I mean without even getting to the burnt smell and the pile of her remains."

Wind gave him a look he couldn't read. He was used to being unable to decipher what went on behind Wind's eyes when they were silent. He didn't know if the look was anger at his levity, or a reprimand at his certain identification that the remains belonged to Flora.

"Well, it's okay to say that, right? The dental records checked out with what was left of the teeth. The burnt ash and bone fragments must be the burnt remains of Flora Ross. Unless they are from someone else and her teeth were put there intentionally. And in that case, Miss Ross can't be in good shape either. So we must assume the rest of the body there goes with the teeth and it is her. DNA should be able to match the bones to the teeth," said Sonny, easily switching gears back into being Detective Ledbetter.

Wind had never thought of the option that it was not her, but to imagine that she was alive out there somewhere without her teeth bothered him in a wholly different way. The thought of her combusting in the quick flash that the fire inspector described was a lot better than if she suffered having her teeth pulled out or some other brutal pain that she must carry with her. Wind looked away from Sonny and out at the apartment building across the street. It was once a public high school and now it had a new life as designer apartments. He looked at the expensive cars in the parking lot—a BMW, a Mercedes Benz, a couple Passats, several SUVs—and almost laughed to remember the time of transition before the building was renewed and drug addicts and the homeless would kick in the windows to squat and crap inside.

"Also, it doesn't make any sense for anyone else to have been involved since the only door and all the windows were locked from the inside. So it must be her and it must have been done alone. So we are left with either suicide or accidental death. You never know with someone, what goes on in their head, but suicide would be strange from what I can read. An obviously high-priced escort, she seemed to be doing well for herself. The place was so clean, almost too clean, and orderly. I bet you felt at home in there with that sense of order that she had? From the looks of the place, she doesn't look like the suicide type. And the pictures of herself, around and under the bed, she looked happy, liked she enjoyed her life. Which isn't such a bad thing when you're paid to have sex. But some of those girls have it pretty rough. From what I saw, she didn't seem like one of those, dependent on the work, like she couldn't do anything else. Those pictures and the decoration of the apartment made it look like she was pretty into what she was doing."

"So then we are left with it being an accident?" Detective Wind questioned back at his partner, egging him on. Detective Ledbetter had his notepad out at this point and his steak quesadilla was nothing but tortilla crust on an empty plate.

"Yes, but what kind of accident could do that? She was a smoker and there was a good amount of alcohol in the kitchen, vodka, rum, tequila, scotch, white wine, red wine. So maybe Inspector Brennen's wick theory could hold up, she was loaded and lit herself up from the inside out. Which is pretty weird, one: since from the fibers found in the ash she could not have been wearing much more than thin lingerie. And two: from the looks of her in the pictures and her weight on her license being 120 at five feet eleven she didn't have much fat to burn up. Let alone enough to melt down the rest of the body. So that damages the wick notion slightly since there wasn't much of a wick on her. Then of course there was the other option he mentioned to us, about a spark shooting out of the electrical socket. But once again that explains the initial combustion, but that doesn't address how the fire could have just engulfed her so completely like that. Maybe it was a combination of the two?"

"I have been thinking about all of that and I agree with you. What kind of accident could it have been then? Do you think it could have anything to do with any kind of cultish involvement? Like what we spoke to the fortuneteller about?" Detective Wind was at this point testing his partner and wondered how much stood out to someone on the outside, without the intimate connection he had. He also hoped that he was missing something, being too close, and that Detective Ledbetter could tell him what that was.

"Well, to bring religion into this reminds me of my mother again. She is such a sweet, kind woman. But she can get downright wrathful sometimes. She would be all praying for this woman's soul if I told her about this and saying how she was 'sure that the poor woman had a place next to God now.' That is, until I tell her that the woman was a prostitute and immediately her face would harden and she would shake her head and just say, 'see, that's what you get, it was the will of God, if you live a life of sin you must suffer his wrath.' And she would have no more pity for the woman because God's justice was done. The woman was a sinner and he burned her up, smote her on the spot. She was an abomination to Him and she deserved what happened to her."

Detective Ledbetter finished what he was saying with a shake of the head. Detective Wind thought he had the appearance of either shaking in mockery of his mother, in agreement with his mother, or in pity for his mother.

"So do you feel the same way?"

"I love my mother, and growing up I went every weekend to Sunday School and every other church function. Once a month we had the pastor over for dinner. Whether I like it or not, I have the belief well-ingrained into me that Jesus loves me and that loving him back will save my soul. And it is always gonna be there, whatever I learned in school or have seen from people while on the force, it's not going to go away. But I have learned to take what I can from my Christian breeding and reject what I disagree with. I have made an effort to not accept the inconsistencies I have found. It's okay, there is enough there for me to appreciate without thinking that I need to believe and follow everything. So to answer your question, no, I do not feel the same way. I don't think God has the time or concern to be bothering with one poor woman in Atlanta who trades sex for money. If he is the God of love that I was led to believe He is, then he forgives instead of smoting or smiting, whichever it is. And anyway, I don't think prostitution is so bad, other than being illegal, it's an act of mutual consent. I don't see God going around burning up child molesters or murderers, those that deserve it, the real sinners."

He sighed deeply and took a long sip from his iced tea, now almost gone. In between lulls of wind the day almost felt hot, teasing with the sunlight.

"That is pretty much what I thought you'd say. I've gotten to know you pretty well. I just like hearing it. Our parents can instill a great deal into us without us even noticing that it is there. It comes up in times of pressure when we are backed into corners and it feels like an animal instinct."

"You're telling me. Remember, my degree was a double major in psych and criminology. I didn't mess around with all that philosophy that you did. But I guess you were going the pre-law route. One philosophy course was all I needed, but I had psych, abnormal psych, clinical psych, and behavioral psych out my ass. I really wanted to be a profiler. I still think of the FBI sometimes... Anyway don't mess with me and don't tell me what a burden the history of one's parentage is."

"Hey, if anything I'm jealous. You know I raised myself on my father's memory. My mom was working. I refreshed myself on all that I remembered before he died. Then I guessed at what else he would have taught me and learned it myself. Until I found my own interests."

"Yeah, I know. I just get touchy about my mom. She is a good woman, but she sees God like she saw her father, a strong, stern, violent man. Ready to beat a punishment into her. My father's not like that. Nope, Cedric Senior is a live and let live kind of guy. He lets his woman do all the carrying on about everything. He always seemed to shelter me from her, and her wrath. I was his Sonny, his junior. She made me strong, scared it into me, but he made me a man. He likes you though. He says that you are forthright. You should come around more. He asks about you sometimes. He likes chatting with you. I'll find a good barbecue to invite you to. They're gonna be planning at least one more before it gets too cold."

The server came and, bringing the check, asked them if they needed anything else. Saying no, both detectives could not help but smile at her as she placed it on the table. She was young and pert, in a white t-shirt, a black skirt and green knee-socks. Both of them tried to look away politely as she bent at the waist to gather up the plates from the table, her t-shirt frayed collarless and hanging low off one shoulder showing more than just her black bra strap. She righted herself and smiled again, telling them that she would be back for the check, before sticking out her lip and blowing upward to clear her short shaggy bangs from her line of sight and turning to go inside to the kitchen. They both went for their wallets and swift Wind produced a twenty before his partner could.

"I've got it, don't worry. It's yours next time." He left the twenty and they headed inside for the door. Out on the sidewalk, Detective Wind spoke. "You have the address? We can go straight from here? We don't have to go back by the station, right?"

"Yeah, I have it. I called and we are expected at about 2:30, so let's just go and do this."

Detective Jonathan Wind entered the squad car on the passenger side, letting his partner drive again. They took turns, driving in shifts. The awkward pleasure of being a passenger made Wind miss New York City. He looked out the window and thought of riding in the front seat of a taxi, all of his college friends crowded in the back. Only if they had more than just a couple of people and were going uptown would they ever deem it worthwhile to split a taxi. Normally, they took the subway everywhere and it went everywhere easily, once you understood its network and nomenclature. All of his friends outfitted themselves with monthly transit passes and found them essential to life. It was a great leap from the two lines in perpendicular fashion that Atlanta prided as MARTA. Wind had explored the new tunnels alone, reading on the trains and popping up above ground just to see where he was. Sometimes he walked back, taking in the city, and sometimes he did not pop up above ground at all, but just rode and read. All of that changed after his four years there when he returned to Atlanta and had to buy a car, for without a car in this city one couldn't really get anywhere.

Detective Ledbetter took weaving side streets, cutting through the green tree-lined blocks of old craftsman houses looking new, a fenced-in lot of overturned earth in the beginning stages of new development with the downtown skyline behind jutting out as if from the dirt, old factories and warehouses half abandoned and half converted into chic restaurants and galleries, into an area not yet touched by gentrification with mostly poor black inhabitants living in homes of fleeting time, and then along the right side of the Martin Luther King Junior Center, all shiny and new; from Euclid to a soft right onto Austin, which becomes Lake, which becomes Irwin, to slide skillfully right onto I-75/85 North.

Out the window, staring at the thick whizzing of lunchtime traffic, Wind let his agitation subside and remembered one night in the front of a New York City taxi; it was a fortuitous night. Looking out at the lights of the city and all the people moving about with so many motivations beyond his conceptions and references, he thought of how far he was from home, from Atlanta. He was in a very different place. The taxi driver must have thought that they were tourists, or at least visitors, so he drove them through Times Square. It was still early, only about twelve-thirty, when they passed beneath the steaming Cup of Soup and the city was in full swing. Supposedly, this was the town in which he was born, where both of his parents were born, and where all his grandparents—whom he never knew—met, married, and aged unto death. That night, he and his friends had all been drinking at a Columbia bar, visiting other friends, and were now heading south. The two girls in the back seat were asleep on their boys and he was alone up front, content not to speak to the driver. Twenty-one-year-old Jonathan felt like an alien just passing through and the alcohol enhanced his peaceful mood. He was at that point of consumption where he felt total comfort and ease, and yet it was a contentment that needed to perpetuate itself.

When the taxi arrived at their dormitory building on Broadway below 12th Street and everyone was roused to pool their cash, Jonathan threw in his share and made his getaway before they went inside. It was the fall of his last year and he was twenty-one. He knew there would be other nights, but his mind was fervently in the moment. Off he went towards St. Mark's, seeking more of what he felt, wanting to hold back time and not jeopardize any moment to the possibility of feeling any less ecstatic. He wanted to do something young and ironically he sought to force some spontaneity. Ducking into bars looking for more friends to enjoy the night with, he finally found some at Yaffa Cafe. Here he was happy to be with others to share his great elation of drunkenness and proceeded to consume even more. At some point in the crowded heat of the cafe, he went outside with his drink to the empty tables to smoke and feel the new coolness of the night. He noticed a woman sitting alone at the farthest table. She had a bottle of wine by her and held a half-full glass. She shivered a little, and from the distance he could tell she had been crying. Feeling bold and in control, young Jonathan strode on up to her and in his clearest voice of trained oratory said, "I am sorry but you look sad and that makes me sad and I would like to change that but all I can offer you is my company and a cigarette."

The woman looked up at him and her large eyes widened, and as her face tightened to smile so did their crow-footed corners, shedding the last tears. While he noticed that she was far older than he, he also noticed how beautiful she was. She accepted both his cigarette and his company and they began to talk. She told him her name was Iris Tamaro and her sadness was from loneliness. Her husband was in Las Vegas, he had gone to bet on a fight, but this was nothing new, he bet on everything. She thought he might be cheating on her, but even if he wasn't, she was sure he didn't love her anymore. His name was Alfredo and she described him as a chronic masturbator who wasn't interested in having sex with her any more. In the last ten years of their twenty married, they had only made love once, on their anniversary. Around the house though, she would find his pornography: tapes, discs, and magazines. Looking at the contents of the magazines she was confused as to what he desired from women and what he didn't desire about her. Every kind of fetish that she could imagine was represented. By her assessment, Fredo—as everyone called him— Tamaro, when not thinking about the ponies, boxing, greyhounds, or cards, was fantasizing about fat, thin, Asian, redheaded, old, young, hairy, shaved, leather-strapped, tattooed, natural, implanted, women's feet. This had finally overwhelmed her and when he had left her this weekend, she had planned to go to the city and find herself a life.

She said that she had never loved her husband, yet still that night, when she journeyed from her comfortable house in Yonkers, alone, into the city to have fun, whatever that would entail, she was guilti-ly frightened. She, at forty-nine, could only experience fear with the excitement of a prospect as unfamiliar as "fun out on the town." And moreover, for a Friday night in Manhattan, the only thing she could imagine as fun would be meeting a man. On this trajectory, she could not invite any of her friends or coworkers. She had been living with the appearance of being "the good wife" so long that the appearance mattered more than the actuality. The actuality was a loveless marriage in clear undeniable contrast to the deep love she once had with her first husband, Ernie. Too young to marry, they were a tragic pairing from the start. Her father did not approve. Not technically Jewish for her community, Iris still referred to herself as a daughter of Judah, born of Gentile mother and Semitic father. It was that father, a husband of an inter-faith marriage, an inter-faith marriage that cost his progeny their history, who forbade her to marry a Gentile. She did anyway, and she was happy and she loved Ernie and he loved her. But the tragic cycle continued to turn as it must and after a year of marriage, Ernie was diagnosed with cancer at the young age of twenty-one and a year later he was dead and she was alone. After no time for mourning, her father convinced her to marry again and made all the arrangements. Thinking it would please her, he set her up with another Gentile, this one of his choosing, who was not only older than her, but already wealthy with a chain of laundromats. Fredo bought Iris a travel agency near their home in Yonkers to keep her busy and there she worked every day, sending people on vacations and never going anywhere, except Florida once a year with Fredo and his family.

Consciously, Iris did not think about the fact that she had gone out to meet a man to remind her of Ernie, a young man steaming with life and energy, the way she remembered him before the cancer, but here was twenty-one-year-old Jonathan and she felt decades younger. In regards to love, she had come to feel like an old maid. She had been promised love, as every marriage does, and as the promise was unfulfilled, she was overdue. It only took one look in Iris's brightening eyes, in conjunction with alcoholic euphoria, for twenty-one-year-old Jonathan to feel an affirmation of his youth and vitality from Iris. The feeling was not unlike that of love. He was a long way from love in his present life and wondered if he had ever really known it beyond the innocent awe he experienced with his high school girlfriend. The previous year, he had ended his second college relationship with the realization that in both he had been living a compromised illusion, or outright lie, in which all he cared about was making the other happy, or reaffirming the illusion of happiness they had offered him. He was at a place where he found romantic relationships a game, subject only to how well they were played. And here, once again, in this first meeting with Iris, he felt that with her he could be important, he could fulfill a true need. He could play that role.

With all of these feelings and realizations flowing between the two inebriated parties, in a cloud of their own smoke and talk, in the ever-biting chill of night, the natural progression was towards a bed, and they chose her home in Yonkers. Heroic Jonathan drove her car; his dominance and control apparent even in drunkenness. They talked the whole way, sharing hopes for a life just beginning and dreams of a life starting almost too late. Iris told him about her husband and his masturbatory habits and how she would love to be desired that way, but she could only find random pleasures weeding through her husband's pornography. He told her about all the girls he had been with and how young they were in their bodies. He told her that she looked like Deborah Winger, with her big eyes, brown hair, and wide mouth. He was to be her Richard Gere and would lift her up and carry her off. She said that she loved that movie and that he was sexier than

Gere. Soon enough, they were in her driveway and then in her house and he carried her to bed.

Twenty-one year-old-Jonathan returned to that bed several more times over the semester and into the new year. Fredo traveled a lot, whether it was to Las Vegas, Atlantic City, Foxwoods, or Mohegan Sun and he worked a lot over the week, whether it was at the Yonkers Raceway or Belmont Park. Many afternoons and a few whole nights, Iris found her way into Jonathan's dorm room, and each opportunity was like time travel to the same university where she had met Ernie. A few times he took her out with his friends when they went to the local bars. She began to find it very easy to forget her other life and her age, and always seemed to be returning late and having people cover for her at work. She was glad that she had no children with Fredo and she began to feel that there was very little to keep her returning home. Jonathan's schedule was a natural fit for hers and they made time between and after classes. When she went home, he had time to study and enjoy his last year in the city. He was learning more from the time he spent with this woman than he had with all the girls before her. In bed, he enjoyed feeling the soft looseness of her aging skin around her hips and belly; and her breasts and how they hung, such a contrast to what he was used to. He would kiss gently the wrinkles at the corners of her eyes and mouth. As much as she was reaching back to reclaim the self she lost in the past, he was reaching forward in time to the man he would become and the women he would know at that point in his life. He explored the future in her body, his future and the future that femininity held for him.

That April, she came to him crying on a night they were supposed to meet and told him that she was ready to leave Fredo. She told him that the time she had spent with him had lifted her up out of feeling like someone abandoned to being a housewife and now she felt like a person: sexual, desired, independent, and no longer afraid of living. She was afraid of many things still, but no longer afraid of being alone and taking chances on her own. Continuing to cry she told him that this meant that she must leave him too. She was going to move out to California, with the thousands of frequent flyer miles she had saved up, and start totally new and fresh. He had given her the strength to leave her husband and now she must use that strength to leave him. Twenty-one-year-old Jonathan was happy for her. How could he not be? She had become a very different person than the one he met that chilly night at Yaffa Cafe. He could see it in her eyes and the way she carried herself, and he heard it in her voice. Over their last five months together, she had given in to the excitement of a new boyfriend and had not only lost weight, but had also bought new lingerie and a new scent, gotten highlights in her hair, explored higher skirts and lower necklines, and even begun waxing her bikini-line. The woman who said goodbye to him that April evening was someone whom he had not fully seen until then; her growth had been gradual, and here she was testing her strength by saying goodbye to her lover, who gave her nothing but pleasure, so she could begin again somewhere far away.

With a kiss and a smile, maturing Jonathan let her go. He knew that she was not really sad, but excited, with a new excitement free from fear, and that soon enough she would forget him. She did not need him any more, but he was glad that he could give her what she needed. He was not sure how to feel. He missed her, but he knew all along that it would not last, that it couldn't, it wasn't meant to. He never let himself go totally. All along he saw it as something for a particular time and a place, roles that must be performed because they were important and necessary. As randomly as she had appeared in his life, she had disappeared again. Back he went to his classes and studies and friends of his own age. Back he returned to love that only existed as theory, and that practice never could fully capture. He was left with the looks they shared and the feel against his lips of the soft loose skin along her belly, pale from being hidden from the world for so long.

Sonny coughed, and then spoke abruptly out of the heavy silence befallen the car, picking up from where he believed the conversation had left off.

"I guess we all have something. I mean, I have the God I have always loved and Jesus right after Him, and sometimes they are one in the same for me. And you, you don't seem to have any inclination towards a God or any kind of higher being outside of your books, the knowledge that they hold in them and maybe that they represent. Your apartment, it's like fuckin' Faust in there. But you have something else other than all that worship of book-learning. You are so composed all the time, and it seems like trivial things don't really matter to you or catch your interest and you always have an answer for everything. You act like you have seen everything, and believe me, I know I can get like that too, especially with as long as we have been doing this job. But there is one last innocent thing I find in you that lets me know you still have beliefs that are not explainable and that don't really make sense. It is that thing that really jazzes me about you."

"And what is that? Do tell."

"The Pez, man, the Pez. Come on, I bet you have one in your pocket right now, probably in the same right pocket of your jacket where it always is. Come on, let's see it."

Wind sighed and gruffly reached into the right pocket of the jacket lying on his lap. From it he drew a Karl Marx Pez dispenser, with white shaggy hair and full bristling beard, on a red shaft body.

"See. Look at that. That's fuckin' Marx, isn't it? Damn, you never fail. To think, yesterday I got you Golda Meir, and the day before I remember you tipping back the head of President Eisenhower to give me a strawberry Pez. You switch dispensers with each new day. That is great. I love how something as silly as a candy dispenser can have representations of politicians and pop culture icons on it and it just fits right in. Plastic people in plastic, dispensing artificially flavored candy."

Wind kept his glare tight and cold, alternating between looking forward onto the highway, as they merged onto GA-400, at his partner, and out the side window at the dirty concrete of the highway wall on an otherwise clean stretch of roadway, a southern extension joining GA-400 within the perimeter to I-85, a process he watched thirteen years ago, as it was cut through the homes, yards, and trees of people easy to sell for progress and the high prices for land it brought.

"So what's with it? You said to me once that your books weren't a collection, they were a library, your resources, and that you used them like tools. And all of that I can buy, I've got a good amount of books myself. But the Pez? There can't be any reason for those other than them being a collection. And if they are just a collection for collecting's sake then why Pez? All this time together and I still don't know what the Pez is about. You've never mentioned it and I have never asked. So now I am asking, what's with the Pez collection?"

The squad car slowed only slightly as it passed through the cruise lane of the only tollbooth in Atlanta. The sensors registered the cruise card on their windshield and they proceeded north at a few miles over the speed limit. Wind sighed again and chuckled, his partner's exuberance cooling his general agitation. With the levity of the new mood, he thought for a moment about his tension and wondered if he needed more coffee or to rid his body of the excess already at flow in his system.

"Well, first, I am glad you are so amused with yourself, and so concerned with what I do. You've been using your skills of detection and reasoning and you have me pinned down. I do have a collection of Pez, they are a true collection, they serve no true function and they are self-perpetuating. As for what is with it all, or why I do it? I am still not sure, actually. I have thought a lot about it though, as you can imagine. I guess it must seem pretty irrational, but I hope not too out of character. My father gave me a Pez dispenser when I was five. It was the early eighties and he was trying to quit smoking, so he bought one to do like a Kojak thing with the lollipops, or like Reagan did with the jellybeans. He saw an Archduke Francis Ferdinand dispenser and thought it was an appropriate choice to replace smoking, since he was the spark in the powder keg. He was amused by it, and elaborated to me on its totem-like and iconic properties to me. I played with the dispenser, and eventually he didn't need the crutch anymore and gave it to me. I held onto it for many years after he died. My mother noticed that I still had it and she bought me another one, a Prince Charles. On Christmas, she would get me another one, as a stocking stuffer, and then it was a thing. After she stopped buying them for me I just started picking them up. It seemed pretty natural, the process, and now I have a collection of them. It increases all the time. The more they make, the more I will buy. At this point, I might as well keep it up, it's tradition."

"How many is that now?"

"The one you picked up for me yesterday made forty-five."

"Wow. And you have them organized by their series or alphabetical or some shit?"

Wind nodded and smiled a sly sliver of lip, exhaling through his nose a stillborn laugh.

"Another thing that I like about them is that though my collecting of them serves no true practical purpose, other than the fact that I could resell them to other collectors, they are individually practical in their own right and I utilize that. I don't just leave them lined up in their formations and not touch them except to occasionally dust them. I take them out in turn by mood or humor and load them up with candy each day. They all get their turn, and I like having one with me. Even though I still might have a cigarette occasionally, I have the dispenser there for a different crutch, I guess." Wind looked down at the bushy beard and hair of the plastic Karl Marx head in his right hand with its red shaft. He thought about how much it looked like Santa Claus—if you ignored the furrowed brow—or Papa Smurf.

"Yeah, that is pretty much what I thought you'd say. I have gotten to know you pretty well. I just wanted to hear you say it. Our parents can instill a great many things into us without us even knowing they are there," Sonny said, without being able to hold a few erratic blasts of a deep, coughed laughter.

"Touché," nodded Wind at his partner's trump. It was hard to be angry with such companionship as they shared, but he woke up this morning raw inside. He could feel comfortable with Sonny to the extent of their familiarity and developed bond, but inside he was not comfortable. Yesterday he never woke up, because he had never slept and his day mounted dark and more confusing as it endured. Today, he woke to a reconfirmation of the reality of yesterday.

"That is my point, though. You too have this thing based on tradition that came from your dad that you do that is not practical. Like me and my mom. It is like faith in something that there is no reason to have faith in. Or belief in something there is no reason to believe in. Don't give me that look. There is something ritualistic about your collecting and lining up of little pieces of plastic that makes you feel a certain way. They obviously do something for you. It's all my psych training. For you there is a payoff in the habit that makes it worth doing, even if you don't understand why or if it is even detrimental. Hey man, don't get me wrong, I love it. You come off so cool and then there is this about you. It's still cool. It's not as extreme, or as really far out as some people get. Like the fortune-teller yesterday. She's in her own world, doing very much her own thing. And if that midget was quite like you described with the Goethe quoting and all, he must be doing his own thing too. It's those folk who make things interesting and a little scary, you know. And yesterday was a little too interesting. What happened to that woman looked like something out of the Old Testament, the things I hear in church, about sacrifices of flesh, burnt offerings. Something so Biblical about it all, just in appearance, without even getting into the idea of sin and punishment."

"Well, if it makes you feel any better about it, the ancient Israelites didn't commit any human sacrifices. God stopped Abraham's hand from hurting Isaac. The Canaanites of the area, they had human sacrifice in their practices and some scholars even think that was another thing behind the Abraham and Isaac story, a denouncement of Canaanite practices. Another thing different is that in the sacrifices and burnt offerings of the ancient Israelites they only used male livestock as an offering. Here we have a woman burnt," responded Wind, with a sensitive tone of authority.

Yesterday was consistently flashing before Wind's eyes while they talked. He worked his memory like the Viewfinders of his boyhood, with each blink a different image projected before the black, a sample clip of what was cycling just below his liminal level of consciousness. Working through memory and imagination, his thoughts were a precarious place to navigate. What he remembered about Flora and what he wondered about Flora became one, and then secondary scenarios approached, and by the time he apprehended tertiary possibilities he was lost in the infinite potential of uncertainty. The more he knew, the more he could control his imagination and quantify the reality of Flora's death, but before then he was beginning to drown in the thrashing cross-waves of ambiguity. That was the anger of the day he was born into, and since it was so thick and clouding, he could not see this truth through it. He was afraid of his own mind because he did not know how to organize the facts within it. Normally, he devised a simple process to allow for the unfolding of a case. In a detached space, he could shut his eyes, or just let his mind clear while driving or jogging or some other repetitive action, and allow the facts of the case to interweave as he scanned for threads, seeing what fit, and following potential threads and connections. Sometimes he would picture a box and put into the box all that was known about the case and through visual equations he could line up the data categorically. Logic statements were made and drawn up in the box to make order of the situation. Since yesterday, the situation was different and it was not data organization as usual. He could not find the ability to detach from this investigation enough to treat it as just another case. He realized that if he were to make a box for the investigation he would be in there looking out among the other facts. And that wouldn't work. He would need to get himself out of the box to think objectively. Wind suspected that the normal box process could not work because he could not just leave Flora alone in a little mental box to be sorted like another datum, and he would want to remain there with her.

When Sonny had mentioned Tia Maite and the albino little person, Wind mechanically separated out the little person, for though he was fascinated by the experience, he had no place for it in what he knew so far. Considering Tia Maite for the moment, sifted out of the images and information churning just below his conscious attention, he reprimanded himself for not asking her yesterday if she knew where Flora was on Sunday night. She would have answered like she answered all the other questions about Flora, that it was not for her to betray the trust of her clients, that he and his partner must come to this information on their own. Regardless, he still wished he had asked, for the sake of protocol, to see her reaction, and out of worry that his judgment might be clouded to his regular methodology.

"When the fall sets in and the wind picks up on these streets it is amazing. You can even catch a little of it, look there. Those gusts, thick with leaves, turning back and in on themselves. It's like that movie *American Beauty*. I remember last year, the streets downtown can be so tight, it was happening all over the place. Leaves and trash, a mess in the air. A whole lot of nothing, looking so powerful, moving in the air. I was on a bridge somewhere, like that one back over the highway, I think it was the North Druid Hills bridge over 85, and the wind was so strong, even in my Explorer, you could feel the wind push on the car and affect the steering. I felt so weak, trying to hold the wheel straight in that big SUV. It's good to think that that season is upon us," Sonny rambled rapturously.

They had exited off GA-400, turned right, and were proceeding east on Holcomb Bridge Road into the eastern side of Roswell. Off the exit were strip malls, the kind that cling conveniently to points of highway access in the suburbs, with gas stations and Waffle Houses, along with the more common grocery stores, banks, and places to take Tae Kwon

Do lessons. Past the commercial cluster, they drove by strips of pine, fir, and slight elms giving shelter to apartment complex buildings, which through the thinning foliage all looked like Monica's building and were probably made by Post, or one of the other companies popular about town. Leaves were on the ground in light accent, bright greens not yet turned, matching the living green of the grass. On they drove, and continued to debate or mutually expound on the weather and the ways in which people are prone to cling to illusion. With Holcomb Bridge Center shopping mall on their left and Pike Nursery on their right, they turned left onto Nesbitt Ferry Road, and proceeded to a right turn into the Rivermont subdivision just before the golf course. Detective Ledbetter took out the notepad from his breast pocket, flipped it to the folded page, and handed it to Detective Wind. Detective Wind read from the page and scanned outside before pointing out the house whose number corresponded to the information that they had. The car was steered into the driveway and brought to rest.

At the front door both uniformed men, one of dark brown skin and one of milky paleness, cleared their throats and adjusted their ties. Standing to the right of the darker-skinned man, the other snapped his neck in a tight limited rotation to both sides, letting off brief crunching noises, before his partner reached out to ring the doorbell. The house was gray with gray-blue shutters and the door matched the shutters. From the outside, it was obvious to the detectives that this was a house original to this neighborhood, that it had been there since the late sixties or early seventies, a ripe old age for an Atlanta house in a suburban subdivision. Wind had grown up in a similar house from a similar period of growth, when his mother was able to afford getting out of their first apartment after his father's death, though it wasn't as large or in such an exclusive subdivision. Properties such as this were affordable investments for the land on which they sat in a city that felt no shame in buying the old to build the new in its place. Rivermont had held its own against the slash and burn of progressive real estate, its status founded in time and golf course, and maintained at a cost for the present generation. Just around the corner sat subdivisions no more than ten years old, like sapling branches cut into the old tree lines, bending and branching, leaving limited yard room with the sole purpose of producing buds of cul-de-sac at each end so the children of young families could ride their bikes safely and securely.

The front door opened and a very tall, pinkishly-pale man stood in its path. His large head was bald on top and thin feathery white hair fit like a half-wreath around its sides and back. Thick glasses with subtle gold panes magnified his wide blue eyes and bushy gray brows. A white oxford shirt with pearly buttons was tucked over his prominent stomach into gray slacks held by a black leather belt. The skin around his neck and collar was white to the point of opaqueness, but his face and hands were freckled and pinkish with the most pink found on the vulnerable crown of his head, patterned with large freckles and liver spots. Before he could say anything, the dark-skinned detective spoke first.

"Mr. Stanislav Ross? I am Detective Sergeant Ledbetter and this is Detective Sergeant Wind. We are from the Atlanta Police Department. I called you earlier. Can we come in and speak to you for a moment? As I said before, it is in regards to your daughter, Flora."

The man in the doorway shook hands with both detectives before ushering them inside, visibly startled and worried, quick to respond.

"Please come in Detectives. You just caught me, I was waiting, but I was about to leave presently to show a house. My work is that of real estate agent so my schedule is demanding. What is this about my daughter that you would like to talk to me? What has she done? What has happened?" His accent was thick, but careful, though he seemed to stammer a bit, caught off guard. Detective Wind knew that Stanislav was from Ukraine and that over the last four decades he had worked dedicatedly on either reducing his accent or at least making it clearer.

"Mr. Ross if we could sit down a moment," said Detective Ledbetter.

"Please, call me Stan. Yes, sit. Sit."

The man moved almost unaware of his size and directed the detectives into the home, plain and neat, with white walls and cream carpet. A landscape painting of gentle hues fit each wall as if from a corporate lobby from the 1990s. Stiffly, the detectives sat on the taupe leather couch to which they were led. The great white man lowered himself into the wood-framed leather swivel chair across the glass-topped coffee table from the uniformed detectives. His great pale hands hung for a moment over his knees before he fit his fingers together and peered back at the visitors. He read the worst in their mutually silent countenance and his long frame tensed, leaning in forward, closer to them. The skin that had appeared so loose when he moved, like tissue paper, tightened to the old man while blood rushed to its surface, rouging his cheeks, forehead, and chin.

"Mr. Ross. I, we, are very sorry to have to inform you, but there was a fire early yesterday morning in your daughter's apartment and regrettably she did not survive," said Detective Ledbetter.

"I see," said the old man.

Detective Ledbetter paused for a moment and looked at Detective Wind before looking back to Mr. Ross, who was reacting in no visible way.

"Mr. Ross, when was the last time you saw your daughter?"

"Well, I spoke to her last week, Wednesday or Thursday. Wednesday, yes. But I have not seen her since August when last we met for lunch." He stammered, and yet though he tried, he could no longer be thoughtful with his words, concentrating instead on his breathing, which had begun to sound erratic. All the blood was instantly gone from his face. Again, he was loose skin, speckled and thin. Detective Wind took keen notice when the breathing abated. For a moment it was as if he'd received a deathblow, his posture slack, his shoulders lowered, his hands hanging from his knees, and his eyes turned down towards the glass table. Detective Wind was about to reach out to the man, to touch his knee, to do something to prove the man still lived, but with the next breath the body twitched back to life and began to rise.

"I'm sorry detectives, I hope you do not mind if I have a cigarette?"

Mr. Ross stood to his full height and stepped to the narrow table lining the wall. On the table's surface was an ornate wooden box with mother of pearl inlaid patterns sitting beneath a metal-framed mirror. He opened the wooden box and drew a green-gray and gold pack of Benson and Hedges. After lighting a cigarette, Mr. Ross reached to the coffee table for the crystal ashtray and returned to stand by the wall ashing and smoking erect and awkward.

"Do you need me to come identify her body?" Mr. Ross spoke after smoking half of the long cigarette.

"Actually, sir, the remains, her remains were not left in very good shape, so a positive identification was made by your daughter's dental records. That is what took us so long in coming to you." Both detectives shuffled slowly with controlled movements while Detective Ledbetter spoke.

"Yes, I see." The old man looked tired and after his first cigarette he lit another one and remained standing to smoke. "A fire... Yes... I see."

Detective Wind watched the great old man from his lower position on the couch. He could see his eyes magnified through the thick glasses, the blue once so bright, now soupy with blood vessels shooting through the sclera. If within the frames were the windows to the man's soul, then Detective Wind could relate to the liquid chaos he saw. As the left assisted in smoking, Mr. Ross's right hand steadied him against the table.

In their nights together, Flora had told Wind about her father. She created an image for Wind of a strong man and here he was now facing a bent giant. He wondered if this was too much for the old man to endure. This man had survived the darkest fighting of the Second World War at the Battle of Stalingrad, receiving the Russian equivalent of the Purple Heart. After the war, he attended the Poly-Technic for chemistry at his home in Kiev, before fleeing for the United States where he was able to get a job at a pharmaceutical company. She described the long hours he worked when she was a child, and even though he retired when her mother died and they moved to Atlanta, he continued to work in real estate to provide as much for his daughter as he could. Wind already had much respect for Stanislav Ross. Sitting in his presence, not only did this respect endure, but a deep compassion for him had come over Wind. As the man's eyes swam in deep pools of tears repressed through a lifetime of strength and diligence, Detective Wind's eyes were very clear. He aimed to redeem this man's sorrow, to give justice to the death and memory of his daughter. For a relationship in which he once had no responsibilities, he now felt totally responsible. Always a thinker in matters of the heart, he felt that Flora needed him more now in death than she ever did in life.

"If you don't mind me asking, sir, is there a Mrs. Ross?" At this point Detective Ledbetter had his notepad out and a pen in his hand.

"No. She died of cancer when Flora was young. We lived in Ohio at that time." With etiquette, he looked toward the questioner when he answered, but his eyes were not totally focused and Detective Ledbetter could tell that he was being polite, that he was not actually looking at him.

"And Flora is an only child?"

"Yes. Flora's mother and I married late by many standards, though she was much younger than I. She was my second wife. There was almost a sibling to Flora. There was a child by my first wife. A girl also, but she died from complications in the last month of pregnancy. My first wife did not live for a long time after that. I have always thought that she died from sorrow. She could not live knowing her own child died within her, she could not help her though she was so close. She had always wanted a daughter and would have loved the woman Flora grew to be. As Flora's own mother would have loved to see her. It seems I cannot keep the women I love alive. I remain alive these seventy-eight years, as if there is no end, through war, two marriages, two deaths, and the parenting of a daughter who is then taken away." He sighed and drew from the cigarette and it appeared that he was not talking to them, but merely talking.

Detective Ledbetter wrote his notes and Detective Wind continued to observe without even pretending to scribble in his pad. If his partner questioned him he would easily be able to recall everything Mr. Ross had said.

"Now, I regret having to ask you, sir, but are you familiar with what your daughter did for a living?"

"My daughter kept no secrets from me, though there were things that we did not normally speak of. I know how she made her living. That was enough. I offered her money, but she always refused. It is awful to say, but I almost think she liked what it was that she did." Then a look of concern came across his face and he turned to Detective Ledbetter, his eyes on him and asked, "Do you think what she did had anything to do with her death?"

"No, I am sorry to have worried you. It seems that her death was accidental. A centrally located fire within her apartment. There is no sign of any kind of foul play or anything. It all seems to be a very unfortunate accident. We are not sure of the cause of the fire. There is some discussion that it is probably electrical. We are waiting for more lab work. I, we, just wanted to be sure that you knew before you dealt with the personal effects in her apartment and stumbled upon anything." The detective looked down as he trailed off, unsure whether he might have said too much.

"Well, yes... her apartment. I had not yet thought about that. There is much I must do. Many preparations to make."

The third cigarette was finished and stubbed out gently against the side of the crystal ashtray. With his broad shoulders leading up and back, the length of the man drew out of his slump to a point of full presence. An amiable smile came over his face and he dabbed at the sides of his eyes with handkerchief from his pocket. From the window, rays of the sloping sun slipped through the room to fall in full illumination over the tall and mighty white man, the wall-mounted mirror providing backlighting so he glowed in full glory, with rays coming through his hair and through the billowy parts of his pellucid shirt as if through his very skin.

"Thank you, Detectives, for coming and bearing this troublesome news to me. It must not have been easy for you to do. You both have been so kind. But I am sorry, I must be off to an appointment showing a real estate property to a prospective buyer. Business does not wait."

Detective Wind, not letting his initial shock at the man's sense of decorum deter him, was the first to rise, crossing in front of his sitting partner to approach the old man.

"Mr. Ross," Detective Wind began, with all the heavy seriousness of justice, "We don't know exactly what happened, but we are investigating. I apologize that there is no certainty yet for you. We are trying to understand, and for you I hope we understand soon. I commit to this and will make it my first priority."

Stan Ross put his hand firmly on Detective Wind's shoulder and looked down at the smaller man before he spoke.

"You understand all that you want. That is your job, to understand. Understanding is not for me, it changes nothing, does no good at this point. For me all there is to do is mourn. Love my daughter and mourn for her." With his left hand still on the detective's shoulder, he ushered him a little towards the door and his partner rose to follow.

At the door, Detective Ledbetter turned back, notebook still in hand.

"Before, when you mentioned the war. Did you fight on the Russian side?" Detective Ledbetter was filling in all the details, even those he only deduced by observation.

"Yes. Before Ohio, I lived in Kiev. My family name is Rostov. When I came to America I changed it to Ross to make myself sound more professional. In a way, it is a tribute to the River Ros that runs through Ukraine, a branch of the Dnieper. From that river comes the name of the Russian people, proudly. I took this new name and having people address me as Stan is a little easier than Stanislav. Of course, I have taken too much of your time. You men must be very busy, as am I."

Again, Stan Ross apologized for meeting them under such circumstances, for his family tragedy worrying them, and for taking them so far from their headquarters to visit him and bear such news. Passing through the door, official good-byes were made on the part of the police force and cards were handed to Mr. Ross. The memory Detective Wind took away from the visit ended with Mr. Ross laying that white hand of condescension upon his shoulder. He found the man's actions and attitude thereafter to be an unmemorable defensive façade; Wind's mind was set on a course of action. The sorrow of a once-great man now laid low was a splash of gasoline onto the fire he already felt inside. The growing toxic flame solidified his purpose, hardening the steel he had erected within to reinforce the mere bone and flesh that supported him. Detective Wind's brow tightened as they entered their vehicle; he was picturing the flame in the center of his chest like a mandala, in the place of his heart, and he could feel it burning.

Back west they rode down Holcomb Bridge Road, until they returned to GA-400, southbound. They had gone up with ease and now they returned with ease, going against the traffic leaving work early, fleeing to the upper neighborhoods of the greater metropolitan area. In the car, Sonny addressed Wind in a relaxed manner. He was slightly taken aback by the way in which his partner made an open commitment to the father of the deceased. This contributed further to his suspicions that Wind knew more about this case than he was saying and that he might be involved with the victim in some way. Out of respect and concern, he observed without revealing his suspicions; he wanted to give his partner the space and time to sort out whatever it was, but he still wished he could help. Yesterday he tried to let his partner know he was there if needed and he was not sure if he should even bother to say it again. Instead, he tried to talk officially about the case. Sonny told his partner that he thought they should go ahead and close the case; that since nothing led to any suspicion of outside involvement, the only viable options were suicide and accidental death, and without any principle cause of the fire leading back to intention on the victim's part, accidental death was the most sensible estimation. Wind nodded along as Sonny mentioned that tomorrow he would look over all the lab results from the Georgia Bureau of Investigation and make sure there was nothing they missed before closing the case.

Wind was no longer listening to his partner because no matter what was recorded in their report the case would not be closed to him. Talking to her father, he felt a new closeness to Flora, but not one that brought him any closer to understanding what happened to her. There was never the question of why it mattered how she died. There was something intrinsically wrong about her death. One moment she was walking about her apartment, naked or in one of her many gossamer nighties, and the next she was aflame. Then she was gone. The ash he saw was not Flora. She didn't live a life meant for accident; she was better than that. He could rest if only he knew the reason. That's what he told himself. What was she doing? What kind of power did she call upon that could incinerate in such a way? He didn't believe in such a God, but he did believe that there was far more to her and her world that was hidden from him. The words of Tia Maite were with him. Ockham's Razor—as Sonny brought up yesterday—was in his mind. He found it most likely to believe in the greatness of the woman he loved, and that this was an adverse side effect of some intention of her own, instead of some freakish case of spontaneous combustion. Whether that intention was totally her own or under the influence or guidance of others is what he intended to uncover.

"It amazed me how well he took it all after his initial shock. That man is a real survivor, all that he has been through. I liked him, I felt really bad to tell him. It was one of those times I wished you'd be more chatty on the job. I understand your caution and you know I have never questioned it. I know you like to watch and take it all in and it's always worked in the past. We are a good team. It is funny though, to think how you can run on at the mouth in any other situation, a fount of trivia and extemporaneous knowledge," said Sonny jabbing again; this time figuratively elbowing Wind. "I bet in a different situation you would have a lot to talk to that guy about, he seems like someone you'd like."

Wind nodded and smiled at his partner. Sonny meant well. Wind deduced his suspicions, but he felt he must continue alone. The comfort of their bond allowed him to relax a little even if he couldn't talk about what he was thinking. They rolled towards, then under, I-285, with branches of traffic splintering into car segments of varying lengths at slow erratic flows up ramps, down ramps, merging and splitting, the longest segments where their squad car was not. It was clearer on their side of the highway, the asphalt gray with black marks like the peeling parts of a birch. Straight, the southbound lanes led up their line of sight until they branched into a bough at the toll plaza.

"He reminded me a little of Father Time, which reminds me of a story about an old friend of mine. He went to NYU with me, Josiah Rand, and he was a philosophy major, not for a pre-law track like me, but one of those real philosophy guys. Logic was his area, symbolic logic, actually, the drabbest track in analytical philosophy. He loved mathematics, too. Anyway, we graduated together and since he had a car, he offered to give me a ride back to Atlanta. He was heading to Florida where his grandfather had a piece of property practically in the Okefenokee Swamp. Josiah's plan for life after graduation was to sit on that property and read and drink all day and occasionally shoot something to eat. It was all going to be guns, books, and booze until he felt inclined to do something else. Maybe he would make some chainmail armor or take up taxidermy. He was a rich kid so it didn't matter much what he did. One day he would pull a Prince Hal and take over his father's company.

"So we are driving the fourteen-hour trip and talking about our lives and reminiscing on the last four years. He rambled on about his dreams, crazy dreams. Of all the crackpot plans he tossed off for his future there is one that I was just reminded of. He said he had a perfect plan for transcendence. He asked me if I ever watched *The Smurfs* and I said of course, I didn't just spend my whole childhood reading. Then he went on talking about this one thing that recurred in some episodes of *The Smurfs*. That in the woods near where the Smurfs lived there was a hut. In this hut lived Father Time and Mother Nature, they were married."

"Yeah, I remember that. It makes sense, them as a couple," spoke Sonny during a pause in Wind's breath.

"So Josiah went on for a while about how this is the perfect interpretation of the relationship between space and time, an organic physics. He said that the world as we know it, our universe hinges on their marital bliss, the union of those two old forest-dwellers. They have spawned us all and control the duration of our lives, their sexual interplay is the cycle of life. Then he started to talk about finding them. He said it was like the Fountain of Youth in the swamp where he was heading, but Ponce de León was a fool. It was not a matter of living forever; it was a matter of transcending the physical world. And the only way to transcend completely was to destroy what you left behind, so destroy the spatial-temporal universe. He must find that hut in the woods, sneak up to it at night, commando-crawling through the leaves, slowly without a sound, like a ninja, cycling his breath through his nose, all in camouflage, wearing his Granddad's old WWII helmet with sprigs and twigs stuck all over it. He would survey the hut when he reached it, peer into every window, maybe with night goggles on, recording the locations of both inhabitants, estimate the distances between them and the windows and the front door. When the time was right he would pounce, kick in the front door and somersault into the room, like SWAT, drawing a bead on both Mother Nature and Father Time with his laser beam-sighted assault rifle. Here he would be faced with the 'moment of truth,' as he called it. He said it was nothing to kill Mother Nature, she was on her way out, men had been putting her down, raping and killing her slowly for millennia. Her day had come and gone and this was a mercy killing. But Father Time, he seemed to remember him carrying a scythe, a scythe and an hourglass. I don't remember that, but Josiah did and it was the scythe that scared him. Josiah noted how legally Father Time had the right to use any such weapon on an intruder who had broken into his home. In this case, his killing of Father Time would still be a defensive action. It's either him or me he said.

"He said he couldn't describe how it would end since the transcendence of time and space was beyond human description and understanding. I just remember laughing at him as he smiled wide at me as if I wasn't capable of understanding such a dream. But he laughed at it too. I am not sure if I even did justice to how well he had the scenario planned, though."

"Man, and this was a friend of yours? Makes sense with what you've told me about New York. Where is this guy now?"

"I don't know. He dropped me off and a few weeks later I got a post card from him of the Okefenokee Swamp and on the back all it said was 'Ponce de León was a Fool!' We weren't very close. I haven't heard from him since, and I don't talk to anyone we had in common who would know about him. For all I know he has disappeared from the face of the earth. Maybe he is out looking for that hut in the woods."

7. CULTUS ET CREDOS

It may even be said that the system can and must encourage
such movement to the extent that it combats its own entropy...
—Jean-Francois Lyotard, *The Postmodern Condition*

A WIND CAME DOWN THE GREEN OF THE PARK INTO THE TREES, SHAK-
ing those full and rattling those part fallen, lifting a few leaves on
the ground only to drop them again and lift others, shuffling a wide
scattered deck before quitting the process and moving on through the
coolness of the shade to touch Jonathan Wind gently where he sat
stone still on a bench. His right hand worked tightly and diligently
over the notepad on his lap with a roller-ball pen on its way up to
a point of stasis in the sheer light of the late morning sun. Across a
shrub-line and a small valley filled with concrete for drainage, sat a solid one-story brick house that corresponded to a darker, ink-rendered
version beneath the pen of Jonathan Wind. Lights that fell openly and
easily from the sky above and about the house, casting it in an aura of
holiness and joy, were not present in Wind's ink rendering. A large
glass ball, like a giant pearl, sitting on a low lawn pedestal reflecting
light and color, a pewter wind-chime bearing a young pert winged
fairy on its crown dangling quartz crystal speckled aluminum tubes of
descending size, and a stained-glass representation of Gustave Klimt's

The Kiss in the window to the right of the front door were also absent. His concern was the rigid shape of the structure, the column-like patterns he inferred within the placement of the bricks, the distance between windows and door, the distance from front step to curb, the slant of the roof. His drawing looked like a prison.

Wind stopped drawing and looked at the stainless steel Fossil watch on his left wrist that Monica had given him for his birthday. He was still getting used to the feel of the cold steel links as his last watch had a leather band. He appreciated the gift, but he didn't care what the watch looked like particularly, all that mattered for him was that it kept accurate time. Every time he saw it he thought of her, but that too he had become used to. The time now read 10:00 am, the time he had been waiting for. Since seven o'clock, he had been on this bench, thinking, watching, and waiting. Awake and ardent, he rose with the radiant call from the east and arrived at Piedmont Park early enough to make certain of the situation. Across from his bench was Goddess Ashtoreth's house, which was also her place of business, and he hadn't taken his eyes off it except to occasionally look down at his pad. He didn't want to bother her too early, he didn't want to surprise her or make her feel like it was a shakedown. There was also the care about her having an early appointment or a client, so he waited for ten to come around, and now waited a little past the hour to see if anyone could be running late. He folded over his notepad to close it, the unlined pages flopping like a worn flip-book, but the only story it told recounted the last few days, drawings from memory of the albino little person, Stan Ross and Tia Maite, the contour drawing of Flora's dusty, ashen remains, and many pages of lists and notes in his black bleeded scrawl as if in an ancient script with accents and vowel markers.

When he had risen from the bench, Wind stretched and tightened his gaze to notice how the day had developed around him. His beige barn-jacket that was, once again, necessary in the coolness of the morning, lay draped over the bench. He picked it up to fit his notebook into the inside pocket and thought of how the weather in this city was bipolar. It was amusing to him to think there was some actual mental illness present in nature, its inconsistencies the sign of a neurosis that could be regulated, a tragic flaw seeking remedy. Earlier this morning it was forty degrees and already now, it was in the high sixties. Last week it felt as if it were summer still, but this week the nights and mornings were that of a southern winter. He imagined that next week might be hot and unbearably humid or maybe nothing but rain. If only the weather could be cured and regulated, reformed and reconditioned, civilized. There would be such harmony if only it was clear and systematic, Wind mused. It was at these times, behind his observational humor, that the deceptiveness of nature did actually annoy him and he felt its lack of consistency to be some sort of betrayal.

Before picking up his jacket again to go, he patted at the seat of his black slacks, feeling dampness from sitting on dewy wood, and straightened his white oxford shirt. His shirt was stiff, with a stiff collar, and hung on him in the same way as the slacks, accentuating his long, lithe form. Even on leave and in street clothes, he still looked like a cop. When he dressed four hours ago he considered wearing a tie, but decided against it; that would be too much. When not at work, he preferred to relax in contrasting the uniform of the workday by wearing jeans, t-shirts, sweaters, maybe even shirts with a little color to really break away. It was hard for him to relax into this new situation; he was still very much constructing an investigation, though officially on vacation. He was dressed for work and work he would do, but not officially. It was waking and dressing when he realized that even without his badge he was still an investigator. The legal implications posed only a slight problem since he could not work a case on vacation leave, unless of course he had a private investigator's license, which he did not. Instead, he would be discreet.

Since Tuesday evening, Wind had been growing to understand that there was only so far his investigation could go officially. That evening, after eluding Monica through complaints of a migraine, Wind partook of another dark night of the soul. He really did have a migraine, though. There was a pain that contracted his whole cerebellum, stabbing into his cerebral cortex, tightening on to the base of his skull and shimmering tremors down his spine to the pit of his stomach, where it bubbled up acid to steam off of the burning in his chest. He paced and ached sleeplessly, pacing and aching, his mind as restless as his body. When the spirit moved him he would pull a book from the nearest shelf or the shelf to where he was heading all along, reading at erratic rhythms, a chapter here, a quote there, standing to read for half an hour from the center of a text on the history of pre-colonial Mexico, flipping through pictures and their captions in *Gray's Anatomy*, scouring shoddily bound forensic manuals he had saved since the academy, picking at the *Exodus* and *Leviticus* parts of a Bible, thumbing through a Spanish dictionary, looking unsuccessfully for fire rituals in Margot Adler's *Drawing Down the Moon*, stumbling briefly through *The Sorrows of Young Werther* before picking up *Faust* and reading the last act, always confirming what he thought as he read, nodding to himself, repeating passages aloud.

Wind was sure that the albino little person was involved, that he seemed to know what was going to happen, that what he said to him was a warning about Flora in the same way Mephistopheles warned about Margareta to Faust. Why the warning; who sent him; did he act alone; has someone been following him; how did they know how to find him? If he could find the midget, he would understand what happened, but to find an unnamed albino midget in the greater Atlanta area of four million people was like sifting sand to find one smaller piece of sand. For a while he tooled about online for the statistical information of how many little people there were in the metropolitan area, but the screen made his eyes ache inside his throbbing head.

When he did sleep it wasn't well, and the following day he dived into his work in tandem with Sonny, going over everything they had from Flora's apartment and all forensic lab reports from the Georgia Bureau of Investigation. The whole apartment was clean of prints besides Flora's, which were on record from a shoplifting charge when she was seventeen. Though the cleanliness amazed them, it helped in no way. It was possible that it had been wiped clean, but Wind knew this was her way, and Sonny never pursued it. They were left with no one present but her, and they couldn't get what was left of her to tell any tales beside that there was a fire of high intensity in a centralized location that did not spread from her person and burned itself out on the fuel that she provided. There was no perfect explanation for what happened and no actual scenario for homicide present. There was nothing left but accident.

As Sonny went about finalizing the case report, with "accidental death" as the simplest verdict for such a mysterious situation, Wind set himself along his own course. He went through the files of mug shots in hopes of recognizing the albino little person, but to no avail. With all the evidence close at hand, he was able, inconspicuously, to photocopy the address book section from Flora's planner along with the last few weeks in the daily organizer section. Ready to proceed,

Wind entered his Captain's office and asked point blank for all of the vacation time he had left starting the next day. Nine days might do it; if needed he would have to start using sick days or take a leave of absence. Standing, asking, almost demanding, with such natural assurance and conviction, Wind seemed to give his Captain no choice. The Captain saw the urgency in Wind's request and he could only agree with the detective that what he asked was going to happen, no matter how spur of the moment, how out of character and protocol. There was a request form necessary and the superior said he would put it through posthaste. With everything finalized, Wind had only to say goodbye to Sonny and leave, out into the late afternoon sun, sinking, blinding, and burning.

That night he read more. His head didn't hurt, but when the telephone rang, he nonetheless dodged Monica and her request for company. He told her nothing about the vacation time, but he knew that soon he would have to see her. He didn't know what he would say then, but that was not at hand and therefore held little concern. He read, but he was really biding his time and fighting away images of Flora. This investigation required fieldwork and whatever information he could obtain from the texts at hand could only be background context for the lived experience actual people could convey to him. Wind wished it could be as simple as reading about pagan groups and putting Flora in a nutshell, but she was bigger than a nutshell and there were intricacies to her experience that would require a thousand books to quantify. Did he not have enough books; would not the Internet suffice?

There were words and text for everything, endorsing and denouncing whatever he could think of. Wind reviewed and discovered new facts and theories. Nevertheless, nothing he could find could give him insight into the lived experience of a person involved in an event just a few days past. Nowhere could he find, in the infinite tapeworm of text, which ate away at him, anything real, anything personal. He had tried his memory and all he found was her face and love. He heard her words and they spoke details of mysteries from the four corners of the globe, every way the wind blew, all across time, but none told him where she went when she was out without him. Books or websites might convey her interests, but none conveyed her life. This was not a case of the street, where he needed to be running around shaking people down, but it was necessary to speak to people, ask questions, get feelings, experience things for himself that she had experienced, touch those that touched her life. Maybe that is what Tia Maite meant, he thought.

Still he read on, ready for the next day; his next move already planned. Wicker men, Corn Gods, Fire Dancing, Purification Rites, Trials by Fire, Burning Effigies, St. Catherine's Wheel of Fire, Wind dug deep into the volumes of his *Encyclopedia of Religious Practice and Iconography*; jumping about, indexing fire, combustion, immolation, until an image filled his view: "Anima Sola." He wondered if he had seen this image at Tia Maite's, it was very familiar and he knew he had seen it before, maybe at a Mexican bodega or a tchotchke shop. The image was so familiar to him that it was as if from a dream, a woman with long hair ravaged by flames. There were chains on her wrists and she fought against them as they pulled her down. Her face was pained and her bare chest heaved out. The hair was darker than Flora's and the breasts were bigger, but he saw her in the image. The "Lone Soul" was a Catholic image, usually a woman, and the central focus of the accompanying text was succor for the dead. The history of the image was a history of the Catholic Church's endorsement of purgation, from the Council of Trent, which declared that souls do reside there and can only be benefited by the favor of the living. It is the work of the living that can aid the dead who died in sin, their efforts can factor into the judgment of God. Further he read, past the Church politics about indulgences and the papal process for the formal petitioning of departed souls; past the question of whether the souls of purgation can intercede on the part of the living, a hot debate that amounts to an agreement that they can, but no one knows if they actually do except for St. Catherine of Bologna. Finally, below all that, he found a voice of relation, as he read about the "heroic act" within the church, where a Church militant offers up to God his works in tribute to a soul in purgatory. There is nobility in acting on behalf of a departed soul damned by sin.

Wind was no Catholic by any means, but he was open to receiving wisdom and inspiration wherever he could find it. He thought for a moment how he would tear down every standing church, stone by stone with his own bare hands, clawing with his fingernails, all the towering edifices to illusion and delusion, if it would bring Flora back to him, put her in his bed right now, and return mass to her dusty ash. He could think of no way of undoing what had been done, she was dead, gone. He no longer thought of his father, her death had replaced his. The death of Nathan Wind was a chain of biological causes that lead to the effect of a hemorrhagic stroke in his brain; it made sense, and was packed off to a point of quantification. With Flora, Jonathan could not go on without closing his investigation.

The city had awoken and come alive in the time that he had his back to it, in the time that he sat, thought, and sketched. Joggers, with and without dogs, the homeless, the morning drunks, and people taking long shortcuts through the park, passed sporadically and cars were a steady flow at the green's concrete borders. There had been no perceivable stirring from within Goddess Ashtoreth's house. The morning was bright, so no lights would have been needed and the question resurfaced in him of whether she might actually be home. Last night he checked her website and it mentioned nothing about being out of town, but she could have spent the night out. From what he knew about her from Flora, Ashtoreth didn't do any full-service or any outcall work, but she could have a boyfriend or girlfriend.

The pace of his shoes on the trail had a general confidence to it as he proceeded to the street. Just beneath his surface, there was a slight change from his usual poise and security. An integral component of his makeup had been altered. The outermost layer of his protective shell eroded in the absence of his badge and sidearm. He could feel a slight difference and when the breeze came back around it raised bumps on the back of his neck, cold fuzz prickles of short dark hair against the warmth of the morning sun.

Wind breathed full and regulating, shuffling the jacket from hand to hand while he popped his knuckles and relaxed the tension from his fingers, approaching the red door to the little brick house. The door opened a good functional crack a few minutes after he rang the bell and he was at once taken aback and drawn in by a soothing bouquet of sandalwood and laundry detergent with a high note of rose hips. The face of Goddess Ashtoreth, which he recognized from her website, smiled up at him from a height only a few inches below his own. Her expression was one of natural awe and examined him from a position of subtle apprehension behind her inviting smile. Wonder and vibrancy resided in her wide brown eyes and pouty lips, but the maturity of her years, though not much beyond his own, cast her countenance in a glow of majesty.

She said hello first and assumed control over the process of greeting, asking what she could do for him, holding the door just wide enough to seem polite while still retaining the ability to slam it if the situation required. He told her his full name, apologized for coming over unannounced and disturbing her, asked her if he could speak to her about a friend of hers, but he had no badge to show her, no authority outside of his own sense of purpose, putting his need into her hands. She continued to hold the door firm as he spoke and she eyed him with caution and scrutiny until he told her that he was a friend of Flora's.

"Yep. I knew it. I knew your name sounded familiar. How is she? I haven't seen her in a while. Wow. Yeah, you are just like she described. Just as cute as she said, actually. C'mon in." And the apprehension was gone, she was all familiarity, an embrace with words and tone and posture.

The door was let open and all the scents were upon him, living, reeking, seeking to acclimate him to the environment so he would not upset its serene stasis. There was the same sanctuary feel he experienced in Flora's apartment, orchestrated and manipulated, but with the purest intentions. She lead him in, in her bare feet, allowing him to shut the door behind himself before he turned to follow her, talking to him about her space as she passed into the living room, holding closed loosely at the waist a pale green kimono with patterns of white flowers.

Wind let his gaze lead his feet in wander around as Ashtoreth went into the kitchen to make some tea. Inside, the size of her tiny brick house seemed to defy physics looking larger than from outside, with twelve-foot ceilings and a wall of windows at the back. The trees beyond the Japanese garden of the small backyard provided ample coverage from the park and he understood that the discretion necessary in her occupation was also obtained through the strategically placed drapes rolled up high above each section of the window walls. He looked around at her books, prints, and the general sense of design and found a model for who Flora was, who she had learned to be. There was a mixture of eastern and western icons and ideals, a sense of universal mysticism, Buddhas, angels, fairies, Ganeshas, Pre-Raphaelite prints, Post-Modern Feminist Art and women in various divine forms from Egypt, Sub-Saharan Africa, Native American tribes, Oceania, and Old Europe. The foyer area merged into the living room and crossed the threshold of a hall that led left to bedrooms, one of which was used as her work place with a massage table like an altar. All the doors were open down that hall, but that section of the home looked darker to him. There was no way he could deny the light of the living and dining rooms before him. There were no isolated streaming beams by which the light of day entered the temple-like space, the radiance just was, as if its source was from within the very house. He told her she had a beautiful home and she thanked him and told him it was from the twenties, "Old Atlanta," she called it and he thought that she was correct for this city, for Atlanta that was old.

"So? What brings you by? To what do I owe the pleasure of your visit?" She went towards the coffee table between her two soft leather couches, so he stepped to meet her there, reaching for the mug until she said it was hot and he sat as she placed it before him. As she leaned to lay the mug on the star-shaped coaster, his eyes were drawn to her neckline before he quickly snapped them away, the robe hung somewhat open even though she held it at the belt. His guilty eyes were down and he kept moving in that direction to blow on the steaming tea, sliding a little on the leather of the couch.

"I need to talk to you about Flora." He called out to her, padding back into the kitchen on slight, bare feet to return with her own steaming mug, smiling over her shoulder through golden and brown curls.

"Sure, what is it? How is she, I haven't seen that girl in a couple of weeks. I've been meaning to call her, but we both get so busy. We barely get together for coffee anymore for our girl talk." Ashtoreth sat at the end of the opposing couch with one leg drawn up beneath her and the other crossed over its knee, the green folds of the robe tactfully arranged. The leg on top, crossing, reflected light from its smooth calf before him. She smiled, comfortable, open; her face was at once the face of a child, full and round, yet with something almost ancient behind the eyes.

"Actually, that's why I've come to see you. Flora has passed away and I need your help." Wind let his eyes fall back down to the tea and he raised it, blowing, attempting a sip. He was blunt and he didn't want to see her face break and her joy and serenity abate.

"Oh... wow... that's awful, wow, I'm just... How... when..." and she moved from her position to sitting more forward with her legs crossed and only stayed there a few moments breathing before leaning back, catching loose tears with the dish towel she brought in to hold the hot mug handles.

"I'm sorry, you'll have to excuse me," she continued to wipe, trying to compose herself, looking upward and widening her eyes trying to stop their flow. The conviction of his words had an instant effect. "I'm sorry, please, can you tell me what happened, I just don't know how to react. This is so weird, so sudden. I saw her just the other week, yep, just the other week, wow... my god..."

Wind told her the most general details of Flora's death and Ashtoreth nodded along, taking it all in, leaning in, processing his words and the truth of them. She gasped a little at the description of the fire and covered her mouth with her hand. He continued to tell her of the inexplicable nature of the fire which is being reported as an accidental death and how he has taken leave from the force because he felt that the job might be holding back his investigation.

"I see..." she responded softly to it all, "but how can I help you? I'll do whatever I can... I'd like to help." Her face still displayed the process of understanding; her big round eyes were thoughtful and the thinking and the desire to help were helping her cope in turn.

"Thank you. I had hoped you would. There are things about Flora's life that I do not know. We talked a good deal, she told me a lot about herself and her life but there are certain areas where she would only go so far. That is what I am looking for, those details of a world she participated in without me, a world she only alluded to. She teased me with the mysterious nature of those spiritual pursuits. I think she liked having some limits on her own terms. At first they seemed only nominal to me, but I believed her that she felt it would somehow dissipate the power by talking about her little points of secrecy and I never pushed her."

"So now you want me to reveal her secrets?" Ashtoreth was calmer now and raised her dark left eyebrow while holding her mug with both hands, pausing to sip after she spoke.

"I would like you to tell me whatever you feel comfortable telling me. The more I know, the more I can work with. I don't want to ask you to betray your loyalties or ethics, but I don't believe that her death was an electrical accident. I don't think it just happened, it wasn't random, whether it was malicious or not. Every effect has a cause and the more I know, the closer I can get to discovering that cause. Flora deserves more than an accidental electrical fire death. And I have seen too much to believe so easily in the accidental."

"No, of course, I said I want to help you and I do. She told me about you. You seem just how she described. Such strength, such focus. She described it as intensity and she said she found it very sexy. I know she trusted you, she talked about you so much, and oh the way she did. She would trust you to handle this your own way. I am not sure how I am going to handle this, but that is for me to deal with later... wow, it's good I have a slow day. For now, I won't stand in your way. So. Sure. Anything you need to know about her life and her work, I will tell you what I know."

"Thank you. I know about her work. I want to say that I know enough, but I don't want to narrow my scope with jealousy. I was never jealous before, but now with her gone, I have been a little more covetous of my memories and my place in them. From what I have seen, it is not likely that any of her clients could be involved. What we have from the crime scene is so clean it almost looks staged, beyond some common crime. It appears ritualistic, cultish, or as someone said, *Force Majeure*. That is why I am interested in her 'reading group' as she called it."

She was nodding along as he spoke, nodding in thought and agreement and she held her pert chin with her right hand, its elbow positioned on her right knee now crossed over her left.

"Sure, what do you know about the reading group, how much did she tell you?"

"The most she ever got into it was over the summer, when she was letting her pubic hair grow back. She mentioned a split in the group and she was going with the side that found the presence of pubic hair to have the greatest purity. That is really all I know. She described it as something like a non-Wiccan coven."

"Sure, yeah, that was over the summer, she might have even moved on from them since the summer. She was interested in lots of things.

She looked at lots of different paths, went to lots of places. I don't know what she was giving her time to most recently. I can tell you all about that group though, but not much about its little offshoot. I only know what she told me about it, nothing firsthand. Right, well, at first when she got turned on to the Sisterhood I went a little with her. That was like a year ago maybe, maybe less. I don't know, she heard about them from a friend of a friend who went. We have a good community of friends, lots of fun spiritual types, sensual types, not too New Agey. And we are always looking to, you know, find like-minded souls to talk about the Goddess with. All of Atlanta is like this big family tree of people who work with sensual energy, we are all kind of interconnected, and I was actually talking to a friend about it the other day and we were realizing some of them only know each other because I introduced one to the other. The friend who had the friend that got Flora into the Sisterhood, I introduced her to."

Goddess Ashtoreth paused for a moment, widened her already wide brown eyes and smiled at Wind. He liked her smile and understood why people came to her, he understood how her presence, let alone her touch could heal people or at least make them feel better. Though she didn't practice sacred prostitution like Flora, her work was only sensual massage, he thought that they must be able to give men the same feeling in their own ways. As she continued to speak, he drew his notepad and pen from his jacket, flipped past the black gridded sepulcher he once saw her home to be, and wrote down "the Sisterhood" on the next blank page.

"The Sisterhood, is that its full name? Usually names of those kind of groups are longer, from what I've seen in my research, what I've read." Wind asked.

"Yep, actually the whole name spells, SUGAR. It's the Sisterhood of United Goddesses in Anthelion Repose," Ashtoreth said, as Wind wrote.

"The founder, Goddess Diana, that is what she goes by, but her real name is actually Diana, Diana Eyre, is a devout astrologer, and writes horoscopes for some small New Agey papers, but she is also really into astronomy, too. That is where they get the anthelion part from, I guess. I don't exactly know what it means other than that it is opposition to the sun, since they are looking to feminine moon energy over the masculine sun." Ashtoreth paused and looked to him allowing comment or question before proceeding.

"The anthelion is a sort of visual trick of light that can be seen on the opposite horizon when the sun is setting, it is at the center of a halo-like glowing circle called the parhelic circle. It is from the Greek, ant helios, or anti helios, against or opposite the sun." Wind spoke to her in his matter-of-fact, somewhat pedantic tone; confident he was telling her something she wanted to know.

"Oh, okay, that makes sense. It makes sense with what I heard about the split that happened, too. I think I heard the term parhelic circle during the few times I was there. But yeah, the name got dragged into everything else that caused the breakup or was a result of a breakup."

"What do you mean?"

"Well, this group was founded by Diana and her girlfriend at the time Goddess Luna. Cute, huh? They shared moon names; they were nauseatingly cute sometimes. Actually, it was Luna who chose a goddess name to be like Diana, though she said it was because that was what the group was about, embracing the moon energy. Her real name is Toni Banford, short for Antonia. So they formed this group together, but it seemed that Diana was the one really in charge, she is a little older than Toni and has more of this compassionate guiding quality to her, a very charismatic leader. Toni is a little rougher, a little butchy. Diana is so sweet, really pretty too, she looks great leading services. Well, they seemed like such a good working couple at first. Diana led the group and Toni handled the details and organizational stuff. It was fun to watch. Their plan was to make a group that was different, not your typical Wiccan coven—which I think they both had been involved with in the past—and call it a reading group, a place for women to share their belief in the Goddess by embracing the individual Goddess within themselves, like reading your personal journal out loud. The moon energy that represents the Goddess was essential too; meetings followed its cycle as all us gals do. This drew an opposition to the sun and the male energy that it expresses and gave Diana a chance to get really into mixing astrology and astronomy. So it was alright, they built a small following, like thirty, thirty-five women coming each week, or whenever the moon was right. I went a few times. Flora took me and it was fun to get all into the Goddess, just us gals, and in good weather we were outside sky-clad, you know nude, in Diana's yard and it could be such good energy. All the women would take a different goddess name and they really took it seriously." She smiled as if the fondness of her memories was both sweet and sour in light of the occasion.

"Why did you stop going?" Wind asked, encouraging her to speak naturally in a steady flow, keeping her thoughts in the narrative of the past. Smoothly, with the skin of her legs sliding against each other and her silky kimono, Ashtoreth shifted in her positioning, her legs now interchanged. So strong was the seduction of her presence, its drawing comfort, the golden flow of her hair, the smell of rose hips and laundry detergent, her love for his love, the words sky-clad, that he began to wonder about whether she wore anything beneath the thin green fabric between them. Were these thoughts a straying from his path or somehow a quicker way to what he wanted?

"Oh, well, I can only take so much of the group mentality. I was raised by Charismatic Christians in Florida where every Sunday was like a revivalist meeting and people would be speaking in tongues, captivated by the Holy Spirit, rolling in the aisles, literal holy rollers. I like to be free to move. I've had enough dogma in my life growing up. I mean, it was great that I was exposed from a real early age to such mystical stuff, the Spirit and all, but I can't take too much of that socially. There is always infighting and bickering and groups of New Agey women, even if they believe in the Goddess, can be just as petty and dogmatic as Fundamentalist Christians sometimes. But anyway, what wound up happening, and it is such the kind of thing that always seems to happen in those best-laid human plans, was that feelings changed. Diana and Toni started fighting and Diana broke it off and started dating this guy, Richard."

"So she was bisexual?"

"Yep, but actually those labels are so pointless when people really reach an elevated understanding of sexuality. Any body can be pleasurable and any soul can be fallen in love with. Diana, I don't know if she was just naturally flippant, but she cycled like the moon itself and her heart, you know, was like the wind, oh, like your... ha, I didn't mean that, but I'm sure you get that a lot. But that is how love is. It's like the wind, it can be so strong and then gone, blown away. No amount of planning can change it. So Toni was furious, really hurt, crushed. I was way out of it by that point, but Flora told me all the gossip. I guess Toni still tried to make it work with the group for a couple of meetings but couldn't handle seeing Diana and couldn't handle being left for a man. Toni is a real diehard lesbian feminist goddess worshipper, not an omni-sexual by any means. So she started talking about changing the group, picking at things they had set up, saying they were Diana's ideas alone and not strong enough interpretations of how to venerate the Goddess. It was a lot like the Protestant Reformation from what I understand. Toni, like Martin Luther, wanted to get purer, more fundamental and really slim down the practices. She had some basic arguments and interpretations, but mostly it was a question of leadership, a power struggle and a lovers spat."

"Interpretation, is that where the whole pubic hair thing came in?" Wind had been writing more at this point, knowing that Flora sided with Toni in the breaking away.

"Yep," Ashtoreth nodded, as she was prone to do when she spoke and thought at once, "the fight Toni started was about—and it might seem so petty—whether they should refrain from shaving their pubic hair. A lot of the women did for some reason or another. There were a good number of sex workers of different varieties present, for some reason they were drawn to the group, I guess we are naturally more aware of the power of our femininity due to our work, and most of us call upon some love goddess in what we do. Toni objected to shaving, first with the feminist stance that women shave to conform to a male idea of beauty and therefore change themselves to fit this awful de-feminized look. But her main argument was theological. She said they needed to stop worshipping the Goddess in all these little forms, you know in all the manifestations that the women were choosing for their names, and worship the one primal mother goddess, the mother of creation, the great womb humans came out of. She said that this goddess was natural and full-figured and had a large triangle of uncut pubic hair and for a model she referred to the Venus of Willendorf, you know, that little statue. I guess she had been reading a lot of Gimbutas recently or maybe Diana leaving her for Richard really pushed her over the edge in her rage against the patriarchy. I am glad I was gone by that point, I love men, sexuality is so much more than one-sided, the duality is so important."

"So that was it?"

"Yep, that was it, from what I've heard. Toni said she was splitting and about half of the women followed her. She said no longer are they the Sisterhood of United Goddesses in Anthelion Repose, they were worshippers of one goddess, they were her daughters, and they did not rest in being parallel to the Sun, they were of the moon and creation and therefore over the Sun. I don't think she shaved much anyway, not from what I saw back almost a year ago, but she let her armpits grow in along with her legs to match her thick pubic bush. The other girls I think were only really required by their new doctrine to let their pubic hair grow since it is not clear whether the primitive goddess statues had hair on their legs or armpits."

"Why do you think Flora went with Toni when she split? Were they friends?"

"No, I don't think they were close friends by any means. As you know, Flora was not a man-hater. From what I could tell, she cared a lot for you. She saw her role in her work to help men reunite with the Goddess and with their feminine sides. No, I think she followed Toni because it would then be a different group and then she would be trying something new. I think she was done with them already, it had almost been a year, you know, since the past fall, and I guess she was ready to move on. This way she got to move on with some people she already knew. She always did it all the way though, she never held back, as I'm sure you know." Ashtoreth smiled sparklingly, knowingly, and the two stray tears she could not contain were of love, and from both eyes they fell in a sparkling instant of a love attached to nothing, a love that rests in its own completeness, a completeness that contains both life and death and is impenetrable to fear.

"Flora showed me her blooming bush proudly, she was so itchy at first we joked about how she couldn't stop scratching, and over the summer she talked about the earliest Neolithic goddesses and all the other goddesses she was getting into from different cultures, some of which I didn't even know, great weird Aztec ones. But that was the summer. I hadn't seen her much recently. I don't know if she was even still going to Toni's Goddess group."

Wind stretched in his seat, sensing the nearing completion of this interview. Ashtoreth looked to him as if she was beginning to experience the news of Flora's death again and again in heartbeats of revelation and acceptance. He didn't want to end their meeting, but he didn't want her to talk about Flora beyond her comfort level. Beyond the normal observations Wind made of body language and the words between words during an interrogation or investigation, he was beginning to *feel* Ashtoreth and for a moment he worried that she was *feeling* him in the same way. He straightened his back and clenched his calves preparing to rise.

"Do you know where Toni's group meets or how I can get in touch with her?" he asked.

"No, I'm sorry, I wish I did, but you should talk to Iliya, Flora's old roommate. Do you know her? She could help, I know she went with Flora."

"I don't know her actually, but I am going to see her today. I have a copy of Flora's planner, which is how I found you and I'll make a call on Iliya later."

"I am sorry if I couldn't help you enough. Any way I can help, just let me know. I care, cared, care a lot for Flora, she was my protégé and became like my little sister and, yeah, whatever you need. And if you ever just need to talk more, I'm good for that too, we can hang out if you would like sometime." She stood, and he could not tell if it was before he began or right along with him, but they both reached their full heights together.

"Another quick question, if you don't mind?" Wind heard himself sound like Colombo, and though it was a tactic that he had employed intentionally in the past, here it came as an actual afterthought.

"Shoot."

"You don't happen to know any albino midgets do you?" And he could not help but smile a little at the sound of his question in this environment, no longer mysterious and very safe.

"No, huh, I don't think so, no, I am pretty sure I don't have that pleasure, but I am always interested in meeting interesting people. Why? Does it have to do with Flora's death? Is it a lead? I am sorry I don't know anything."

"It's alright, it might be nothing, but I try to consider all possibilities." Wind leaned into her as she leaned up to him at her door. Her weight was against him, on him, and both of her arms found his back. He thought of her kimono hanging loose, and how close they had become in such a short time. Goddess Ashtoreth kissed him on the cheek, with lips soft and slightly open and he could feel her breath stirring the skin, engorging his senses, before they hugged. The hug had a pronounced duration beyond when he stopped it and he felt as if he pushed her off him as he reached for the door. The more he wanted to stay the more he needed to leave. Her body fell from his; he was rigid and stern now. The temptation to comfort her was strong, but he was ready to move on. His will was an ideology, a dogma behind his methods and agenda, and it dragged him away from her and what she represented, the persuasion to take life in stride and accept its natural flow.

8. MOKOSH

That way of thinking likens the Great Goddess to a boundless ocean of formless energy, which is always pregnant with the potential of becoming. Whatever exists pours out of this ocean of energy at the moment of creation and returns to this ocean at the moment of death. Creation happens not once but continuously. So, too, does death. The cycle of nature never stops.

—Lanier Graham, *Goddesses in Art*

"WELL, IT SEEMS THERE ARE, UM, TWO KINDS OF SUCH PRODUCTS. ONE kind that is meant to be discarded this way and there is another that is not." He paused to dab at the beads of perspiration on his brow with the back of his sleeve. "It is the ones that are not, that have created the problem here, ya see. If you all can refrain from throwing out those in this way and wrap them up and put them in the trashcan then this won't be any problem any more."

The man was tall and pink-skinned with a round balding head, streaks of thin black hair stuck by sweat across the great dome. His white t-shirt, subtly advertising Orlando's Sea World, was clinging to the corpulent torso beneath his arms, and the lower cuffs of his overalls were damp like his work boots. Lapping at the rubber soles, at the bottom of his brown boots, a shade deeper from the wetness, were the flowing tides of septic water released after a blockage, backup, and leak onto the concrete basement floor, now a dark brackish pool smelling of earth, birth, and feces with bobbing moments of color from the pink plastic tampon applicators that were not meant to be flushed among the brown cardboard ones that were permissible.

The landlord of the building thanked the plumber from the dry safety of the stairs without shaking his hand and turned back up into the foyer to a small group waiting and listening by the open door. Present were the managers of the occupying offices with all of the female employees from each floor. On the various faces, made up in colors and jewelry, he read a mixture of anxiety, shame, and annoyance. The managers had the look of troubleshooting and taskmastery they believed essential to being the men of the office and running an effective workplace.

"His name is Gene Freshwater, of Freshwater Plumbing, and I will give a copy of his card to each of y'all office managers in case we have anything like this happen here again. I'm sure if we all just do as he mentioned then this can be avoided in the future and I'll let the office managers handle any kind of special procedural details or, you know, specifics for each of the bathrooms. Maybe special trashcans, I don't know, I'll let you all deal with that yourselves." The landlord handed out the cards bearing the Freshwater Plumbing name and number and ventured back down into the thickness of the moist basement air, as the crowd of women and their managers returned by respective channels to their offices.

Iliya Chernovsky returned to her desk shaking off the initial guilt of womanhood she felt in sympathy with her female coworkers. Publicly, she felt shame at most things, hanging her head and hiding her eyes out of habit and defense; it was easier to divert most gazes than it was to acknowledge them. Her hair did well in this act of concealment, letting her bangs fall with the strategy: if I can't see them, they can't see me. However, this was an area where she had done a great deal of work to overcome shame and on top of all that, she was pretty sure it wasn't her tampons disposed of incorrectly. She noticed the awkwardness in returning back to work for her female coworkers after such a diversion at the end of the day so close to the weekend. Apparently she was not the only one to notice, for as she was getting settled into her cube desk, her boss came in to make an announcement that since they were still trying to fix the plumbing, and it was almost five anyway, everyone should just wrap up what they were doing and call it a day.

Iliya still had to urinate, which she had to do since right before they noticed the plumbing problem, so she quickly closed down her computer, grabbed her bag and jacket and walked out into the street, putting on her black sunshades to fight the lingering brightness from the west. The pressure of her bladder was tolerable as long as she remained in motion, but she was not looking forward to the ride home. When her eyes adjusted to seeing again, she noticed Jonathan Wind in front of her building looking at her. She looked at him and smiled awkwardly, thinking she recognized him and then thought maybe what she read was only his recognition of her. She slowed as he approached.

"Hello, Iliya? Are you Miss Iliya Chernovsky?" He asked.

"Yeah, do I know you?" She stopped, looking up, her posture at a slight hunch.

"No, not really, but I was hoping I could ask you some questions."

"Are you a cop?"

"Yes. Well, yes, but no. I am, but not right now. Right now, I am not. I am on vacation. Can we talk?"

She seemed to shrink initially at the possibility of being questioned by a cop, but his indecision in answering put her a little more at ease. He walked along by her side eastward on West Wieuca Road without questioning where they were going, conforming to her step.

"Are you here about Flora?" She asked as if that had been what they were already talking about. He looked at her and answered, yes, interrogatively, to which she replied, "I knew I'd see you soon enough. Mr. Ross, Flora's father, is good friends with my father, so he called my dad and my dad told me what happened. That is how we knew each other. We met at the Ukrainian church in Roswell, St. Andrew's, where our fathers took us."

"Yes, actually, Flora had told me that. About you both bonding after church and smoking cigarettes. I am Detective Sergeant Jonathan Wind," he smiled at her, trying to let her know that he was a friend.

"So you're the cop, her cop. Yeah, she told me about you, too. You're the one I expected but in case you weren't I couldn't let on. Even though she is dead I still have some tact about her secrets. I was surprised I didn't hear from any other cops earlier. I expected someone, but hoped it would be you."

"Well, I am not here officially. There is no reason to question her friends. Officially, the case is closed. Accidental death, but as you can imagine, since I am here, I am not entirely confident in that pronouncement. I suppose you're having similar thoughts since you have been expecting someone. Do you have some reason to believe that what happened to your friend was not an accident?" They stopped for a moment and from the right pocket of the jacket on his arm he drew out a Mikhail Gorbachev Pez dispenser and with his thumb on the bright purple birthmark, he pulled back the Premier's head and as a gesture of openness, offered the pink brick of candy it held to the shorter, paler woman before him with wavy black hair, darker than his own. She took the Pez and dropped it on her pink tongue and flashed a quick smile with her hair out of her face, the sun striking off her tiny stud nose-ring before she put her head back down and walked, leading, talking.

"It is all pretty strange. But Flora was into some strange shit. Since we were kids—I've known her like ten years—we were always both into strange shit, but it seemed like recently she got into stranger things and would always drag me along. Not that I wasn't into the same shit, I liked it all and I went along, but she always found these things first and was always exposing me to them. It just seems pretty weird and coincidental that with all the stuff Flora was into she should die in some freakish, horror show kind of way. I mean, what way is that to go. Her dad has been to the apartment already and he told my dad about it. Like she was the only thing burned, the rest of the place was fine, he told my dad. He said the cops told him that she was alone and it was an accident. An electrical fire. That's just too fucked up. She knew lots of really out-there people that I never met, but sometimes I would hear about them. I don't think this was some kind of black magic thing or anything, but maybe, I don't know, who knows what was going on with her."

"Is there anyone in particular you worry about, someone who seems the weirdest?" Wind took a Pez himself, pleased with how quick she was to speak, how comfortable she was becoming beyond her first apprehension.

"No, not really, I mean, no one I can think of. I don't know everyone she spent her time with. It's pretty cool you are doing this. I guess when some prostitute dies in some really wack way most of your types don't give a shit, one less whore to worry about. But you have different circumstances that motivate you, don't you?" Wind winced a little at her tone and the word whore, but it was evident that she was just making a point, venting hurt.

"What did you think about her career choice? She used to work in an office like you do, temping, back when you both lived together, after you both moved out. She told me all about it. It seems she left you high and dry to make rent when she was able to change her position for the better." Wind snapped back, sternly and tactically.

"Hey, I was happy for her. I found a new roommate, another friend from home. Not as good a friend, not as fun as Flora, but it worked out. Flora was doing her escort thing, the high courtesan, the sacred prostitute, and she needed her own space for that. I mean, I didn't want to see her bringing men home all the time and I would've been in the way. She did try to include me when she got settled, but it wasn't really anything I was into. I joined in on a couple of her calls that were into, you know, dual goddess action and that was fun and I got some cash out of it, but overall that wasn't me. I couldn't just give love the way she could and be real with just anyone. She had a role she played well, she really gave those sad men the impression she cared. God, the first time she had me help her out I took two Percodan and just numbed out and hid in my hair and let them lead me around, play with my body... I'm sorry, I bet that is not the kind of shit you want to hear about. She talked about you a lot. She was good at what she did, and cared about her role as some kind of love-giving, love goddess, but since she had been doing it she wasn't really able to date. Most men didn't get it. It was only a job, and for her a really spiritual job. She only went on a few real dates and then there was you and she never went on a real date after that, just spent more time at home, for both work and pleasure, sorry, you know what I mean, work and you. Well, when she wasn't out at some movement or class. That was stuff she always had time for. The great weird shit I mentioned before. That girl saw a lot. I don't know how she found some of those things. It's a wonder she ever had time to sleep."

"Did you go to the SUGAR, you know, the Sisterhood, reading group with her?" What was once a strawberry Pez, was now a dark, saccharine syrup in saliva and it slid seamlessly past the palates of both speakers as they reached the corner of West Wieuca and Roswell Road. Their footing and chemical compositions were corresponding, his step short like hers, with pauses due to the pressing of her full and needy bladder.

"No, she didn't bring me along with her until the end of the summer and they already had split off into the worship of the Eternal Goddess Mother. I have only been twice and I'm not an official member yet. I'm not even sure if she is, was, still a part of that scene. I think most recently she was into something else, something weirder. But she hadn't told me yet. I am sure she would have dragged me along eventually. I always got into things late. I had to wait to see how they went for her. I love to dive into things and really take things on and so it's best if she went first, you know, to tell me how the water is. She was only like a year older, not even really, my birthday is February 24th, I'm a Pisces, and hers was May 21st, so it was just like nine months almost exactly, but it seemed best if the Gemini showed the Pisces around. This way always let her be just a little more experienced with everything than me. Since we stopped living together, and she went off on her path, I knew I would never catch up with her. It's sad that now I can…"

"So where are you heading? Do have a minute more to talk? Maybe we could go somewhere, are you parked nearby?" Wind asked, looking around at the rush of cars from all directions blowing through the intersection at this awful time of day to be driving anywhere in Atlanta, let alone North Buckhead. He scanned the streets unsure of why she would park so far from the office building and where she would find a spot on a road like Roswell.

"I am heading right here," Iliya said, crossing her legs as she stood still, putting her hand on the MARTA bus stop. "My car is in the shop, it's pretty fucked up. I can give you ten more minutes to talk, unless the bus is early." She looked at her watch as she responded.

"I am parked back by your office, I can give you a ride home and we could talk on the way, if that works for you, or go somewhere else to talk? I have a few more questions."

"Today I'm pretty busy, I got a lot of shit to do at home and I have to get some money out of my dad for my car. You can ask me all the questions that you want tomorrow in the car on the way out to Douglasville," she said flashing her same quick smile, like it was a coveted punctuation mark for only the most special words to come from such a serious face.

"Douglasville?"

"Yeah, I figured you would want to see with your own two eyes, experience with all the senses, the last reading group that I'm actually positive she went to. Tomorrow is my initiation, the fourth quarter of the waxing moon. Powerful energy shit. You gotta be there. Maybe someone knows something? There are lots of weird and creepy women at these things. I'm pretty disappointed that Flora won't be there for me, but I'm already committed to this shit so you have to come to support me." She pleaded and before he could agree she reached into her bag to get out a pen and an old shopping list, to write the address of her apartment in North Druid Hills on the opposite side of, a seedy location he recognized as she wrote. Bumping in her glossy black vinyl bag, she started her Discman and through the headphones within Wind could recognize the music.

"Is that My Bloody Valentine? Flora loved them. You two are so very similar. Is that Loveless, even?"

"Yeah, it's hers actually. I borrowed it last time I saw her. Growing up we each would buy like one CD and just share it, handing it back and forth, but we were always together so it was like it was really both of ours. It was the same with clothes and books and lots of stuff. One cigarette pack for the both of us when we went out. It was pretty hot. Once she had this idea that we would be blood sisters. Not with cutting though, though we did go through a cutting phase, I guess all girls do, or the fucked up ones at least, you know, slits on the thighs. She is pretty good at covering the scars up now. But no, she said we would be true moon goddess blood sisters. We were like fifteen. We both dripped into the same jar when we had our periods and gradually filled up this little jar. We kept it at both of our houses in turn, a little symbol of our sisterly connection. I have it now. It's a comfort since I found out about her."

A large smoking, bustling MARTA bus pulled jerkily up to the sidewalk beside them. Black dirty liquid dripped from its undercarriage while it hove a sigh and rested with doors gaping towards Iliya. She looked up at the taller man before her in the shadow of the bus and smiled in a new way to him, without the intention of leading or distancing.

"So I will see you tomorrow at my place at 11:00. PM. Don't be late, the Goddess is a stickler for promptness and shit."

Wind gave a slight wave and nodded, letting her be sucked up into the bus that jerked back onto Roswell Road taking her away behind its tinted windows. The air it let out was thick and dark and he turned his face while waiting for the rapid movement of air to rise up and take the clouding smoke away. He could not be passive and he could not wait for another air system to form and make all the dirt in the city go away, he had to stay in motion himself. So he walked back down West Wieuca Road, and mused on the Atlanta legend he had once heard, that the street was named by its developer with the two first letters of each of his three daughters' names: Wilma, Eugenia, and Cathern. Wind was blowing directionally opposite of his home, but he required the speed of wheels and combusting fuel to get where he was heading. The traffic was the last thing he needed right now, but he wanted to get home. In the car he would think, but the anxiety ubiquitous in his thoughts this week would be greatly enflamed by the stopping and going, clutching, gassing and breaking, along with the general anarchic melee of driving across the jewel of the southeast during rush hour, when it seemed all the floodgates had opened from the center out and steel streams were pouring and squeezing and banging against their own backflow. So from the context of his location he brought forth happy memories out of his past.

In the direction of his car, past Ilya's office building, was Chastain Park. He knew that it was once a Creek Indian settlement, a place in tension with the neighboring, dominant Cherokee, until they were all forced out by the U.S. government in 1821. Eventually, the area became a prison and the fields now for play were for harvest by the prisoners. Wind's personal memory picks up much later in 1993, when he frequented the park to pick up his last high school girlfriend at the end of her school day. Cecilia attended Galloway, a private school located on the park grounds, its oldest buildings once belonging to the prison. At that time in his life, his mother worked nights at the Postal Facility and he used her car while she slept in the day.

He was remembering the fall of 1993, the beginning of his senior year, and Cecilia's too, he at Riverwood, she at Galloway. They met over the summer at a party of mutual friends. New sexual waters were tested by the pair and they relished the giving and receiving of mutual innocence. Only thrice had they broken this new ground, only thrice before the day Wind was remembering, and already they thought themselves old pros. The day he remembered, clear through still depths of memory, was in late August, almost the season of his present, but in full blister of the Indian Summer, burning brighter later and later. He struggled for the very day of the week in his catalog, breathing to relax, letting the image rise up through the clear, still depths: Monday, most likely. They spoke on the phone Sunday night planning that he would pick her up after school, meeting her at the art studio where she often worked extracurricularly on her sculptures. The expectancy he felt in class that day was almost overwhelming in a glandular way, and his pallor surged red with all of his limbs alive and shaky. The minimal romantic planning made his mind constrict upon his body a will and energy far exceeding that required for schoolwork and a drive down the shady stretch of Lakeforest Drive. He parked where agreed, away from the school buildings, and she was waiting at their rendezvous picnic table. From his car he pulled a Mexican blanket that a friend of his mother's brought back from vacation for them as a souvenir. Cecilia, a young girl with golden curls, took his hand, and they walked back into the wooded area, through a path of thick, low bush before they were in an enclosed clearing. They looked around, listened and kissed, giggling awkwardly. The blanket was spread on the ground and he remembered marveling that without any such discussion on the matter beforehand she was wearing a skirt for the ease and melioration of their plan. Down they went on the blanket and he remembers her saying to him, "we have to be quick in case someone comes."

With anxiety, self-consciousness, and the feeling that he might have a greater sexual investment in this act, beyond what might be for her just the thrill of "doing it outside," the young-man Jonathan pulled down his pants just below his knees and helped her pull down her underwear. They were yellow. Instantly, he was on top of her and they kissed and had sex on the blanket, in the clearing, in the woods behind the picnic bench. His fear made him worry that he might take too long to cum, but he persevered and she moved in a way that he figured was an excitement out of her own fear of getting caught. By the point of his flood crest, it was clear that in all their devising as "old pros" neither bore any form of contraceptive, so at the time of unstoppable torrent he bark-moaned the word "now" and she scooted back holding her skirt high and free of the blast while he hobbled to his knees in panic. His worry-weighted spunk burst and fell in rivulets on the Mexican blanket until it was down to a seeping trickle on his rapidly shrinking penis, which he stuffed back into his pants. Quickly they folded the blanket and placed it in his trunk. Their nerves were raw and the sounds of trees and cars and birds increased the pitch of their anxiety. They didn't know how to ford the new awkward divide between them in his car as he drove her home and the need for the rush from adventure had been extinguished for some time after.

In light of this memory, Wind wondered how his constant preoccupation with death this week could have possibly dredged up such sticky feelings of sexual guilt. It was too Freudian to ponder and his attention should have been on the investigation, not self-analysis. Here he was distracting himself, through the traffic and the car-coffin heat, with a memory that had become more foul than fond in this harsh light of age. There were new worries now: was "doing it outside" all his idea, did Cecilia go through with it for him, was she uncomfortable; were there other times that she was uncomfortable; did she have any regrets from the times with him, feeling too young or unready; where was she now; why didn't he have friendships with any of his ex-girlfriends; how did he push them away; why did they not need him; when Cecilia and he both went away to school and finally gave up trying a long-distance relationship, did she replace him sooner than he did her, and did that matter; did she have as many lovers in college as he, and did that matter; why did Monica not want to hear about his past, did he paint it so darkly early on? He could find Cecilia, with her he knew no better than to love honestly. But to what end would finding her serve; the past was just information, safe and secure in his catalog, notebooks, journals, and the dossiers he had recorded on everyone he has ever known. Of only Flora did he never write, he didn't want that kind of quantification, he had wanted her to live constantly in the sense memory of his lips and skin, even when kissing and touching another. But it was also out of guilt that he never recorded on paper anything about her; more has he written since her death.

Forty minutes after he left West Wieuca Road, Wind pulled his plain Honda Accord off of Highland Avenue behind his apartment building and parked in his regular spot next to the dumpster. He grabbed his jacket and folded it in a securing fashion, conscious of the notepad in the inner breast pocket, as he locked the door and turned to let it slam tight on a vehicle he purchased out of necessity, in a city he once walked in his youth, then dreaming of a place like Manhattan, but now he rolled over, enclosed and detached from its smells and texture, almost one hundred miles on an average day, his squad car taking the brunt of those miles, an added occupational bonus. Walking, he passed the sidewalk and the door to his apartment building and headed onto Highland, where he turned south. The traffic ran thick up and down the Avenue with people leaving work late and heading home or to happy hour in the neighborhood. Wind crossed at the crosswalk right up to a wide white building which was originally a movie theater decades before his birth and now stood divided into a Ben and Jerry's Ice Cream and a Starbucks Coffee.

Inside the Starbucks, Wind was greeted by his first name from behind the counter. He was beckoned up to the counter as the other customers moved to the left to wait for their drinks.

"Hey, how have you been?" asked Jack Thoth, matching Wind in height and thinness. "Want something to drink?" and he reached for a cup, hoping he could provide for his friend in the only way his job allowed.

"Yeah, sure, just a cup of whatever the house blend is. You know me, I don't care. How's work been?"

Jack filled a venti cup with the steaming dark brew and when receiving a nod from his friend, threw in an extra shot of espresso, left over from the last purchase, turning the house blend into a "shot in the dark." Jack had a stature similar to his friend's, but a face of distinction, sharper, bird-like, easier with a smile, appropriate with the social aspect of his job, entertaining the endless stream of customers, most far exceeding the economic stature of their barista, but craving a connection through him with the marketing of youth and hipness.

"You know. Work is the same old shit, customers, coffee, killing time by amusing ourselves. If not for the kindness of the neighborhood bartenders, none of us would make it through a shift. But, oh, yeah, we were just talking," he snickered over towards his fellow employee, a young guy with black horn-rimmed glasses, "and maybe you would have a good take on this, I asked Lao earlier, and his response was pretty funny. Alright... how does female ejaculation make you feel?" And he smiled waiting with little breaths escaping.

"Fine... I guess. What do you mean, like as a concept, as an event?" Wind played along, knowing he would enjoy where his friend was going, feeling out the terrain.

"It doesn't threaten you? You don't feel like ejaculation is something only you can do as a man and women are stepping into your territory? I mean, it's a fetish to watch in porn, but no one is talking about the dark side, who it hurts, what it does to us men. We are one-trick ponies at best, and this is emasculating."

"What did Lao say?" Wind looked around and no one was listening, the patrons all rapt in their own conversations.

"Oh, it was great, he not only was right there with me, but he picked up those scissors and ran with them. He said that he thought it was just a myth, like the female orgasm. 'They're just peeing,' he said, 'trick photography.' A feminist myth! It was pretty fucking funny." Jack said, clearly well caffeinated and maybe a little buzzed from alcohol. He laughed on to himself, electrified in his own orchestrated joy, a trick to making the dehumanization of his job bearable. His laughter was so great and familiar that it brought Wind to let out a few audible laughs. "Sorry, I just thought that was great. It can get pretty slow here. What have you been up to? You're not in your work clothes, but you have that possessed look on your face you get when you're working."

"I am actually on vacation leave now, but I am still working on something, something personal." Wind sipped from the coffee, which he wasn't allowed to pay for.

"Something personal? Wow. Sounds like you're on some sort of vendetta. Vigilante cop shit."

"Well, it's not like that entirely, but close. I felt I could get more done not being a cop for a little while." Wind shifted, not sure how much he should say, not sure how much he was ready to say. It was pretty clear, the path directly before him, but he worried that with the next step beyond he might end up groping in the dark. If he began to speak it to his friend, it could all pour out in a muddled burst of words, some of doubt, infused with fear, and they would then be out there, real, in the world, forever beyond his control, beyond his ability to suck them back in.

"Hey, if you want to talk about it, I have a break coming up soon. We could get a drink. You know, whatever, it's cool, I'll listen."

"Thanks. Actually, tonight I'm pretty distracted. I've got more to do. If we start talking it would take more than your break, anyway." He shuffled and sipped, the warmth of the coffee opening his throat, adding volume to the burn within him. As he relaxed he remembered that just sitting and listening to Lao on Monday helped him feel less alone. "This weekend looks full already, I have a lot to do, but maybe we could make time to get together for dinner next week. If that's cool with you, your schedule?"

"Hey, yeah, sure, that could work. I work early in the day on both Wednesday and Thursday so either evening is fine with me. We could call those troglodytes, Lao and Tammy, see if we can drag them out of their cave and make them socialize a little. Damn, they can be such freaks."

Wind agreed and thanked his friend for the coffee. The increase of people out on the street was noticeable; Thursday night a prelude to Friday. Wind walked north past Surin, The Dark Horse Tavern, and Limerick Junction. Energized by coffee and the stimulation of a friend, he took in everything, conversations, perfumes, colognes, facial expressions, fashions, processing all that he read into character analyses and mini-histories until he crossed the street after The American Roadhouse. He thought maybe he would keep walking, but the practical notion crept over him that no matter how far he walked, that much farther he would have to walk back. He would rather be in his home, where everything is where he left it, where he was in control, where everything he could need was at his fingertips. So that's where he headed. He would make use of his time until he slept; he was ready for the day to be over, ready for tomorrow, ready to follow where his path unfolded. But as he explored what he had learned today he made a point of rejecting the metaphor that kept occurring to him, that he was pulling a thread and watching it unravel. That metaphor ends in nothing but chaos: a pile of thread with no form or meaning. Instead he created for himself the image of following a waterway up river, into the darkness of undergrowth, wherever it may twist or bend, to its source at some seep or spring. Everything had a source when you went far enough back, everything.

Hours later, as the dark night of Thursday had officially darkened deep into the early morning of Friday, Wind instantly crossed the ephemeral threshold from his restless sleep into anxious waking, as if there was no separation. His thighs clenched hot around his hands and he felt the need to purge his bladder. Not since childhood or drunken college nights had he woken in the night to urinate, but he followed the urge and stood up in the darkness to amble slowly out of his room. He walked down the hall towards the bathroom and the smell of smoke. Maybe someone was smoking outside and it was coming in through the open bathroom window? From scattered dream fragments, and the raw material of the world around him, he had a memory of being at Flora's on just another hot night in early June when their love was still in its early stage of discovery. Walking down the hall of his apartment was walking from Flora's bed to her bathroom. As he peered into his own empty bathroom he was peering into her bathroom, looking left into his bathroom he saw to the right around the doorframe into hers.

Flora sat on the toilet, her hair slicked back from sweat, making it look darker. The light came from behind his view, produced by the swaying candles in the bedroom and its warm light rubbed across her naked body, featuring the slick oily shine of her flat sternum, the dark tips of her small doe-nosed breasts, the shadowed wells of her deep clavicles ringed by light. The light ran down to the small round bump of her stomach, past a horizontal shadow where her torso bent at the tiny navel, to the hairless pubis that cleaved slightly around her dangling labia. Her left knee was lost without candlelight, but her right, directed towards him, was split by shadow, and the lit calf shined as it clenched, as down her leg her long delicate foot held her whole position at balance on its tippy-toes. The sound of her urine being expelled with pressure into the splash of the bowl's pool rang out with command and presence, and the slimy residue of their sex drained downward with the flow. Smoke rose around her as she withdrew the cigarette from her mouth and smiled, exhaling, her face turning from its half-lit position to full revelation. After all the work with sex and words it was in this moment, as Jon stood naked and sweaty before her, his penis small and red, glistening and swaying, its drips catching onto the matted hair of his thighs, that he beheld a picture of deep intimacy. They were not only bare before each other, but with each other. He approached her and she laid her cigarette in an ashtray on the sink as he bent to kiss her. She drew a violet hand towel from the sink and caught his drip, before drying his penis, testicles, and thighs. She then kissed his penis on its now dry head, as if she were making a child's wound better. Standing up to flush, she dried herself with the same towel, their fluids coming together again.

Wind stood before his own toilet, in the same position he remembered, and urinated alone. If someone was smoking outside the window downstairs, they were now gone, and he could smell nothing but the night air and dry leaves.

9. FERTILE GROUND

I was talking about time. It's so hard for me to believe in it. Some things go. Pass on. Some things just stay. I used to think it was my rememory. You know. Some things you forget. Other things you never do. But it's not. Places, places are still there. If a house burns down, it's gone but the place—the picture of it—stays, and not just in my rememory, but out there, in the world.   —Toni Morrison, *Beloved*

"THE FIRE THAT WE ENCOUNTER IN SHC AND ALLIED PHENOMENA IS fire which is directed from a clearly definable point of origin, and against a specific victim," Jonathan Wind read in Michael Harrison's *Fire From Heaven*, whose title is a reference to how God's wrath is often described in the episode of the Bible when Elijah faces the unbelieving Baalamites. That was only page ten and he grumbled to himself as he read on, reading how he normally read, rapidly and thoroughly. On page sixty-four, grumbling through the sixth chapter, he stopped at the line, "we may now ask the question: is there any connection between the mass destruction by fire of the cities of Sodom and Gomorrah and the individual destruction, equally complete, of Ms. Euphemia Johnson, sixty-eight, of Sydenham?" Wind did not want to ask that question and he did not want to read any further to see how the author answered that question. He had sought out a book the Fire Inspector had mentioned and now he was closing it half read. Before he began reading, he had skimmed the whole book, looking at the sources cited at the back, the index, and the titles of chapters, and now he had no desire to read further. Wind understood where Harrison was coming from, in his desire to ally somewhat random-looking phenomena to some sort of teleology. However, in his grief he passed judgment and thought it all to be silly moralizing, beneath even sillier allusions to poltergeists, energy centers, and other mystical staples. The book did provide photographs though, and detailed accounts of spontaneous human combustion, including eyewitness testimony and interviews with fire inspectors and police reports. The documented cases were from the 20th and 19th centuries and the black and white photographs showed bodies incinerated, one of which the legs remained crossed and untouched beyond the point of burning. Nothing was as thorough as what he saw in Flora's apartment, nothing so clean. Harrison would have a field day with this case, he thought.

This is no act of god, men bring results upon themselves; effects are from causes, human effects from human causes. Humans are just another part of nature. Wind was very clear on all of this to himself. All of the logic and analytic philosophy he had ever studied from Plato to Wittgenstein broke down quite simply, especially in regard to divinity. Situations present themselves and the outcome for man is how man reacts to what is presented. One thing grows out of another. In this godless world, nature works on systems and structures and with enough facts, and a great enough view of each situation and all the connecting parts, an understanding can be reached. In this world, there are limits and parameters of structure. There is no connection between what happened to Sodom and Gomorrah in the Bible, a work of fiction, and what happened to Flora Ross, a woman he knew and loved.

Wind rose from his seat at the study table and walked confrontationally towards the stacks before him. The light behind him came west through the tall block windows of the eastern wall of the Central Fulton County Library. Behind him through the window stood a short, white corner building with a black marble fountain before it, next to the Marriot Residence Inn, a little peninsula jutting into the awkward intersection made by Carnegie Way and Forsyth Street colliding together at Peachtree. On his right he passed the concrete crossing stairways leading up one more floor to the fourth and down two more to the ground, but Wind was set on more text with the time he had. When he reached the section of OCCULT PSYCHOLOGY SELF-HELP, he returned the book to its place on the shelf. The next section of shelves was marked PHILOSOPHY RELIGION, and he was reminded of the region in which he lived by rows of Christian Bibles in different printings and translations. He was in the Bible Belt. He knew the world that lurked inside of that book well, but it was not his world. He knew it firsthand and he knew it as legacy. At NYU, young-adult Jonathan took a minor in World Religions along with his other studies. They were easy classes to excel in as his father, Nathan Wind, completed a doctorate at NYU in Religion before moving the family down to Athens, Georgia where he taught Philosophy of Religion at the University of Georgia. For the five years they lived in Athens until his father died, the little Wind heard his father preparing his lectures and lesson plans and absorbed as much as his thirsty sponge-like mind could of the world's religious traditions and the philosophy behind them. The world of the father flowed like family blood into the body of the child. Mature Jonathan knew that he was not to complete his father's work or follow the same career path, but he was never too far away. His study in the area of religion was for general knowledge and a greater understanding of humanity—which he pitied as compulsively religious—but was also out of a need to feel close to his father's ghost. Now he, like his father, investigated mysteries that humans created for themselves.

The book before him was no mystery. Within its black spine were just black marks on sheets of bone white, a text like any other. Its contents were to him verse, verse and artifact, and it contained no more meaning than the aesthetics and wisdom he valued in the best poetry. He knew where he could find all of the mentions of fire from heaven the wrathful god used to punish and he had reviewed them all recently. To his mind now came the Book of Job where the fires from heaven destroy faithful Job's flock. Wind sighed and shook his head at the notion of a God, who though omniscient, must test the merit of the faithful. His head continued to shake for he knew that this was considered the wisdom literature of the Bible, but there were those many people that he pitied for taking such a tale literally. Even as a story with a moral, an example of Hellenistic-Semitic thought, characterized by the notion that it just makes sense to obey God, he could not understand it as a place for belief. While man is at the whim of a god who tests, how is he to live while enduring his tests, like a stone with patient strength, with bronze flesh? Wind knew Job's words well. Should the faithful continue to suffer to no end, trusting, loving, and not questioning? And Job is faithful, he never gives up his faith in his god, never rejects or curses, he only wonders why. Why him? Why should his god bother and care to bother about the strength of his belief? For why else would bad things happen to good people, than for people to suffer the challenge of faith? Though that is the end result of the story, there is the grand *deus ex machina* climax where God is nothing but swirling hot words out of swirling hot wind appearing before Job. This is where Wind respects the figure of Job, for this is where he asks the big question, the big Why? Is it not mine to wonder why, more than just to do and die? And it is that question, and that asking that threatens the whole universe, its hierarchy, for it enrages Job's god in such a way that he pretty much answers with a "How dare you question me." The smile is ever quick to come to his face as Wind pictures that bombastic primitive deity flying off the handle at a man plagued, yet standing before him and asking, why me, why should you bother, why should you care what something as comparatively small as me feels, but the gusting whip of godly words never really answer, they just boast and blast.

Wind is confident that he has a clear method for making sense of the story: do as we have done since the cleansing light of the Enlightenment, remove the divine from the story. If people are fighting over what a god said, then remove that uncertain, unreliable variable from the equation and the solution is human, real, and attainable. Without some father, there on his sad height to refer to, people are going to have to get either far more creative or far more honest. Then it becomes time to look at history.

Wind was comfortable with all of these thoughts, they were not unfamiliar and they were how he naturally operated. He took a materialist view similar to that of Tolstoy, but with a deeper belief in free will, a good ole' American Pragmatist by self-definition. Wind knew the stories of religions as the fictions they are and yet he still felt a little guilt at shaking his head at the belief of others. He was surrounded by man's collective history, marked on the page and on everything else he could see around him. That is all we are, he mused, descendants. People reacting to the reactions of the past, backward *ad infinitum*. A well of history we drag behind us by the bucketful as we try to climb free. Lao was right; we cannot build on the old with new without understanding what went before. Back to the Bible: not destroying but completing. We must understand where we are and what was there before us. For I too am a transplant here, in this place, this city, this state.

Wind turned back towards the stairs, his sure footing, quick eyes, and muscle memory directing him through the labyrinth of stacks, reading their labels and Dewey's decimals counting upward, unfazed and unfettered by the noise and bustle across the great room, citizens using the computers, surfing the net, socializing, staying out of the sun without having to purchase anything. With few turns he was alee the rows of American history and after one false start he walked down the aisle going up on the left and down on the right where the ends would meet at the period around the Civil War. This was where Wind knew he could find the beginnings of Atlanta history, Atlanta's destruction and becoming. It was a city born true and anew out of conflict, but the land was old and as sad as Lao made it out to be. He turned to his left and there were volumes on colonial Georgia surrounded by books of the whole country's beginning. Lao told him to listen to the land, but that was hard to do considering how thorough the conquerors were. Lao spoke of the Mississippian tribes that roamed this region and left mounds and shards and spirits when they went and Wind knew they were well to rest for behind them came the Cherokee, from the word Tsa-la-gi, the people of Kituhwa as they called themselves, their minds always on the ancient city of their own past. Written history, written by invaders, remembers them of their original lands as fierce and bellicose, pinned in by colonizers and pitted against other tribes, but they were true to the land and took nothing without asking. The mound-builders' memories were tucked in respectfully by the Cherokee, as the lands were retained and used again and anew, a process that he remembered the psychic, Tia Maite, related about her Aztec ancestors at Teotihuacan, a process she said she and her people were enacting again here in Atlanta.

If there was anything that could sadly shake Wind's head, more so even than foolish belief, it was the dark history of his country and its treatment of its indigenous inhabitants. Wind knew much of these people, all that these books could offer, but knowledge does nothing, and that is where his sadness lay. The Cherokees completed what had been left by the mound-builders, a legacy of land veneration, and now they are gone, most to the next world, many to Oklahoma. The Cherokee were not without their own beliefs. They are a people of balance and a cosmology that recounts a beginning with only sky and water, where all life crowded in the sky until land was drawn up and dried and someone powerful fastened that land to the sky by rope at each compass point so it would float and hang in harmony with what was above and below. That powerful someone made man and woman after animals inhabited the dry land and a sun and moon were drawn from behind the rainbow in the sky. All was going well until the Europeans came, they had balance with nature and operable balance with their neighbors. Fortunately, their cosmology contained an eschatology, and it became understood that the European man was the harbinger of imbalance and his coming will bring a tear to each of those four ropes attaching land to sky and all will eventually be submerged again. Sometimes this was not that unattractive a notion for Wind, he worked in a field with consistent reminders that humans will never change nor disappoint him in their capacity for bestial acts.

Would Lao attribute this city's history to a metaphysical or spiritual imbalance, Wind wondered. Would Lao, a self-declared poet and prophet, explain and contain Flora's death by and within this land's restless darkness? Looking further at the history of his location, Wind saw a city carved out of the wilderness, created in fear of the dark; a history he was provided with on one level in Georgia public schools and on another by participation and empathy. First, it was Fort Gilmer, then Fort Peachtree, an outpost on the Chattahoochee River, aiming musket barrels at the shadows flitting behind the pines, leery of the red savage in the Cherokee settlement of Standing Peachtree, yet securing the northlands for the rest of the state. The 1820s saw surveyors and the early 1830s saw a few settlers. From such humble beginnings in primal fear and defense, a city grew, on whim and ambition, slowly at first, but with the momentum of enterprise, a contrived metropolis amassed to sustain transit, for the capital was Milledgeville in central Georgia and a rail connection was required with the northern location of Chattanooga, Tennessee. By the end of the '30s the southern end of a rail line was established in what was then called Terminus, after Colonel Stephen Harriman Long drove a stake in the ground for the line's zero-point less than a mile down Peachtree Street from where Wind now stood. As line was laid, the only obstacle in the northern expression of this lust to connect points of commerce were the Cherokee, living cautiously on a land they never thought of as their own. Easily and efficiently enough, they were moved, all neat and legal like for the state. As for any good reader, history was alive to Wind and bitterly he recounted the Trail of Tears of 1838-1839, when the federal government graciously gave armed escort to the Cherokee population in helping them move to their brand new home on a reservation in Oklahoma. 1,500 died before the move in a military stockade. Over the long, hard walk another 4,000 perished, but the rail line finally reached Chattanooga and supplies could effortlessly attain points north from points south and vice versa. The sad trail from Georgia to Oklahoma is marked by a *Rosa laevigata*, or the Cherokee Rose, and they bloomed from the falling tears of Cherokee mothers, a sign of hope nourished by sorrow, recording their history in nature: white petals for their pure tears, gold center for what drove the land-lust of the invaders, and seven leaves per stem for each branch of the Cherokee people. In 1916, in the ultimate act of appropriation or, as Wind some times refers to it, a sick joke, the Cherokee Rose was named the state flower of Georgia from the support of the Georgia Federation of Women's Clubs.

It was a place not to be, but a place to move through, a crossroads, this Terminus, and those that stayed were tough and raw. They were railmen and mechanics, laborers and merchants, investors and profiteers, and they all felt entitled to this frontier that they had carved themselves, dressing up their prize like a painted pig with drinking holes, brothels, and gambling houses. A change of name came in 1842 with Governor William Lumpkin lending that of his daughter to the burgeoning depot town, now Marthasville, a feminizing departure from that Latin word for boundary, which was an ill-fitting name for a city free from confinement, growing steadily outward from its zero-point day after day. Only three years did the name last, when the opportunity was taken to honor the true inspiration behind the young city of commerce, the railroads that lured opportunists to its black, scorched and scarred railroad earth. The tale went for Wind that the Western & Atlantic line gave the inspiration for the new name, which was softened and feminized into Atlanta.

She was already an important city, out of step with the rest of the south due to the speed of her growth, when the state seceded fourth in line from the United States to the rebellious Confederacy. In this new fragile country, born of insolence and pride, her position of significance could never be surpassed, and her basic function as crossroads and center for industry ready to transport, made her the jewel and hope of a young country grappling with identity in the shadow of its former governing body.

The hostile neighbor to the north would not allow another revolution for independence to shatter the union created by the last revolution for independence and so committed all of its might to returning the new nation to its south to the original union they once established together. Atlanta played her own glorious part in the struggle, becoming the nexus of the supply lines throughout the Confederacy. She gave everything she had in all four directions as the wind blew, labor, arms, her sons and daughters ready in a minute to serve in hospitals or fields of battle, tightening her every belt, prohibiting that which corrupts, securing all persons of suspicion, and committing the rest of her populace to martial law until she met her end, giving all that she had left to give to the miles of consuming flame that took her glory, beauty, and hope. Her enemies too, understood her throne of steel and what she represented both materially and symbolically for her new country.

The recollection of her burning took Wind to the end of the aisle before such titles as *Ordeal By Fire*; *Atlanta 1864*; *The Atlanta Campaign*; *The Battle of Atlanta*; *Season of Fire*; *The Siege of Atlanta*; all of which told him, as a seasoned resident of Atlanta, nothing new. Everyone knew how she burned, how nothing remained standing but thirty buildings. His imagination of this time period, like everyone else's, was developed from tragic retellings full of northerly-directed hate, the tour guide's battle narration at the Cyclorama (an Atlanta attraction that contains the world's largest oil painting built into a three-dimensional diorama), and of course footage from the movie *Gone with the Wind*. However, the Technicolor of his memory was made more vivid and darkened at the edges by his own readings, specifically about the man, regarded as the Devil, who set those hell-fires upon the Confederacy's precious flower, violating that Southern belle like only a barbaric, ungracious Yankee could.

Wind had always been intrigued by the distinct figure cut by William Tecumseh Sherman. He was an Ohio man who when the call had come, made a career out of war, yet always staying clear of the distasteful world of politics, unlike his Senator brother. He was a man who rose to every occasion, doing what must be done to get the job done, making the most of what was before him. He was a man full of contradictions that he resolved in his own time: named in tribute to the Great Unifier of the Indians of the Ohio Valley, but he became the Great Divider of the post-war west, conquering and relegating tribes to reservations; a failed banker in New York, yet a beloved superintendent of Louisiana Seminary of Learning; a hailed graduate of West Point, but in the War of Sedition he led an unruly volunteer army; a man whose name was lent to a method of rail-line mutilation, but who later enabled the building of the intercontinental railroad with his military protection; a fierce commander against Generals Johnston and Hood on the field of battle, but after the war he dined with them and helped their careers in the government and military of the reunited country. William Tecumseh Sherman was described in papers as insane during the war and when one of his subordinates complained to President Lincoln on one of his visits to camp, the honest President told the man not to argue with the stern general, if he threatens to shoot you, believe that he will. Total war was the method of this industrious "modern" general, preferring to drive back Johnston's forces throughout the summer of 1864, from Chattanooga down into Georgia, flanking and cutting off lines of supply and communication, challenging them to a fight on open ground all the while bent on finishing Atlanta militarily and economically. General Hood was in control after Johnston, and Sherman beat down his forces, laying siege on the city for a month until it was his. He knew that once the will to fight was conquered, so was the fighting body. Responsible for much destruction in his life he wrote and spoke unrelentingly against war as a crime against humanity and the embodiment of Hell. Still, it was his job and he did it well and thoughtfully, weighing what he believed to be the highest good in his conducting of total war.

Wind remembered that in Sherman's famous letter to Atlanta Mayor James M. Calhoun in September of 1864, he followed up his order to evacuate the city with a declaration of military complicity for the whole city. He saw no innocence in a city built around the industry of war and the transportation of war goods. Atlanta's destruction was a necessary deed to prevent the loss of more lives; this center of commerce would not be allowed to hold under his control, and from that implosion he foresaw everything else falling apart. In the letter he acknowledged the cruelty inherent in war and that the only way to bring about the peace that he so desired was to hit hard, fast, and thoroughly, leaving no possible recourse on an enemy's side. Only with flames could the machinations of and spirit for war be burned down and only with flames could a people understand that the war, which they brought upon themselves, was truly Hell on Earth. This was the action of William Tecumseh Sherman in regards to Atlanta. She was just another victim of a war he didn't start but would sacrifice anything to end. His order for fire, along with his zealous, unruly volunteers lit her up like a celebration and the evacuating rebels threw in their own share of spiteful incandescence. Left standing after the smoke cleared were very few buildings compared to what once supported the town of 20,000; mostly what remained was City Hall and such churches as the Catholic Church of the Immaculate Conception, St. Philip's Episcopal, Central Presbyterian, Second Baptist and Trinity Methodist.

The man of action and the man of rationality came together in "Cump," as he was affectionately called by his friends and respectfully remembered by Wind. That synthesis was what the detective sought in his investigatory police work, to be more than a mind, but a mind put to use in solid actualities, to leave his tower of text and abstraction and find some outer truth. Looking at the books present on Cump, Wind found such titles as *Sherman's Battle for Atlanta*, *Sherman's March*, and *Sherman's Horsemen*, but his favorite he couldn't find, *The White Tecumseh*, by Hirshson, a fellow Yankee who gave the world a detailed and sensitive biography of the man laid bare, not of the legendary military tyrant. It was this book that solidified the kinship Wind felt for Cump. Wind was a Yankee by birth and heritage, though he moved to the south at the age of two. He lived here always feeling like a transplant, as his parents reminisced on their lives in the north. At eighteen he left northward but eventually made his return, his self-perception and identity split across a geographic line. He saw this same passage back and forth in Cump, who once visited

Marthasville years before the war and even stopped at the Etowah Indian mounds on his way north because they reminded him of the mounds in Ohio he experienced in his childhood. Cump briefly lived in Louisiana and traveled extensively during that time. He was the Yankee who returned again and again to the south musing on the differences, before his most famous return, burned in the history of this place forever.

Wind understood the care that went into Cump's decisions about Atlanta, and wondered if this understanding could help him in any way, for here and now he was faced with his own fire. It was a fire that he believed he wasn't responsible for, though he felt a responsibility towards. In his work, he made connections between pieces of evidence and always stayed away from thematic generalizations, but in the presence of towering rows of creative history, all fictive in their own subjective ways, he allowed his mind to play with the idea of history repeating. Here was a fiery act directed towards a feminine body, scorched beyond recognition, another horrific burning in Atlanta. If at least by thematic coincidence, Flora's fate was tied to that of the city she called home. Wind could see how easy it was to interpret the first burning in a moral way. Atlanta burned for its sins, the sins of lust, corruption, greed, genocide, appropriation, pride, and slavery. Atlanta was burned to purify her civic soul. The infernal act of aggression defined the young city, branding it the Phoenix, her municipal symbol and the epitome of resurrection and resurgence.

Wind was familiar with the Phoenix. He grew up reading the stories from his father's books and encountered its image in the neighboring metropolis to the west of quiet Athens. The two generations of Wind-men would whisk into Atlanta on weekends to visit museums, bookstores, and Piedmont Park, and sometimes so the earlier generation could do research at Emory. Around town they traveled, exploring the sites of note where they were constantly faced with the city seal, its circle broken by the wings of the burning, unburned bird, its head raised in a mighty cry and its base all aflame. Above the mythic figure read the Latin word "Resurgens" and on each flank were the dates 1847, the year of the city's first charter, and 1865, the year she rose mightily from the settled ash. Upon returning home, father Nathan would read from the Histories' of Herodotus to his young son the story of the phoenix Herodotus learned in Egypt. The inquisitive boy would follow that thread through his father's labyrinthine library marveling at the potential universality of a myth. In Vietnam, the Phoenix was Phoung, in the Chinese version it was Feng Huang, and for them both it performed works for mankind, helping the world progress and return to the heavens. Adapted from the Chinese, the Japanese have in their tradition Ho-Oo, who is a dual-aspect bird of masculinity and femininity and represents fire, justice, and obedience. On the Arabian Peninsula, the bird is Cinomolgus and her nest is made out of cinnamon, a common spice associated with its mythos, as are myrrh, frankincense, and ginger; items that tie it in with the Christian resurrected god-man. Bennu or Benu, it is known in Egypt, its home in Heliopolis, and at times, it is understood as the soul of Osiris in flight, another resurrecting god. To the peoples of this land beneath his feet, the bird has taken many forms. Some tribes saw the tricksterly Raven as fire-born-blackened by flames. Many others revered the Great Thunderbird who ruled the sky with bombast and lightning under its control. Closest to home was the Tlanuwa of the Cherokee, a great hawk with the magical abilities of speech and shape-shifting, who meddled in the affairs of men.

The West has been fascinated by the scintillating figure at a safe distance from Hesiod to Herodotus, from Pliny the Elder, who has Senator Manilius try to rationalize the fantastic phenomenon, to Sir John Mandeville, in whose travels the story is reiterated Christianly, with three days of death for the great bird on an altar to God, an act he proclaims a miracle. Wind shared this fascination and cataloged what he knew in a way that would make both his father and Flora proud if they were both not gone from him. The Phoenix is a dense semiotic intersection, at once a masculine symbol of the sun that dies and is reborn daily and a feminine one that creates the situation of birth, her own birth and eternal transmission. A confusing image perfect for an area that when Cherokee, viewed the sun as feminine and the moon as masculine and now has turned that world out of balance with a western tradition that reverses those roles.

Rising, he walked his creaky legs to the end of the aisle and turned left and up the rows of ancient Greek and Roman history. Did any of this "research" help him, or was he just killing time until evening? He really couldn't say. Wind followed the trail of his thoughts up through ancient history, but the burning thread he followed in his mind seemed to be taking him further away from his actual investigation. His thoughts were on Ovid now and the blending metamorphosis of time and narrative. On careful footing, he turned right at the intersection of another cross-aisle, reading titles and Dewey Decimal numbers, and abbreviated categories, until his labyrinthine ways deposited him before the upright rectangles reading "Ovid" in the section labeled WORLD LITERATURE. Passing over the Loeb Library editions, housing the original Latin, but often yielding dated translations, he found the nice paperback Horace Gregory translation of *The Metamorphosis* he had at home. Comfortable in his hand, he flipped to where his mind was leading: Book II; its beginnings on page fifty-seven; set in the Palace of the Sun. The hours, seasons and divisions of date majestically stood in flanking throng of blinding light and beauty, all royal purples and golds, as a boy met his father for the first time and demands proof of patronage. Guilt a motivating factor even for a god, the father could deny the boy nothing. The boy wanted to drive the sun and he couldn't be dissuaded. The father relented and handed the boy the reins. Phaeton, half-mortal, took the power of a god, his father Apollo, into his young, brazen possession. Headstrong, yet weak in understanding, the poor boy was quick to dispel all of his father's advice and admonition. He tried to be more than himself, more than his stature, more than his mortality, and the result was loss and destruction. Phaeton dropped the reigns, never in control of the blazing steeds anyway, and could do nothing to prevent their erratic path scorching the Heavens and the Earth below. In this time, as the day made its way, across the sky and sinking low, everything took cover, as there was no place without fire. Moist Earth steamed, hiding within herself, and screamed out in fear for the powers on high to put an end to the searing that threatened all life as the incandescent chariot streaked ever closer. Apollo watched on, her cry answered as fire was fought with fire; Jove casting his forked lightning bolt down to the chariot, shattering it all and letting the boy fall like a burning star to the ground. There was no light from the sky as a father wept and the charred Earth cooled.

This is what Wind had come to think of, a father making reparations for his absence and a rebellious son thinking only of himself. He now for the first time saw this story in the history of this city. The Seditionists were sons of the Union, southern children of the greater host, headstrong, brazen, and insurrectionary. Their prideful irreverence for the greater body and desire for self-government, whether legal or not, was the prime cause for the resulting destruction. Would this make Cump into Jove or simply the lightning bolt, he wondered? Does this fit the causal moral logic he considered earlier, the acts of seditious rebels bearing responsibility for the fire that took Atlanta's body away, burned away in fire then washed away in ash by wind? Was there any sense in inferring redemption through fire as many did? Cump saw its purpose expressed in its end-all nature and for him ends mattered more than means. Many have used hindsight to find good in the bad. Wind would have to suppose far too much cosmology to apprehend spiritual purification resulting from a world turned to ash, and this slash and burn moralizing was what he knew many would see in what happened to Flora, for good or bad. Tia Maite perceived a positive process of purification and he knew the negative sentiment that someone like Sonny's mother would bring to it. Here were two women from very different worlds and very different worldviews who can use the same phenomenon to support their own distinct beliefs. Flora's death was a semiotic sign of the same density as the Phoenix, as useful a myth for those that had use for such things. Wind didn't want to find in Flora's death another reflection of the world as he saw it. He didn't want to find again what he always expected. He wanted to find the truth, but he stopped himself before he could explore the paradoxical notion that he was always looking for the truth and in his quest for an objective reality, he had still never escaped the subjective.

With the book in his right hand, he turned the pages slowly with his left, scanning and skimming. Was he too a rebellious son? And what would he ask from his own father as proof of love if he ever stood before him again? From any guidance that his own father had given, he did not believe he had strayed, but here he was, uncertain in a world of information, cleft in ways outstanding from those whom he loved: physically from Flora; spiritually, sexually, and emotionally from Monica. His sister, at whose apartment he had left a message every day since he received his mother's postcard, he could not find and they hadn't spent much time together in years. His mother was gone away, but her present physical distance added very little to the great emotional one that he had felt for over a decade now. There was the urge inside to move from this place, from the book he held, as if in that action he could change the emotional direction his thoughts were heading. Unless he was going to act to remedy these relationships, which presently wasn't possible, he found no purpose in thinking about them. Before letting the book close in his hand, he remembered another path of mind that led him to this place; Ovid also spoke of the Phoenix. Turning to the back of the text, where the moral of resurrection through the changes of time was well laid out, Wind scanned through the middle of Book XV. The great bird was Ovid's unattainable ideal, it was always reborn again in the same form, though it changes like everything else, following a cycle. This view of cyclical time is very comforting to many, thought Wind, and he had studied a great deal of dialectic history in Plato, Vico, Hegel, Marx, Joyce, and others. Still, he always felt the most secure with the mentoring words of Lao, who at the age of nineteen attributed the positing of cyclicality to an impotent fear of death.

Wind found that cyclicality was like the promise of an afterlife, it was a solace for those afraid to live life in the present. There was a broken spirit of the South that he saw perpetuating itself on an expectation of return. "The South will rise again" is the pitiful cry, the death-rattle, echoing out of a misunderstood dream, which Wind has heard many times all over this city, but especially on its outskirts, often emanating from tilting porches or red pickup trucks, both decorated with the flag of the Confederacy and occupied by old white men with bitter pinched faces full of misdirected anger and regret and their young counterparts full of nothing but anger. To them, nurturing a rebel's heart a century and a half too late, claiming "heritage, not hate," and trying to stoke a fire that was extinguished so long ago that no one knows anymore what they would do with their own separate country; to them, Wind can only ever respond that the South will not rise again, not that way, not like it was, not ever again.

But alas, the South has risen again in another way; Wind was quick to check himself. Atlanta, at least, is a towering marvel, the jewel of the Southeast once again. This building in which he stood was a testament to that, as was the view out of each window. Through such local brand names east to rattle off like Coca-Cola, Delta, UPS, Georgia-Pacific, Home Depot, and Turner, she has become the economic and cultural center of the Southeast with industry supporting growth and growth supporting an expanding population. The Centers for Disease Control alone figures her as some last hope in several potential post-Apocalyptic future scenarios. Hartsfield-Jackson International Airport, one of the busiest airports in the world, makes Atlanta a crossroads to such a degree that there is a joke that a person must layover in Atlanta on the way to the afterlife. After the Civil War, the motto of the "New South" was "reconciliation fueled by competition," but it seems the citizenry of Atlanta saw success as the best revenge.

The city entered the 20th century strong, and soon the mobilization for the Second World War took local industry to a greater level with General Motors, Bell Aircraft, Lockheed, and Ford. The Atlanta that Wind knew was independent of any of the facts he had learned. It was a home and a place of memory. Moving to the city in 1984, a young Jonathan was able to grow up and watch his surroundings change and explode into a monstrosity of development and urban renewal from the late '80s through the prosperous '90s until now, when he could constantly find a part of town altered beyond his last recollection. With the population of metropolitan Atlanta exceeding four million and the city geography swelling to include twenty counties, Wind was not alone in seeing his residence reaching the ranks of such urban behemoths as Chicago, San Francisco, Los Angeles, or New York. Now when he traveled, or when Monica pinned him down into watching cable television at her apartment, he understood another way that Atlanta had grown into a capital among capitals: Hip-Hop. On the local streets he has heard his city referred to as Hotlanta, the ATL, Phatlanta, the Dirty South, the Dirty Dirty, and A-town, but to catch those epithets in passing on the streets of New York City or to see stars such as Usher, Ludacris, Da Brat, Bone Crusher, Killer Mike, Lil' Jon & The Eastside Boyz, Outkast's André Benjamin and Big Boi, J-Kwon, and Jermaine Dupri on MTV give a shout-out, holleration, or otherwise represent his adopted hometown, he could not but feel pride along with the understanding that the Phoenix had risen and its wings were spread far and wide.

Wind closed the book and returned it to its ranks to stand with the other upright volumes like stone soldiers in a tomb waiting for a call to action that may never come. Under the buzzing glow of the fluorescent lights, the colorful spines of each erect volume blurred together like static between the hazy institutional shades of the carpet, shelves, and walls. Weaving through the granite gray of the stacks, Wind headed for the center of the room, no longer experiencing this maze as a trap. Passing down the great crisscrossing concrete stairway, he made his way across another computer-laden research room before going down the side stairs walled to one side by windows, out which he could see the Carnegie Building (that family too had money in the 20th Century growth of Atlanta). On the ground floor, he eased through the turnstile while people to his left were hassled emptily by the security check as they entered, flashing the contents of their backpacks and purses. Through the front door, he broke from the air-conditioning and the cool concrete smell into a day in full fire, bright to his squinting eyes. He stepped north, clean away from the library and its oddly menacing shadow. Designed by Bauhaus architect Marcel Breuer, the library, or "People's University" as the slogan goes, was dedicated in 1980, a small avant-garde nod in a relatively staid downtown environment. Crossing Carnegie Way towards the Peachtree Center MARTA station, Wind was not yet ready to dip down into the subway and inhale more processed air and that same cool concrete smell. Onto Peachtree Street, he turned and continuing north, he let the breeze and afternoon sun wash away his scattered thoughts. He knew that quite often his mind was just a big toy box with which to amuse himself. He inputted data and watched his mind work, sorting, referencing, cross-referencing, breaking down repetitions and spiraling off even more connections from what was broken down. On the job he could control the break down and arrive at the most logical connections from inputted data. In directionless hours like how this afternoon was spent, full of waiting and thinking, he let his mind run wild, sweeping noisily through whatever he took in.

As had been his daily routine this week, he drew his mobile phone with the intention of calling his sister's apartment. Wednesday when he called, he spoke to her roommate Kerri who hadn't seen Astrid in some days, but Kerri said it wasn't rare since they're on different schedules. Kerri told him that Astrid was working Thursday night at Zappoli's, but when he called there the next evening they said she had not shown up and someone was covering her shift so he left another message on her home answering machine. Now, dialing Sonny's mobile phone number, Wind was moving further into action. He was familiar with his sister's lifestyle and no stranger to tracking her down, but still this time he worried because of his mother's worry. Over the last few years, he had been trying to give her as much freedom as she needed. She had never cried wolf, but neither had his mother's intuitions. Nevertheless, she hadn't called him back all week.

"Yeah, Wind, what's up? How's your vacation been? You calling to see how I'm doing on your cases? Can't stop thinking about work, can you? Don't think I can handle it all without you? Ha, ha, what's up, man?" Sonny sounded sincerely happy to hear from his partner. Wind could also tell by the background noise and Sonny's speech patterns that he was answering while driving.

"That car lonely without me there next to you getting nauseous from your driving? You know I had enough of that stop and go cabby crap in New York." Wind matched his partner's mood.

"Yeah, well, I'm crying myself to sleep at night. So, how you doing? What's up?"

"I'm alright, I just need a favor from you if you don't mind helping me out?" Wind continued briskly up Peachtree Road past the Hard Rock Cafe on his right and the Westin Peachtree Plaza on his left, careful of the precarious reception his mobile phone managed downtown in between these buildings, heading for the sun, beyond the shadows.

"You name it, buddy. What you got?"

"I need you to check up on my sister. Speaking to her boss and roommate, no one has seen her all week. I haven't spoken to her in a while, but I've been leaving messages. It's been over forty-eight hours, but I don't want to fill out a report yet. You know what she's like, but I was hoping you could check around. Run her name with the usual places, morgue, hospitals, arrest reports at the other counties, you know. Maybe even send a patrol by her apartment."

"What do I do if, when, I find her?"

"Well use your judgment based on the circumstances, but I trust you. Call me anytime and let me know what is going on before you do anything?" Wind was quickening his pace to get past the white Southern Company building to his left and cross Baker Street, to feel the sun again and to walk through the slight grounds of Hardy Ivy Park, a place named for Mr. Hardy Ivy, a South Carolina man remembered as the first permanent resident of Atlanta. Peachtree Street angled to the right, giving the park a little room before straightening out again in front of Max Lager's American Grill at the corner of West Peachtree Street.

"Alright, don't worry. I'll take care of it. I'll call you after I know something and before I do anything. Is there anything else, you okay? I mean is there something else going on? I never figured you for a spontaneous vacation guy." The voice on the other end crackled in and out giving Wind an easy exit.

"No. I'm fine. Everything is fine. I just need you to check on my sister, that's it. It's probably nothing. She's probably just doing drugs with some guy somewhere. Hey, you are breaking up, so I will say goodbye before I lose you."

"Okay, call me if you need anything and man, take care of yourself," said Sonny, and Wind responded to his partner's goodbye with one of his own and closed the mobile phone with both hands.

His eyes went to the ground before his feet as his hands moved, one slipping the phone into a pocket and the other fishing for Pez.

Dazedly, he walked up to the marble arch before him, a square frame of four triumphal arches "erected and dedicated to the advancement of learning." The area above the arch in view read "The Advancement" in deep engraving with the name "Carnegie" below. The other sides bore the names "Dante," "Aesop," and "Milton" below their respective portions of the commemorative phrase. Sucking on the peach Pez candy drawn from the Ulysses S. Grant dispenser, Wind wandered up the steps into the space between the columns. Looking down at the brickwork in the monument's center, he read the names of the nine local institutions of higher learning, each in its own circle surrounding a smaller bare inner circle.

"Hey! Yo! Yo! Hey! Hey! Yo! Yo! Hey!" came loud from behind the next column and a kick hit Wind on the left shin.

Wind, startled, stepped back, jerked his leg, and reached reflexively for his sidearm, patting at his bare hip, and looked up with scanning, examining eyes trying to read the figure emerging from behind the marble. Hunched over with bulbous back and long stringy brown hair, a man of indeterminate age rocked low and edgy before Wind. The detective recorded the shape of the man, his ruddy face and squinty eyes, the oversized, striped shirt, once favored by skaters, and baggy cargo pants above work boots. For a moment they both hovered nervously on the balls of their feet, but before Wind could speak the bent man did.

"With long-forgotten woe my spirit groans, I shudder at the load of mortal ill. Here she is lodged, behind these clammy stones, and all her crime an innocent blind will. You shrink to seek her in this place, you fear to meet her face to face! Delay not! Else may death his doom fulfill. Goethe said it once before and you must bear it ever more!"

Wind was about to react with grapples and a barrage of questions like: who sent you, does this have to do with Flora Ross, what happened to her, why Goethe; but after the gruff and jittery man let loose his prepared speech, he unchained his insecure footing and turned to jump down the short flight of steps from the arch, hop a few feet and then jump down the next flight of steps to land alongside a brick building where he darted around a corner, bounded over the low brick wall and sprang into a green dumpster. Wind made a step to the column, looking where the hunchbacked messenger went, and staggered a moment on his left leg from the pain in his shin. A resonant metallic bang rang out and Wind watched the swing of the long greasy hair as the figure flung himself back out of the dumpster and went skipping like a wounded gazelle across the parking lot and down Simpson Street.

Deeming the expenditure of effort to pursue the man who already had a two-block head start impractical and pointless, Wind hobbled down the opposite side of the monument towards Peachtree Street sending over-the-shoulder glances down Simpson. The hunched and hopping form was long out of sight and the shock of the experience, so strange, but now increasingly familiar, had the limping investigator in an exhilarating haze. Gone was the liberating daze the sun brought in the freedom from the stuffy library. He was cerebral again, turned inward, comparing what the hunchback had said to what he remembered from the little person. It seemed to be the same passage from Faust but in a different translation, neither the one he had at home. He crossed West Peachtree and passed the door to Max Lager's as late lunchers came out and early happy hourers went in. A dark-skinned woman with thick Jheri curls parted far on the left side of her head passed by to his right wearing a black t-shirt reading in erratic and urgent colored lettering, "Relax, God is in Control." Wind barely registered the content of the slogan beyond the lettering, as he drifted by the woman, lost again in thought.

10. NIGHT VOYAGE—SELVA OSCURA

What are these, So withered and so wild in their attire, That look not like the inhabitants o' the earth, And yet are on't? Live you? Or are you aught That man may question? You seem to understand me, By each at once her choppy finger laying Upon her skinny lips: you should be women, And yet your beards forbid me to interpret That you are so.   —William Shakespeare, *Macbeth*

FROM AN EMPTY LANE OF NORTH DRUID HILLS THEY WERE GIVEN luck and a green arrow allowing them to turn with ease without stopping from the bridge down the concrete ramp onto I-85 South, the darkness of the sky lit by the crossing currents of Friday night traffic, and Iliya Chernovsky proceeded to speak about the troubles with her car, as she had been since Jonathan Wind picked her up at her apartment only ten minutes ago. She seemed so inherently awkward that he didn't know if this was nervous talk on her part, nervous about being with him, nervous about what awaited her tonight; or whether this was her in a place of comfort, relaxing into banal details of everyday life. He listened and let out noises to let her know he understood, peppered with the occasional appropriate question to keep her elaborating, talking, and seemingly comfortable. As I-85 merged into I-75, sharing the dual identity of I-85/75 making the stem of a "Y" shape, the urban wilderness opened up before them with a great glow of electric light running along the buildings, the streets, and the undercarriages of passing cars. Driving through Midtown, the streets along the highway were alive with people out for a Friday night, in the sunless dry comfort of the emerging season. Typical for after-hours and weekends, the visible portions of downtown were abandoned as the business districts rested. When the chance was given past Grady Memorial Hospital, Wind exited onto I-20, cutting across the great Y's stem, heading west in the direction of Birmingham, Alabama.

"It's a good night for this, it looks really clear. I hope it stays this way. Tonight is the fourth quarter of the moon. That is when they like to do initiations. I was lucky that this month it happened to be on a Friday." Iliya had reached the point of comfort to be able to talk about where and why they were making this trip together. Wind nodded and gave her one of his listening looks encouraging her to proceed.

"Their idea—I say they, but it's all Toni—is that for the initiates it is best to be eased into the flow of the moon cycle that everyone else is already on. It's like they meet often enough and get so in tune with their periods and each other that they are all ovulating and ragging at the same time. So I have to come in on the fourth quarter, as the moon is waxing and then somehow get into their flow. No pun intended." She smiled out half of her mouth and he smiled in his own small way back.

"Do they know that I am coming?"

"Well that was the tricky part." She let out an audibly restrained breath, her version of a laugh. "I called Toni and I was like, hey, I have a friend that I want to share in my initiation with me, yadda, yadda, yadda. And I was like, *but* this friend is a man. And I could hear her sigh, which I knew she would do, but man, I know what these people are like and, shit, it was great, I think you will love this. Flora would have. Anyway, sorry. So I told her that you were a Ph.D. candidate in Women's Studies at Columbia University—I had heard you went to school in New York—and that you are writing an article for Harper's on goddess worship in the New South. She ate that shit up and tried to act all official, asking if they would all have to fill out consent forms or releases to be used in your article. I told her verbal consent was enough, just making shit up, trying to sound just as official as her, like it was some business negotiation. I swear it sounded like she was nicer to me after that than she has ever been before."

"Alright, I can play along, go undercover. Why did you say Harper's?"

"I didn't want to name anything with any chance of connection to someone there tonight. It is a damn small world when you get into specialized circles and I needed something believable and still cool sounding. I rehearsed all this before I called. I am familiar with their no boys policy, no exceptions, but I was pretty sure she would make one."

"Just so you know, I went to NYU, but it's okay, I have always wanted to pretend that I went to Columbia, it being Ivy League and all."

Iliya let out a pity laugh and another awkward half smile to acknowledge Wind's attempt at humor.

She let him know which exit would be best to take into Douglasville and he followed her directions off the highway and through Douglasville and out towards farm country. The final street they turned down was unlit and rural with large acreage between each house. He could barely see beyond the limits of his headlights except when they approached a house, since most were lit with floodlights on the porch or above the garage. Wide spaces followed each house; dark spaces, of either fields with fenced-in shapes of standing, snorting, sleeping beasts; or thick walls of Georgia pine free from cow, goat, or horse, but alive in with smaller animals of craft and cunning. She told him to slow down and they gradually pulled up to a long line of cars parked on the side of the road around a driveway. They both exited the vehicle, and from the passenger side Iliya rounded the front of the car so as to be next to Wind. Down the row of cars they walked, quiet as the night, their breath lower than the creak of the life teeming in the peripheral dark. Wind recorded what he saw of the cars behind which they parked. Ten vehicles total for both sides of the driveway other than his. The two late model Grand Cherokee Jeeps and a Ford Aerostar Minivan were outliers, but the other cars all seemed befitting of the practitioners he imagined: an old white Volvo station wagon, a new yellow Volkswagen Bug, a red pick-up truck, a silver Toyota Prius hybrid, a humble green Ford Escort, and a couple of modest late model Honda Accords. He noted the bumper stickers arrayed in varying degrees across the spectrum of vehicles present, some he recognized, while others were new even to him: *Blessed Be!*; *Just Say No To Sex With Pro-Lifers*; *Righteous Babe Records*; *U.S. Out of My Uterus*; *My Other Car is a Broom*; *Magic Happens*; *It's A Druid Thing*; *Xena for President*; *Lick Bush*; *No War in Iraq*; *Towanda Lives!*; *Buy Organic*; *Eve Was Framed*; *I'd Rather Be Home-Birthing*; *This Is Not My Boyfriend's Truck*; *Eve Was Framed*; *Midwives Help People Out*; *Less Bush More Trees*; *In Goddess We Trust*.

"Not much for carpooling, these goddess worshippers," Wind whispered as they passed the last car and reached the driveway to the house, a plain colonial with yellow walls and pale blue shutters, standing bright before them in the fierce glow of a floodlight.

Iliya walked a few steps in front of Wind and he took in what she was wearing in a way he couldn't while driving. She was dressed simply in black jeans and a loose black shirt that matched the color of her hair. On her feet she wore black Chinese slippers with brown soles and she carried the same purse as yesterday. In the car, he had noticed that she had on more black eye makeup than yesterday, no lipstick that he could discern, and a shining silver hoop was in her nose in the place of the small stud. She looked back over her right shoulder and smiled, making sure that he was still close behind her in their shared silence. They walked up the long driveway and right past the house in the direction of a red barn clouded in the din. Immediately behind the house was a small yard with some patio furniture and after a few yards was the tree line, a crusty barrier of pine running parallel to the house and broken only by the length of the red barn. They walked straight to the entrance, discreetly located on the right side just within the tree line.

"This is Toni's sister's place. She's not much of a joiner, but she lets them use her property," she said over her shoulder.

He wondered if Iliya had spoken to break the tension of walking through the wooded dark. She had her hand on the door and it appeared to him that she took a deep breath and held it before she drew the swinging planks out. The play of the shadows around him kept his body poised to react to any sudden approach.

Within the barn, Wind followed Iliya beneath the overhead light, just an exposed bulb at the end of a hanging wire. The boarded floor was smooth and well swept except for the occasional tawny remnant of hay and to both sides of where they entered there were freestanding racks of hanging clothes with pairs of shoes beneath. Without saying anything and with her back still turned to Wind, Iliya put down her bag and took off her top and hung it on a hanger to her right, adding her bra to the same hanger. Still turned, she unsnapped her jeans and bent forward, sliding them over her full buttocks and off one leg at a time as she balanced on the other. As she had begun to strip, Wind had turned himself around and busied his mind with speculating that she must be more nervous than normal in here alone with him, since this barn served as a threshold, a transitional state, before the openness outside, through the other door, which she had experienced before. This is the place you leave a part of yourself behind before going on. Iliya hopped on her right foot for balance as she took her black panties down her bent left leg. When steadied, she spoke over her left shoulder.

"I don't know why I'm being so shy. You're gonna see all of me out there, more than you'd ever want to." And she let out a small forced chuckle.

Wind looked over his shoulder, they smiled at each other, and both slowly turned towards facing, his speed of turn matching hers. Her shoulders were hunched and her hair draped across her face like when he first saw her leaving work yesterday. Her arms were crossed under her white bulbous breasts, like blue-veined onions, and her hands clutched her sides to cover her slight stomach roll above her black and bristling pubic hair. He looked for her eyes to make and hold contact, fighting the reflex to draw his sight down her body.

"Should I disrobe?" He asked and she told him that she was pretty sure he should not; he was a spectator, not a participant, and they probably have some ideas about what masculine energy could do to affect their cultivation of feminine. She told him it was probably best for all concerned to keep his maleness covered, and they both loosened up a little at the acknowledgment of her humor.

Wind felt relief, for he had worried on the way here, and his worry increased as Iliya undressed and a natural stirring occurred in his genitals, an amassing of blood and heat. He was not in uniform at a crime scene, surrounded by other busy police officers, feeling totally on the job. He was stepping into an encounter that was outside of his sphere of experience and all of the associations he had from Flora were amorously and erotically charged in his memory. The jeans he wore were tight and discreet and the white shirt he wore with his barn jacket made a subtle enough combination to support his cover as student and journalist.

She stood naked before him in the swaying light of the exposed bulb above their heads and though she still smiled up through her carefully careless black bangs, he saw that in her eyes her attitude had changed, it had gone solemn and serious and when she asked if he was ready he just nodded. She walked barefoot to the door at the opposite end from where they entered, giving the barn even more of a threshold quality as she opened it to exit. He walked behind her on the path up a slight hill between the trees. The swept and trodden path was delineated from the pine straw of the woods by rocks and the occasionally placed votive candle. The path was steep enough that as Iliya walked before him her bare buttocks shifted where his eyes fell with each of her steps and he saw, as the rising Moon slipped through the trees, that it was as pale as the rest of her and squared off and flattened by the weight of her hips and the thickness of her short thighs. The consciousness of his footing became tied with the consciousness of her swaying haunches, side to side as the trail twisted in the tall pines, but she never looked back and the crunching of his shoes kept her aware of how close he was.

The distance was not as far as it felt and in no time at all they were at a clearing in the trees where a circle was marked by burning citronella tiki poles and fifteen shimmering figures stood within the flicker of the pungent flames awaiting them. The Moon was just past the highest trees around the clearing, winking down in Her state of becoming. The sounds of conversational chatter came from pockets of the circle but gradually faded as the approach of the man and woman was noticed and acknowledged. Iliya led straight for the table draped in purple at the path's end, an obvious centering location as the ring of fire seemed to open to its placement. Clearer as they neared, Wind could make out, in the smoky flicker, a blending of fleshy naked forms of different proportions and his eyes flitted, fearing where to fall for too long. At the table two forms turned to greet them.

"Why, hello, Iliya. It seems that the Great Goddess has blessed your journey. You are right on time," said the shorter of the two as she leaned in to hug Iliya, pressing bare breast against bare breast in a way that it appeared to Wind should cause the recipient unease; he saw the awkward girl as quicker to retreat into herself than to connect with others, especially bare breasted, yet here he found her relaxed in the embrace of initiator, giving herself up to the experience in a way that seemed at odds with the person he met yesterday. The taller woman carefully leaned down to kiss Iliya hello on the cheek and withdrew without any spectacle or delay as the shorter woman greeted Wind.

"So, you must be Iliya's friend, Jon Gale. I am Goddess Luna. Iliya has told me a lot about you and the Great Goddess blesses your arrival. I hope you will be respectful and accurate in your reporting of our rites. Men are not usually welcome, but as you are here to support our initiate and share our love of the Goddess with others we will allow your observation. I have made the others aware of your presence, and they all give their consent." As she spoke, Wind broke eye contact for a moment to look at Iliya who smiled full yet close-lipped, waiting for his glance in recognition of the final joke she forgot to share. His eyes were back on the woman whom he realized was Toni Banford and he held her glance, resisting the urge to observe her body beyond her musky and dense redolence.

"Well, thank you, Goddess Luna, I am very grateful to be here and appreciate how gracious you have been in welcoming me at the last minute. I hope I can capture in words the sincerity in your practice and be able to convey to my audience what the Goddess means to you and the others in your distinct interpretation. I have heard how excited Iliya has been by the process and the sense of sisterhood that she feels here and I was hoping I could give her my support, as she becomes a full member of your group. So thank you again. Do you mind if I take some notes and maybe if I have any questions I could ask you after?"

Wind's eye caught Toni's small, loose, empty breasts quiver as they shook hands and she agreed to his requests. Her brusqueness he took for coyness and he could tell that she was putting on a facade for his benefit. Toni then told him that they were about to begin and he kept his eyes high as she took Iliya's hand and lead her a few feet away to round the purple-draped table outfitted with a large silver goblet, a hefty moonstone, four red standing candlesticks, a sculpture of the Venus of Willendorf the size of a small baby doll. Remaining together, he and the other woman, whose height reached his own, finally acknowledged each other.

"Hi, I'm Guinevere. Call me, Gwen."

"Hello. Jon. Is Guinevere your Goddess name?" With her at his height it was harder to make eye contact; he was used to his eyes falling to meet the eyes of others and now his eyes kept dropping to her full tan breasts with dark bumpy areolas and taut nipples.

"No, that is my given name, Guinevere Hedge. My parents were pretty flaky, with lots of Celtic pride. My Goddess handle is Rhiannon, Celtic Goddess of horses and the moon, but I know what you are thinking. It's true, cheesy, but true. I always loved Fleetwood Mac. I've probably modeled too damn much of my life after Stevie Nicks. And now I am Goddess Rhiannon. Oh, well. Hey, it's okay. You can relax. I am used to people seeing me naked at this point in my life. I've done a lot of wild shit. So I don't mind if you look, this old body's got nothing to hide. Once we get in that circle, there is a lot to look at, all those bodies. And I'm always checking everyone out, all the women always are, some are horny, some are envious, some are just catty. Hey, wanna hear a joke? Why do witches go commando?" She paused dramatically. "To get a better grip on the broom!"

She laughed and Wind laughed with her and she spread out her hands invitingly and presented herself while Wind conducted a sweepingly obvious look at her body from head to toe. Gwen's hair was long and dirty blonde down the middle of her back and most of her skin was well tanned and weathered to the point of leathery. Freckles covered her wide shoulders, arms, sinewy hands, chest and breasts that hung in their full weight to the bottom of her ribcage and the top of her tan stomach. In her body, voice, and manner he found traces of the aged hippie or biker. The signs of sun-overexposure stretch down her long legs, covering her whole body except for a pale veiny bikini strip curving down from the middle of her firmly protruding stomach to the dark hairy shadowed patch that ended where her thighs met. Figuring her age to be close to that of his mother and impressed by her friendliness, Wind readily trusted Gwen; and her humor temporarily delayed the potential arousal her body offered.

"Good, now that we got that outta the way, lets get into the circle.

Once she is done talking to Iliya, Toni—that's Goddess Luna's real name—should be ready to get this show on the road. Should be any minute. Come with me, you can hang back and watch right over my shoulder, you'll see just fine, you're like an inch taller than me. A man looking over me. You're not married are you? I don't see no ring. I'm just kidding. I'll show you around and let you know what is going on. I'm kinda the mother of the group. With some of these girls, I feel like the grandmother. I'm not even the oldest, but I somehow got myself in this damned position. Toni's a little scattered, she's got her hands full, and as you can imagine, some of the women who show up at these things are more serious than others and a group this size needs someone to ride herd. C'mon."

Wind followed Gwen into the perimeter of the tiki poles, watching her body as she moved, the black stallion tattoo on her right shoulder blade rearing on its hind legs, the rose vine and barbed wire tattoo around her left ankle; and noticed how firm her large body was, even her wide hips and buttocks, though no wider than her broad shoulders. He found her great in stature and was glad that she ventured to be his guide through this night's events. As she stood in what seemed to Wind to be her usual place, at the point where the circle of poles opens to the table, he watched as the other women followed her lead, dropping their conversations, shuffling their placement, and shaking loose in their new spots with their attention on the two women at the purple table. A breeze rose as from the Earth herself, filtered through the twisting trees, reforming as one movement, exalting the clearing with energy, the lashing of the toxic flames, the swirling wafts of chemical citronella, and the women instinctively all joined hands for a moment and cast back their heads letting their hair flow to the wind, letting the potency of luscious Nature charge their energy and sense of commitment.

"So how much do you know about us already?"

"Iliya hasn't told me too much, but I am familiar with other groups of Goddess worship. I know that this group was once part of a larger group." Wind hovered behind Gwen until she let go of the woman's hand to her left and could turn a little more over her shoulder towards him while still facing forward.

"Yeah, things were a little different when Diana was around. Toni, bless her heart, she tries real hard, and really keeps this group together, but she isn't as creative as Diana was. I always thought it was pretty cool the way she worked out the whole anthelion repose thing and really made sure we were on track with all of the astrology going on above us. You know, she was a different kind of leader than Toni. But that's okay, I mean, I'm here. I was interested in seeing what Toni would do differently and I always sympathize with the jilted lovers, the underdogs. I was looking out for her, I wasn't sure if anyone else would follow her, but it turned out she had more friends than I thought. It is understandable now, looking around at who is here, who made the, you know, transition. But it's been good. Real basic, hardcore Goddess worship. And Toni has made it really her own thing while still feeling out the climate of the group here and what they would all go in for. The kind of stuff Diana wouldn't have liked at all. I mean, we are women hear us roar, kind of stuff, hardcore feminists... Well, you know, most of us."

Wind listened as his eyes slowly adjusted to the tiki light and he found himself glancing subtly around over her shoulder, cataloging the initial distinctions he observed in the women present. It was a natural way for him to feel at ease and make sense of new surroundings, describing to himself and recording, and here the quantifying helped to abate arousal. Most of the flesh he saw was light in coloration and even when obviously browned by ultraviolet ray, he pinned down the recent descent of those present to be not far from totally European. From what he already knew about this group in particular and what he had read about these groups in general, they were far from the serious inclusiveness of the womanist movements and deeper within the feminist western European tradition of modern goddess worship, not too dissimilar from Wicca or witchcraft, no matter how hardcore they claimed to be. But he wasn't here to pass judgment, but to learn. Wittgenstein came to mind, his words: "don't think, look"; so he looked. To the left of Gwen stood another woman about the same height, but wider, and from his view behind and along her right side, her flesh appeared to be overflowing, pushing beyond the boundaries of the skeletal frame, out and down, stretch marks like tiger stripes. Wavy black hair, stringy and frizzing, poured well down her back as more of the same substance stood out of her armpit and covered her legs, which rubbed alongside each other from her low-hanging dimpled buttocks down to her knees to diverge and meet again at her hard rounded calves before ending separately on rough pink heels. Gwen could read his subtle movements.

"Where are my manners? I'm sorry you guys. Jon Gale, this is Ellen Douglas. Ellen, this is Jon Gale. But I don't know, she may want you to call her by her Goddess name, Goddess Dana."

While shaking hands, the woman turned briefly towards Wind and he was able to read her face, eyes, smile, and countenance as she said to call her Goddess Dana and that it was nice to meet him, before turning her attention, in a no nonsense manner, back to the purple table. Her face was softer head-on, away from the extreme angles of her long chin and nose in profile. Her breasts were like elongated winter squashes, not wide like her buttocks, and fell onto the first dominant roll of her stomach, salmon areolas and fingertip nipples out and upturned by her stomach's shelving. From her bulging navel, ran downward a trail of dark hair that he assumed covered all of the area below her second stomach roll. Now acquainted with her, he stood closer and looked over both of the shoulders before him, into the ring, watching where all the other eyes were directed.

"Goddesses! Living Incarnates of She who birthed us all, from whose womb the universe was born, from whose womb all life emerged! We bare the names of her manifestations, but we are all avatars of the one true Mother! Give your attention to her creation, give your attention to the living Goddess in her creation all around us! Blessed be, all Her daughters present!"

"Blessed be!" Everyone responded back to her in solemn unity.

"All praise the One Great Goddess!" She called.

"Praise the One Great Goddess!" they responded, with a little less solemnity and a little more cheer.

"Tonight is a special night, as are all nights special in rapture with the Goddess. All of our nights together stand out in their own ways. This night we welcome a new feminine voice into our holy chorus, that her voice and story might sound out along with ours in praise of the Goddess and all of the Goddess's creation. With more energy, we are greater, louder, and stronger. One daughter at a time we are closer to the Mother. Allow us now to close the circle with the initiate on the outside before we welcome her within our ring of power and love." She then whispered to Iliya and they both lifted an end of the purple-draped table and walked it slowly and steadily, as it wobbled, bare feet to grass, into the middle of the circle as the women all moved either to their right or left to close the circle at Gwen and the woman now next to her while Iliya slipped out between the two women closest to her. Wind hovered behind Gwen and to her right, finding an easier view over the woman now there, her height about five foot six.

"Alright. Blessed be, sisters, daughters of the one and only Goddess, our Mother," Toni called.

"Blessed be!" all responded.

"Now, our initiate, like a young girl, prepares herself to enter womanhood, total womanhood, within our circle. She will begin her walk around our circle, counterclockwise, winding down and backwards into the origins of time and the universe, winding backwards until there was only Goddess, the Primal Woman, our Mother. After three circles around us, she will enter. See her begin. Feel her energy move behind us. Feel her getting closer to us in her descent." Iliya began at the opposite end from where Wind and Gwen stood and began her slow serene walk within the tiki poles and around the circle of fifteen women.

"Now as she redraws the circle for herself, aligning herself with us, we will ask the Goddess for blessings to her four directions and her four elements." Toni moved her stocky body closer to the table and lifted a lighter in her left hand. Her form was low in its thickness and center of gravity, with swinging slushy breasts, like pockets full of change inside loose pants, nipples pointed down to the Earth, the direction her large dimpled buttocks and hairy thighs were sagging, as if the Mother was calling them home to Her. Wind quickly noticed this general trend among the women present, especially the older ones or heavier ones. The women were sky-clad and free, with no underwires or support, shaped beyond the boundaries of clothing and social constraints. It seemed either that gravity was the greatest enemy of a woman's body, which expressed its femininity in its curves, or that a woman's path of aging and physical development was leading her back to the origin of all life.

"We consecrate this circle of power. As our initiate winds around us counterclockwise, we will consecrate in the other direction, meeting her and matching her."

Iliya moved slowly behind Wind, her careful, intentional movements stirring a breeze of her own, and he could smell the sweat of her anxious body.

"We call upon you, the Easterly Direction and the Element of Air, to witness, protect, and empower this circle." Toni lit one candle in the square shape she had arranged on the purple-draped altar table. A chorus of Blessed Be filled the space as the wick caught hold of the flame. She then moved towards the next candle, farthest from her with the lighter.

"We call upon you, the Southern Direction and the Element of Fire, to witness, protect, and empower this circle." Another candle was lit and another chorus of Blessed Be rose mightily. Toni reached with the lighter carefully to the right of the twitching flames.

"We call upon you, the Western Direction and the Element of Water, to witness, protect, and empower this circle." Again ignition, again Blessed Be. One red candle remained directly before Toni and she took a moment, an obvious breath of air before finishing the consecration.

"We call upon you, the Northern Direction and the Element of Earth, to witness, protect, and empower this circle." This Blessed Be was the loudest yet and Wind felt the circle of women shake with the force of their words. Iliya, passing behind him for her third time was heading up to the top of the circle.

"Around us we have air and fire. There is earth beneath our feet and in this glass is sacred water, perfumed with rosewood. These elements are the essence of life and they make up each of us as women as they make up our great Mother. We draw now from their power as we welcome our newest member." She made a full turn towards the top of the circle and Iliya stood just behind two women, waiting to enter.

"We now open our circle and with love allow the entry of an avatar of the Goddess. The love with which we allow her to enter, is like opening ourselves up for the one and only Goddess to enter. She enters the circle as Her daughter and a new sister joins us! Open, praise the Goddess, and allow our initiate to introduce herself with the story of her name, and we will enter that story into our own." Toni nodded to the two women blocking Iliya who then parted to give entry.

Iliya made three steps into the ring of flesh and a chorus of praise to the Goddess went up around her.

"I am Goddess Ros. I have chosen to be the avatar of this manifestation of the one true Goddess as a tribute to a dear friend. Ros was an ancient Ukrainian mermaid of the River Ros near Kiev. She was the wife of Perun and mother of Dazhdbog. It is through her that the Russian pantheon persists and that the Russian people take their name." She stood waiting in the moonlight, trembling but on her mark. For three minutes she stood in silence, glowing pale under the moon, whipped by the lights from the tiki poles and everyone else stood the same way, staring silently and waiting, while Toni counted the seconds.

"Praise the one and only Goddess! Welcome Goddess Ros!" Toni called, breaking the silence.

"Praise the one and only Goddess! Welcome Goddess Ros!" Everyone responded.

"Close the circle and now Goddess Ros will walk clockwise around the circle on the inside and we will each greet her in turn with an embrace." Toni again conducted Iliya, leading her to the woman who closed the circle at where she just entered.

Wind felt Gwen's head turn towards him so he leaned in for her to narrate. She told him that the woman Iliya was hugging was eight months pregnant and she had been coming here since she first started showing at about three months. It was a little before the split and she bonded with Toni so she followed her. She took the name Goddess Nut, the Egyptian Goddess whose belly was the arch of the sky. Her real name was Stephanie Sullivan and all the members loved watching the belly grow, drawing allusions to the Egyptian Goddess, saying that they were all within this belly that she was the Mother in action. They all looked after her, all mothers to the mother.

"With the split Toni really seemed to draw the wild ones, and a lot of girls who came along are in some part of the sex trade. It makes sense though. We are all women empowered by our femininity and especially our sexuality, some more empowered than others. Bring sex and religion together and these ladies lap it up like kitties to milk. Take a story back to Babylon and temple prostitutes and everyone is suckered in, eyes wide, all ears, even if they don't really know what the hell you're talking about. Most of the girls are pretty smart though, and we get together early most nights and look at Toni's books. That's how we first saw a drawing of Goddess Nut, it was perfect for Steph and her swelling belly. She was a prostitute, an escort actually, well I guess she still is, but she is taking some time off right now, living on savings. Getting pregnant was what brought her to us, it hit her hard and she saw it as some sort of miracle. She was on the pill and that one percent of inaccuracy went her way and bam, pregnant. The father was one of her clients so she hasn't even bothered to contact him. That kid is coming into a lotta love being born into this group, boy or girl, we are gonna raise it right. And as soon as she has the baby we are gonna initiate her. She isn't fully a member yet, but she already picked a Goddess name, it was too obvious not to just jump on."

Wind hovering at Gwen's right, enjoyed his clear line of sight around the circle over the low head of the woman next to her, following Iliya's movements and taking in the smells. Iliya was at the third woman down of the six women between Goddess Nut and Gwen. The process was slow as she hugged each woman and they kissed on both cheeks. He leaned in close to the shorter woman before him, putting a hand gently on her shoulder out of courtesy as his mouth went towards her left ear.

"I hope you don't mind, I've got a good view here. I'm Jon Gale," he whispered.

"It's okay. I'm Goddess Hestia," she whispered back in his ear, shyly, leaning in to his stooped shoulder, as her clean straight dark brown hair brushed its chemical fruit scent against his face.

"Goddess of the hearth and home," he whispered back through her hair.

"Yes," she said proudly and cheerily, "I'm a mom and a real homebody, it seemed fitting. This is the most excitement without the kids I get all week." She turned back with a smile, already seeming more comfortable with him above and behind her. As she moved he saw her body. She was petite and thin, her skin, free of tan lines, seemed to be naturally olive-hued. Her waist was pronouncedly compact compared to her low pot-belly and round weighty breasts which, after knowing she was a mother, he wanted to describe as matronly. Her aureoles were a shade deeper than her skin and as she turned back he marked the deep dimples of her smile and her deep brown eyes. After she turned, his eyes ran down her back, down the smooth skin of her back and the buttocks that no longer reached out but down and her thighs, where among the dark scattered hairs, reluctant for regrowth after a lifetime of shaving, slight waves of weight broke the smoothness with sensual ridges.

Iliya was now in front of Goddess Hestia and she smiled at Wind as she hugged her with her head on Goddess Hestia's left shoulder. After both cheeks were kissed, Goddess Hestia whispered sincerely into the other's ear, welcome Goddess Ros, and she was thanked in the same passionate tone. In their embrace, breasts were pressed together and burst out the sides under their crossed arms. The strong scent of Iliya's body mixed with the freshly washed smell of Goddess Hestia and Wind's senses were all going wild. He felt drawn to all of them and he wanted to hug and cry with them in the sweet moments he witnessed, but his reaction was mostly glandular. The spirituality and the sensuality of their sisterly love was working on him, the sacred space they were creating of love and power was familiar from his time with Flora, and the smells of flesh, the smells of womanly things, the candles, the esoterica, were taking him outside of his mind into the rest of his body.

Iliya had her turn with Gwen and then Goddess Dana and kept on moving. Wind's eyes went straight across the circle and the altar, where Toni muddled around straightening things, to the pregnant Goddess Nut. He had never found a pregnant woman so sexually attractive. Her belly was big and shiny and bursting in its roundness, her breasts proudly on display, resting on their womb shelf, great round burnt umber aureoles and nipples staring back at him out of white skin swimming with blue serpentine blood vessels. Her belly was practically pink with a red line sprouting hairs down from the outward belly button to the wild darkness spread out across her thighs. He could not see her vulva, but his eyes searched hard for it in the dark shadow. Guilty, he drew his attention back to her face, which he also found glowing in the framing of her long raven hair and severe bangs. Goddess Nut reminded him at first of Cleopatra and then of the High Priestess on the Tarot card Tia Maite dealt out to him. She smiled at him and it was a friendly look that in any other circumstance he would take for flirting and his impulse would be to look away, caught in the act of staring, but here he didn't and he smiled back at her. He was saved from looking too long by Toni's voice as Iliya finished her round.

"Tonight we attune ourselves to the natural rhythm of the Universe and allow Goddess Ros to enter her voice into ours on this night when the Moon is in Her fourth quarter. Look up at Her, the reflection of our Mother. She is almost full and we can feel within our very own bodies the drawing near of fullness. Now that she is one of us her cycle will become like ours and we will all bleed together." Toni spoke to the group then up and out to the sky and Moon. Iliya stood next to her at the altar.

"Blessed be," the group screamed, and Wind wondered if this is as much participation they all normally have, his cynicism a reaction to and distraction from his growing physical excitement.

"Here it's about to get pretty hardcore," Gwen said quietly to Wind. "You see those two older women over on the other end, to your left of Goddess Nut? They just love all this because I'm sure it's their little secret to giggle about at the country club. They are older than me, the two oldest women here and they act like such kids sometimes. This makes them feel so controversial and provocative, even if they can't tell anyone about it—well they aren't supposed to talk about it and they probably don't. The two Joans. Man, they are a hoot." Toni spoke quietly to Iliya and Gwen kept on talking to Wind as he kept on listening. "The two Joans didn't even know each other before they met in the old SUGAR group. But did you see those two matching SUVs out front? Just one of the many coincidences that those two get so tickled about. Same car, same first names, same initials. Joan Bridgewater is the tall one and Joan Beckforth is the short one. And you see, they both drove, even though they both live near each other by Chastain Park, they both drove. It's a marvel that they never met before, Atlanta is so small in some circles. When Joan Bridgewater chose Gaia as her Goddess name, saying she would be the mother of us all, Joan Beckforth chose Maya saying that at least she could be the mother of Buddha. Goddess Gaia and Goddess Maya, it's just too much. Both went to Diana for readings. And they never met, never passed on the way out or in. But here they are now. They act like such giggling little girls; I even have to shush them sometimes. Just look at them, like they are about to bust out at any moment. Toni had to incorporate more clapping actually into the rituals, because those two will just start up a good supportive clap whenever they can. It's great when they are enthusiastic, I mean both of their husbands are lawyers, one is a tax attorney the other is criminal, I don't remember which goes with which Joan, but this seems to be their own mid-life crisis. Men buy a Corvette and take a young hoochie as a mistress and these two old broads play Goddess-worshippers. I can't say that they are just playing, they do get really into it, but come off like weekend warriors. I tell ya, I seriously wonder how much of that enthusiasm for the Goddess they take with them into the rest of their week. I bet they never encounter any lesbians or strippers or escorts or burned-out biker chicks like myself in their high society lives. But they did go through all this right here that you are about to see. After Toni started things her way we all had to do a new initiation."

Wind examined the women, both with expressions of proud giddiness, both with puffy round hairdos of gray hinting towards blonde, both from the neck up looking like self-satisfied matrons at a church picnic waiting for everyone to sample their homemade recipes. Similar patterns could be noted in their jewelry-laden hands, ears, and necks, along with well-manicured and polished nails. They were even physically similar except for height; Joan Bridgewater was a beanpole and in comparison Joan Beckforth was a pumpkin. The difference was a matter of spine and legs, as both had stomachs of perfect elliptical shape like buoyant watermelons, bright in whiteness compared to the fading tans of their arms and upper chest. Breasts like tiny falling tears of tissuey skin were found in equal proportions on both women. On Joan Beckforth the breast tears dangled to the white watermelon stomach, rubbing it as she swayed, but on the other Joan, the distance was unspannable. Wind was beginning to see that Joan Beckforth was fundamentally of the same body, but the extra mass that her twin carried in elongation, she carried packed into the density of her thighs. Allowing greater liberties and comfort in his study, Wind examined the vulval areas of the two Joans. He was developing a theory that commitment-level to the group could be determined by degree of body hair. Both women, beneath the bowl of their stomachs, had woolly bushes of gray hair and whiskers of varying shades ran down to a defined line in the middle of their thighs, inconspicuous within average skirt length. He could see no armpit hair and measured their conviction at the level of closet worship.

With Toni's voice, he turned his attention back to the center of the circle and the altar.

"Goddess Ros deliver your offering to the one true Goddess, our Mother, the great Progenitor, the Never Closing Womb, She Who Suckled Us At Her Breast and has made us in Her image. Goddess Ros give her what it is to be a woman, what it is to be like her, what it is to be creation Herself!"

At that, everyone seemed to take a deep breath and Wind looked on intently as Iliya spread her legs into an upright squatting position and put her right hand in Toni's for balance as her left reached down between her legs and, disappearing into her thatched labial folds, rummaged about with a concentrated effort. Wind's eyes widened and his pulse sped, what was she doing, he wondered, and he couldn't look away, but could smell his own sweat and feel his jeans tighten against his firming groin. She drew her hand back up from the dark and sweaty depths of her vulva holding an object for all to see and righted herself. Wind saw in the delicate grasp of her fingertips what looked like a brown cordial glass with stem but no base, like a dark rose cut short for a lapel. She held it up as in a toast and everyone watched silently her ritual movements. She walked to the altar where Toni lifted the silver chalice and Iliya poured blood from the little receptacle into the greater container. Toni held up the chalice before them all and Gwen reestablished her role as Wind's whispering narrator.

"You ever seen one of those? It's a menstrual cup. It's called the Keeper and made by a woman in Ohio, Lou Crawford. We all have one. Toni turned us on to them for the initiation, but a lot of the ladies here have gotten into using them all the time. They are perfect for women like us who are totally okay with our bodies and have no problem putting our fingers up inside our vaginas to pull these things out during our moon time of the month. There is another brand some of the girls use called the Instead cup. Those are disposable so there is no washing the thing and reusing it. The Keeper is made out of natural gum rubber and supposed to last for like ten years. A lot of us are pretty environmental, which makes sense, the Earth is the Mother, and think of all the waste a cup saves from tampons, pads, panty-liners, all that stuff. And if you are good and confident with your body, you can get that thing out without spilling any, like she just did. She's been practicing. They are cleaner than messing with anything else if you do it right. Man, I'm sorry. I'm sure you are really glad you get to see and hear all of this. But I guess with your work you are used to all this woman stuff. You must be such a snag catch, you know, a SNAG, a Sensitive New Age Guy. Your wife must love it? Or your girlfriend?" She smiled inquiringly and nudged him with her elbow. "It's okay, my old man is used to it all too. He's gotten pretty into it actually, loves my Goddess self, and he's gotten all into loving my bloody side. Which is good, because it's almost over. He's in touch with the power in a way a lot of guys aren't. Some of the girls, they use the Instead cup, which looks like a diaphragm, but with a deeper pouch. Those you can use while having sex on your moon and it keeps things clean and blood-free. I'm sure it's rare with this group though. We've all learned about the sexual power of blood and most seem to be training their men to it, the straight ones, that is. Maybe the girls who do work as escorts use the Instead while on the job. But they can still work the blood power. You men know its power too, you can sniff it out like dogs." She smiled and elbowed him again as they recommitted their attention to the ritual.

Toni had begun to speak and Iliya was holding the moonstone.

"Goddess Ros is of the same substance as the Great Goddess, our one and only Mother, even in her reflection as the Moon. The Moon too bleeds as we bleed. She sloughs Her lining, rebirthing Herself, as we slough the lining of our uteruses and are cleansed every month. After this initiation, when Goddess Ros is one of us, she too will cleanse along with the cycle of the group, the cycle of our great Mother, who is at once the Earth and the Moon. We bleed without dying, riding Her cycle, and we too have Her life-giving powers. With our new sister, Goddess Ros, we will all bleed as one, a complete circle, strong and unbroken, like the Moon above us, and we will channel that power together. Within this silver chalice, itself a symbol of our Mother's womb, Goddess Ros's essence is mixing with water, a sacred element that is visibly drawn to the Moon's power. Lift the moonstone above your head Goddess Ros while I anoint you with blood and water into our circle, a circle of Goddesses, a circle of empowered women embodying the one and only Goddess, the Mother of all life. This circle is her womb and you will be born again from it, Her avatar."

Iliya raised the moonstone above her head and held it there. Her body was bright and glowing and it seemed the light from the Moon was refracting through the stone bathing her. Wind's eyes beheld more of her clearer than even in the red barn. With her arms stretched up high, the tufts of black hair in her armpits stood out straight and reaching and wild like the first plants of the Earth, hungry and musty, and their smell traveled to Wind's olfactory sense stronger than ever, bringing with it deepening desire. Iliya's breasts still hung in a slight bob as most of their mass disappeared into her taut torso. Toni dipped the first and middle finger of her right hand into the chalice and drew them out shiny and crimson.

"Blessed be her eyes that she may see your path," said Toni, and dabbed a single red finger to each of Iliya's shut eyelids. Blessed Be said the women of the circle and Iliya.

"Blessed be her nose that she may breathe your essence," and she drew watery blood down Iliya's nose after dipping her fingers again. A chorus of Blessed Be followed.

"Blessed be her lips that she may speak your truth and love and drink of you," she said as she redipped and dragged her fingers across Iliya's lips, deep red blood coating like lipstick. A round of Blessed Be went up, Iliya parting her painted lips to join it.

"Blessed be her breasts that she may be faithful and potent in your work and her works," and Toni brought her glistening index finger to Iliya's right breast and painted slowly around the aureole, changing pink to almost brown, finishing with a bead on the tip of the nipple and then using her middle finger on the left breast. Blessed Be rose all around.

"Blessed be her loins that brings forth life as you bring forth all life," and her two fingers dipped deeper in the chalice, emerging shining crimson to the second knuckle, and they were directed, with an almost medical care, to the space between Iliya's legs, where they were slowly drawn up. Wind's lips parted as Iliya's did, showing her front teeth, and he could tell by her expression just how slowly Toni dragged her fingers through her vulva, painting her labia. When the chorus of Blessed Be rose in unison around the circle, both he and Gwen seemed equally surprised that his voice had joined in.

"Blessed be her feet that she may walk in your ways," and saying this Toni was on one knee and dragged one finger down the instep of each foot. Blessed Be was said again for this anointing and self-consciously Wind refrained. For a moment before Toni had moved to Iliya's feet, he was totally lost in the process, his mind narrating what he saw and at one point it was his fingers smearing blood on that sensual gothic alabaster body, her pubis and her eyes, mysterious and dark.

"Goddess Ros is now our sister, an equal member of this circle and we have nothing but love for her. She has been initiated into the Goddess with her own sacred blood, blood that is summoned and drawn forth by the Moon. She is painted in the color of life." Toni motioned for Iliya to lower her arms and, taking the moonstone, moved to the table where she exchanged it for the statuette. "The Venus of Willendorf, formed twenty-seven millennia ago by worshippers of the Great Goddess just like us, was originally painted completely red and traces of red ochre are still found in her folds. In being the avatar of the one and only Goddess, Goddess Ros is completing work that has been done for all of time." Toni returned the statuette to the altar and then kissed Iliya on both of her cheeks. Holding hands with Iliya she took a breath and continued to speak to the circle, pivoting to address everyone.

"In the first great world patriarchy of religious oppression, Judaism, the blood of a woman, her femininity, her cycle, her connection with Nature and the Great Mother was deemed impure, dirty, and taboo. They instituted a mikvah or ritual bath, to imprison women during this time. A jealous act in fear of the potency of a woman's sacred blood. She was contained, for they knew she was a threat to their order and oppression. We are turning this crime against women back to the true source. The original menstrual huts and circles were about empowering women and invoking the Goddess as we do here. We have given our new sister, our initiate, a ritual bath in her own flowing power, her blood power, her Moon power." As Toni spoke Gwen brought her lips to Wind's cheek, warm breath with the smell of cigarettes and sweat. The force of her breathy speech brought goose bumps and chills across the nape of his neck.

"She is really laying it on thick. She never gets into so much of her lunar mysteries stuff. True to the name Goddess Luna, she is researching it all the time. This must be all for you. But really, she must imagine you know a lot of this already. I guess she is trying to give you a real sense of our intellectual base, but really we don't usually spend so much time on this. It even looks like she is trying hard not to look your way. Normally, she is looking at me a lot, trying to get my okay for what she is doing, but she seems to be avoiding this whole area."

Wind listened to Gwen more than Toni at this point. He was quite familiar with the connections she was drawing and less interested in the information than the environment, which was captivating him more and more by the moment. His hungry eyes grazed over the circle of women, rescanning the ones he knew already, cataloging body parts and mannerisms that whetted his appetites. In rapaciously gobbling at the sensual stimuli, his attention moved to the figure of Joan Beckforth to his left. She had a beautiful flat smooth face with pale blue accents of makeup and well-tanned skin. Her blonde hair was dark at the roots and fell past her chin straight and intentional in styling. He beheld perfect circle aureoles inside perfect sphere breasts, sitting high and fake over a long rib cage and cut abs. The bronzed and manicured hairless body still had a fluff of pubic naturalism that captured Wind's eye in a way the others had yet to. Like a naked mole rat in its burrow, there was a hairless segment that moved freely in the pubic scrub and it hung like a peanut pod from the rest of the body. Wind spoke to Gwen when she was finished, their heads still close.

"The woman next to the shorter Joan, her face is quite beautiful and very feminine but it looks like she has a penis."

"Good eye. She does. That's Nikki Lesci. She was once Nicholas. She is transgendered, you know, a pre-op tranny, as she bills herself. She's eventually gonna have that thing just snipped right off."

"And how does that whole penis and masculine energy thing work in the group here? In some obvious ways, she is still a man. Does it affect the circle? How does Toni justify her presence? How as the initiation performed?" He was curious about the technicalities of the group process, but on some level, he understood everything before Gwen answered him. His basic understanding was glandular and regardless of Nikki's penis he saw her as a beautiful woman, attractive and stimulating. She swayed as all the others while Toni spoke.

"It's funny. We like to say that Nikki is the ultimate convert. Everyone here was led to the Goddess for some reason, from something else that didn't satisfy. I might be a rare case. My parents never took me to church, they were actually into Spiritualism and I got a lot of that growing up. My Granma, my father's mother, always thought my parents were into witchcraft and she wasn't half wrong really, so when I was really little she took me to church with her, a real God-fearin' Lutheran church with a lot of hellfire and sin and all that really tormenting stuff for a little kid. This was in Roanoke, Virginia, a tiny German community of hardcore Lutherans. So I have always been kind of ready for this group here, from my parents interests, but I have at least seen what the other side is like. For a lot of these girls, the younger ones, this group might have saved their lives. I mean, if you don't know who you are or why you are living do you really have a life? Being raised in a repressive Christian patriarchy is like a death wish for an open-minded, sensitive woman. Nikki had trouble with that stuff at the same time as being labeled with the incorrect gender. As Toni at her most dykey likes to say, just because Nikki was born a man doesn't mean we should hold it against her. She is our ultimate convert, not only was she converting to worshipping the Goddess and the role of avatar, but also converting to femininity. She is proving how much she wants to be here and how much she loves the Goddess with every dose of estrogen she takes.

Even before the physical work of transformation started really happening she as an escort for men looking for someone like her and she continues to get clients as she changes. It's like Babylonian temple prostitutes I mentioned earlier. They would sleep with men as a way for the men to experience the Goddess, a real avatar position. Nikki, and some of the others here really feel like that is their calling. I channel the Goddess for one man only, but they do it for any in need. Nikki took the name Goddess Hi'iaka after she visited Hawaii with a client. She was captivated by the story and has now made it part of her identity. Hi'iaka is the Goddess of the hula and sacred sensual movement, so that is also how she sees herself. One day, biologically she will be all woman. After getting to know Nikki, Toni was really into her joining us, I think she sees it as a point scored for the Goddess, one more for us, one less for the patriarchy." Gwen was totally relaxed in her interaction with Wind and felt no guilt in speaking softly to him at the same time as Toni, her attention equally split between the inner circle and Wind's curiosity. His left hand was on the small of her back now, acknowledging their comfort level and keeping close without the risk of losing his balance. With his open hand pressurelessly resting over the inward curve of her spine just above the ridge of her buttocks, the anxious sweat of his palm was mating bead for bead with the perspiration from her heated body in the cool night air; their bodies were alive and, through this limited physical interaction, in sanguine communion.

"But about her initiation?" Wind asked again, pulling her back on topic.

"Wait, listen. I think she is getting to that now." Gwen kept her head against his and her eyes on Toni while nodding to her direction.

"Tribespeople of Africa and Aboriginal Australia had rituals where they painted themselves red and poured blood on sacred stones to recreate this mystery of womanhood. Some tribes of Australian aboriginal males emulated the process of women by cutting their penises and inserting stones to keep the wound open. This is even where the rite of circumcision comes from, ancient Jewish males trying to usurp the power of women and their genital blood potency," Toni was in the middle of saying.

"That was actually pretty close to the essence of Nikki's initiation with us. I have a friend who is Jewish and she got married to a guy who wasn't, but he converted for her, and as part of his conversion, even though he was already circumcised at birth, they had to cut him just a little. He had to bleed a little to enter the faith. That is pretty much what we did for Nikki. Toni had a sharp knife on the altar and gave her a little slit on her little wee-wee there and let it drip into the chalice. This blood ritual is very important for understanding womanhood and our Goddess worship. That is why Goddess Nut is not a full member yet, since she's been with us she's had no periods so we will wait to initiate her after the baby." Gwen stopped speaking as she noticed his head carefully moving around the circle again. Wind had taken some last laps at Nikki, up and down her shiny legs and taut sensuality, cutting an angular fashion pose, smiling with blinking blue eyes and breasts floating high. If he were to estimate commitment for her based on body hair, she would receive low marks for her pubic nest and otherwise smooth form, but he took into account her expenditure on body augmentation surgery and he could not deny how convinced he was of the depth of her covenant.

"Matriarchal power is power with, not power over, as it is in the patriarchy. Matriarchal power is the power through. We are free like Lilith, who left paradise because it was not complete, because she would not be under a man in his oppressive missionary position, and by the time she climbed on top she was already beyond him." Toni was still orating and Wind was still searching, grazing among the sites of womanhood he had yet to embrace with his ocular appetite. His jeans were tight and murky and his upper lip, shaven this morning, was irritated by the sweat beading on the vulnerable skin, the sweat also dense at his hairline. He discreetly stretched and ran his hands through his hair, smoothing the short dark strands back with the wetness of his perspiration.

To the right of Goddess Hestia was a younger woman of the same height and to her right, a few inches taller, was another young woman. Wind put them both in their early to mid twenties, twenty-three to twenty-six. He was no longer holding back in saying to himself how beautiful he found everyone he observed. Taking in the crowd, he found beauty and desire everywhere. The circle was steeped in pheromones, all movements stirring the pot of pheromones, and his deepest sexual, sensual, and amorous hungers were being drawn up to the surface of his skin, his taste buds engorged and saliva flowing freely, copiously. The taller of the young women was blonde, golden blonde. She reached up, while still facing Toni, to take down her hair, but turned to her left feeling Wind's eyes upon her and caught him staring. When her hair came down it was like spilling waves of gold. The waves spilled only to her shoulders, but their cascade shimmered on never to stop, and Wind couldn't look away. She smiled at him and that too was golden, the shine of her teeth lighting her auriferous skin. Was her look of elation part of the rites, beaming freely from her, leveled on any in her line of sight? Or was it he she was looking at? Had she been watching him all along too? He was lost in the moment, unable to comprehend how sexist he might be, that the desire he perceived in her must be for him, since he was the only man here. He saw mirrors of what he felt; even faced with all these women, he could not escape the Self. The blonde's smile expanded and her look was locked.

Before she had caught his stare, he had taken in her whole brilliant body, singing the description to himself. She was thin like thistle, but her breezy body was toned tight against her frame, with tight tiny breasts drawn to aureoles-less nipples, dark chocolate kisses poking out of wheaty flesh. Her arms, stomach, and legs were shimmered with downy waves, hair like refined white gold. Her prominent labia hung down visibly wearing a crown of rose gold comprising all the shades of filament her body produced. Locked in her gaze, he could only bow to her as if she were a queen, a slight bow of the head and his eyes lowered and closed briefly and when they returned they found hers gone, back to the center of the circle.

"That is Reggie Power. Doesn't she have beautiful hair? That is why she took the name Goddess Sif. It is from a Norse story about Thor's wife. She had beautiful hair that was envied by all and jealous Loki, the Trickster, cut it all off. The other Gods took pity on her and had the dwarves make her new hair out of gold. Reggie's a dancer, just look at that body, she knows how to use it and she takes a lot of pride in it. She is pretty open about admitting that too. You gotta be pretty secure in your looks to pick a Goddess story like that to latch onto. She does these great artsy, erotic burlesque shows that really draw the crowds of men and women. I am a little surprised she doesn't get into stripping, it would be better money, better then waiting tables. But see, Reggie is the perfect example of what I was saying before about Nikki. She is someone who came running to us from something else that was so restrictive and detrimental to her health, I mean it, not just spiritual health, but physical, mental, and emotional. She was raised a Jehovah's Witness and it was just awful for her. She never even had a birthday until like two years ago. So for her, like for a lot of the girls, this place is a real spiritual rehab. I know her better than most of the others here. I knew her before she joined.

"She is a friend of the girl next to her, to her left. That is Miranda Breads, her mother and I go way back. She is from Columbus and I met her when I lived there for a little while. I still get out there to see Jody, Miranda's mother, but I mostly hang out with Miranda now, here. It's funny how these things work, I tried to get Jody to check this group out, but she wasn't into it, but Miranda was, and after she joined she brought in Reggie. They are both hot young things, aren't they? It's okay for me to say that, I'm like Miranda's aunt almost. Her mother is a looker too, that's where she gets it from. They were a great little family unit with me tagging along. Now Miranda lives in town, waiting tables with Reggie. East Atlanta. Such talented girls, and real smart. Miranda paints, she has a BFA from UGA." Gwen chuckled and proceeded with maternal pride. "She likes to say that she paints like Hemingway wrote. Great paintings, they subtly invoke the Goddess. You should buy one, or photograph one for your article. Her Goddess name is Eris, Goddess Eris. It's her little jab at Reggie, they keep each other in check. You know, Eris, the Greek Trickster Goddess, the Goddess of Discord. She was trying to make Reggie a little paranoid, identifying with a Goddess similar to Loki."

As Gwen spoke of Miranda, Wind directed his dejected yet resilient attention from Reggie to the shorter body next to her. Without the aurous air of her friend, he still found a beauty in the unassuming demeanor of Miranda. A shaggy brunette haircut gave way to her face, pink at the cheeks with excitement; looking closer, her face resembled a heart. Short and smaller, her body was almost that of Flora. His mind ran wild with his eyes and his nose and he could even taste the mixing of citronella, fresh cut grass, shampoos, conditioners, body washes, and deep sweat. He thought of freeing himself, stripping down and running around the circle, touching, smelling, until he would enter and they would close in on him and he would just cry and let them take him. There were more faces and bodies for which he had no names. Corpulent faces and cushioning bodies, small tits and angular portraits, bouncing boobs and big bellies; and hair flecked like accenting brushstrokes across the landscape of female flesh. They were all beautiful, every part of all of them and he held back on tears like he held back hermetically on all of his distended glands and vital reserves. He returned his eyes straight ahead to the bulging belly laden with life as Toni made reference to her.

"At pregnancy, like our own Goddess Nut, a woman is of full moon and does not need to bleed. She is cultivating her power, using that power in the act of creation. The most ancient of our ancestors even believed that the blood was nourishing the baby in the womb, which in a way it is. The life of a woman is a threefold cycle in harmony with the changes of the Moon. We have all three of these stages represented here in the ages and life stages of our sister Goddesses. Some of us are the Maiden, the New Moon or crescent. Some of us are the Mother, the Full Moon, and some have already gone past this time to a time of great reverence, the Crone, of the great Waxing Moon, a time of menopause and wisdom. We honor our bodies, our cycle, our Moon time. Now we honor the Goddess and ourselves to a greater degree by including our newest member Goddess Ros!"

Wind focused on Toni's words and when she was done, she invited the circle to say their Goddess names including Iliya, who would then be adding her name to theirs along with herself to the circle. As the roll call went, Wind was bringing himself back into what the moment was supposed to be for him and drew his notepad to record all sixteen Goddess names: Luna, Ros, Nut, Athena, Astarte, Isis, Sif, Eris, Hestia, Rhiannon, Dana, Freyja, Aphrodite, Hiʻiaka, Maya, Gaia. A last ditch of desire in him regretted not having made sketches of the bodies he beheld. His heart was slowing and he felt the night breeze against his forehead cooling. Hands were grabbed and held up high and a moment of silence was had by the women, as Wind scribbled down some notes and observations. The silence was broken as all at once the women said, praise the Goddess, and Blessed Be, in closing. The circle held loosely as people approached Iliya and welcomed her again and Wind stood around with Gwen as she stretched her legs. After all that he had asked and all he had learned, he thought it was entirely inconspicuous and innocent enough at this point to tender a very practical question to Gwen.

"Gwen, do you know a friend of Goddess Ros, Flora? I think she goes by Goddess Chloris? I was hoping she would be here and so was Iliya, I mean Goddess Ros."

"Yeah, sure, I know her. Flora, great gal. She was a looker, gorgeous through and through. Full of love, that gal, and same line of work as some of the others: dispensing love. I wasn't too shocked that she was a no-show tonight. I haven't seen her in a while. Since maybe summer, like late August. On September 23rd we had a Mabon celebration, a seasonal pagan calendar event for Autumnal Equinox and it's one of our big to-dos. I remember thinking of her then, that if she didn't show up to that she was long gone. She was great though, real enthusiastic and not squeamish about anything. I think all the girls who like girls had secret crushes on her, but then again we are all girls who are really into our own womanhood so we are all a bit girl on girl inclined—except for the Joans, maybe. It's natural, we see in each other what we love in ourselves, the Goddess."

"Do you know if any of the other members were particularly close to her? Goddess Ros mentioned all this to me, I think she wanted to get in touch with her."

"I don't think so. She used to come to SUGAR with another gorgeous Goddess with golden blonde curls a while ago and I've seen her leaving with Goddess Ros before, but no one else I remember. These kinds of groups are weird, and this one is no exception, all the same stuff us humans, and particularly us women, drag around with us into everything we do. We can all be so close here, in the circle, and even after in Toni's sister's place, but when it comes time to go, all those sentiments stay behind. It's so weird, it's like it's important for them to be here, but it's still a part of their lives that's roped off from the rest. But I can't speak for anyone, what they do in their own time. I'm only guessing really. I just feel that it would be nice if we all did hang out more, outside of here, since we're all so like-minded. But I guess it's like they say, what happens in the naked Goddess worshipping circle, stays in the naked Goddess worshipping circle."

Gwen laughed at her own joke in such a way that Wind had to join her, out of empathy and enjoyment. She moved away and he let her, the looseness of the circle and the scattered attentions seemed to draw her back to something that he was not really a part of and he said goodbye.

Toni had made her way away from the other women, some stretching and others clamoring to talk to her, and approached Wind to ask him if he enjoyed the rites and if there was any other information he needed. She seemed to be feigning aloofness while fishing for the chance to speak further about herself and her work. Wind wasn't taking the bait. He felt drained and wasted, forced to backtrack out of this investigatory cul-de-sac that didn't give any new direction to follow. He had tasted a part of Flora's life tonight, sampled with so many sense receptors a buffet of what she once offered up to him through her body and words. He was spent.

Iliya wound her way up through hugs and kisses and words of encouragement to a point where she was ready to stand with Wind at the end of what was once the circle, now as a cohort again and with her back turned to the others, cleaning and clearing the altar, she spoke close and in confidence.

"I am ready to go. No one I spoke to knew anything about Flora. And man, do I need a shower." Her arms were crossed, her breath was on him, and his right hand was on her spine as she spoke. The awkward nakedness in which she stood was different from how she appeared in the circle, and yet it looked to be more natural for her. The blood red streaks on her face were already fading and looked like crusted old war paint. They said goodbye to Toni as an aside with their attentions back on each other.

"Was that everything you expected it to be?" he said in a way for her to take as either an attempt at levity or more investigation.

"Yeah, totally. My inner-Goddess is now outer, and I could really use some clothes, a cigarette, and a tampon. Let's get outta here."

I I. ST. BRIDE OR THE VIRGIN BRIDE

For in these three is contained our life: nature, mercy, grace.
From these we get our humility, gentleness, patience and pity.
From them too we get our hatred of sin and wickedness—it is
the function of virtue to hate these.
> —Julian of Norwich, *Revelations of Divine Love*

IT WAS ONLY THE FIRST FEW MOMENTS WITHIN MONICA'S APARTMENT
that were dominated by an unconditional expression of love, no matter
how reflexive it might be, where she lauded upon him hugs and kisses
and descriptions of how much she missed him in the time since last
they were together, before a point was inevitably reached of questions,
demands, verbal navigations, concealments, appeasements, and the reflexes of relational rhetoric. Jonathan Wind played happy and played
along, not sure where to begin in answering her questions of how he
had been, where he had been, why hadn't he answered his phone last
night, so he skirted and applied vagaries, turning her questions back
to her. Through omission he lied about work and the vacation time,
and he allowed the natural course of their night together to play out
as he bided his time and chose his words carefully. He was not sure
how to come clean and how clean to come with Monica; there was a

certain limit to honesty that he felt their relationship required and to tear at any facades erected in the name of compromise might erode the whole foundation of their relationship, as many supporting beams were deceit-reinforced if not originally framed from placation. He was prepared to let light shine within the darkest nooks and viper nests of their relationship, to bathe in that light himself and be cleansed by harsh truth. Yet as prepared as he was for a mini apocalypse, for all to be revealed, he was allowing one last supper for her and one last temptation for his cowardice, to tease himself with the notion of settling into this life, a life out of his control, but of devotion and service to her will.

Monica asked, but Wind did not want to go out to eat, and she agreed since she only asked as a way of appeasing him and gaining emotional currency; she always preferred to stay home, unless there was the option of visiting her family, so they followed a common alternative for how to spend a quiet Saturday night together and ordered pizza, one for each of them, just how they both liked it, the phone number on her refrigerator and no discussion about toppings, only a question of whether to get another two-liter bottle of Coca-Cola to supplement what was left in her refrigerator. On the couch they sat more comfortable than close, waiting for the pizza, flipping through the channels on her television to see if there would be anything to watch at nine as they ate and easily enough a film was agreed upon, something they had seen before together, but not for some time, a romantic comedy she knew all of the lines to.

When the pizza arrived they sat on her carpet before the television and ate their respective dishes. He cleaned what remained, putting leftovers in her refrigerator, decked with photos of Monica and him and Monica and her parents and sister, while she narrated to him what he was missing, as if the actors were her friends and their experiences were the cause of great emotional tension in her life. After he refilled both of their glasses, he rejoined what was left of the carpet picnic. Soon enough he was sent up again to retrieve Ben and Jerry's ice cream for her and returned to watch the rest of the movie as she ate, only interrupting the steady flow of the film twice more when he had to get back up to return the ice cream to the freezer and when she got up to use the bathroom as he mentally recorded what she missed to relate it back to her when she returned. By the end of the film it was eleven o'clock and he was full and tired and had no circulation in his right arm from where Monica sat back against it.

"Do you want to go *be intimate?*" she asked, using their own label for the sex act, a name distinct enough to them to be romantic, and cryptic enough to keep it verbally desexualized in accord with Monica's sense of decorum. Although he used the expression too, whenever he heard her say it a voice in the back of his mind always thought: if that is when we are being intimate what does that mean for the rest of our time together, especially considering what an awkward and selfish twenty minutes it usually is?

"Sure," was his inevitable response and they both rose to fold the quilt in which they had cuddled, drape it on the couch, and make their respective ways, him to the bedroom and her to the bathroom. On the rare occasions that she initiated the sex act, he jumped to seize the opportunity. She must have been trying to make up for the fight they had last Sunday, as initiating *being intimate* was a bold move on her part. He entered her bedroom and closed the door half way to give him access to the hooks on its back where he hung his shirt, partially shrouding the face of Jesus that was nailed up there. Behind the door was the perfect private place, fit for the bluntness of an image she regarded so sacred. The walls held prints of Raphael's angels, like the one that she had given him, and other subtle representations of her Christianity, like prayer cards of the Pope and Mother Theresa on her dresser and a cartoonish print of St. Brigid, her patron and favorite saint, next to the bed. On the other side of her bed, the side where she slept when Wind was over, was a nightstand with pictures of her parents and sister and a picture of him alongside C.S. Lewis', *The Great Divorce*, her newest love of faith professed. Other than the Christian images, her bedroom walls were like the walls of her living room, decorated with framed prints that once hung without frames on the walls of her sorority house room at the University of Georgia: a black and white of an Italian woman walking fast as men leer and whistle; Anne Geddes' chubby babies dressed as flowers peeking out of pots; and an Everything I Need To Know I Learned In Kindergarten poster. The newest decorative flourish to adorn her walls was above her living room couch in the form of an early release poster of the upcoming third *Lord of the Rings* film, "Return of the King."

Wind sat on the soft fluffy comforter, white with a lavender lattice pattern, and removed his shoes, placing his black socks into the shoes and laying his pants down in a fold over them. His shirt and boxer shorts completed the pile and he slipped naked under the soft sheets folded tightly onto the bed. Only a short time did he wait before Monica entered the room in her Victoria's Secret bathrobe, a white robe of fluffy terry cloth adorned with fluffy hearts of varying colors that hung down just past her knees, a robe she picked out their first Valentine's Day together with the gift certificate he gave her. She smiled quickly as the light went out and moved swiftly to her side of the bed where she slipped in and dropped her robe to the floor in one practiced move.

They met in the middle of the bed, heads on pillows, and faced each other in the dull gray dark, his penis stirring reflexively as her leg moved up along his thigh. Her brown eyes gazed into his across the distant worlds between their pillows. His hand was laid on her waist and while she gazed into his eyes she spoke to him, calling him Her Buggy Bear and apologizing for pressuring him when last they met. She was making a move of diplomacy, he thought. She just loves him so much, she told him. It was times like this that Wind wondered how she could be so deluded, how she could see so little beneath his surface, or maybe she did see and did not care, she preferred the facades. Could the images he cast up before him be that effective, he wondered? She was a believer, a great and ardent practitioner of belief, in all its rigid forms that transcend reason and pragmatics. Did she just believe in what he wanted her to see or did she choose to believe with the prayer that he would change; perhaps their relations were a form of missionary work? With words, Wind could handle any situation created by her belief; he could find what she wanted to hear, though often after failed navigations around sharp and rocky edges of her somewhat arbitrary dogma. With words like wind he would blow at the fires of her passions, careful to direct the flow by observing her reactions, fearful of spreading the flames into other areas, sparking other passions. He was convinced there was a rationality to her mind in relation to her faith, but most of what he found was habit and hand-me-down. Monica did and thought as she did because that was what her parents had told her; her opinions were not her own. Quite often, he found evidence that even her parents did not live by the standards she had set for herself, the same standards she worked diligently at imparting to him. There were times that it seemed she was trying to mother faith into him.

All of these memories and musings were fresh with him as he noted how serious she was about her penance, their brief kisses leading to her naked body straddling his. She was to control her own forgiveness, give what she thought he wanted and take the remainder of emotional debt left from his gratefulness at her apology. He gave himself up to the cycle, allowing her to be on top physically and morally. From the warmth, it was only an instant before he was erect, his arousal compulsory, breasts on his chest, her hips moving side to side, back and forth, smooth legs against his own. Monica smiled down at him without speaking, pecking kisses, letting her dark curly hair fall against his face and neck, an action softer in intention than actual contact. His hands went to her hips, then traced down her back, following her lead before she broke abruptly away smiling, excusing herself to reach down below the bed and grab a tube of KY spermicidal jelly. Pushing back the sheets from her body in a moment of urgent haste, she sat up on her knees and squeezed from the tube onto the fingers of her right hand. With thoughtless accuracy she dragged the jelly within the slightly hidden folds of her labia and covered the whole area with a smearing action. The tube fell back to the floor and she moved back into place at his waist.

At her motioning, Wind brought the sheets back up to give her cover and warmth. Monica's knees at his hipbones and her breasts dangling against his chest and her own, she moved into place against his penis, sliding against it, rubbing, pressing it into the bristly hair of his abdomen. His eyes, keen now in the dark of the room, reeling from the shock of her rare brusqueness, watched down into the catacomb made by their dual flesh and he could see his penis appear and disappear beneath the hang of her stomach. Her cool, yet moistening, breasts obscured his view, swelling out of his hands as he attempted to hold them back. He outlined her wide pink areolas with his thumbs and watched for a reaction upon her face, but she was in her own world, at work, with her eyes closed, lower lip pushed out, convicted. She stopped and stumbled back to center, her weight on her left leg. His hands went to support her at the hips and she smiled out of embarrassment. Regaining her kneeling position, she left the sheets where they lay and hunched her body in an awkward contortion as she attempted to place his penis beneath her so as to rub on the other side of it from a sitting position. Frustrated noises came from her and she balanced awkwardly with her forehead against his shoulder while utilizing both hands in a careful endeavor towards eventual success.

From her difficult position, she was able to build a steady rhythm moving to her own plan, possessed. Wind tried to watch her, the tendency to study and examine creeping over him. The pressure she applied was intense, pressing his swelling penis down, stretching the tendons, aiming it at a forty-five-degree angle in the direction of the opposing wall. She rode like this and his hands grew tired from reaching to touch her breasts, swaying and bobbing, her nipples like eyes, in and out of focus. The tip of his penis tingled in the cold air as it was rhythmically exposed, but the glands down the back of it in the grip of her loins were on fire, burning with pressure, tensions, over-stimulation. Her body moved upon him and he was taken along with her direction. With spine straight, her head went back with her chin towards the ceiling, closed eyes not visible, and her body looked like a statue of flawless marble, its whiteness shining in the gray of the room, and down to her pubis, her hair trimmed so neat and tight that it looked like it was painted onto the marble. Wherever she was, his body was with her and his mind was dragged behind. No longer was Monica Maria Kildara upon him, but just a sensation and the sensation took over his whole body, a live wire surging with connection. A frantic pressure was building in his testicles and his whole body acted behind the pressure. Her lubricated slit moved against him tight, jerking down and away, pulling, and he pushed with the pull. Body thinking for him, muscle memory, he rocked with the pulling, the pushing, tugging against the sheets, the bed frame creaking metal against metal with the bump of the mattress and box spring. He saw images, his brain and eyes jerking, opening and closing with images becoming words, thoughts and memories, interchangeable... her chin in the air, some drool down the side of her lips, breasts swinging, more breasts, breasts from last night, so many sizes, so many shapes, colors, shifting, shrinking, growing, and her vulva, its grip and all the words for it, if only he could go inside, her vagina, her cunt, the hair so neat, so different, pulling, all the while going faster, her body up and down, scraping, pushing down, stretching him, tearing against him and he could smell her and with the smell was the women, all the women, their bodies, Iliya, the blood, the Goddess, and they were one, with many breasts and one smell, so murky, like shit, like sweat, like cum, like cunnilingus where all three come together but deeper, stickier, saltier, and he was fucking that abyss where they all came together; he saw faces with sweat upon their brows and they danced and the body connected to his swayed and danced and he ached and the pressure he felt became white heat of total completeness and from the breasts and bellies and bristling bushes he found one face and he released his tight jaw to breath deeply out:

"Flora."

And that was it. Wind's discharge fell to the bed where Monica squished down upon it, startled and looking at him with a face changed fiercely in its passion.

"What? What did you say?"

"Flora." He stared back at her, matching her.

"What is that supposed to mean?"

"It's a name."

"No shit, whose name? Who is she? Why did you say her name? Were you thinking of her just now? Is that where your mind was, on her? Is that where you were last night?" She moved erratically and he tried to lift himself upright towards her, but she pushed him back down again, moving furiously like a rabid beast with little movements shaking all over her body, across the bed to her robe, and covering herself.

"Is this why you don't want to get married? Are you seeing someone else? Who is she? You were with her last night, weren't you? That's why you just changed the subject." To the light she bustled, clutching the robe tight over herself, barking questions and accusations. Wind was too late to cover his eyes before she hit the light and he rubbed and stretched his brow to quickly adjust his sight and keep his posture.

"Were you with her last night?" She paused to ask, imploring, adding a sweetness of voice to her plea. She leaned on the dresser and paused to look at him after opening her underwear drawer.

"In a way, yes." And as he said this he held his ground in honesty, but his eyes added the weakness of shameful apology in their blink.

"Bastard! Ugh!" Monica said and threw, with all her frustrated intensity, the balled up pair of panties in her hand at him. Wind caught them and left the silky black pair on the bed, like a dark stain on the field of white. He stepped off to his left, to the side of the bed where his clothes were piled on the floor, giving him and her distance, and he watched her from that distance as she shook her head and mumbled to herself about how she knew it, she knew it all along, and how stupid she was. She had pulled another pair of panties out and stood on one foot at a time to put them on, beneath her hanging robe, and he watched, careful to not be drawn in by the sway of her breasts, hanging in view, careful to not let her see him either, careful. The panties were dowdy, full-cut cotton, white with little red hearts, the universal sign of love, and she pulled them up around her and against her, absorbing the spermicidal lubricant and vaginal secretions. He was trapped by her actions, she wasn't going to the bathroom to clean up, they were here to settle this, so he matched her actions and pulled his boxers up around his wet drooping genitals.

"So where did you meet this whore? At work, is she some street-walking whore you picked up at work? Maybe you busted her and then started fucking her?"

"I did meet her at a crime scene on an investigation, but she was a witness. She was not a street-walker, she was an escort. I've never busted her." He gave this to her forthright, calm and controlled.

"Oh, My God! Are you fucking kidding? I was fucking kidding! She really is a whore; you have been fucking a whore? You fucked a whore last night and come to me tonight, fresh from that, fresh from fucking a whore, bringing all her gross whore diseases and filth into our bed, my bed! My God! I can't believe this. You bastard." Her eyes were wild and in her fury she threw again, this time a small silver heart-shaped jewelry box, which Wind caught and laid down on the bed by the panties. He watched as she ignored it, her eyes either on him or on her own little frantic movements.

"She died last weekend. Last night I was investigating her death. I was at a group of goddess worshippers that she used to attend. I have not seen her in two weeks, but she was very clean." He spoke slowly and hoped his calmness could bring her down.

"Oh, great, so I should be happy. You have been fucking a pagan whore, the fucking whore of Babylon, but I should be happy because she was very clean. No wonder she is dead, God doesn't let such filthy people live. How long had this been going on, you haven't seen her in two weeks, so it was going on longer than that I would guess, how long?" She trained her eyes hard on him.

"For a while. Almost five months, since May." Though still cautious, his honesty came from a place beyond fear.

"Five months! Since May! What, since your birthday? Did I not give you enough? I guess I didn't give you what some whore could? Yeah, you respect me, respect my faith, my purity, respect my desire to wait until marriage. Of course, it's easy for you, you're fucking some whore witch. You don't mind that you can't put your dick in me, though you've tried enough GOD DAMN times, you're sticking it every which way in some loose skanky whore who does it for a living! And after I give you so much. My God, I've given you so much of myself, more than anybody else. Did you love her, you called out her fucking name, do you still love her?" When she asked this last direct question she stared at him waiting for an answer.

"Yes, I loved her, and I still do," he said simply.

"Bastard, fucking bastard!" Tears formed for a split second at the corners of her eyes, but their progress was cut off prematurely as she let out a guttural noise and hurled herself on the bed at him, landing on her knees and hands in a way that scattered the black panties and the silver jewelry box and allowed enough recovery time of balance for her arms to raise up, tipped with little viscous fists, and swing in Wind's direction. He caught both of her wrists before her hits could land on him, but to his shock she still moved forward, fighting with what she had left, and bit him on the right shoulder. He pushed her back off him, controlling her body by her wrists, wincing more from the shock of the bite than the actual sensation of teeth to skin.

"Let go of me, you're hurting me," she yelled and after he had done so she just swung again and again, both fists flying and he blocked each swing, blocked without grabbing so as not to hurt her. His tactics were not effective enough, and he deflected all of her most conventional-seeming blows until one of her small vicious fists conked down on the top of his head sending his top front teeth crashing into his bottom teeth. The impact created a small chip and the shimmer down the tooth's nerve cut deep shaking a tiny yelp of pain out of him. This seemed to satisfy what fed her fury for the moment and she sat down on the bed in front of him, clutching closed her robe that had fallen apart in her attack. Wind held his chin and he ran his tongue slowly, surveying, over both rows of teeth.

"So you're just going to sit there? You think everything is going to be okay? You call out another girl's name while we were being intimate and then tell me that you've been cheating on me and lying to me and that you love someone else and you are just going to sit there? You are such a coward, a fucking coward. That's it, you tell me all of this and that is it, we are just supposed to go on? Why don't you just lie to me some more? How do we go on now?" She spoke slower and breathed, allowing her lungs to calm between each sentence.

"I don't think we can," he said softly.

"What do you mean?"

"I don't think we can go on. I can't go on, not anymore. I am sorry." He spoke softly with a small humble smile, nothing more than creased cheeks, and after making eye contact as he spoke, he brought his eyes back down to the space on the bed that lay between them.

"What are you trying to say? You're sorry? You love some dead whore and now you want to break up, you have been lying to me and now all of a sudden you are totally honest? Don't you love me any more, Jonny? Don't you want to be with me, don't you love me?" These last questions she asked pleadingly, in her sweetest voice, tears returning to the corners of her eyes.

"I am sorry, I don't. I think this is for the best," he said, eyes still lowered.

"I want to hear you say it, you fucking bastard, I want to hear you say it," her voice raised again and she swung a right slap at his face, which he caught. "Don't stop me, you said you would always give me what I wanted, this is what I want, don't you fucking stop me. I want to hear you." She held his chin with her left hand and kept her right palm raised and open. "Tell me!"

"I don't love you anymore," he said and she slapped his face. She asked him to repeat it.

"I don't love you anymore," and holding his chin, she slapped him again. She wanted another.

"I don't love you any more," and after she slapped she let go of his chin and fell to crying.

"I can't believe you don't love me. I can't believe it, all this time, you are such a liar," she sobbed out loud, in between sentences and words. "Did you ever love me? Was this just some game, maybe eventually I'd give it up, you could fuck a virgin, is that it, some sick game. All these years, three years, wasted, thinking about our life, planning our future, our life together, and you just want to throw it away, and you have been throwing it away. Did you ever love me? Was it all a lie, please, really, tell me."

"Yes, I loved you."

Wind either believed that he once did love her or believed that he once believed he loved her; it didn't matter which. It had been over three years that he had been with her, and for the majority of that time he had watched the slow degeneration and falling action from what they once were when they took this trite stage. While they ran their slow and steady production, they conducted themselves blindly and stiffly of each others true feelings and motives, and Wind rationalized that if he really did love her once he would still feel that same way, and as that was not the case, then what he once experienced must have been a momentary fleeting passion that was charged and contained by a random mix of lighting, physicality, character motivations, and the other myriad factors involved in plays about love at first sight. After that moment, everything they knew of each other as individuals and as a couple was more falling action, coasting in a mutually choreographed pattern of complacency and short-range improvisational blocking. Even before the subplot of cheating, a relatively young enterprise in the length of their relationship, he had learned his role with her and learned where to put the parts of himself that did not fit hi designated character. They were both acting, and though their form was that of trained method actors living every ounce of their parts when together, he at least was aware of his splintered true self (maybe too aware, he'd never know). When most compatible, their staging and pacing was slow and profane, emotionally free of highs or lows. Rare scenes of passion were more common over the last year, especially since deepening the petty deception of lip service by the frantic concealment of adultery. The case of last Sunday night stood as the most common scenario, she trying to promote her plans of taking things to the next level and he assuming the role of resistant boyfriend with a fear of commitment. At those times he worked hardest to hold his grip on living his character; whenever she spoke of marriage the fourth wall was broken for him and he felt the urgency of truth and reality come rushing in.

Although the skills of deception necessary for ongoing relations with Flora were already in use in support of his splintered self, the work, energy, and weight of guilt that it required was tremendous; it was a weight from half his life that dragged at his whole self, an uneven cargo, always leaning and pulling down, wanting to rest, wanting to be placed, to be unloaded, but he continued to transport it, trying to alleviate its excess tonnage in constant motion and recirculation, keeping it alive in the air, disguising and passing off the burden with the veil of constant attention to the point where the rhythmic shuffling movement of his greasy guilt burden was a dull white noise contained and amounting to no more than an annoying fact of life. In the beginning, last May, when he first began to load this new cargo into his secret compartment, the lading charge of guilt he had to pay to himself could only be paid in intense paranoia. The truest manifestation of paranoia, it was felt in his every living nerve and cell and touched on that feeling of connection to all life everywhere; it was all the living at once in one, pantheism, and one end of the universe was never any farther from the other end than it was from itself. Atlanta was a city of four million and he saw the same people all the time, recognized the same strangers, and as he traveled about investigating, he felt like everyone else must be having the same realizations as they all moved in overlapping circles of familiarity.

Light without heat, that is how Wind now recalled the depths of his paranoia, he could remember all of his frantic thoughts, but thankfully could no longer feel them. His skills of detection and investigation, though practical and rationally based, ran far and wild with his fears to create so many improbable yet possible situations. *What if* was a prefix for all of his thoughts, and though he trusted Flora, when he was away from her and trapped in the multidimensional universe of his mind, rotating swiftly on the charge of his nervous pulse, he could conjure any unlikely situation. He saw Monica and Flora meeting from so many angles at so many natural, one in a million moments and could at times even convince himself that he heard Flora's voice in public or smelled the approach of her scent. This was what his work was about, connecting loose ends; in every human endeavor there is always a paper trail, always a trace, evidence; as a cheater, he was truly experiencing the criminal mind firsthand. When finally his guilt had calmed from the dissonant screeches of paranoia to the tolerable hum of white noise, it was back to the same old staging and tempo for them, running the same lines.

Monica leaned and reached for a tissue from the dresser, holding the puffy white robe closed. Head down, back to the same way of sitting on the bed with one leg beneath her and one crossed in front, she sniffled and blew beneath the dark curls. She sighed, trying to breath through erratic nasal passages, and he watched, respectively and wearily silent. There was no way of telling how stable her condition was and he was guarded for the next eruption. His cautious mind and body watched and mused. His image of her had been eroding the more he violated her trust. Maybe she went through the same process in her own self-delusion, he wondered? With the passing of time, over the last couple of years, it had begun to feel to him that he could no longer actually see her any more, they had become so routine, so set in repetitive actions and dialogue that she had almost become one of Monet's landscapes, confirming his awareness only from a distance, never close-up, and yet through that growing emotional distance he still felt a fear of her; maybe it was that fear that really maintained his attachment to his role in their drama. The more he had pulled away and the colder he had gotten, the more she talked about marriage and the more she tried to hold and bind. This he figured was her particular method of self-delusion, her ingénue-turned-shrew character arc. All along, this was their dynamic, their cycle of stage setting; it would have been too boring without it to keep the audience they themselves played attentive and sated enough in a drama about mutual complacency. It was the story of opposites attracting, loveless lovers magnetized in reversed polarities. The triteness added to the smoothness of performances and on and on it all rolled until here they sat, with curtain down, footlights off and the knowledge that neither would be coming back up. The show was over, the plot revealed, and no longer were there any actors or audience members present; only critics remained.

They began to talk calmly, he following her lead. She said she was sorry that his friend had died. He said thank you and pursued no further, waiting for her to speak again. She asked him again if he ever loved her and he assured her he did. He told her that he had been with her longer than with anyone ever and said that he could not have done that if he did not love her, a rationale he thought up quickly on the spot. She seemed to accept his logic and smiled a little, looking up at him for a moment through her hair. He was careful not to go on too far ahead of her in what he was saying, feeling out the sincerity of her calmness. He waited for her to speak.

"So you were serious about not getting married anytime soon," she said, jocular and tearful, and he smiled a little, but not much, continuing to give his most lugubrious countenance. She brought up other plans and smiled at the joy she once felt in them and teared at their dissolution. He held her left hand in his and rested them both on her left knee. As she talked, he consoled her as if there was a death in her family, as if they both agreed that these feelings belonged only to her and he was there to support her own process of grieving. Long gone had been his guilt, routine had become his betrayal, but now, faced with her expression, just sitting there on the bed before him with such wet sadness and broken smile after seething red rage, it was all back. He had confessed his crime and he was ready to feel the pain of it with her. He could not cry, but he lowered his eyes and continued to smile sullenly as she spoke. Guilt she would understand, guilt and fate, so he tried to carry both in his face, but she was in her own world already, divorced from him and dealing with her own mixed emotions.

He knew she could never appreciate his honesty for its own sake, but he felt so good relaxing his faculty for deception; the cargo was deposited and teamsters with crowbars were attacking the crate, prying with deft movements until it was no longer, just six slats on the floor and its insides were out. Finally here, being honest, baring everything, showing and telling outwardly what had always been inside, not only did a weight lift—strained muscles relaxing that had been contracted for so long—but his view also cleared. He felt a slight elation and euphoria. He could not stop, he didn't want to hurt her, but he wanted to tell her everything. He wanted to say, this is me, this is who I am. He felt a unity in himself, in honesty. He wanted to introduce himself and say hello we haven't officially met, but this is me the true total me. All that I suppressed to make you happy, to not upset you, I have no reason to hold back any more, I have openly defied my duty to you so I can give all the rest up too. Above all, he wanted to tell her that there is no saving or converting him, he is not the Augustine to her Monica. But sadly, he said nothing, and here, even at the end, he deceived a little, lying by omission, giving appeasement and solidarity of misery as a last gift and act of compassion. They both sniffled together and hand in hand wandered down a sweetly staged lane of memories, lingering over flowering beds of brightly colored days, like their weekend trips to Asheville, Savannah, and St. Augustine, and other beds of duller days, at her family barbecues and out shopping, painted and perfumed brighter for the occasion. It had seemed like their whole relationship ran past their lips and from her eyes and nose, but it was only the night slipping away from them, the darkness receding, and when it seemed to him that she had expelled all of the tears and mucus that she could in the hours that passed, she rose with a kiss but no word and left the room. Alone he put on his pants and shirt.

She returned from the bathroom and sat on the dresser, after moving some of her knickknacks over to make room, and she was sitting against the window with a slight glow around her. From Wind's angle looking up, lightening early morning sky crept in through the cracks in the blinds and framed her. He thought she was beautiful like this, her pale skin and dark hair, so sad and beautiful, almost like the Pre-Raphaelite work that she loved, but darker, more baroque; the light was fighting for its place around her. Yes, she was beautiful, but even more distant now than he had ever seen her. There were no more emotions shared between them. In the past, to see her like this he could not have kept away from going to her, taking her up in his arms, waiting silently and consoling her. In the present, he felt nothing, not even a sense of duty drawing him to her and he could only see her this beautiful across the great distance between them now. He stared at her not wanting to move yet. Her beauty was fragile and precarious; like Monet's Japanese Garden across an empty room or the colored dust on a butterfly's wing, he could not get any closer without ruining the beauty with truth and reality. Hers was a cold stone marble beauty, and from where he sat on the bed, her expression now pained and looking down, it could have been that of Leboeuf's Eurydice. He had only her profile and he supposed that she wasn't looking at him to prevent more tears. Aurora, the bright dawn, rose around her and it was no longer a halo creeping across her flesh, but piercing rays of living light streaming through the blinds attaching themselves to her. Wind rose soundlessly from the bed and said goodbye, grabbing his shoes and socks, but she still didn't look his way. Instead, her eyes went upward, tears flowing down, and her smooth marble faced looked, in that last moment he saw her, like Bernini's "St. Theresa in Ecstasy."

12. MAHA-ATLANTA

The world does not require to be reformed; nor are its laws to be disregarded. All of the various planes of manifestation of the absolute can be beheld in a dispassionate spirit. The solid, the liquid and the gaseous states of the one substance, under differing conditions, producing differing effects, are accepted without moral or emotional preference.
—Heinrich Zimmer, *Philosophies of India*

DRIVING EAST THROUGH DOWNTOWN DECATUR, THROUGH THE CHIC little shops and cafes, he followed Ponce De Leon Avenue all the way from his home on Highland. Past the Hare Krishna Temple on his right and then the Coptic Church on his left, he enjoyed the late afternoon under the canopy of trees along parks and refined brick homes in the most elegant neighborhood of Dekalb County. Over the phone, Sutra Diamante had given Jonathan Wind directions from the proximity of the most well-known Decatur landmark, The Dekalb County Farmers' Market. She would meet him less than four miles away and these were the most straightforward directions she could conceive of if he was coming from Ponce. The scenery became more industrial and before the Farmer's Market he turned, as prescribed, left onto Dekalb

Industrial Way and followed that until it merged and blended into Lawrenceville Highway, presenting him with the familiar strip malls of the area and making him realize he could have found his own quicker way to this same location. Watching the street names at stop lights he turned left onto Harcourt Drive into an older residential neighborhood typical for Dekalb County and looked for Mount Olive Drive to find Shamrock Middle School, tucked up on his left at the top of the hill. The front of the school was as quiet as a Saturday should be, but when he drove around to the side, he saw several cars being loaded by people in colorful dress, families rooted in the sub-continent of India, moving in clusters, small children orbiting like car satellites, mothers reprimanding, carrying trays covered in aluminum foil and cellophane, while fathers and sons held coolers by each end.

He nodded hello to no one in particular and passed the side door from which they all came and walked around to the front of the building towards the figure on the bench he had passed as he drove in. "Sutra," he called to her back to make his approach known, and she stood and said hello.

"Hi, I'm Jonathan Wind. Thank you for meeting with me. I didn't really get to tell you what this was all about on the phone." He put out his hand and she shook it with hers, soft and narrow with long fingers, her palm more yellow than the deeper honey-kissed yellow of the rest of her visible skin.

"That is only because I wouldn't let you. I am sorry if I seemed enigmatic. I stopped you because I don't like talking on the phone. I don't trust it for first meetings or most interactions at all. It's too impersonal for me, and I can't stand email, don't get me started. I thought it would be better face-to-face, anyway. Moreover, I actually wanted to meet you." Her eyes were still serious, but she smiled. "I have always wanted to meet you. From what I have heard about you, I always thought we would have a lot to talk about. I like meeting interesting people and Flora said you weren't like other cops, you read too much to be like other cops. I was led to assume that if more cops were like you we wouldn't have a lot of the problems we do in this country. It's a shame she never introduced us before, that we never all three got together, that would have been fun and some good conversation, but I guess she brought us together in the end here." Her arm returned to her side and her posture was straight and narrow, her thin body angular with grace, like she was posing for a temple painting, moving from one tableau to another. Her face was long and thin too, framed by straight, dark hair, parted down the middle, and on her forehead she wore an orange bindi coiling upwards like a flame or a double helix with a green gem at its bottom and silvery sparkles up the thinning coil. High round breasts held tight against her chest by a cropped skin-tight orange blouse beneath the wrap of a sheer chiffon orange sari with a silvery woven border of paisley and rose-shapes. Orange pants with the same border near the cuffs covered her legs beneath the wrap of the sari.

"Thank you. The sentiment is mutual, she referred to you as her best friend and coming from her, I always supposed that meant a lot. She mentioned a lot of people in the stories she told, but your name came up the most. That is why I wanted to talk to you, if anyone, maybe you knew her the best." He paused, and then looking at her he looked back down at himself. "I feel a little underdressed here," he said, standing in brown boots, blue jeans, a black t-shirt, and his barn jacket.

"It's okay, we are actually done here. We ended at five. That is why I asked you to meet me at five-thirty. They're just cleaning up inside and I slipped out."

"What was going on here today? I thought it was kind of odd that you asked me to meet you at a middle school, but since the parking lot it has made a little more sense that there was some sort of Indian festival going on."

"We book the cafeteria here since we're a community group, the Bengali Association of Greater Atlanta. But I actually went to middle school here, my parents still live off of Lawrenceville Highway. This weekend is the Durga Puja, it's been going on since Friday night. It's a celebration for the Goddess Durga, she is a pretty big deal in Hinduism, especially the Bengali community."

"Yes, I have heard of Durga. I have read that Durga is one of the oldest recorded names for a goddess, comparable to the Greek Gaia."

"That's true. Today is the last day, Dashami, and this morning we sent the Goddess away to where Shiva lives in the ritual of Bisharjan. Then we have a big lunch with all the other families and talk about what's going on in the community. And thus ends the festival for another year, not that there aren't other festivals that come up."

"Are you a strict Hindu?"

"I am not a Hindu at all really, but in my love of my parents I have a certain respect for their feelings and practices. It took me a long time to get here, to be like this. I also respect their community and like to help out if I can. It doesn't hurt me or conflict with any of my beliefs to make them happy at the same time as acknowledging a little pluralism."

As if on cue, the front door to the school opened up and a small brown-skinned girl in a teal and lavender sari came running out towards them, her eyes on only Sutra, so similar in face that they would easily be assumed as family.

"Sati, Sati," the little girl called out in a high child's voice and reached her arms up to Sutra, a motion showing that she desired to be lifted; a request instantly understood and obeyed. The girl hid her face in Sutra's shoulder and peeked at Wind and hid again to whisper in her carrier's ear.

"This is my sister, Kamalika. She is shy around men and most people she doesn't know. That is why she is whispering," said Sutra turning the girl so she would have to look at Wind. "This man is my friend, Jonathan, do you want to say hello to him? Huh, do you want to be polite and say hello?" She addressed the child, but Kamalika turned away from however she was positioned and wouldn't look at him.

"She was sent to get me and to tell me that my family was ready to go. I would have invited you in to check it out but I thought we could talk better at this time and now there is really nothing for you to see inside. Do you have anywhere to go now? I expected you would have some time since you said we could meet wherever and whenever I designated."

"Yes, I'm free, I have nowhere to go. I came to see you so, as I said, whatever is fine. I just need to talk. What do you have in mind?"

"Kamalika, tell Mommy and Daddy that a friend came to see me and that he will give me a ride back to their house later, okay?" She kissed the child and put her down. Half way back to the front door the little girl turned in a colorful swirl of her sari and waved at Sutra and directly at Wind and then turned back to go inside.

"She must have liked you, she waved at you. That is a good sign. For you."

"Thanks. She is very cute. She looks just like you. She called you Sati. Is that as a term of endearment? I wondered if Sutra was your real name or not. It was what Flora always called you, but in her world there seems to be a lot of name changing and aliases."

"You are deductive, I guess you *are* a detective. I was born Sati Patel, you can't get a more common Indian name than that combination. I didn't become Sutra Diamante until I was eighteen, in college, when I changed my birth name. It's my legal name; it's who I am now. It's not just some Goddess name that I dance around with once a week. It's what everyone calls me, except as you just saw, my family. It would really be too much of an uphill battle to get them to change, and though I am not one to run from a battle, believe me, it's better left alone. At this point, it would confuse Kamalika. Where is your car? We should go."

She walked towards the parking lot and he tried to lead her while still keeping close enough a stride to pursue questioning. Wind found her of the type that wants to give more information than she lets on but needs it drawn out by others. She is not scared to talk, to give, but must know it is asked for, desired. Maybe she likes the attention, but seeks to deny such a joy.

"Why did you change your name, if you don't mind my asking?"

"Oh, I don't mind, not at all. I am proud of my choices and make them without fear of them being shared with the whole world. I find no purpose in dishonesty or deception, a life lived in shame is a life half lived. I know that *you* must find some way to justify deception, but I cannot." She spoke with such confidence and assurance as if he was an intimate relation or a student in her charge to be lectured.

"Hum. You really cut right to the point, don't you? Alright. Good. I have nothing to hide from you and I'm glad we don't have to mince words here. It's that one, the Honda Accord." His words steered her at the last minute and they got into his car. She told him to head back to Decatur the same way he came. Then she resumed where she was in the conversation.

"That is what I do, though, cut to the point, sharp and indestructible like a diamond. Most of the problems in this world are from people lying to themselves and then others. I know who I am. I pride myself on my honesty and wish others were more like me. I lead by example. Flora appreciated it, she wasn't a big fan of lying, but of course in her work she understood discretion, which does walk the line at times." She was giving him another jab, keeping him on his toes. She spoke this way naturally, her tone saying, *this is me, and if you cannot handle it then fuck you.* "The story of my name change is the story of my awakening to life in my family and other such hypocrisies. My birth-name is fraught with problems. I mean, Patel is like Smith or Jones in India, East India, at least. So common, I was lost in that name. It said nothing for me or of me. My father was born here, first generation, but his family was from East India, near Calcutta. He was raised a good Hindu and took the traditions like any other son of immigrant stock raised in America would—land of the free, cable TV, and the all you can eat buffet—he pretty much ignored it all until a crisis of faith or a moment of weakness brought him back to it. Meeting my mother was that for him. She also was first generation here, but it was more complicated than that. He saw her from a distance, at a supermarket actually. It's really that corny, that is the way I have always heard it. He saw her and she was beautiful with long straight black hair, curry-colored skin, eyes of green and some other flavor to her that he could not denote and he was sold, head over heels. That was it for him, without even speaking to her. Sold. Love. But he went over to her and spoke to her, asked her out, she said yes, and it was only when getting her number that he noticed an odd lilt to her accent.

"He called her and they got together for their first date and it was finally then that he had the great humbling moment of his life. He had spent the day talking about this amazing Indian woman he had met, he was sure she was even Bengali, there was a spice to her. With great excitement, he picked her up and immediately in the closeness of the car when they started talking he realized that she wasn't Bengali or Indian at all, she was Mexican. He must have felt like such an idiot, for as much as he strayed from the traditions of his parents, he knew this would not be well accepted, he had crossed the line. But he still loved her, it was really was love at first sight; or so they say. I often suppose stubbornness is hidden behind love at first sight, but anyway. The only thing he could think to do to make it all right for everyone was to marry her, and fast. That would prove his seriousness in his feelings and if he got her to convert and had a real Hindu wedding, he could win his family over. So that's what he did. It all went as he planned and it was like his re-conversion, his return to the path. My mother, bless her sweet subjugated soul, being a better wife than Catholic, converted for him. They had a very nice and traditional Hindu wedding. Her family practically disowned her. Only now is there any contact with them and that is through me alone, but she didn't care, she was happy, she had a man, a husband. They both pretty much ignored the will of her family and traditions in all of this." She took a breath for pacing only, very used to speaking with such wind, and proceeded, paying no attention to the very familiar scenery of Lawrenceville Highway passing around them.

"I was soon on the way and my father confirmed his faith again by giving me one of the most common Hindu girl names there is, Sati. As I grew up and my eyes opened, I bore that name with shame. It is such a typical name for girls because it means 'good wife.' That was the first problem. I wasn't going to be labeled and identified as nothing more than a good wife like my mother, as something in relation to something else, especially not a man, a husband, a keeper. The second problem gets into why that name means good wife, what it was to be a good wife historically in India. It even goes all the way back to the *Rig Veda,* the story of Sati, the wife or consort of Shiva. I can understand how it is seen as a story of devotion and an act of dignity from a loving wife who was defending her husband to her own father. That was something earlier on that I related to, as a child, when I first heard the story. An act of vengeance and insurrection against my father, like it was expected and therefore okay if I finally couldn't take him anymore and burned myself, got out of my home situation by jumping into a fire. But to make a model out of it for wifely duty is sick and sad. Even in Indian culture it was a right extended only to women, men couldn't self-immolate legally. But I'm glad the British outlawed it in 1829, even if it was just some colonial power-play, white men protecting brown women from brown men. Fuck a culture that plays with women's minds in that way, conditions them that way. I don't mean the whole culture, there is a lot of female goddess representation in Hinduism but people gravitate to what they want from a tradition, they pick and choose. But that's not for me, any of it. I have sympathy for the women, but want no part in any of it, especially not the bearing of the name for it.

"I could think of a few things worth dying for, but certainly not some dead husband... nor, come to think of it, for some patriarchal God waiting expectantly in the afterlife. I'm sure you've read Josephus, his *Jewish Wars.* At the end of the Battle of Masada, when Eleazar is trying to get everyone to follow him into the backwards dignity of suicide, he mentions that they should be as brave as the Indians who have philosophy and stoically self-immolate at the end of life. I mean, what crap is that? My copy of the *Jewish Wars* has a footnote for this that says that Josephus got the idea from Aristotle that the Jews were descendants of the Indians. I don't know where Aristotle, or Josephus, got any of that but I find no glorious self-immolation in India's past except for the poor wives." She was really getting heated now and took a breath that was more than just pacing, but necessary to regulate her breathing.

"In Buddhism, the Sanskrit word sati can be used to mean mindfulness, as in the right mindfulness of the Eightfold Path." Wind interjected hoping to both calm her and return her to her train of thought.

"Yes, it is. Samma sati, right mindfulness, that's the Pali expression. It's just a word. It's not all bad. It was just given as a name to me in a certain context. That does bring me back to where I was going, as I am sure you intended. Your point illustrates mine. My name change was a clear move from the Hindu origins of my father, the product of someone else's karma, to an act of my own doing, my own karma, and a fuller sense of how I see myself. I mean other than reading Hesse's *Siddhartha* in high school and buying music from bands that wanted to help free Tibet, I didn't get into Buddhism until college. There I was, eighteen, out of my parents' house, far enough away in Athens that no one was dropping in on me, and I was free to do whatever I wanted, as long as I kept my HOPE scholarship. Out of my home situation and I didn't even have to light myself on fire. My freshman year, I came in with such big ideas of studying political science and woman's studies and doing something with social action and I really wanted to avoid anything as fluffy and exploitative as religion, something that so many people hide behind like my father, but I was somehow drawn to taking a religion course. Maybe because of my hatred, so I could mock it, tear it down, and seem superior.

"My great mistake in taking the class, considering my hatred, turned out to be my great fortune in the end. I wound up burning away part of myself. I picked a high-level Buddhism class, and maybe my choice was equal parts curiosity and spite, since Buddhism was such an Indian thing to me from my limited awareness, yet my very Indian father and his family never spoke of it. The very first day of the class was amazing, I was bought and sold. The professor, Dr. Phil Ruen—isn't that great, Dr. R-U-E-N, pronounced ruin, I'm finally comfortable calling him Philly now, like his friends do—scared half the class away that first day. A few of the kids got up and walked out as he spoke. He encouraged them to, actually. He asked which of them was a theist, who believed in God? Then he told them that they would be studying the thought of a figure who considered theism to be not only foolish, but probably a disease and if they couldn't handle that kind of attitude towards what they believe then just leave. And they did, it was great. By the end of the semester, I was a religion major, fully committed to this work in multiple disciplines. Not only did the class and Dr. Ruen convince me to study religion, and I did so on a Comparative Religions track, but also to practice Buddhism.

"That year, still a freshman, I began attending the Zen Center in Athens and meditation groups led by Dr. Ruen. On this new life, this path that was there all along but was only now visible to me, I decided that if I were to leave the Hinduism of my parents I must also leave the Hindu name they set upon me. Taking my karma consciously in my own hands, I exerted my rights as an eighteen-year-old and had my name legally changed to what it is now. I admit that my actions were reactive ones, rebellious ones, but they were still what I felt was right and comfortable. Sati Patel was no longer, I paid my surcharge and from then on Sutra Diamante existed. She really had existed all along, I just didn't know it. The name choice was a very careful one for me, I do not do things lightly; even the times when I am rash I really commit to them. The Buddha in his time was a rebel, an iconoclast, breaking with tradition. That sat well with me. I loved his criticisms and deconstructions of the Brahman Hinduism of his day. Especially his problems with religious structures and hierarchies that always turn out oppressive and unbalanced. In my study of Buddhist history and tradition, I found this sense of political rebelliousness of the Buddha against Brahmanism again in the split from Theravada to Mahayana Buddhism. As a good populist, I easily sided with the Mahayana stance, the Great Vehicle anyone could climb on, their belief in anyone's ability to achieve awakening in the normal walk of life without having to adjourn from the world to a monastery. So elitist, not everyone can fit on that Small Vehicle, that doctrine of the elders. Other than the Buddha's life itself, this became my favorite time frame, the Mahayana split. It cut right to the heart of the teachings, cut its own middle path in the world. That is where I found myself, while reading the Diamond Sutra, translating it from the Sanskrit, finding such crystalline truth without any flourish. I saw synchronicities with the tradition and my own life as well as with the etymology of the word sutra itself, meaning to bind or tie things together, the root of our word suture. That is what I was doing at the time, tying things together. I felt comfortable with the name and it rationally fit.

"The renaming I was doing also gave me a chance to declare my own expression of my mother and her culture. Diamante sounded better in Spanish than just diamond in English and now I have a Spanish last name as my mother once did. I have always felt more for her than my father, though most often sadness. But from then on, through the next three years of school, I made sure all the transcripts were changed to my new name and that whenever I had to fill out an official form, I no longer put Indian as race but other and choose to not fill in what that other was. The religion department was deeply supportive, especially Dr. Ruen who was constantly trying to push us out of the comfortable nest of institutional learning and into the world to really learn and experience. I hope that was a satisfactory answer to your question, longer than you expected, but real questions have real answers. I think we both deserve better than something simplified and false just to be polite." She smiled with a cock of her head to close her lecture.

"I appreciate that. I too wish we could have met under better circumstances. Especially with how long it seems to have taken us to get through the introductions." He remained looking forward while driving but quickly flashed her way the easy smile he commanded when the need to charm was at hand, a smile for women, usually tough women. "I've liked hearing about your education and your confidence of identity. We have some similar tendencies in our backgrounds. You definitely live up to the approbation our mutual friend held towards you. As you might have guessed, though, I was hoping to talk to you about Flora's death." He kept his eyes on the road, deadpan, waiting for her to proceed.

"Oh, Bhikkhus, all is burning, all the world is on fire, but it's all just sensation," she said shaking her head as if it was just her way of sighing after a pause of thought.

"To Carthage then I came, burning, burning, burning, burning, O Lord Thou pluckest me out, O Lord Thou pluckest... burning." Eyes straight he delivered, still deadpan, waiting for her to react, feeling her out, suppressing a breath of laughter.

Her brow darkened by furrowing, not an angry expression, but one slightly confused and surprised at her own confusion. He noted her confusion and responded to it.

271

"That's T.S. Eliot. It's how 'The Fire Sermon' from *The Waste Land* ends. He was referencing what you were referencing." His laughter fully suppressed, he kept his own expression staid. It was the way he handled himself, not only in interrogating, but also in dealing with someone unfamiliar.

"Yes, the Buddha's 'Fire Sermon' from *Samyutta-nikaya*. I'm not used to being shocked by people, nor impressed, especially by men. Or by a cop. You seem to be a contradiction, a well-read cop. It's like military intelligence."

"I see no contradiction. Just because I know Eliot and the Buddha doesn't mean I don't believe in law and upholding law to run a safe and orderly society. Laws protect people. I deal in hard objective realities. As a Buddhist, you've got to respect that. I investigate crimes and figure out exactly what happened, no metaphysics, not lofty speculation. I just bring to light the concrete world how it actually is." He was familiar with this attitude toward cops; he had a diverse group of acquaintances and some pretty radical friends. He knew many cops who were dangerously ignorant regardless of their education on paper and he knew of others who were wise open-minded people who would never crack a book to save their lives. Part of him relished blowing her mind in regards to his badge. It felt good that she would take that away with her.

"Wow. I might start thinking you're a Buddhist, if you keep talking that way. A Buddhist-cop, it sounds like a bad television show: Buddhist-Cop."

"I am no practitioner, but I've read a little. I'm an investigator, a detective, so our areas of investigation and inquiry might overlap sometimes, me and the Buddhist, but I claim no faith."

"That is too bad, your lover, our mutual friend claimed almost every faith, but I guess then in a way she really claimed none. A perfect couple, you are a religious eunuch and she was a religious polymorphous pervert, to misuse a little Freud. Here I am mixing sex and religion in metaphor just like she did in life. She's not around, but that wheel of karma just keeps on turning, nothing really dies."

"Is that what you believe? Is that what you feel about her death? The circumstances of her death leave me feeling very unresolved to say the least. I will not give up my own capacity of understanding to a God or a cosmic wheel so I was hoping that you could tell me something, give me a little help at enhancing my understanding of what could possibly have happened to a person we both loved very deeply. I will not settle for answers that involve such vague excuses using terms like accident or supernatural phenomenon or act of God, and I don't think Gotama would go in for any of that either, that at least is my reading."

"Do you know what nirvana means?"

"Yes, unbinding."

"Yes. Again, I'm impressed. I guess I should get over it already, but you didn't say anything flowery or western about ecstasy, serenity, or some enlightened state or paradise shit. The word itself in Sanskrit originally—although the Buddha would have said nibbana in Pali—is from the prefix and root *nir* and *va*, roughly *blowing* and *out*, blowing out. Unbinding is good, some of the best translations use that. My mentor Dr. Ruen is doing a new English translation of the *Dhammapada* and he always translates the word nirvana, never just leaves it in the Sanskrit, and when he does he translates it to 'unbinding.' The word itself was used as an expression for, or a metaphor for, a fire being extinguished. For Indians at the Buddha's time their physics of fire was pretty advanced. I come from a clever people, I'll give them that. Unbinding works well though, not being bound to life, the world. Experiencing without being attached to the experience. The experience rises and when it passes it is gone like a flash of light or a clap of hands. To not be attached there is no fuel for suffering, and that is what attachment is, the fuel of suffering. If you are a wick in wax and there is no more oxygen to bind that spark in agitation to you, then it passes, it goes out. Sparks flash like lightning or a clap of thunder, but they only burn you, only stay burning on you in the tension of their condition, their balance of fuel. It makes a lot of sense, the word roots, the metaphor. Attachment to the impermanence of all things in life, since they all are impermanent, is the cause of all dukkha, all suffering. And it is not like a flame even ceases to exist. It just relaxes from its state of agitation. The Brahmins understood a flame like this and the Buddha knew his audience would get the reference. Attaining nirvana, experiencing nirvana, is an act of freedom, the flame is freed from its state of unrest, as is a person from suffering, or really the attachment to suffering."

Wind was about to speak, about to question why she would be explaining Buddhist concepts after he had asked for more information about Flora's life and death, and why she thought this notion of nirvana was relevant in this situation, when *BAM!* a face banged against the driver's side window.

The car idled in the left lane at the intersection of Dekalb Industrial Way and Decatur Road, a red light hanging and keeping the cars in their directional flow at a state of tension, ignited, but stopped. Wind's eyes were on the light as he slowed to stop and his mind was on Sutra's words, both attentions keeping him from noticing the approach of the figure. Through the empty oncoming lanes he must have come, but what Wind first saw was his face pressed against the glass, mouth open and lips in a wide circle gripping like a suction cup.

When Wind and Sutra looked in the direction of the bang, the lungs of the man exhaled and filled the pressed mouth, inflating the cheeks against the window like a blowfish.

The man's eyes rolled wildly in circles and comical patterns while his tongue danced, exploring the space of his distended cheeks. His head was shaven poorly in patches and clumps and he beat on his bare chest in his squatted act of puffing. Wind lowered the window and the buffoon unstuck his mouth and blew a gust of garlicky air into the car. Wind turned his face for a moment from the blast and the buffoon slugged him on the left shoulder and shouted, "A horror, long unfelt, comes o'er me, and Man's collective woes o'erwhelm me, all. She dwells within the dark, damp walls before me, whom better feelings made a criminal! What! I delay to near her? I dread, once again to see her? On! My shrinking only brings her death the nearer. Goethe said it once before and you shall bear it ever more."

Wind reached out to grab the man, but the buffoon jumped backwards, tottering on the line between the lanes and as the light had just changed, the line of cars behind Wind had begun to honk their horns. Reluctantly, Wind drove on, casting glances back at the buffoon who waved from his precarious spot before bounding through the traffic and off into the Walgreens parking lot.

"What the hell was that? That was fucking bizarre. Do people often hit you, rant gibberish, mention Goethe, and run away?"

"More often than you'd think."

They sat in silence for a few minutes, her waiting for him to say something more about the experience and he thinking about the buffoon, the hunchback, and the little person, about how they all appeared to have been reciting the same passage but in different translations. He calmly wracked his brain about every aspect of each interaction, and from the wracking he brought order by creating quick mental Venn diagrams and flowcharts of the cataloged information he had compiled without letting any of the internal bustle break the surface of his face or demeanor. At this point he had to assume that he was closer to something, as whoever was delivering this message to him was getting much better in their timing of his location and if they were following him they were doing it very carefully.

With his unfazed coolness after such a startling experience, he was testing Sutra, sitting there next to him, equally unfazed after her initial comment and he was hoping to read something in her slight movements. This was the first messenger that someone else had witnessed and that made him wonder further if she had any connection to this most cryptic aspect of his rogue investigation. On many occasions he had mulled over how they always knew where he was and were always there ahead of time, but in this instant he had been following her directions. He listened to her as she looked out the window, glass keeping her eyes safe from the windy world outside it and he could tell that she was listening to him, listening for him. He moved back to questioning, taking control and taking her back to where they were before the intrusion to see if what she had to say was any different now from how she spoke earlier.

"I am sorry, you were talking about nirvana, about the flame metaphor. I think you were about to relate that to what happened to Flora." He spoke kindly and with a warm tone, warm and assuring, a tone he used when checking his facts back to suspects so that they believed that he was listening and thought that he was believing. From there, he could attempt to lead them.

"You had asked about Flora's death and I was sharing some applicable metaphors. From my own life perspective, it is easy to see things in such a way, or think towards such things. I can get a little didactic in any conversation, Dr. Ruen at UGA let me lead some classes and employ that very Buddhist and Socratic method of learning by interaction and questioning. My point is that I don't know exactly what happened to Flora, there are so many factors that go into everything, so much you don't know about someone else and their life, their karma. However, I don't believe that anything ever dies, not even the Buddha was released from his karma. Otherwise there would be no Buddhists, to name one problem with the notion of him entirely breaking the cycle, even after experiencing nirvana. Karma in the Buddhist usage is just action, the interplay of cause and effect. It is the cause and it then is that effect because that effect just becomes another cause. Even after death, causes one created before death still create effects after. In some ways karma is all that we interact with others through and that doesn't end so easily. Flora is physically dust, but look at you and me: she has set in play our actions through her own. Some people call this morphic resonance, the traces of our interactions, but in Buddhism it is often called dependent-origination. This is why compassion is common sense, because all things are connected." Here he could tell she was pausing for effect in her lecture. It appeared, or she was making it appear, that she had forgotten all about the buffoon.

"See, I wasn't talking about some abstract absolute impersonal wheel of fate or some awful judgmental asshole-god directing traffic from heaven when I bring up a notion like karma. We are nothing but something that originates anew every moment from the circumstances around us, and the circumstances that we were born into, not only our own karma, our own actions, but the actions and karma of others too. Dependent-origination makes a lot of sense, especially in looking at death. It's just an effect of so many causes. Everything is impermanent. Everything breaks down. We project what we want onto death since no one really understands it. It's like anything else, a zero-point for us to project all of our own experiences onto. It just seems like a very personal zero-point because we value others so much and feel that it is so necessary to be attached to them. In Buddhism, in some texts, in my namesake for one, there is the Sanskrit term nimitta, which means sign, as in a symbol or a referent point, something that stands in for something else. It can also mean a false perception, since a representation of something is not the thing itself. To me, that is what death is, for that is what we do to death, as the non-dead, ignorant onlookers, we make it a sign and create false perceptions. My sutra says that we should be acting in the world openly and generously and from a place not supported by a sign, or the notion of a nimitta. This is the greatest illusion and deception, that the suppositions and artifice we use to describe the reality that we do not understand is actually real. Well, any more real than any other dream, thought, or sensation. So I don't know what happened exactly to Flora, and I don't believe I can ever know, all I can know is what she and her death mean to me."

"One of the main points that you didn't really emphasize is that of choice. We make our own karma, other than that which we are born into, but we have the power to choose. Even in dependent-origination, even with a finite set of choices, we have the ultimate power, and that finite set of choices is pretty large," Wind added.

"That is true. Flora made many choices that I can never know about, and I will say that she made the choices that resulted in what happened to her, in some way, somehow," said Sutra.

"Many wouldn't agree with you, it was ruled an accidental death, but it seems that your worldview allows no accidents."

"No, no accidents at all, I will agree with that insight of yours, Jon."
She smiled.

"I was hoping you could fill in some blanks for me though. I don't believe in accidents either, I try not to even use the word. I am trying to find the path of karma that led Flora to a point of immolation in her apartment that night. I am trying to tie pieces from her life together and look to place her death in that framework. I have been to the goddess group that she was attending for the last time over the summer, but I believe, on the testimony of others, that she had been involved with something else over the last couple of months. That is what I was hoping you could tell me about. I believe that she went somewhere earlier in the night she died and I was hoping that you could tell me about that, where she was, whom she was with.

"She never told me what she was into recently, over the last few weeks it never came up. It was a side of her life that only came into our conversations when there was a reason. Maybe she was telling me all along or references were coming out of her speech, but I don't have enough context to read allusions and references into the last many conversations we had. Do you know where she went? Can you help me?" Towards the end of his request, his words were as honest and sincere as they could ever be. It was in part still a tactic, but he was truly asking for her help and had to be vulnerable and open to receive it. She was too strong and set in her ways for anything else.

"I feel good about helping you. You are asking me for something and I would like to give it to you if I can, as long as I don't hurt or betray any others in the process. See I am using right mindfulness in this, Samma sati. All actions harm someone, I just want to harm as few as possible. I will see what I can find out, and I give my word that I will do all that I can for all parties. I will call you on Thursday, early probably. I have your mobile phone number. I will do what I can. Leave Friday open just in case."

Wind felt now a confirmation that Sutra knew something and he was a little elated, lighter. On the wheel, his hands were for a moment looser until his mind projected forward. He would be restless in waiting until Thursday for her call, but he was putting his power in her hands for this time and he trusted that she would respond according to that trust. The days ahead, without his power, days in waiting without control; would be insecure, filled with a proliferation of thoughts and expectations, creating false perceptions about the result of her call and findings. Still, this was the most direct avenue into Flora's life he was left with and he needed to embrace it without attachment, to hold on without clinging to make it through.

She directed him off Ponce de Leon onto Oakdale and he followed her lead conscientiously.

"Just up here on the left," she said, pointing to the white stucco building.

"The Hare Krishna Temple, I should have guessed, and maybe on some level I did. Flora told me that you both met for the first time at the Hare Krishna Temple. I guess on a Sunday like today, she liked to go there for chanting and the free spiritualized vegetarian dinner."

"Yes, we bonded instantly. That was years ago, when I was coming into town from Athens for these Sundays and at times to visit the Vajrayana Buddhist Center in Decatur. She definitely got me back here more often, got me to see much more of this city than my sheltered childhood allowed. I loved her perspective on things, her sense of devotion while understanding how to be part of something without being restricted by it. She was always herself, with everything she did and participated in, she was always herself, always honest."

"That she was, that she was," he said and found it hard to stifle his emotions. He got out of the car with her after parking and they walked beside each other after she came around.

"Are you coming to join me? I was going to ask, but for some stupid reason assumed you wouldn't be interested. After all I've learned about you today, I guess I shouldn't think that way. You're pretty open-minded, but I shouldn't be so shocked, Flora wouldn't have loved you if you weren't the way you are. She had good taste, good taste in everything. You are welcome to join me though, I'd like that." She had stopped while walking up to the building.

"It's funny, actually. I was instinctively following you. I need to ease into waiting for your Thursday call and I have nothing else to do, so I guess I was just naturally following you. Maybe I thought you might let some more information slip," he said smiling. "I would love to join you."

"That would be nice. We are on time for the Arati and Bhajans, so you will have to chant a little, but it's a good meditative exercise, I'm sure you can handle it. It'll help with your waiting anxiety. And then Prasadam, dinner, is at 6:30. What about your girlfriend or fiancée, or whatever she is, won't she be expecting you?"

"Actually, we just broke up yesterday. I came clean."

"Wow, that is some timing you have there. It's pretty funny, funny and sad, your timing."

Wind agreed with Sutra Diamante through a humble smile and a sullen nod of the head. They walked up to the building. The ruggedness of his American street clothes with work boots and barn jacket crashed like a dry limb on a fire behind her as her orange sari blended with the orange, yellow, and red robes of the congregating crowd. They were just getting out of a Bhagavad-Gita lesson and his contrast

281

fueled the flames of interaction, robes flapping in introduction, bow-ing, and hand-shaking, but soon enough a calmness was resumed and the phosphorescent colors eased in their flux and chanting was ready to begin.

13. ETERNAL RETURN

Ride home, Odin, and be proud of yourself! No more men will
come to visit me, until Loki is loose, escaped from his bonds,
and the Doom of the Gods, tearing all asunder, approaches.
— "Baldr's Dream," *The Poetic Edda*

HE HAD WAITED UNTIL MORNING HAD ALL BUT ABATED, WHEN THE
traffic was lighter everywhere, but in the direction he charged little
stood in his way. I-85 north of the loop passed exit by exit, shopping
center by shopping center, from the strip of home furnishing on the
Dawson Boulevard access road on his right up to Malibu Grand Prix
on his left before the consumer explosion dominating both sides of the
Pleasant Hill exit until the lanes finally thinned along with the shopping opportunities where the city's outer edge gave him the choice to
angle east to Athens. On Highway 316, University Parkway, he rode
in peace among few other cars with the other side of the highway
conveying a thick and constant flow of vehicles back to the city behind.
The first site to strike him on this straight flat four-lane thoroughfare
was a massive car dealership just past the first of 316's stoplights. A
compound ready for deployment, it looked like a steel-field lying at
the bottom of the hill, light reflecting and clashing in every direction

across more cars than there was room in which to drive them. High above this presence flapped violently a gargantuan American flag, behind which towered a billboard, all white except for giant capital red letters reading JESUS. As he passed he looked in his rear-view mirror and saw that the other side was also white with bold red letters that read COMING SOON.

He felt no shock at seeing together the mixed encouragements of patriotism and an announcement of Jesus' imminent arrival. Though it still made him wince a little inside, it was a familiar pairing from life in the South. This ride, especially, he felt as an inter-zone between the New South metropolis of Atlanta and the small, isolated liberal academic atmosphere of Athens. Between Atlanta and its satellite, were indications of the rural field house, farm, or trailer life that consumed the rest of the state, except for maybe Savannah. Jonathan Wind's eyes beheld god's country, particularly of a Protestant Christian god, and the Bible Belt buckled as tightly around the University Parkway as it did around the rest of the non-urban areas of the state. Other than the 1992 election year when Georgia went blue for an Arkansas-born southerner, it had been red since its first homegrown President failed to win a second term, and Wind knew that surely it would go red again next year. He could see that other than Atlanta and Athens, isolated islands of blue anchored in seas of red, what colored the crimson conservative tides lapping at their shores was the plankton of fundamentalist Christian ethics. The rest of his ride revealed all-black billboards bearing in white such witty phrases attributed to "God," as: "Don't make me come down there;" and "I don't question your existence."

Wind discovered this connection between politics and the Christian religion in his adopted state as a young man, years after the death of his father. Driving to Athens was more than driving to the first place Wind had ever verbally called home, it was making a move back in time into the choices of his father, for Nathan Wind loved Athens and after uprooting his family and moving to an unknown place, in the northeastern corner of an unknown state, in an unknown region eight hundred miles from all that he had ever known, he felt remarkably comfortable. Athens was his father's fabled island that he discovered abroad in a treacherous alien sea, a promised land of low buildings, clean air, pine trees, and cicadas, where he could raise his son, expand his family, love his wife, and do his work. After being the next of four generations of New Yorkers, all of whom made their living with their backs more than their brains, this was as far as Nathan had ever imagined the antithetical journey of his life taking him. In Athens, the senior Wind had a school, a department, an office, a community, a neighborhood, a street, a house and a family, all of which he was an active and appreciated part. Even as a young boy, Wind could never imagine that his father died anything but happy.

There was an intersecting road leading in the directions of towns named Carl and Bethlehem and as Wind approached it, he remembered the last time he was here. It was mid-July and he was taking Monica to visit some of her old friends from college. She had two friends, Kimberly and Chelsea, whom she once roomed with, and they still lived in Athens while doing graduate work, Romance Languages and English Literature respectively. Preparing himself for the frivolous and jocular manner he must summon as disguise and defense in the presence of three old sorority sisters at a college town bar, Wind made a small joke. Pointing in the direction of Bethlehem he asked Monica if they should head that way to a Comfort Inn maybe and ask them if there was any room? At first she made a grunting noise since she was anxious to see her friends and thought that he was making an overture towards having their distinct sexual relations at a hotel. When she read the sign and realized the joke her anxiety took another turn, away from the conflict of sexual awkwardness, but just as familiar. She responded by telling him that just because he had no faith of his own did not mean he was entitled to mock the faith of others. His only outward response was to drop his smile of jest for a smile of civility, and after telling her that he was sorry, remain quiet until she spoke again or until he could think of something totally unrelated on which to converse.

This was a familiar tactic for him and driving underneath the light accessing Bethlehem, he replayed thoughts about Monica that he had had that night, a diatribe he worked in his mind over the years, to which he was always adding more points of evidence, but could never convey while together without fear of really severing their connection and even though he wanted so much to say these things last Saturday night, to finally get it all out, he knew it would have been too painful for her, for it was a purge that would have bordered on sadism. The diatribe was a critique of her faith and politics and the shoddy logic that he saw as barely holding it all together. To him it was all derivative for her, she voted and believed as her father told her, which was a further display of her devotion to a wrathful patriarchal god and an almost monarchical obedience to a bellicose president. He couldn't sit with any of the blind observance he perceived and though he knew that he could never know what went on inside her head, he believed that she only thought about these things after accepting the original premise that her father was correct and infallible. Wind found in her the perfect extreme example of *the faithful*, and agreed with Nietzsche when he said that faith meant not wanting to know the truth. She had a truth, which she accepted for no reason he could see and she followed it wholeheartedly. He found this unexamined and unstable core to be the catalyst behind other failures of logic or inconsistencies in her life, about which he extemporized in his diatribe. Her pro-life stance on abortion did not correspond to her views on capital punishment or war; her views on premarital sex fit only within her own definition of what constituted sex; and even her allegiance to Christ-like compassion had very obvious limits and qualifications. For Wind, as they got more committed to their relationship and he learned more about her, he began to see their time together as an exercise in Buddhist compassion and nonjudgment. To chill the boil of the diatribe that was always ready and simmering beneath the surface, Wind would concentrate on his breathing and try not to think about anything except maybe a mantra of love and acceptance. On this highway, that night three months ago, just as he did now, Wind calmed himself with thoughts of Flora, once a living mantra and mandala, and as his pulse calmed that night and again this morning she was as real to him as she ever was.

As far as Wind's own worldview, if politics had any sort of overlap with religion it happened in a theoretical way. Other than his own role in civil law, the enforcement and upholding of it, contemporary politics interested him less and less the more and more futility he found in it. His education in political science had as much to do with how people acted and how societies operated as did his study of philosophy, religion, and literature. Deeper than his role as investigator, his theoretical worldview has always been sympathetic to a very liberal combination of Plato's philosopher-king and Joseph Campbell's hero with a thousand faces. Wind tried to avoid seeing himself at their intersection, but there is a cyclical nature to his conception of self and his conception of this ideal. The philosopher-king is the perfect leader because he would not seek that power out, he would be called to serve, and the archetypal hero returns because he must, to bring enlightenment. He thought it to be a naive ideal and didn't share it with others, the dream that there could be a leader worth following who was all three, philosopher, king, and hero. Mostly, he agreed with Nietzsche that if the world had a goal it would have reached it already.

Wind followed 316 expectantly until the overpass above the 10-Loop where it exchanged its name for another and within this loop, itself a small and ovular I-285, and he felt no longer like he was seeking, but arriving, and proceeded to take this same thoroughfare now called Epps Bridge Road until it merged at a joint into the Atlanta Highway, a road which with one more name change would take him straight into the heart of town from the east. Climbing the hill after Atlanta Highway became Broad Street, Athens, for one moment, looked like a metropolis, or a city at least, the horizon blocked by the few tall buildings. Settled on the plateau of downtown Broad Street, it's again in the proportional context of a small college town of about 100,000 people, approximately 35,000 of whom are students. Wind drove through it but wanted to walk it, feel the town beneath his feet and breathe it in his lungs. Students crossed the street around him on foot and bicycle. Passing the emblematic arch on his right, representing the school and the entrance to UGA's North Campus, and the center of downtown on his left, Wind drove slowly, scanning for a parking spot down to Jackson Street where he turned left. After the next street, a one-way, he turned left where he could and then left again, doubling back on College Avenue, heading straight back into the center of downtown towards the arch and luckily found a spot right before the road ended into Broad.

Wind walked across College Avenue to Blue Sky Coffee and with every step he took he couldn't fail to acknowledge that he had stepped in each place before as a child, that this town, though not the place of physical birth, was a place of many little births leading up to his father's death, his second great birth. The late morning sun was swelling towards a noon sun and students sat smoking, talking, and reading at the tables outside of Blue Sky. He passed through the clouds and entered the cafe immediately in line for counter service. This morning Wind woke from the soundest and longest night of sleep since Flora's death and restless to be home, got in the car straight from showering. Now he needed coffee, it was his prime directive in reaching downtown after letting his soft tired mind ramble on the highway. The line moved and his hunger for food grew with smelling coffee; it was a hunger linked with his sleep, a body craving energy, but it was also a stronger craving for food than he had felt in a week. Each new day he was waking up a little more.

When he reached the register and the smiling face waiting at the end of the line, he had decided to just get coffee and go elsewhere for food since the snacks they served here were not enough for what he needed. For a moment he looked down and thought before ordering and when his eyes rose to graciously ask for a double espresso, the fresh young face was still smiling. The skin of her face had yet to stretch or fall, and its youthful promise looked and smelled so clean to him that he could even pick up the scent of cucumber melon moisturizer through the clouds of steam and coffee grounds. As they interacted with smiles and pleasantness, her face in its nuances was clear to him, unfettered by hair, a mass of brown curls held back and mane-like by a black headband. Her airy eyes were made even more blue by the cerulean Blue Sky t-shirt, and he followed her small nose down the center of her face to a small chin point, drawing together

her wide jaw and high and wide cheeks, free and wide with promise. He lowered his eyes as he took his change and brought them back up to say thank you, have a nice day; a bashful act, and flirty, saved by its welcomed return. From the register and the store he walked, feeling as if that beautiful young girl was an old friend welcoming him home.

Outside he stepped a few yards to the left and bought a paper. Walking back past Blue Sky he caught bits of conversation from those at the tables, scattered pieces of dialogue, what a professor said, what a friend did, what happened over the weekend, what band played. Some smoked, some drank coffee, some read quietly and the sun, reaching towards its peak, shone down on them all equally and in the light they all looked familiar to Wind, like friends from school or friends from Atlanta. He could know some of these people, he thought, maybe he should know some of these people, in their hipster dress and their familiarity with indie bands, but he felt so much older than them all and insecure with the self image of police officer for a moment. However, two appetites drove him: one of emotion and nostalgia; and the other of literary bodily hunger; so he made the rational effort to bridge both and keep on walking. Turning right onto East Clayton Street, he walked down to a restaurant on the left where the street ended. Before the last building on Clayton was a vacant lot and he could not remember what was once there, if anything was once there, but the gap on the street felt like a gap in his memory, a vacant lot he could not fill. After the lot, he was back to old bricks, basic rectangles, but worn and sandy in color, and as he saw a blonde couple in t-shirts and sweat pants enter the restaurant before him he almost jogged the rest of the way to secure his place in line for a table he was so excited.

There was a table left, one for two, in the back corner by the window facing out onto Thomas Street beneath the blue bird logo and the restaurant's name, The Blue Bird Cafe. From where the host indicated for him to sit, Wind could see all around the rectangular room and out both windowed walls onto the intersecting streets. He couldn't remember it ever being this crowded inside when he was a child, but he tried to take into account the reduced size of his last perspective. There was hardly room to walk around and the servers had to weave carefully between the tables carrying coffeepots and plates. How well did he fit as a child? Did he hide and play between the tables when there was no one sitting at them? He couldn't picture his childhood here, but the feel of the room was the same with the same walls and carpet, and even the tables seemed to be the same. With these pieces of his past all around, he hungered to escape his present and all the complications of life, and ease back into the feelings that tingled his skin. He hoped the food would take him comfortably back, he was so hungry and he wanted to eat his way into his past, like Alice eating the right cupcake or drinking the right potion to make her impassibly adaptable to a new situation. He wouldn't be ordering the same things he did as a child; the menu had to have changed since then.

The waiter in a robin's egg baseball hat, a beaded necklace, a Frisbee football t-shirt, and baggy blue jeans stood before him and spoke in a voice stoned, bright, slow, and pleasant.

"Hey, do you know what you are going to order yet? Actually, let me get your drink order first. So, do you know what you want to drink?"

"A coffee and a water, thank you."

"Alright. I'll come back and see what you want to order when I bring back your drinks."

Wind didn't need more coffee to feel more awake, espresso for him kicks in almost immediately, psychosomatically, just from the smell. He was ordering more coffee because he wanted the whole situation. It wasn't rational, but he wanted to step into the whole set-up that he imagined for himself coming back here, the whole scenario mixed from memory and imagination of sitting in here and sitting in the place of his father. The extra caffeine intake would have him wired, but he'd try to regulate his system with water. Either way, it was no price to pay, being a little wired for the rest of the day in which he had nothing to do but wait, all so he could feel this homecoming.

It was longer than he liked—but as long as he expected with the amount of seated clientele and the stoned vibe of the waiter—before he was able to place his order. He had looked at the menu thoroughly and could not tell if anything had changed in twenty years since last he was here. He wanted breakfast foods and the first page was covered with an international roster of omelets. His glazed gaze centered at the bottom of the list, around the Huevos Rancheros and Breakfast Burrito. Like the last generation of Wind-man to patronize this establishment, he was enamored of the abundance and quality of Mexican food in Georgia. Where the father's proclivity for the cuisine emerged out of an allure of the unfamiliar, the son's was born out of his actual environment. An observation he made in college while living in Manhattan, was that it lacked, in comparison to Atlanta, the diversity and aptitude of Mexican restaurants. His basic hypothesis was that the farther one travels from the border, especially north and east, the lesser the Mexican food. New York had a large Latin community filled with Puerto Ricans and Dominicans, among others, but it had nothing as Mexican as La Buford, where he found Tia Maite, whose advice and calendar governed a sizable population of whose number he could only speculate.

When the sweet and slow waiter returned, Wind ordered the Huevos Rancheros and, expecting another long wait before the food was actually brought out to him, he picked up the *Atlanta Journal-Constitution* that had sat in the empty place on the table. The front page predicted clouds and scattered showers to go with the high of seventy-one. For the sixth day of October, it was what he had come to expect from the region and though the clouds outside had yet to solidify or break, he was ready for it to happen at any moment and either pass away instantly or last for the next three days. What really grabbed his eye beyond the raining cloud graphic in the top left corner were the headlines that corresponded to the thoughts on his drive here, the headlines of religion and politics. Bold above the fold, the biggest headline read ISRAEL HITS SYRIAN TARGET, while beneath it another headline read 3 DIE IN CHURCH SHOOTING above a big color photo that led under the fold for the story. Foreign and domestic religio-political violence sharing the same page. Instead of reading the international account, which he imagined had a higher casualty rate, he was stuck on the photograph of women dressed for church, crying and embracing, their walnut skin and attire so Southern to him.

The story was nothing sensational, just sad, random, and true; the kind of incident he had seen dozens of times. All they knew was that a woman brought a gun to church, a .44 caliber handgun. She was newly out of a mental health facility, returning to church for the first time, and shot the reverend, her mother, and then herself. The actions were clear, in how they happened, in the details, but as far as this day-old story was concerned, there was no understanding as to meaning, what caused the actions to happen, what led to their arising. The woman was dead and free of the pain she caused, free from what pain led her there in the first place. The article conveyed the sentiment that we will never know why she did this unless she left a diary. With this Wind couldn't agree. No ends are ever loose, everything is connected, everyone and everything leaves a trail. If he didn't believe this there would be no point in his job, he couldn't do it, or he would be lying to himself and of this, every once in a while, he had to remind himself. Over the last week, he had reminded himself every day.

What he found to be the saddest part of the article, and intentionally so, was that the lead line read, before it went on to tell the reader that the parishioners were mourning outside the taped-off church, "They were supposed to be inside their church singing 'Nearer My God to Thee.'" The irony of the line was a little insensitive for him, but it too was as true and sad as what had happened.

With flushed cheeks on bone-hued skin, the waiter returned carrying a wide plate. Placed before the view of the hungry mind and body was the order of Huevos Rancheros that filled the whole circle of the plate, a warm wheat tortilla beneath a thick and fluffy disc of yellow eggs covered in pinto beans, tomatoes, jack cheese, sour cream, and jalapeños. Ten inches in diameter, protein packed, carbohydrate based, and cheese covered, all salty, savory, spicy, and sweet from the cream. It was exactly what he wanted, what he needed, and unable to pick it up he cut into it and did not stop cutting until he was done. He took time to chew and breathe, but his fork and knife were never put down together. If the knife went down to allow that hand to raise the water glass for sipping, the fork was always poised and ready. In the moment while he ate, he stepped out of time, as can happen for him at a crime scene, while reading, sketching, or when making love to Flora; and in this moment out of time there was no decay, no recession, only what there was in a state of total being and though while in the moment it was impossible to acknowledge it without losing it and stepping out of it, he would acknowledge the second he finished. Flora had often said that their lovemaking was not just a unifying act for the two of them, but also an open-eyed meditation for each of them individually. Sometimes she used a term that Sutra taught her to describe these moments out of time that they shared and experiencing individually. The term was "bardo," and she told him that in the Tibetan Buddhist tradition it meant a space, like interstitial space, between one life and the next incarnation. It originally came from the Bun tradition of pre-Buddhist Tibet, but the term found a place in other forms of Buddhism beyond reincarnation to express that space where anything is possible, a moment, even the most quick and flickering one, where someone has full control over their karma. Of course most of us, she told him, fall into habits and repetitive actions in those moments of bardo and fail to embrace the multitude of possibilities.

Presently, he embraced the moment by fully experiencing it, while eating he thought of nothing, felt nothing, and experienced nothing but the Huevos Rancheros, their taste, their texture and the feeling of satiation as they filled his mouth, stomach, and then whole being. Flora had quite the effect on his life.

The check came sooner than he expected. When he was done eating it was already there. He must not have noticed when the waiter came slowly and silently by to leave it. He got up and paid and left. He was full and ready to go. Not too full, but sated in a way that still left a little hunger for movement, smells, and sensations. Out on the street, the clouds had yet to cluster and feeling the sun unfettered through the thin teal of the sky made him question if they would today. The slope of the white parted plastic hair on the head of the Jimmy Carter Pez dispenser anchored his left thumb, the whole dispenser being gripped lightly around its peanut butter colored stem. He popped the peach brick from the neck of the sweet smiling President and as Wind crunched and swished the flavored saliva in his mouth he thought of how pleased his father would be to see that face on a Pez dispenser, that smiling face that made his father feel welcomed in a state he once governed. They had arrived in the summer of 1978, in June, with time to settle in before the semester, and enough time and distance from the last Wynnton Stocking Strangler attack in Atlanta to feel safe—though right before the Atlanta Child Murders rocked the whole region. Regardless, Nathan Wind's faith in his choice was reinforced while during his second month into the semester the Camp David Peace Accord was brokered.

All the way to his car, he felt that he had just gotten started in town, that his Athens experience was in motion despite the fact he had no exact plan for his visit. He liked seeing the town though, the downtown blocks very much the same as they always were and though the names of bars had changed and there were stores he didn't recognize, the actual buildings were untouched. The initial boom for Athens, beyond just being a football town, was with rock groups in the early '80s when Wind was growing up here; and though he was too young to enjoy the bar or club scene, he still felt the charged energy of the place. Part of the charge for him personally was his father's own love of the place and his interactions with local artists and musicians.

Driving north within the blocks of downtown, Wind was rolling over streets he once ran beside, but he was no longer thinking of this, he was merely looking at the buildings, the signs, and the students walking around, noticing how much everything had changed, like Atlanta when he came back from New York. He turned left at Dougherty Street and after the intersection of Pulaski Street it became Prince Avenue, and he cruised on autopilot, his sense of direction reflexive; he knew where he was going. Out of the immediate blocks of downtown, this strip showed its southern colors with a Baptist Church, then a Catholic Church before getting to another Baptist Church. After the first two churches, on his left he passed four pillars of blue lights and read that they belonged to Go Bar, a corner establishment behind bushes and part of a historic looking building, that it shared with a restaurant called The Grit; which though new since he last lived near, he heard about all the way in Atlanta for its southern vegetarian cuisine and landmark status.

At the third church on the street, he turned right onto Grady Avenue and was overcome by how little it had changed. Of course it was smaller, but also it was cleaner, brighter, and shinier than it held up even in his fondest memories. He paused in front of the only apartment building on the street, the small two-story De Ville Apartments. Some of the houses he saw were being renovated, but they all had a look of clean newness like he had entered the Disney World version of his past. He swung a U-turn at Dubose Street and stopped the car on Grady along the backyard of the Taylor-Grady House, a historic colonial that faced out onto Prince. Beneath the sheltering bough and scenic array of maple, dogwood, and sycamore trees, he walked in the shade on the sidewalk down his street. He first physically opened his eyes in Queens, New York, and took his first steps there, but this is where he saw the world for the first time and ran fast and free across its surface. Passing De Ville again, he walked on the west side of the street. He was looking for his house, which he had not lived in nor seen in the last twenty years. Almost halfway down the street he found it, not by its appearance, but by the street number, 169, which he had committed to memory as a boy of four so that in the case he was ever lost he could find a policeman and tell him that he lived at 169 Grady Avenue and could he please be shown home.

The house had the shape that he remembered, but it was very different to behold. It stood like a shed, like a movie set that was only painted board and concealed behind support posts and the illusion of a third dimension. The memory he retained and stoked at life moments overcome by nostalgia, insecurity, or the mourning of his father, was that of the pictures his mother had of the house, and now he realized it was not the house as it stood in reality. It was painted white still, a fading chipping eggshell white, and renovations were in the beginning stages. His childhood home was not only aging along with him, but it was being reborn without him, reborn for others, for their lives, pleasures, and pursuits; yet it was still the same house. Looking at the yard, the overhanging sycamore trees, it was difficult for him to summon up the young Jonathan, the boy barreling, skipping, and skidding; Big Wheeling, biking, and skateboarding through the powder-fresh, golden days of perpetual youth and knavery before the death of Nathan Wind brought that all to an end.

So as not to draw suspicion, Wind, ebbing between youthful and present self, walked past the house, still on the west side, with the intention of doubling back on the east side when he got to the avenue's end at Boulevard Street, to steal another look. As he walked, he tried to think of all the things that transpired within its two-storied frame. There he first learned about the other peoples of the world, interesting people, artistic and intellectual, who attended his father's department parties. He learned that his parents were not alone in their knowledge and he needed to study more to keep up. Books were the most common, natural part of life in this house. Not that the physical dimension of life was neglected, the young lungs of transplanted-Yankee Jonathan pumped as much as any other boy his age, but at the park, going for a walk, or relaxing in the living room there was always a book in accompaniment to either of his parents. While Nathan tried to share as much of the world's great works with his son from the age of two, when they first taught him to read, it was his mother who rounded it out for him in works that though still educational, were more fitting for a child of two through six. The father, never one to coddle or baby, aspired to create in his son the contemporary embodiment of such famous prodigies as Jeremy Bentham and John Stuart Mill. Always on task, when Nathan thought it nice to relate to young Jonathan's interest in animals the animal stories he choose to read to his boy consisted of Aristotle's *Animals*, Darwin's *Origin of Species*, and Orwell's *Animal Farm*.

The mother was there with all the devices in her maternal arsenal to make sure the boy did not go mad in the ways that Bentham and Mill did. She read the boy Dr. Seuss in his earliest days and progressed accordingly in complement to the father's teachings. As little Jonathan aged, she stepped to her husband's shelves and drew works that interested her and that she also found important to her son's upbringing. Interested in the place to which they moved, she read aloud, with him on her lap reading along, Native American folk tales and mythological stories, particularly of the Cherokee. It seemed to him now that she was listening to the land, like Lao had said. She was responding to what was there before they got there. He didn't think that she thought it out or intended it the way Lao said, but she was doing it naturally as a considerate and empathetic human. She was going back all the way, to get all that the land had to say. It is easy to soak up the western, European influence, tales of conquest are practically the same across the land and that voice is loud and manipulative, but the voice of the land that was there before, the voice of those that were there before and was almost entirely snuffed out, now barely more than a breath or sigh; that was the challenge of listening that young

Jonathan's mother accepted. Drives and walks helped them investigate this new place to which they moved, to see the land and to feel it, but the wife of Nathan Wind made sure the investigation was also conducted on a textual level.

The picture he held most vividly in his head from the Cherokee readings he and his mother performed, was that of their cosmology. The image had been tugging at the peripheral of his visual mind since last Friday in the library, but now standing in front of his childhood home, looking at its square frame from the opposite side of the street, he could see the image from where he first possessed it. Age three he remembered in little bright patches of scenes with nebulous lines of demarcation. He could not tell you the day of the week or even the month, but one day that year he sat on that porch, on the lap of his mother, on a white wood bench no longer there, swinging from the overhang by creaky steel chains. She held the big book open along his thighs, the cover was cool in the air and he could recall the feel of it on his skin; so it might have been summer or at least not winter. When the chains creaked, he would look at them, at the little bits of rust flaking off at the joints as if the sound was from them and their movement. He could smell his mother, no perfume, for she rarely wore it, but the smell of her skin, her hair, her deodorant, and the soap on her hands, all one smell of mother. When his mother read he followed along, matching the words on the page to the sounds she was making as he had been instructed as far back as he could remember. He made the sounds in his head and kept still his lips. They swung and read, swinging like the world of the Cherokee story before them, a land drawn out of the sea and tethered to the sky in its four corners. The story told how the Cherokee made baskets because of this, with four main ribs like the four supports that held the world intact, in balance. The young Jonathan could picture this so clearly, swinging in the safety of his mother's arms. He saw the whole continent, or his amorphous version of its shape, that he knew they had just traveled almost halfway across, hanging from the sky and rocking in a gentle balanced sway with the ocean's tides.

Notwithstanding the exposure his mother gave him to the voice of the land before the arrival of Europeans, she was also responsible in providing his own mixed European heritage back to him. She would tell him that it was there anyway, so he might as well embrace it enough to understand it. In these Edenic Athens days, young Jonathan did not yet understand colonial-guilt white people or Holocaust-guilt for those of Germanic origins. Nevertheless, Nathan's family line was once the family Windauga, a genealogy through Germany, Norway, and back again; its "wind-eye" translation, pointing to only one sure fact, that one of his ancestors built windows. Wind always wondered if that piece of genealogical and etymological tidbit contributed to his becoming a stoically observing investigator. His father provided the scholarly trivia, but his mother's myth-readings gave it color and form.

Walking back to his car, he thought of the story of Ragnarok, the Norse eschatology, which his mother read him out of the same book of mythology as the Cherokee account, and how intertwined they had become in his mind. Judeo-Christian, Muslim, Hindu, Shinto, Meso-American, and an array of other cosmologies found their way into that book, together side by side with the same treatment, as if they were all fictions, but beautiful, important fictions. Ragnarok was part of his genetic memory, but just as much a part of his physical, spiritual, and creative one as the Cherokee worldview. He acknowledged that he was the product of many pasts, and maybe this was the intention of Lao's "listening to the land."

There was a pressure in the corners of his eyes, a welling that he resisted, but he knew that it was true, no matter where she was now, what boyfriend she was off with, or how little they talked or related to each other anymore, it was true that because of her he was the whole person he is now. His father was the mind, the science, but she was the heart and the myth of his upbringing. That was before she had to become both, and after which he felt that the heart suffered. Where was she now—other than sailing around the Caribbean—where was she in her life, and where had she been since he left her and home for school, to return a man and a stranger. It had been so long that he couldn't sort out who had really changed since he left, himself or her, but wasn't it supposed to be him at his age?

He sat in the driver's seat of his car on the street on which he grew up. Part of his mother died with his father, in most ways that part was totally gone from the world except how it lived inside of him; it was there, her heart, her love, and that identity he could not see any longer in her present life and action. And it was that part of him, from her, that had the adult Jonathan poised and ready within his own imagination and conviction to ride like Sigurd with no fear in his heart. To turn the key and gun the engine, without need of warming, his feet on clutch and accelerator like golden spurs, he felt at once like a Nibelung or the bearer of Nibelung craftsmanship on Honda's fleshless recreation of Grani. His Brynhild was never far from his mind as he presided over his past, for his Brynhild too was a spiritual warrior, a reader of dreams, and one who was damned by some god's wrath to a fate of fire or love; but she could love only the fearless. So fearlessly he changed lanes on Prince Avenue, gauging the lines of cars ahead, estimating movements and motives, speeding up, stopping, changing lanes again, always with a blinker, always careful not to tailgate, but encouraging them with his closeness and signal, and if he could not move them he would find the right timing to route and shoot farther down the Avenue. There was a ring in his path, a ring of fire and like I-285 wrapped around Atlanta, that ring of fire wrapped around the one he sought. He would charge that ring, fearless like his mount, and through its fire he will not be burned, but delivered to her, what is left of her, what he does not have, what he does not know. With the conviction, courage, and grim determination of Sigurd, and all the Burgundian, Norse, and Teutonic kings resounding within, he drove out of Athens, out of his past, back to her, back to the ring of fire, back to Atlanta.

14. LOGOS

The origin and primitive form of the language game is a re-action; only from this can more complicated forms develop. Language—I want to say—is a refinement, "in the beginning was the deed."

—Ludwig Wittgenstein, *Culture and Value*

THE SUN, PHOEBUS, AT POSITION, WEST, LATE, WANING AND DECLINING in his tired route and intensity, was still able to make a shadow with what power he had left, striking the yellow umbrella, which stood by means of a wooden pole out of the metal table, and causing a lightless reproduction of its shape to fall just beyond the stitched borders onto the floor and the neighboring chairs. The two men sat at the table with their arms under the umbrella and their legs turned east into the shadow, their backs to the Sun so their eyes could avoid the blinding of his glare and the nape of their necks could feel the warmth of his light. The two men were talking and they had been talking since before they were seated, since they met at the Starbucks on Highland Avenue and caught a ride down here with an employee ending his shift and heading in this direction. In the car they gave some obligatory attention to the driver, asked him about his night, where it would take him, his off day tomorrow, but if he were to lull, they returned to their own thoughts locked in discussion. Six o'clock being early enough on a Thursday, they were to be seated immediately, and smiling at the young attractive server, they proceeded silently up stairs behind her until they stood, before they took their seats and resumed spilling words, on the roof dining area of Six Feet Under.

"Oh, man, so that guy I work with, Cullen, he's a great guy, a DJ, a really great guy and we have a lot of good times at work. He has this amazing taste in music, really open-minded and versatile. All the bands I know, he knows already. He has over a thousand records. I've met some hack DJs, but he knows his shit. And he has actually opened me up to a lot of dance music, played me a lot of the good stuff, that now I can appreciate, not listen to all the time, but appreciate. So talking to him about music is great and even movies, not really books, he doesn't seem to read more than he has to, but movies, he has some great taste in, likes the French New Wave stuff a lot, the Godard, and all the American stuff influenced by that French stuff, a little too much Tarantino for my liking, but that's cool. Anyway, my point is that culturally he seems like this progressive open-minded, really sharp guy, but occasionally he will say some things and it turns out he believes in Hell. Not in some fun heavy metal way, but really believes in an afterlife Hell and Heaven, the whole shebang, end of days, God's Judgment, second coming, Jesus' love; all that shit."

Jack Thoth was taking his turn to direct over-flowing thoughts through words at Jonathan Wind, or Jonny as his old Atlanta friends called him, and his break in thinking and speaking came right as the waitress approached. She wore a blue t-shirt with yellow Six Feet Under lettering, and smiled wide and perkily to the two men seated before her. She put her left hand on the back of Wind's chair so he had to turn dramatically to listen and from this place of power in discourse she asked them if they wanted anything to drink while they waited. Appreciating the restaurant's appreciation of the local breweries, they both ordered draught beers by Sweetwater.

"Baptist?" asked Wind, resuming.

"Totally, and really in touch with its Calvinist roots. He was raised that way and seems to have no intention of growing out of it or letting it go. I mean, he doesn't wear a cross or proselytize or anything, but it is there, just what he says he believes. He still drinks and smokes and even smokes dope with me sometimes. I don't even think he goes to church regularly, but apparently it's all there all the time. One day, it was great, I just started pointing out people who came in and asking about some we knew and getting him to tell me who is going to Hell and who is going to Heaven. So I had him playing Judging God and he was all about it and most people we knew are going to Hell. I am. He wasn't though, he seemed to know some way to Heaven, some sort of path to salvation. I mean, I like the guy. Whatever, I don't care what he believes or says he believes."

"I agree. Whatever. Believe what you want, but I prefer if people are consistent. I don't mind theists, as long as they hold it down the line. Those, I can talk to. I don't even mind crazies if they are consistent." Wind spoke quickly, feeling the approach of the waitress and then she was there with her smile and their beers, beaming. Both men said thank you and Wind could tell, as she stood between them, that Jack was looking at her bare legs reaching down from a dark denim skirt. When she moved around Wind to the stairs, he turned his head quickly to see her slip through the doorway, ponytail bouncing. He turned back to Jack who was drawing up his glass and Wind went to match him.

"Yeah sure," Jack sipped the top off the amber froth in the tall draught glass. "I don't care what he believes because we get along well. Which is kind of my point, why I brought him up. It doesn't match as consistent to what I would suppose from the other stuff about him, but what do I know. I guess he's a dogmatist. Well, yes, I will say, yes, he is a dogmatist, but he isn't oppressive, he isn't trying to convert anyone that I know of, or change anyone's beliefs. He just thinks that everyone is going to Hell, it's negative, but ambivalent. Humorously ambivalent, is what I enjoy the most about it. I've tried to bring up some other issues with him, the war, capital punishment, abortion, especially abortion, and he just isn't too into philosophizing or theologizing really. He does tow a pro-life party line, but he takes it down the line. That you'd like. As a pro-lifer, he doesn't just reserve it for fetuses. If he voted he would vote Republican, but that is because he is anti-abortion. He's still against capital punishment and the war in Iraq. So at least that is consistent," said Jack.

"Remember, Sartre always sided with the underdog, just for the sake of consistency," Wind added.

"That old Fartre, Sartre. Isn't that from a Tom Robbins book, Skinny Legs maybe? The old Fartre needed to read his Emerson, he was a big mind, a great mind... or maybe just a good mind, but those still have their hobgoblins too." Jack punctuated this with his own version of a hobgoblin-like expression, his typical "crazy face" that exhibited how intense his eyes could be and how tight and sunken his cheeks could get, with the help of his thin long neck, a look like that of a meerkat peeking up out of its burrow.

"Nice hobgoblin, but you still look like a meerkat. Your Starbucks tale does remind me of a guy I knew at NYU though. He was a sweet guy, really crunchy and hippy, from Western Massachusetts. Everyone liked him because he was really nice, but he was a little stony and spacey, not much with the long- or short-term memory and that would drive me nuts, as I am sure you can imagine, but I hung out with him occasionally. He was pretty smart, with a good mind, smarter in situations than he seemed interaction-wise, but when his mind focused it really honed in. Beneath the stoner veneer his mind was a machine and created exacting visual art and was slowly leading him away from creative pursuits into the realm of higher math and computer science. Mostly he did really exacting stuff in those fields, and I liked to talk to him about it, but nothing too abstract or theoretical, more engineering than psychics and very little philosophy. So whenever we did run into each other in a mutual friend's dorm room, I would try to see if he was taking any of that rigid math and engineering stuff, that can get so tedious to me, and applying it to bigger pictures or cosmologies, test-driving it on the streets outside of its very limited systems and structures. I would ask about physics and philosophy and it would really irk me that he had all this knowledge and was such a nice guy and then would say something about *the meaning of life*. The big question, *the meaning of life*, and the goal of science and philosophy to discover this *meaning of life*."

Wind was worked up, working through his memories and back to the comfort level he felt with his own body of knowledge in college, and gestured largely with his hands as he said the words "the meaning of life," for emphasis and comic appeal to try and avoid the unavoidable attitude of condescension.

"Man, yeah, that's a loaded statement, or just extremely vague, did he ever elaborate what he meant?" Jack responded.

"No, at the time I never pushed it. I tried to steer towards some exact existential or theoretical questions and avoided such a dangerously trite phrase. I always held my tongue. He was a nice, sweet guy, so I never railed into him with the usual line of questioning like: can you define your terms; and why are you starting from the supposition that there is a meaning of life; and why with that supposition are you positing that there is only one meaning; and what do you mean by life, do you mean human existence..." Wind trailed off, feeling like an asshole, and sipped his beer.

"I am sure he eventually got beyond it. I remember by his senior year he had gotten into mathematicians who were pretty philosophical, you know, some Gödel, Russell, and Whitehead. I am sure they added a much fuller take to his question."

"What was his name, did you ever mention him to me before?" Jack asked.

"I don't think I ever mentioned him, we weren't that close. His real name was Abram, but his nickname was Piz, he came in with it. Everyone called him that too, he was introduced as Piz." He chuckled as he said the name.

"What did it mean? How did he get the nickname Piz?" Jack was laughing too and shaking his head.

"That is the funniest part, he didn't remember. His friends back home gave it to him, stoners in Western Mass. At some point he was dubbed Piz, but no one remembered how or why it came about. He had a friend from home visit once and I asked the kid, hoping his memory was better than Piz's or at least if it was as selective it had retained his friend's name's origin, but no. Nothing. He had been Piz for years and no one remembered why. I always assumed that it was zip backwards." Wind too shook his head now as he laughed.

"That is how tradition happens, no one cares about origins, as long as you keep up a tradition. It's seniority that matters. Speaking of Piz traditions, you still sporting Pez?"

"Right here," Wind said, as he reached into his jacket pocket and drew out a Pope John Paul II Pez dispenser with rosy pink plastic cheeks, movie star smile, and white ringed hair under the white skull cap. "I thought the pope was fitting today, thought you'd like it. Want one with your beer, it's kiwi-lime flavored, yum, great with beer, ki-wi-lime?" Wind looked down at the Papal face and tipped the head back to show Jack the neon green brick in the neck shaft. After he shut it he stood it up on the table between them facing Jack.

"Man, that shit kills me." Jack laughed and shook his head smiling wide, a middle arc between his jaw and cheek lines. "It's so funny. You, a cop, Detective Jonathan Wind, trained and licensed to carry a gun, but what else does he have in his holster, a Pez dispenser. Your own little tradition and superstition, you always have one of those. Don't leave home without one, without your secular religious apparatus. Like all that other religious ephemera that looks like crap to some and to others is regarded as sacred. Is that from the world leaders series? Or religious leaders? Man, put that shit away, I don't want JP II looking at me any more," said Jack, chortling as he spoke.

Wind grabbed the dispenser by the stem and clicked the head up and down a couple of times at his friend before returning it to his pocket.

"So, man, how've you been recently? Last week you didn't look all that hot and now you look better, but it seems like there is still some cloud around you you're walking around in. Is it work stuff?"

"Yeah. Some work stuff. And some other stuff. I'm taking a break though," he lifted his beer to Jack and took a big gulp. He swallowed and sighed, looked down and back up. "Monica and I broke up. Actually I broke up with Monica." He said it like an admission more than a confession, just giving plain fact, something for Jack to chew on.

311

"Huh. I'm sorry, man. I guess. How was that? Wow. From what I know about that girl, that couldn't have been easy. How did it go?" His face now serious.

"No, ha, it wasn't. It was a long rocky night to end a long and rocky relationship." Wind shrugged slightly and half-smiled.

"She must have been shocked, or you been holding out on me. From what you had told me, with all her marriage talk, she couldn't have seen this coming. I'm surprised you got out of there alive." Jack made a slow clawing motion with his free left hand. "That girl could be vicious and didn't care who saw, either. Man."

With knowing nods they lifted their beer glasses and sipped deeply, leaving such small amounts that quick concerned looks came from both faces as they wondered where the waitress was before Jack continued.

"Man, I'm sorry. I feel for you, I do. I've been through it all before."

"Thanks, I know you have. I'm okay."

"I am just shocked you lasted as long as you did. What, like three years? Three years with a virgin, a Catholic virgin. You are a more dedicated man than I. She never even wore a Catholic school girl outfit... that I know of." Jack cocked his head interrogatively and Wind and shook his head. "I just can't believe you could handle being with someone so Catholic, and conservatively so. She was a true believer and you are a dirty godless liberal atheist."

"I'm not an atheist. I'm an agnostic, a Clarence Darrow agnostic by his definition. He wrote an essay conveniently titled 'Why I am an Agnostic' where he gives his great critique of religion, particularly Christianity. He established himself as a doubter and goes on to tackle the flaws and inherent silliness he sees. It's a little weak and dated in the religious scholarship area, but he wasn't a religious scholar anyway. It's also a bit condescending too. He can't fathom how the intelligent rational person can take any of what he sees in a religion seriously. He ends it well though, he says, 'The fear of God is not the beginning of wisdom. The fear of God is the death of wisdom. Skepticism and doubt lead to study and investigation, and investigation is the beginning of wisdom."

"Yeah, sure, that's great, but you are not a doubter."

"Sure I am. I get it from Descartes. What's the line?"

"De omnibus dubitandum."

"Yes, all is to be doubted. He used it in his work, skepticism as a place to start from. A place to reason from. I guess we can take it all the way up to quantum physics, Gödel's 'Incompleteness Theory' and Heisenberg's 'Uncertainty.'"

"Yeah, again, that's all great, those are great theories and who could ever fault Clarence Darrow—which was nice, by the way, referencing Darrow—but that is so not you. It's so not you. You might like those ideas and maybe ultimately agree with them, but it's not you. You are all about certainty. You might like to speculate, but you solve crimes for a living. You *solve* them. It's all hard facts for you, no loose ends. The physics you mention and this agnosticism is all about loose ends. You can't handle that."

"Maybe in regards to daily life I stick to the parameters of logic and reason, I operate the system as the system dictates for maximum efficiency. But in the case of a transcendent ultimate reality, metaphysics, a deity, for all of that, I am agnostic."

As if the discussion was resolved or ended, Wind drank the last of his beer, but he knew it was not over. The waitress emerged from the doorway to the stairs behind Wind and Jack waved her over. She had two more Sweetwaters already with her and told them that she took the chance that they both wanted another. They thanked her, letting her know she was right.

"Ah, certainty," Jack said before they both sipped. "She took a chance on it and it paid off for all of us. You are a dogmatist in your own way with your causality. You are the worst kind too, hiding your dogma in pragmatism, in the idea that it isn't dogma: 'It's just common sense, it just makes sense.'"

"Oh yeah, well at least I am actually doing something, producing something, engaging with life and the world. You're a dilettante of the intellect," said Wind.

"I prefer sensualist of the mind, thank you," Jack interrupted.

"You work at a Starbucks, but you read ancient Greek, French, and German. Your BA is from St. John's College and you excelled in that great books program. It's a cooler degree than I have, one I always envied. You read everything and occasionally research graduate programs you're interested in for cultural studies or film or history or political science or philosophy or classics or art history and yet you never actually apply to any. I always thought it was great, back before we went off for school, when you used to say that you didn't want to actually ever produce anything. You said to me that I had law school and Lao wrote computer programs and Stew played guitar and Nigel wrote poetry and you didn't want to do or produce anything. You didn't want to have a thing. You just wanted to think, and then relay those thoughts to others at your own will. But the only place you can do that is in an academic environment and you're not doing anything about that. Now you are just serving coffee and occasionally making your customers feel stupid."

"What can I say, I am worse than modern man in the crisis of too much freedom. I am the postmodern man in the crisis of hyper-reality. Maybe I am just too lazy and cheap to apply and pay application fees. Or maybe that whole academic world is all a big mausoleum, and if there is no more metanarrative any more, everything is equally valid and right, and every thing is just text, then I can read the world from anywhere, even a Starbucks. Marshall McLuhan said that the text is only as complicated as the reader, right? We read with and out of our past."

"Don't get me started on that crap. Most of it's forty years old and I think we are all ready to move on."

"You're right. I'll give you Heidegger though. He wasn't a po-mo, but they wrestle with him a lot and invoke him and try to keep breaking him down. He, like Nietzsche, was just trying to go Greek, without the mentoring of young boys part, though.

"He did have the Aryan youth. He did cut a scary, attractive visage in his SS uniform."

"Man, that weirds me out. I can agree with so much he wrote and then, BAM, seeing him like that I want to burn it all. I guess we all have our flaws, our kinks." Jack used his hands to accentuate the word bam and kept them moving to gesture the act of wiping away to support burning all of Heidegger's work before exaggeratedly shrugging at the end. "Kinks, yes. He did seem to think Hitler was the Absolute. But come on, Wagner was a raging anti-Semite, but are you going to burn the Ring for that, it's beautiful?"

"Well no, yeah, but you know what I mean. I can separate the artist and the work, but it almost seems that there is a difference with an artistic mind and a philosophical one. Knut Hamsun was a Nazi sympathizer and so was Céline and their fictional writings are brilliant and stylistic and vile, they characterize the world, but don't necessarily advise on it. Heidegger, as a philosopher, is characterizing reality, hu-

315

manity, the whole universal experience and then he was a Nazi. It's hard for me to reckon with."

"Some believe he was going along to save his ass and keep his position. Jaspers pardoned him."

"Yeah, and his wife was a Jew. If he could do it, I guess I can ignore it or overlook it in some way too."

They sat silent for a moment, blinking, drinking, and watched as Phoebus rounded his slow burning chariot towards home.

"Back to you and your causality. You are right and pretty honest about operating a system the way a system dictates. That is logic and math, structures that have rules, laws, problems, and a solution for every problem and as long as you follow those rules the system will support you. And I would guess that that might work for the more forensic aspects of a crime scene, but logic and math is all still its own language game and does not necessarily have any corollary in the actual outside world. I can't imagine that you use the same kind of logic and reasoning in all parts of investigating. People are chaotic and not entirely rational. They are very irrational most of the time. The world is just a big contingent mess and it seems like you are taking logic, something in the head and trying to bring all these independent contingent elements in constant flux into a linked system, a causally connected whole."

"I find what you are saying to be so pessimistic. I am much more into Whitehead, what he did it *Process and Reality*, that all things are entirely interconnected, involving need and necessity. I see structure, and I believe that when I don't see structure I just need to look closer or bigger from farther away. I am not going as far as Aquinas on teleology, but to think of logic being just a game of the mind, seems to me to separate man from nature. We are just organic matter, just

316

like dirt or anything else, and I think it naive to assume that these structures and games of logic and math and language only show up in the human mind. Of course, it's all we have so we want to see it other places, but it seems far too random that it's a freak occurrence of nature that just happened to us. Mostly though, when I am on the job, investigating and talking to people and trying to figure out how something went down, I am thinking about Dostoevsky. I have seen a lot of ugliness, the gross human ugliness that is all too human, and that he catalogs so well. Some of it can be random in its grossness, people can do awful things for no reason at all. If the final why is never solved, why someone would torture their own child to death or some of the other grotesque things I've seen, at least I can figure out the when and the how and the where. And then if the person tries to escape justice I can figure out how they did so, where they went, and get them back. That much of the world I can fathom with reason and engage."

Wind sipped long on his beer, only his second, but the alcohol on an empty stomach was doing what it naturally does and he was experiencing deep emotions in thinking about the horrors in Dostoevsky's work and the horrors he has seen in his daily work. Tears teased at the corners of his eyes.

"I have been rereading Dos recently," said Jack

"Dos, what, are you guys buddies now? Dos, like Bukowski called him. Are you going to start calling Bukowski Buk now, too? And Hemingway, Hem?" Joking helped keep the horrors back.

"Yeah, why not? They are mine, I own their words and works. They are dead, they can't speak. I possess them. You know, like Modigliani said, 'to paint a woman is to possess her.' Kinda like that, they are mine."

"You are getting a little solipsistic and a little hermeneutic too. So, it's all you, huh? The lone eye looking out at the world, your creation. Back to the death of the author birth of the reader stuff, I thought we got beyond that."

"Yeah, we did, I'm just messing with you. I've been rereading a lot of Dostoevsky and Kant too recently, kind of going back and forth."

"You must not be sleeping much."

"Yeah, not really. Kant was in some ways doing what you are doing, especially with your claim of agnosticism. In the *Critique of Pure Reason* he says sure I'm a theist, there is a God, yeah yeah, but let's leave that over there for now, that stuff is over there." Jack gestured to his left with both hands as if he was carrying something and placing it, as he saw Kant to be doing with theology. "But I am dealing with this, reason. He draws this great box around reason, and everything associated with the faculties of the mind, the whole human experience." As he finished, his hands were in the middle giving two sides to the box in which Kant would contain human experience.

"I like that about Kant, and that critique. This idea that a god is possible, as well as so much else, but that it might just be outside of the human experience and we will never know because we can never be outside of the range of our own experience. That is my agnosticism. I am not ruling it out, I am only deeming it irrelevant," said Wind.

"Yeah, sure. What was that example that Lao used to use? I am sure he ripped it off of someone else. That the question of whether a God exists is an invalid question once you have more information, like the question, 'where is the end of the world,' was a valid question back when people thought the world was flat, but once they found out the world was round the question became invalid," Jack interjected.

"Kant's box can also account for resolving freewill and predestination with the existence of an omnipotent and omniscient God. With a theistic model man is totally free, but only within the conditions of being man, being human. Totally free within our cage of flesh. In contrast to the rest of the universe we are probably so tiny it's like we have no knowledge or power at all, but within our limits, which we barely understand anyway, we are totally free," said Wind.

"I am with you on that. Rereading *The Brothers Karamazov*, I wind up relating to Ivan so much."

"As do I in my work, but you do because you are both arrogant assholes," interrupted Wind.

"Yeah, there is that. And you wouldn't know *anything* about that. But he just cuts right into it all. Things are so bleak and ugly for us in our experience that not only does that not justify free will as a benefit to loving God and his grace and kindness, but if there really is a God we might as well just get rid of him because he must be a sadist. If he is outside our experience and we will never understand him, fuck it, fuck Him, we shouldn't bother. I just keep drilling over 'The Grand Inquisitor' chapter and the one before it, 'Rebellion' or in some translations, 'Mutiny.' For Dostoevsky, he uses all that stuff to get to reasons to believe, towards faith, but myself, as an atheist I admit it's an attractive stance." Jack nodded like he was saying something of common acceptance.

"Of course the theists have it so easy, what to do, what to believe. They have souls, they are never alone, they have God. There are so many people who believe that you can't have ethics or a morality without a God. That is crap, but it sure makes things easy if you take the burden off yourself." Wind too was now nodding as he spoke.

"You sound like the tired stand-in for the patriarch, God's steward. I guess you are in a way, you assess, establish, and enforce law. But see, there you went and brought it all back to causality with you. It's okay; that's just you, it is part of what makes you such a great guy, there is something heroic about your desire to assign and especially accept responsibility. I'm sure that causality is useful in your work, but you see theism attractive as an excuse for causality, all that Aristotle and Aquinas, Prime Mover teleology crap. I find it more important that a belief in God makes it okay for life to be illogical and irrational. Having something like a creator or just any influence outside the human condition is therefore outside of such human conceptions as math and logic. It is such an important and essential role belief in God can play. There is always an undiscovered territory, an unknown, a variable. It's going on in quantum physics today, there are things that can't be solved or known. Like work with the particle. It's those kind of little areas that are perfect places to assign to a God, those things that reach us from out of the box around humanity and the human experience. Most especially, theists have it easy because they have something to defer to. They have a solution to uncertainty, like you with your causality. Theists have an easy way out of a world that might be wholly contingent and meaningless. I might imagine that ancients and primitives with gods and goddesses for everything might have been more happy than monotheists trying to explain the ways of one very mysterious god or our science and current physics with no god or meaning. As Lao Tzu said 'Heaven and Earth are ruthless and treat myriad creatures as straw dogs.'"

"If we are going to get into it, 'Like flies to wanton boys, we are to the Gods, they kill us for their sport,' Shakespeare." Wind parried.

"Oh, yeah, well, Shakespeare also said 'There is no good or bad, but thinking makes it so,'" said Jack, with a counterpunch.

"'The mind can make a Heaven out of Hell and a Hell out of

Heaven,' Milton. So take that," Wind landed as a haymaker causing both friends to laugh and take big gulps of their beer.

"Really though, it's easy to envy theists sometimes, but so many of them look so sad and confused and miserable like pouty children when they wrestle with their faith. Or they sound like crazy fanatics like they are paid-off spoiled bratty children. I will not go as far as Freud, but he and Marx really plumbed how bad people can be worked over by organized religion and the dependency it can breed and manipulation it can empower," said Jack.

"I have always felt that most theists bring in God too soon. Theist scholars and philosophers, historically in the Western and maybe Eastern traditions brought God into their discussions way before they ever needed to. There is so much we can figure out, explain, explore without having to go beyond the physical, to shoot at a metaphysics. Sadly, most of the great Western thinkers had to watch what they said or they would have been burned so they had to quickly show they were theists," said Wind.

"Sure, you blow your wad by bringing up God too soon and then what, your whole philosophy is impotent and post-climatic. What really gets me is the normal everyday believer, they don't believe what they say they believe. Maybe they want to, they try to, they fool themselves that they believe what they say they believe, but they really don't. Does Cullen really believe in Hell or know what the Hell he is really talking about when he says it or did Piz have any idea what he meant when he referred to the meaning of life or the pursuit of it? In looking at *The Brothers Karamazov*, it's amazing how those scoundrels talk, those Karamazovs. Most people who think of themselves as religious don't talk that way or care about that crap. Religion most often is a superstition people often don't choose to follow. Most people don't believe the tenets of their own faith. It's like they don't believe in anything except that they should be believing in something. They don't believe in God, but believe that they should. It's not just that people are wrestling with faith, but what religion really is, is so much simpler than all the artifice used around it. Why is it raining on a day I planned a picnic, why did my brother die, why don't people like me, why me, why me. Or the please let my baby be born healthy, please bless those I love, please don't let me die alone. Those are the reasons and situations where normal everyday people turn to God or get religious. They are not philosophizing, theologizing, pondering the place of evil in regards to free will and predestination; trying to understand how God can be three equal persons in one entity; how Jesus as the Christ can be wholly man and wholly God in one soul and body and why that is necessary for salvation; what the soul is, and where it goes when you die. People want to get through the day, they want to pay their rent, feed their kids, watch television, and vacation at the beach. They want to know they are safe and loved and they are special."

"Yes, I am with you on all of that, I have encountered so many varying degrees of the deceivers, deceived, and self-deceiving, but you really are showing your Marxist Freudian stripes now." Wind smiled and encouraged further his friend's tirading.

"Freud and Marx were just the tip of the iceberg. Remember when we were talking about this before, the cognitive stuff I was getting into. Cognitive philosophers and cognitive scholars of religion, guys like Boyer, Pascal Boyer, and neurologists talk about how the actions and needs that get expressed in religious practice are things we would naturally do anyway. Just brain functions functioning, doing what they do to promote the life of the organism that they are a part of. Biologically, it's all right there. Of course, those neurology people really seem to have found the key to the universe and all questions just by tearing apart the brain and stimulating its various parts. They really got their own science dogma going, no room for doubt when it's all biological." Jack shrugged and drank, showing his ambivalence to the circles in which they kept talking.

"So is this what you have been thinking about most recently?" Wind asked.

"Well I really only read a few articles, the Boyer most recently, but I have been practicing the only art you like to remind me for which I am fit, aphorisms. They have been close to what you and I have been talking about."

"So you have been writing more aphorisms? You better watch out, in a couple of decades you might have a whole book."

"Yeah, man, I'm working away. Remember the one I called you with the other day. It reminds me of something Ivan Karamazov said..."

"It just keeps coming back to Dos with you, doesn't it?" Wind interrupted.

"Hey, Nietzsche said that Dostoevsky was the only psychologist he ever learned anything from. But as I was saying, in the beginning of the chapter 'Rebellion' Ivan mentions how he can't understand the whole idea of unconditional Christian love of one's fellow man and of this saint, John the Merciful, caring for a disgusting beggar. And then he says something like what I wrote and called you about the other night. He says, 'If I must love my fellow man, he better hide himself, because as soon as I see his face there is the end of my love for him.' Just like my most recent literary endeavor, 'The more I know about someone the less I like them.' I had read *The Brothers Karamazov* so long ago maybe Ivan was just trying to resurface. Ivan might have liked my wording though in regards to the Christian God, those

323

sentiments. He is right though, arm's-length love is best and safest. You never really know anyone else, so it is best not to deceive oneself with the idea of intimacy. Keep it safe, simple, quantified, and qualified. That is what is keeping me happy and loving my fellow man and ladies." Jack nodded solemnly at the end as if he had laid something very serious on the table.

"You are only saying that because you were dumped. If you had done the breaking up with Gretchen you'd be singing a different tune. But that would be a different situation, where she would be a different girl, one that you could dump and you would be whining and pining for someone to love as you have in the past. Wanting someone to love after you just dumped a girl who loved you, but wasn't what you wanted. Now though, you're all cool and cold since you are the one that got hurt, you're on the defensive. I know your wily ways."

"Yeah, I guess you're right. Very good, Detective Wind. I am a dickens aren't I?"

The both let their mouths take a break while they tried to calm their minds. Women was a subject that both were sensitive on and they magnified that sensitivity as they each superimposed it on the other. Looking away from each other, they both finished their second beer and allowed their thoughts to turn to the rooftop environment. The temperature was falling, but both men felt nothing as the beer provided the illusion of warmth. In the wake of Phoebus' chariot, its trailing light no more, the owl of Minerva rose with the dusk, and with violent wings, beat its gray upon gray against the night sky before moving on.

15. THE PNEUMATIC ABATTOIR

Any phenomenon associated with the acts of remembering, commemorating, and perpetuating an unanimity that springs from the murder of a surrogate victim can be termed "religious."
—René Girard, *Violence and the Sacred*

THE THURSDAY DINNER AROUND THE HIGH STEEL TABLE AT SIX FEET Under was boisterous and bright regardless of the darkness of the night, Jonathan Wind's dilemma of waiting, and the great cemetery in view across the street, past the edge of the building. Oakland Cemetery, the original six acres established in 1850, was now eighty-eight acres of historic burial in the rural garden style of its first days, with the intention of being for the living as much for the dead. Art programs occurred within its stone walls and tourists visited the historical residents like thousands of Civil War soldiers, newly deceased Mayor Maynard Jackson, and beloved novelist Margaret Mitchell. Four months ago, Wind made the mistake of having brunch here on Father's Day, and sitting in this very same seat he watched family after fatherless family approach marble markers bearing flowers. He had had a drink as soon as they started serving at twelve-thirty as he waited for Monica to meet him after church. It was her Sabbath and his day of rest, and he rested in slight inebriation, hiding his exhaustion and guilt after a night with Flora as Monica rambled on about gossip from her work, oblivious to the fatherless families. His own father was buried in Queens, New York, in a sprawling urban hillside on view from the highway, smiling down on Van Wyck traffic.

Appetizers had just arrived and another round of drinks followed. This round was the fourth for Wind and Jack Thoth, but on Lao Benjoseph's lead they were drinking Six Feet Under's specialty Ragin' Cajun Bloody Mary's of peppery vodka and house mix, rims coated in cayenne and salt glinting in the artificial light. Tammy had wine and her friend Lisa was enjoying a potent, bitter-syrupy-sweet Bourbon Lemonade. Wind sat facing out, with Jack to his right, Lao to his left and the girls next to the boys. For the first few minutes after the appetizers arrived, the only conversation was about passing the plates and who preferred what. Tammy said the crisp and greasy hushpuppies were better than her mother's and the serving plate remained in front of Jack as he handed them out. Fried green tomatoes sat in front of him too as across the table Buffalo wings were being passed.

Wind and Lisa both moved on the wings at the same time, breaking apart the little hollow bird bones joined by strong and sinewy dead fibers. She held the greasy spiced shaft delicately with her fingertips and pulled with only her teeth while he yanked with teeth and lips and instinctively sucked as he tore the meat from the bone. They both sucked at their fingers before going to their napkins and the process was repeated again on the next wing on their plates as it was by Lao and Tammy. Buffalo sauce, fry grease, chicken juices boiled and drawn out, went into the four mouths and onto the many fingers before making it back into the mouths. Barely chewed strips of sinewy flesh, worn from heating, freezing, and heating again, slid down throats, while some pieces lodged in between teeth to flap in the heated flow of breath in and out. The Buffalo oysters were soon moved from place to place beginning in front of no one in particular and riding on their pungent spiciness, distinct from the chicken prepared in the same sauce, the basket making its rounds to deliver red nuggets past Jack to the other four plates. With relish, the four popped the oysters into their gaping mouths, breathing faster to cool the heat-like spice oozing from the fried and soaked mollusk. The salty brine carried the Texas Pete's flavor around the four corners of the four oral worlds as the now fried, but once mercurial and gelatinous, sea-life was torn and ripped apart amid the vibrations of rising sighs and moans of gastronomical pleasure. Soon only one fried Buffalo oyster was left.

"Gahd help me, I love this place. Isn't everything so good." Tammy laughed at herself and her own excitement. "Jack, you should try these things. I can't believe you won't even try them! They are so good! Oh, my Gahd, they are so good!" She spoke like she spoke, every sentence or phrase, its own burst of energy between short rests, and now while eating she chewed during each break of speech.

"Tammy, no. I don't eat meat. I've told you. The other apps are great, look. Yum, fried green tomatoes and more fried food, look, yum, hushpuppies." Jack spoke scoldingly, as he did often, from a place of confidence and dominance. He bit from both of the meatless options and chewed exaggeratedly, demonstrating to Tammy.

"Shut. Up." She said with a slamming beat on each word. "I've seen you eat fish before. Oh, my Gahd. You know I have. It's just a stupid little oyster." As she got flustered her voice went higher, louder, and faster.

"Actually, Jack, the oyster is a very simple organism. I mean, it's barely alive. It's really not meat at all. A glob of cells, practically a plant. It's like a zygote, a clump of cells, and no one minds killing zygotes, or farming them for their stem cells. Or actually it might be the phlegm of a larger sea animal and marine biologists are really just trying to trick us. It's just tubercular fish spitting up in shells. Pearls are just sand and spit," said Lao and at this point, he too was spitting. His goofy laugh had been building with rising volume and momentum as he found funny his own jokes and coughed out erratic air while he smoked, spoke, and spit.

"Fine, I'll eat it. Shit, will that make you happy? I am only doing this for you two. Great, yum. That Buffalo oyster is delicious." He popped one in his mouth. "I eat fish or seafood very occasionally, if that is what you are thinking about, Tammy. Usually only if there is nothing else to eat, no good veg options. But see, there, I ate one. It tasted good, I never doubted you guys." Jack took a sip from his Bloody Mary when he was done chewing and speaking. He washed the spicy tomato and liquor solution down with a sip of water after and shook his head at Tammy as she smirked back at him.

Lisa and Wind watched and laughed lightly. Then there was a moment shared where they all drank at once, the appetizers down to scraps, sauce, and fried crusts. Wind had been eating with his stomach, but not his mind. The conversation he had earlier with Jack and the fourth drink he was now working on had fueled his hunger on the most basic need-based level. His movements were out of physical habit for physical need and his softening thoughts for a moment turned to his lack of mindfulness and he felt a sense of guilt and sadness. He had always respected Jack's vegetarianism and it, like so many things, made him think of her. Flora didn't eat meat either, and though she could be anyone a client desired, she wouldn't ever playact so far on a dinner date to actually consume the flesh of an animal. She didn't wear any leather either, unless she was respectfully accepting a gift from someone who did not know her that well, but in the strength of her character, she was quick to educate those in her circle. The leather she received she often regifted since she was not confrontationally righteous in her beliefs. She didn't lecture anyone else, nor did she give unsolicited advice. At her apartment, he ate what she had at hand and if they had ever crossed the bridge of actually going out to eat he always supposed he would be respectful enough to not order meat though she told him she ate amongst carnivores all the time. It was her holistic view of the world, and it, like her other attributes, was very infecting. She spoke like Sutra at times and spoke to his own rationality. She said that if all life is connected, then compassion is pragmatic. There is no difference in suffering. He cried once when she said that. It was almost dawn and they had just made love for the third time that night. They were covered in each other's fluids, slick against each other with the air-conditioning on and the summer heat squeezing and cleansing like a sponge outside her apartment. She said that they were one flesh and she made sense of compassion in simple words he could never have conjured.

For a moment now he was lost far beyond the food, drinks, friends, and the glowing, beckoning darkness of the cemetery and he was back there with her and his mind continued to soften in alcohol and compassion and memory. Her voice, her face, her tears were before him, calling to him. And then she was gone and he was back and Lao's voice boomed and thundered across the table, Bloody Mary spittle all over his gray beard.

"Oh man, Jack, you really buckled pretty easily, no conviction. Oo, oo, that reminds me of something. Oo, oo, I got this great idea for a movie I want to make and you guys can help, but you have to read 4

Maccabees. Jack, Jon, have you read 4 Maccabees? Well, you should, you need to, it's fantastic. So you know Mel Gibson is making that movie about the death of Jesus. Well, it's supposed to be really gory and brutal, showing in-depth and graphic detail the torture of Jesus' last twelve hours of life. Well, if it does well, and it should—Christians eat that shit up, they love blood you know, almost vampiricly—then the time will be right for my film of 4 Maccabees. It'll be a big hit, we'll all be on easy street, no more programming or coffee making or police work for any of us, nope, easy street I say, fat city.

"But first you guys have to read 4 Maccabees. I'm sure you both have it somewhere, any decent Study Bible or Bible with Apocrypha should have it. It's really great, really crazy, and has this very strange moral. Visually, I want to make it like a splatter gore Russ Meyer film, a slasher film, lots of flaming bloody visuals. You guys know the first two Maccabees, so you get the context. Same idea, Antiochus IV Epiphanes being mean to the Jews, trying to Hellenize them and get them to renounce their faith and convert. In this one, the story is set up like one big sermon about how rational faith should be. Pretty much Antiochus takes his guy Eleazar and says, 'renounce your faith and eat this pork,'" and Lao does the Antiochus voice loud, like a cartoon villain. "'And Eleazar says no, never, I will not,'" the Eleazar voice higher in a pitch of protest. "And then they keep torturing him and trying to get him to eat the pork and he keeps saying 'no, I will not eat the pork.' And it goes on graphically to describe how they tortured him. They whip him and cut him and scourge him and kick him and burn him and pour stinking liquids down his nostrils. And all the while until he dies he won't eat the pork. After all of that the narrator says that Eleazar is right. It's rational to control your emotions. If he had listened to his emotions he would have given in and eaten the pork and then there would be no place in heaven and God's kingdom for him." He starts giggling and lights a cigarette only to laugh the first drag of smoke back out of his hidden mouth and nostrils.

"I don't know about you guys, but I would have eaten the pork. That story is crazy." He kept on laughing harder, choking a little, and caused the others to laugh with him, while Tammy, laughing, hit him and told him to stop acting stupid. "The book is amazing though, it goes on to tell about a mother and her seven sons and all seven are tortured in front of her because they too won't eat the pork. And this is all seen as good, it is better to be rational than to fall for your irrational emotions. The sons are tortured in different graphic ways like stretching until limbs are dislocated on this wheel, which is described as dripping gore and pieces of flesh from its axles. Another is eaten by a leopard and then his flesh was flayed off and the others are worse, bodies broken in half, raked, catapulted, disjointed, poked with burning rods so their entrails are on fire. Finally at the end even the mother, since she isn't faint hearted, says they did the right thing and she is proud and doesn't mourn them. This is the sovereignty of reason, the story goes. I don't agree with it, but isn't it amazing. You guys have to read it. Just picture it as a movie, EAT THE PORK! NOOOO! ARGGGG! And then close-ups on the faces, agony, blood splatters the screen and there is a close-up of the blood on the sand, and then we can have like a voiceover saying that they did the right thing."

As he finished, everyone was laughing and Tammy was hitting him again and calling him an idiot and telling him to stop laughing in such spasmodic contortions in public. The waitress had come as his story was closing with the different voices for both the martyrs and Antiochus and she laughed too, having no idea what they were talking about. Now as they all calmed down, their food was before them. Jack was signaling the waitress to return so they could order more drinks. He asked Wind what he wanted next and they both returned to beer. Tammy ordered a Coke and though Lisa and Lao ordered more of the same, he would not rest at that.

"Oo, Jon, Jack, do guys want to do oyster shooters? Let's do oyster shooters. Lisa do you want one. They're great. Guys?" Jon and Jack nodded passively. "They have a few different ones, look on that menu, which do you want? Jon we did the Firecracker once, right. That was good."

"Yeah, and I remember that you shot it weird and you were crying from the Tabasco going up your nose."

"I don't remember that at all. Let's try a different one. Look at the drink menu and give me one. There is the Six Feet Under, which has the spicy vodka, Bloody Mary mix and an oyster. Then there is the Oyster Cholula which has vodka, a little bit of Cholula, lemon, and an oyster. The Deep Throat has spicy vodka and Clamato juice, Worcestershire, horseradish, and an oyster. The Bloody Bass-tard has Bass and horseradish with Bloody Mary mix and an oyster and the Kamikaze has lemon vodka, Triple Sec, lime, and an oyster. Jack what do you think, which one do you want?"

"I don't eat meat, oysters included!" He spat sternly at his friend and instantly tried to shake and laugh his tone off.

"Jack, you caved pretty easily before. You are no Eleazar. Let's just take this temporary bend in ethics a little further. Oyster shooters are really good." Lao kept control of the ordering as the waitress stood idly by, shifting her feet in a limbo of commitments and obligations.

"Whatever, I'll have whichever one you guys have. I don't care," Jack said, resigned with a shrug.

"The Kamikaze is fine with me, it's like a Margarita shot," said Wind.

"Yeah, with a dead mollusk skimming the bottom. Lisa, you're having one right?" and before she had a chance to say no Lao ordered four Oyster Kamikaze shooters from the waitress, releasing her from her state of tension and allowing her to scribble on her pad as she went inside down the stairs.

Their food was before them. Wind had ordered catfish tacos, keeping with the predominantly seafood theme of the restaurant and his new apprehension towards other meats. He had had these before and he loved them. Three grilled catfish on warm tortillas with melted cheese covered in jalapeños, cabbage, and a cucumber wasabi dressing. His sense of order was appeased in a meal well contained in a folded bread, providing a full palette of coverage, salty, sweet, savory, spicy, chewy, and crunchy. On the side were the homemade Six Feet Under potato chips, straddling the warm soft French fry sensation with the compact crunch of a potato chip. His mind and perception had been softening more and more with the alcohol and the food and its many tastes and textures consumed him as he consumed it.

For the first ten minutes that the entrees were present no one spoke. The sounds were of slurping, biting, crunching, sipping, coughing, swallowing, nose-blowing, napkin-rustling, and fork to plate clinking, chiming, and grating. The smell of the table was one dominant mixture of fried food and the sea, but all each person smelled was their own plate before them. Lao had a Buffalo chicken sandwich with the same homemade potato chips and with each bite of the bread-contained meal he had to wipe at his mouth with his napkin or his sleeve, his beard collecting most of the color of the sauce, mixing it in with its dull gray, white, and black tones. Tammy faced-off at her a massive blue metal cup containing snow crab legs, bristling, and reaching beyond the curved surface. She pulled each leg in turn, cracking and bursting it for all its meat and juices and biting and sucking its insides. Lisa cut at the BBQ salmon sitting delicately on her wide white plate among coleslaw and shafts of whole fried okra. The bites were small and properly mouth-sized as she portioned and served each one to herself. To Wind's right, getting in his elbow room, were Jack's plates, more plates and baskets than anybody else, since here the vegetarian option was sides and Jack made a meal out of fries, corn on the cob, and asparagus. The beer and other drinks were back before the shots and everyone took a break from chewing to enjoy their fresh beverages.

"I like this place and some of these veggies are good, but really, especially not eating meat, everything here is so starchy and fried." Jack was the first to speak, his corn done and his concentration falling on his fries.

"Um, it's good," Lao gasped through bites and breaths.

"I like it, but I see what you mean," smiled Lisa while picking conscientiously at her own food and looking down at Jack's plates.

"Oh, stop complaining Jack, Jeez, you are such a little girl, just eat your vegetables. They're good for you. Do you want to try my collard greens I got on the side? Yum, they are good, and they are so good for you," and then with no response she repeated pounding each word indignantly on beat. "Jack Thoth, stop complaining and eat some of these collards, they are so good for you."

"No, I am good, and that is an argument that I have never understood. Lots of things are good for you, why eat one of them that you don't like? I don't like collards. Maybe if people used that, it's-good-for-you argument for a food that possessed something beneficial that no other food possessed, sure, but there isn't anything like that." He pushed her plate back towards her.

"Well, I like them. I think they're good. And good for you. So fuck you. More for me." She smiled and moved from her snow crab to take a bit of her drippingly moist collards.

"Well, I guess she told you." Wind said to Jack out the side of his mouth, smiling, getting giddy with his new fullness.

Before Jack could even comment, in a break from his fries and asparagus, or before Lao could interject an anecdote or further attack on Jack's eating habits, the waitress arrived bearing a tray of short murky glasses.

"Here are the oyster shooters. I'll just put them down and you all can sort them out." Hurried, but personable, the waitress delivered the four Oyster Kamikazes and moved on after quickly checking if anyone else needed anything.

The four glasses were distributed in front of Lisa, Jack, Wind, and Lao who all readied themselves and raised their glasses, making them clink in random orders and accidental repetition careful not to miss anyone. Tammy put her Coke glass up too and tapped at the others.

"So what do I do exactly?" asked Lisa.

"You have to shoot it," said Wind.

"The whole thing," said Jack.

"Oyster and all, all in one shot," said Lao.

And they shot. The boys put it back instantaneously with ease, and slammed their glasses with exaggerated force down onto the table. Lisa shot and made a bitter, scrunched face and gagged for a moment and everyone stared motionless as she tried to smile and her eyes watered and her hands were too slow to stop the oyster from shooting back out of her mouth and landing on the table in front of Tammy. All around the table, breath was abated and the pause hung for a heavy three seconds until Lao reached out and grabbed the oyster off the table and ate it. The laughter that had been building since the oyster emerged from Lisa's mouth covered the table. Tammy struck Lao on the shoulder and back a few times and called him gross and Lisa laughed through her red eyes as Jack asked her if she was okay.

"Wow, Lao, you just took an already gross act and made it grosser, very impressive," jabbed Wind. He didn't know, but his cheeks were flush. There was a general heat about his face and his ears tingled. The shot added to the alcohol saturating his blood stream, moving fast in absorption from his stomach, amid the small but growing mass of food. Already his hands were lighter and his movements, so well trained and controlled, felt reckless and beyond his restraint. He had returned to eating along with the others and the action of looking down at his plate felt faster than it really was. In his drunken awareness his perception trailed behind his vision. His focus was keen on his tacos and chips. The area right before his eyes was clear, but his peripherals were a blur. His drunken awareness was similar to how he had felt over the last many days since Flora's death; no matter where his head turned there was only what was before him.

Lifting his head now he looked out across the table at Lisa while she ate. In his foreground of vision the cemetery was a blur in the background. When he shifted his focus to the marble-speckled green lawn, Lisa was a dark blur. The movement between foreground and background felt like a paradigm shift. Back and forth he moved his eyes and perception, cemetery to Lisa, Lisa to cemetery, there was no escaping either, women or death. His mind was sloppy in its inebriation and as he made connections they were contaminated by sentiment. Where were his women, he thought, looking in the foreground. Switching to background he thought that his life was death, his job, his raison d'etre. He thought of Sartre's atheistic words, that we are what we become and since there is no afterlife, we are nothing for that is the end for all of us, nothing. There it was before him, a park with arts programs and walking lanes over the dead, consciously over the dead, grinding them down further into nothingness. Back to foreground was Lisa. She was beautiful. Her hair in a short dark bob, with bangs similar to that of Goddess Nut last Saturday. His mind snatched the reference and he tried to picture Lisa naked. She looked up from a bite of fish, and caught him staring, and they smiled at each other and he faked looking away as she went back to her plate.

Where were his women, he thought again, as he looked at Lisa. Her skin was pale like Monica's and her hair was dark, but she was easy to talk to like Flora. He didn't know her well; she was a friend of Tammy's, but he had met her before. It was around her birthday, she was an Aquarius like his mother, which didn't matter to him, but it was one of the few things he knew about her. Without any real prodding she did a shot she wasn't interested in at all and it was this daring acceptance or maybe obedience to men that reminded him of his sister. Lisa was gentle and precise in her actions, her cutting and biting. She had a natural elegance to her that was similar to Flora. Her hips and bosom were fuller, but in the slipping firmness of his mind he thought she reminded him of Flora; but really the only familiar was her womanhood. Her femininity drew him and as she sat before him, he missed her, and since he couldn't touch her he felt nostalgia and loss for the many others he had touched. With the sporadic gusts across the roof, he tried to smell her and wondered if there was some excuse he could make to go to her and at least hug her, to get her scent on him and in him. His whole body, including his face, was relaxing and he looked out past her to the background of loss so as not to cry, for if a woman could finally make him cry, the well-groomed

337

field of death would stymie such emotions with different sentiments, those of grim determination.

Somehow I lost them all, he thought, and he had never felt so alone. Even surrounded by his closest friends he thought this. His mother gone, a new life, a new boyfriend; Monica gone for good, cut out of his life by deception, then honesty; Flora gone but ash and memories, dead and burned, and there was nothing he could do to stop it or save her. And now he couldn't even find his sister. He was surrounded by those that loved him, he knew they did, but they didn't understand him and what he needed to do; they couldn't. Looking at Oakland Cemetery he let his mind cherish the order with which humanity controlled death. The plots all lined up and grouped by family or time period and labeled and kept neat and tidy. I do that, he thought, I control death. Not that he really believed that there was anything beyond this world, but he thought for a moment that he, in his job, steps beyond this world into the next and brings the dead back to the living light of reason. No death is random and no one is gone if the truth behind the seemingly randomness of a death is exposed. I bring that truth, went his heroic thoughts, I find it and record it. No one dies alone if death has meaning. He thought of karma and dependent origination and how she said that compassion made sense.

Staring at the cemetery his thoughts ran to tomorrow, its nearness and its relevance. The friends and the drinks held back the flow of time, but now again it was running to him and away from him. The cemetery and tomorrow beckoned. He was ready to lay Flora to rest, to give her back to the world through truth and meaning and under-standing. Sutra had called earlier: tomorrow was the day. He was to pick her up at the Avondale MARTA Station tomorrow at 11:30am.

She would give him information on where to go tomorrow night, he hoped. She told him before to leave Friday night open and he was ready for whatever instructions she provided him. He would brave tomorrow with strength, prepared for whatever it brought, and in his focused mind he hoped that it brought that cemetery and its certainty.

He looked around at his friends as they cut and bit at their plates. Jack, always a glutton, had finished all from his own plates of vegetables and was stabbing at Lisa's coleslaw and slurping down her remaining breaded shafts of okra as she continued to methodically cut, raise, and deposit pieces of fish into her mouth. She was mannered in her movements, but Wind could see into her mouth as she made just a small opening to accept the food. Within was mashed and masticated fish flesh, tossed and rolled in the dark sauce, clinging in miniscule detail to her teeth and gums and darkening her tongue. Next to her, Tammy, was working diligently, drawing a leg, snapping it open and sucking salty juice and meat from the cavity of the exoskeleton. Leg after leg she pulled, snapped, and sucked at the snow crab, butter running down her fingers and her eyes focused only on the big blue mug. She offered some to her husband at her side, but he was locked in his own process. Lao's face looked like the substance Wind saw in Lisa's mouth, dull and gray around his mustache, beard, and lips with the same dark sauce, deep red like fresh spilled blood, combed and wiped throughout the hair in clumps and highlights. His mouth was open as he chewed and with each bite more stingy pieces of chicken were visible as his teeth ripped them and tore the flesh.

Wind continued to eat as they did, trying to make an effort to chew as his body drew the food in with each breath and only exhaled to gain the strength of pressure to draw in more. He sipped again at his shrinking beer, letting the flow of sweet and malty grain juice run with the macerated fish and vegetables down his overworked throat. As he gave more and more way to the alcohol, he was living for each moment and while eating he was fully present. Lao was done with his sandwich and chips and after roughly wiping his face he lit a cigarette and sipped at the remainder of his Bloody Mary, licking at the crusted salt and pepper.

"So what else is going on with you guys, is anything new?" asked Lao in the direction of Jack and Wind, taking the floor as he was the first to finish and everyone was still picking at something on their plates.

"Well, Jon and Monica broke up," said Jack as he finished the last scraps of his fries and drew up his new beer.

Group sighs and moans of lament went up around the table.

"Jonny, are you okay? I'm so sorry. How did it happen?" asked Tammy.

"I never liked her. She loved Jesus not enough and Yahweh too much for me. A weak dependence on a weak deity. Cthulhu dreaming in R'lyeh would devour Yahweh," said Lao, and Tammy laughed, patting Lao weakly, laughing more.

"Be nice, Jonny needs you. Can't you be more sensitive?" she said.

"It's okay. I did the breaking. And I am not too broken up about it. It needed to be done and was a long time coming," said Wind.

"Well. Good then. I'm sorry Jonny, but I am not that sorry. I tried, but I didn't like her much either. I always thought she was judging me," said Tammy.

"In his house at R'lyeh dead Cthulhu waits dreaming and when he wakes he will drive mad all those Christians as he devours their God. He will eat Yahweh raw, mind first," said Lao.

Jack laughed at Lao and leaned in towards Lisa, taking her lighting of a cigarette as a sign of completion, and asked if he could finish her okra. Lisa was quickly finishing her Bourbon lemonade as the waitress came around and cleared some plates and nodded as Jack told her to bring another round. Hearing this, Lao told her to bring him a beer instead of another Bloody Mary.

Lao continued to rant about Cthulhu and Wind laughed, but tried to ask him seriously if he had been reading any Lovecraft recently and Jack listened on as Tammy and Lisa whispered.

"Ph-nglui mglw'nafh Cthulhu R'lyeh wgah'nagl fhtagn," Lao was in the process of saying until Tammy interrupted.

"We have an announcement too, y'all. You guys, y'all listen now, it's better than Jonny's news," she began. "I am pregnant again."

"Yep, I'm potent. My boys can swim. Jack, Jon, have either of you ever inseminated anyone? Huh? I didn't think so, we know who is the most potent here," said Lao.

"How long?" asked Wind.

"You two, at it again. Another shot at a kid, huh?" said Jack.

"It's been about a month. I just found out. My period was late so I went to the doctor and he ran some tests and there you have it. We didn't plan it this time, but I've been really healthy and we think this could come to term," said Tammy.

"I noticed you weren't drinking. That's a good first step," said Wind.

"I'm glad you approve," said Tammy.

Everyone else was drinking though. Wind couldn't remember how many he had at this point and he caught himself before he tried to count. He didn't want to know. He wasn't sure why he was drinking so much. He was letting the night and his time with his friends take him, letting the dinner of revelry run its course. Things were in place for tomorrow, as in place as he could imagine them being. There was a contact time and place with a person who knew more than she had said where she would give more information than he had before. He would follow her instructions and go where she said. This plan was rehearsed as his mind slipped more and more into the situation at the table. The drunken feelings were familiar, the desire to make the night last forever, that there would be nothing beyond this, that everyone felt the same, and there was no judgment, no consequences. Continuously sipping from his beer, he could not stop the progression of drunkenness, but knew he risked giving in more to this situation, the talking, the lack of control, the looseness of lips, the gluttony, the emotional flow, as well as risking how well he would function tomorrow after living so much for the present moment.

Looking at the women he felt a love for them, Tammy in her friendship, Lisa in her beckoning femininity, then looking at the cemetery he wondered again where the women in his life were, for these women before him were not his. Had he driven them away? Monica, yes, and that was honestly best for all, but Flora, how could he feel responsible? It was still his deception, his duplicity that was a factor. If he had left Monica already, would he have been there to prevent what happened to Flora? Maybe he could have gotten her out of the life and they could have been a normal couple. These thoughts came fast and he knew he was surely drunk. What Flora did was more than a job for her and he was not responsible for her death, his responsibility had come after. He felt far more responsibility for his sister, but still he didn't know where she was and he was chasing down Flora's ghost rather than actually pounding the pavement for his sister; he farmed that responsibility out to Sonny. Maybe he was resistant because his mother asked him to check on Astrid, he was being passive aggressive against his mother and taking it out on his sister? Psychoanalyzing himself was tiring and as he kept drinking he was trapped between the women and the grave. Of the women gone, the one he wished for the most was his mother; he knew where she was, but he couldn't reach her. He knew it wasn't that simple, but in his state he wanted it to be. He wished he could just call her and then all those years of lost understanding and chilling intimacy would be erased in one act of humbled pride. It would not work, he knew. His emotions were starting to seep, and he felt them threatening to drown him. They were a temptation away from his purpose. He was a detective, an investigator, a police officer, he told himself, focus. Bring the mind to the present, the matters and company at hand.

Across the table he looked at Tammy. She smiled as she listened to Lao speak and commented in her own way to Lisa. These were his friends; this was a happy occasion. Lao and Tammy are having a baby, he thought. He honed his vision. Beneath her breasts, hanging free and braless in a scoop-collared black t-shirt, lurked her abdomen, not yet distended, a small pooched-out tummy, and in it a clump of cells, changing, growing, every second different, not more than that fried oyster, or a ball of phlegm as Lao described it, an embryo clinging to her womb's wall as a timeless process enacts around it and through it. He held his view away from the graves, the 70,000 decomposing shells, one of which the clump of cells will one day be, those wood-locked piles of bone, hollow now with the meat and juice long sucked out, like the crab legs in Tammy's big blue mug, there was no life beyond flesh, nothing but meat. But he shook free of those thoughts and the cemetery, the beckoning of that not too distant hill of judgment, and concentrated on the life before him and the potency of both of his now life-giving friends.

"Jon, I've always wondered, but I never get a straight answer from Lao, and Tammy told me just to ask you. Why did you become a cop?" asked Lisa.

"Well," Wind began, pulled out of his focus and trying to acclimate to another while still careful with his words. He felt her eyes on him and with them her attention, real attention, and he became nervous and self-conscious to answer her. His thoughts ran with the moment and the attention. Was she flirting? She knew he was single now. He barely knew her and neither did Jack, but all night it looked as if Jack was making his move towards her and any pang of jealousy he experienced was just one of feeling left out and alone. To look out and see Lao and Tammy together and Jack eating off Lisa's plate as if they too were a couple. But now her attention was on him and he must be cool. Mostly he decided that he should just be normal, forthright, and the word professional came to mind. Her question reminded him that he was an officer of the law. He had a social role and responsibility and he must be faithful to that. He would exhibit control and precision of speech.

"I know why he became a cop," interrupted Jack before Wind could speak.

"Oo, oo, so do I," began Lao. "As a child he was a huge fan of the Village People and would dance around to that YMCA song because he went to summer day camp at the YMCA and loved to stay there and play there. And he always dreamed to give something back to that YMCA he loved to play at. But you see, Jonny never understood that the group the Village People was not actually connected to the YMCA. He thought they were the spokesmen of the YMCA and he believed that he could speak well on behalf of that place so he tried out the represented careers. He tried on cowboy and Indian, but didn't like the whole old west thing and construction worker was too much for him and biker was not active enough so he was left with cop. It was only after he completed his training at the police academy that he realized there was no actual connection between law enforcement, the Village People, and the YMCA. He was very sad about all this, but we encouraged him to stay on since we thought he looked good in his uniform."

"Yeah, maybe. Could be. But I think the real reason is that he did it for the ladies," said Jack.

"No, c'mon, seriously," pleaded Lisa.

"No, seriously, he did it for the ladies," Jack said again.

"It's all for the ladies. He's a savior of the ladies. It's not just about the uniform that allows him to save them from their loneliness, but a good percentage of homicides are women. Or women are in some way affected. Detective Jonathan Wind protects all the women out there by finding killers and taking them off the street. Even the women who kill, he takes off the street to save from themselves. It's his messiah complex. With the death of his father he stepped into that role and saved his mother and sister from being alone and husbandless and fatherless. It is simple psychology. He must be the hero, the man of the hour, and he will save the world one woman at a time."

When Jack was done he raised his glass and the others followed, with Wind moving in a display of reluctance, and they all toasted to heroes and the police. The waitress had come while Jack spoke and cleared away the rest of the plates and smiled as they toasted, used to the patronage of Atlanta police officers at Six Feet Under. She asked them if they wanted any dessert or another round of drinks and chatter rose up around the table with the men making drink suggestions and the women cajoling the men into splitting desserts with them. Lisa ordered the icebox Key Lime Pie and Tammy ordered the

Mom's Chocolate Mousse and two Diet Cokes, while for the men it was a round of fifteen year old Dalwhinnie Scotch.

"So do you have any names for the baby yet? Are you thinking of any of those names you never got to use before? Like Robo or Magneto?" asked Jack.

"Robo? Magneto?" questioned Lisa.

"That was such a good name. Magneto Benjoseph. Such a good ring to it," proclaimed Wind lovingly and drunkenly.

"No! We are not naming my damn baby Magneto or Robo or any of that shit!" shouted Tammy across the table at Wind and Jack. Lao just laughed.

"Yeah, those names work well for a boy or a girl. But since I have been reading the Old Testament recently I have been thinking about Elijah," said Lao sounding more serious than anyone was ever used to.

"See, now that's a good name. That we can agree on. I like Elijah," said Tammy, still loud, but calmer.

"Elijah Benjoseph? Why not just name him Jewy Jewerson for Christ's sake," laughed Wind with Jack and Lao following.

"That kid is totally gonna get beat up," Jack continued to laugh.

"And he wouldn't get beat up if he was named Magneto?" Lisa added in attempted defense of her friend Tammy.

"Not at all, Magneto is a power name," said Jack like he was pronouncing law and he kept laughing with the other men.

The desserts were placed before the women, but far enough in front to appear communal and the Scotches were all put in front of Wind so Lao and Jack had to reach for them. Wind watched the placement of the desserts and it was like a miraculous apparition to look down and just see the Scotch there. He sipped at the Dalwhinnie and felt the taste open up to the full expanse of his oral cavity and burst down his throat where the sensation of radiation gave way to a creeping slither. His trachea burned, it was the burn of stress and the Scotch was stoking the inner fire. He sipped again and let it roll over his tongue, tasting the wood of the barrel and the grain as he had trained himself to do. The burn and radiant awareness reached into his sinuses and his eyes and nose and lips were invigorated. He felt more sloshed than ever, as if he were rocked in a drunken boat, and as Lisa passed some of her pie to Jack to taste and he passed it on by to his left, Wind received it, reacting without thought.

"That is so good. I get it sometimes. The mousse is good too. Jonny you gotta try it too. After you try that," said Tammy to Lisa and everyone and no one in particular.

"Sure," said Wind as he bit from the icebox pie, its coldness moving about his raw mouth, cooling and drying. He sipped from the Scotch then bit again, a cycle of contract and relax, overtaking his mouth until it was no longer clear which contracted any more. Lao and Jack smoked and Lisa bit from Tammy's mousse and they both chewed and moaned in enjoyment together. Wind was alone among the smoke and sighs in the night beginning to chill, surrounded by four, two couples going forth not alone, so he drank, losing himself to the moment, the night, the sweet coldness of the food and the bitter clarity of the Scotch. Past the women and the grave, they handed him their mousse plate, the offering they shared. He handed back what he had to share and took from them. He bit and lost himself further in the gluttony, the act of devouring, taking in more of what was solid and present in the moment, hoping to keep up as it seemed to run on with his friends and without him. Lisa and Tammy enjoyed the pie and asked him if he liked the mousse. He smiled and tried to say yes it is good. He gaped in speech, then gobbled and gasped; gasping from garrulous movement to gluttonous impediment; cough, cough, coughing and cutting away at the flesh within his flesh, the only way he knew how, cutting with air from in and out, contracting and cutting, climbing constantly with a gurgling grind; air and will wearing away, breathing and sucking, spit starts to slide; and the substance is down within him and breath continues. Then his right hand moved in and drew upward another bite.

16. TLECUAUHTLACUPEH

(She Who Comes Flying from the Light Like an Eagle of Fire)

I think Rodriguez has his Alfaro and for every Alfaro there is
always a Rodriguez. They do not always remember.
—William S. Burroughs, *exterminator!*

IT WAS HIGHER THAN THE HALFWAY POINT, BUT IT WAS FLAT AND A
good place to look west out over the whole city. In the center of the
horizon the skyscrapers looked like one mass, casting light in all
directions, and that mass was like another mountain, an inhabited
mountain, to complement this one: a mountain of glass opposing a
mountain of stone. From here, the shimmering downtown was silent,
cold and silent, a still place abandoned by the god-like men that once
inhabited it. A loose chain of skyscrapers, like foothills, ran from the
central peak north up to Sandy Springs where the Landmark Towers,
the "King" and "Queen," shone like crystal chess pieces with their
genders and power positions illustrated in their white headdresses. To
the south the airport was indicated with the landing and lighting of
planes, a clear flat place where the planes looked like swarming and
feeding gnats, as if they were the same planes going back and forth,
careful of a precarious trough. The flow of the bodies resting at the

349

point of plateau was consistent in its thickness and constant movement; a transitioning. An uncharacteristically thick flow for a weekday, for a Friday just after noon, going up or coming down. They all glistened a little about their arms and brows and napes, some shinier than others, gnats to and fro on the stony plateau. A sparse tree line bordered the lower edge of the plateau. Spots of fir and pine, sprouted from cracks and craggy crevices in the rock, the sharpest edge of the cluster thin and wind-cut.

Jonathan Wind, vacationing homicide detective of the Atlanta Police Department, breathed heavily, his ass parked on a flat rock at the over-mid-way point of Stone Mountain's walking trail, and tried to remember the last time he drank as much as he did the night before. All he could conjure was that it must have been some night out with Monica and her friends and though he might have drank a lot out of awkwardness or guilt, he would have internalized all feelings and effects of alcohol and not let it take him as away as he let it take him last night. Though he was with his dearest friends, he still felt a pang of regret today for letting himself be so off guard, so relaxed, and he kept replaying everything said to make sure he didn't betray anything about his investigation. Except when necessary with Sonny, Wind didn't like to talk too much about a case until his thoughts were in order and all his connections were made. Breathing on this rock he bent his head down out of the high sun and felt its warm rays against the dampness of his neck, and as the sun drew out more beads of perspiration the strong crosscutting winds washed them away.

"Hey, tough guy Mr. Police Officer Man, are you alright? I thought you guys were supposed to stay in shape. In case you have to chase someone down. Roust some punks." She clapped. "Come on, let's go! Not much farther now, little Smurf."

He rose with the sounds of his knees popping and slowly rotated his neck, letting it pop too as he walked around the bench-like rock to Sutra.

"I'm sorry I had a long, late night. You look pretty spry, like you've got a lot of energy. A formidable foe. Normally, I'd race you and beat your ass up this rock."

"Well then. Flora always said your greatest weakness was pride, and we all know that it's pride that will bring the proud down."

They walked up the steepest portion of the trail to the summit. It was only their second meeting, but they were joking so freely with each other that endorphins must have been playing at least a small part. Halfway up this last leg, walking side by side, he shouted at her, "race her to the top," and took off running. He was thankful that he wore hiking boots and khakis instead of jeans, although he had no idea where he was taking her after he picked her up at the Avondale MARTA Station. Hopping between the bigger rocks as he ran, Sutra was close behind him so he let out a burst of energy from deep within his body and sprinted to the top ahead of her. As she walked up to where he stood on the flat summit, he was leaning with his hands on his knees and wheezed a little, cheeks pink and cool, his brow moist.

"That was a great use of energy, very productive. But here I go, walking past you and you have to catch up to me again. Come on."

Wind righted himself and walked behind her. She walked towards the concession window and met no rebuttal when she suggested that they needed water. They walked towards the benches with a city view and without speaking, made a mutual choice of seat that was sunny, but shielded from the wind. He sipped at the water she handed him.

"I love it here, regardless of all the cheesy stuff, the legacy of hate, and the fat, out of shape tourists," she looked slyly and sideways at him. "All that, and I still love it here. This big pointless rock has a lot of meaning."

He felt that he understood where she was coming from. Wind had been here several times growing up and remembered all his moments of angst and spleen in regards to this place, as well as random moments of joy. After how he had already heard Sutra speak on their last meeting, he could imagine all of her various complaints and had most likely shared in the majority of them. A park had formed around this rock, a mountain of rock, Stone Mountain, the world's largest piece of exposed granite. A town had always been around this rock, as long as colonists were here, a town called New Gibraltar until 1947 when it was changed to the town of Stone Mountain. The town and the park, however, don't just celebrate a world record in granite exposure, but another world record all together. The park holds the honor of being the world's largest Confederate Memorial—to which Wind always wondered if any other countries even came close—but part of that memorial is also the world's largest high relief sculpture. On the baldest, smoothest, steepest face of the mountain is carved an effigy to the three greatest defenders of the Confederate dream, mounted riders in the carved stone likenesses of President Jefferson Davis, General Robert E. Lee, and General Stonewall Jackson; a Confederate Mount Rushmore by the same hand. To the top of the rock, a cable car and a walking trail, and at the top, an information center, historic film, and concessions. The surrounding park is filled with crafty shops, restaurants, an old timey-themed train, a man-made lake with beach and water rides, an ice skating rink, and other such entertainments mixing down-home flavor and modern extravagance that all somewhat smelled like fried chicken to Wind.

Once as a child, as the park provided good cheap fun with a sum-

mer laser light show and fireworks display for the price per car entering the park—the lasers projecting onto the carved face of the mountain and the fireworks coming off the top—his mother had brought
he and his sister. There were warring prides inside of his mother, and
while one pride would not let her move back to New York after Nathan died, to seek the assistance of his family, for she had none of her
own; another pride was committed to making do and depriving her
children of nothing on the meager salary that she made. That night,
which he remembered as being in the summer of 1986, at the laser
light show, they got to know their city in a way they had not known
it before, as pickup trucks loaded with Ku Klux Klan members made
their presence known, indiscreet and incognito, watching the show
and cheering for their heroes; then booing when the laser show closed
on the last strains of "Dixie" with laser-drawn General Lee breaking his saber and throwing its halves to the bloodied battleground
in resignation, before returning to his place with the other horsemen
and the green beams gave way to lights glorifying the sculpture and
an eruption of fireworks. Here, young Jonathan had seen his share of
kitsch, hate, and overweight tourists, but now looking around Wind
tried not to judge.

"What meaning does it have for you? I am guessing that's why
we're here. There is some point to our meeting and coming to talk
here, something the mountain has for you. It seems that you have a
flair for lecturing and I assume this is a teaching tool, to help you cut
right to the point?" He asked, because she told him nothing before,
nothing but to pick her up at the Avondale MARTA Station and
from there she said to drive to Stone Mountain. In the car she gave
her own quicker directions of side streets and he squinted through the
windshield, having forgotten his sunglasses, an oversight he regretted

less now than he did all the way up the mountain, the sweat running blindingly along with the sun over his brow.

"That is me. I cut like a diamond. Good memory. I'm glad to see that your mind stays sharp even when your body is sluggish. You seem to keep coming to me for stories, so I'll tell you another one and this is a good setting for it. You might try to tell me that what you want is information, but it's all just story, all packaging. Now, I have a lot of duality in me. I am a Gemini like Flora. It was just another thing we had in common, the twins. And we were each other's twin a lot of the time. We were light and dark as twins, like how night and day make one whole and blend in and out of each other." He looked at her strained and tired, but his expression was one of intention, like he was trying to mentally record what she said. "My point is that I told you all about the Indian traditions that I embrace and define a large part of myself with, traditions that come from my father's line, though not his guidance in particular. No matter my take on him personally, or how I get along with him, my Buddhism has some cause in him, if only by reaction, and protest to his Hinduism. In a way that is half of me, what I have come to practice, how I have come to live my life, but it's still only half, the Indian half. There is the other side, of me, the Gemini duality, that comes from my mother's side, the Mexican side. Water?"

He had finished his bottle of water and she offered the remainder of hers to him, his head turned to her out of the sun, squinting in reflected glare.

"Are you sure?" He asked politely, and took her bottle as she nodded, sipping the clear pure water slower than before to let it coat his mouth and lips.

"Last Sunday I only mentioned that I chose a Spanish spelling of diamond in my personal renaming as a tribute to my mother, a little representation of her heritage, but it goes further for me than just the name. She might have let her traditions go for a man but I will not and I've brought them back and embraced them for myself"

A wind came up fiercely from the east and south, charging up and at the mountain in an effort to wear at its rocky surface, an action that it had been repeating for thousands of years and with it sounds were carried, created in its interchange with and against different surfaces, the dull thud as it hit the walls of the building, the flapping of signs and paper, the stripping rustle of fir and pine needles, and the resonant tock of Wind's empty water bottle tipping and striking the rock against which he propped it. With the wind came a chill to the exposed skin of both bodies, but along with that a feeling of elation and exaltation.

"Feel that. That is why I wanted to come here, I love that, that power. This mountain is just a rock, and it's practically treeless since there is no soil for roots to grow. It's like a bone of the Earth poking out, the inner Earth reaching out and as we sit on top we bring the power of Earth and Sky together. In Meso-American traditions, ancient Mexico, mountains were called altepetls, which literally means 'mountain filled with water,' but the word was also used to refer to a community or city. That is what they were doing when they made pyramids; they were trying to recreate these mountains with the belief that the gods and all life came out of the Earth, out of mountains. They would keep their dead in the pyramids along with icons of the gods. Some were designed so rainwater would run down the structure and collect around it like a canal. The Aztec found gods already in the pyramid at Teotihuacán and named it that because to them that was the place of the gods, where the gods lived. I have felt wind like this when I stood on that pyramid of Teotihuacán, that energy it brought was amazing, that feeling of power you know the ancients felt. A whole cosmology of mythic stories came out of that wind, that invisible hand of god, invisible gods themselves touching the surface. I felt it even more so at Tepeyac, not a mountain or pyramid, but a hill, a natural one. That was the actual research work I did in school."

"What was that work, specifically?" Intrigued and reassured, his mind energizing his body, Wind asked her a question to keep the process active and move her along as he guessed she wanted.

"Technically, I was doing post-colonial studies, and in the religion department, as a major, I did those under the concentration of Religion and Literature. My major professor wasn't actually Dr. Ruen. I took a lot of classes with him and brought that Buddhist side of my life forward because of him, but my major professor was Dr. Toni Medecin. She was amazing, a brilliant woman, and so supportive, from Louisiana and married into such a great French Creole name that really fit her, she was both a doctor and the medicine. Dr. Ruen and Dr. Medecin, great faculty names to learn from, made you think the themes that we discussed were in their blood, part of who they were in their roles as teachers, purveyors of knowledge. They were both relatively recent additions to the department though, not anyone your father would have known."

He snapped a sharp look at her with his brow tight and furrowed. He hadn't mentioned anything about his father to her today or on Sunday, so whatever she knew about his father must have been from Flora. It was natural for it to have come up in conversation, her being a student there and Flora knowing his father taught in that department, but it made him wonder how much more she knew about him and what she planned to do with that information, however much she had. She acknowledged and dismissed his look with a quick smile and went on talking.

"Watching the Indian side develop and beginning to honor my mother's side with my new last name, I decided to go further academically. Dr. Medecin helped me realize that academically. I was interested in the post-colonial and looking at the places where cultures met and overlapped, points of conflict and growth. I myself am one of these points. I am such a product of the post-colonial, an Indian Mexican in Atlanta. So I took to it fast and did so much more than just literature with Dr. Medecin, not that it isn't all just literature anyway, but we got into all the postmodern theorists and I worked my way up through all the bullshit Western philosophical jargon to get to a point where I was ready to understand notions of interstitial space and how they appear with groups and cultures and religions. For examples of this, I looked towards Mexico, into my background. Dr. Medecin exposed me to Mary Louise Pratt's notion of the contact zone, the space of post-colonial dialogue between the indigenous and the conqueror. The colonization of Mexico was a perfect example of Pratt's notion and I spent the last two years of school looking at both sides of the experience, doing a lot of research. My heart is with the oppressed, as you might guess."

"Jean Paul Sartre said he always sided with the underdog for the sake of consistency," Wind added in a quick break between her breaths.

"It's a good policy that I agree with. It was easy for me to side with the indigenous of Mexico, the Aztec and other Nahua tribes, seeing what happened to them by the Spanish, butchering and beating conversions into people for the honor of their god and crown. Revolution is part of all parts of my blood and though I came to learn about the Spanish side, I have never really understood or agreed with it.

357

Technically, my mother is a mestiza, of both Spanish and indigenous blood, but to me she is all Mexican. Her family is Catholic, the religion of their conquerors, and sadly, most of them have no concept of a pre-Colombian heritage. Just like she let go of her past for my father, they seem to have let go of their own past. I guess they did it for the Pope as a father, or patriarch, in a similar way. So the work I started doing was looking at discourse in the contact zone. I was trying to find ways in which the indigenous speak back to their conquerors through the language of the conquerors. Pratt calls this autoethnographic expression. I was looking at these instances as revolutionary acts, but on a cultural and religious level. Other than fighting back with guns and fists, I wanted to see how people could fight back more covertly. Eventually I started looking at the figure of the Virgin of Guadalupe as just that revolutionary act. That is what brought me to the hill of Tepeyac in Mexico City, Teotihuacán was just a side trip away from my school research."

Investigator Wind listened, lining up the connections, watching them tighten in his head, and felt that he was finally on the right path now hearing a second person mention similar things as a first, and though this connection of information was not very esoteric so far, they were both very distinct threads to align during this limited and strange investigation.

"It was all paid for, I got a grant. It was an award actually. I applied and my professors wrote letters and the money was for undergraduate thesis research. I put it to good use and went to Mexico the summer before this last one. I didn't have enough to go in July for the canonization of Juan Diego, but I went down in August and was kind of relieved to visit the shrine of the Virgin on an average crowded day and not during an international canonization with the Pope and his whole ridiculous retinue. That man sure can draw a crowd, especially in Latin America. I missed him though, went down on my own for five days in the heat of August and just worked. In Pratt's terms, the Virgin of Guadalupe would be textbook autoethnographic expression. Through the crafty syncretism of the early missionaries, a miracle story is recorded in both Spanish and Nahuatl that tells of the Virgin Mary appearing in the new world to an indigenous peasant, but it's laced with references and symbolism native to the colonized people. It became an amazing conversion tool and really led to the success of Catholicism in Mexico."

She paused and he handed her back her water bottle, thinking that as longwinded as she was being, she might need it more than he did. Apparently, she did.

"I was going down to interview people at the shrine, the devoted, the faithful. I wanted to know what the Virgin of Guadalupe, specifically, meant to them personally, and compare that to how the Catholic Catechism describes the Virgin Mary, generally. I was doing the normal fieldwork questions, age, sex, occupation, but I was also asking about heritage, if people had any Aztec heritage or could speak Nahuatl, the language of the indigenous, or if anyone related to them could speak it. It looked like a possibility, it is the largest spoken indigenous language in North America, and over one million Mexicans speak it. After asking about the Virgin, who they were obviously there to see, I asked about two specific Aztec goddesses, Tonantzin and Tlazolteotl. Tonantzin was the Aztec Earth Goddess, a mother figure who also helped bring the rains from her shrine on the hill of Tepeyac, where the Virgin's shrines now stand. In the story of the Virgin of Guadalupe those early priests sure did their homework and the goddess Tonantzin seems well preserved in the new Virgin. The Catholic take is, of course, that the Virgin appeared there to a newly converted peasant; it was a miracle. Maybe those Aztecs had been worshipping her there all along under the mistaken name of Tonantzin until she came to clear that mistake up in talking to that peasant Juan Diego. The paper I wrote to graduate, my senior thesis, was all about how the Mexicans were preserving the cult of Tonantzin and continuing to worship her under her new name, the Virgin of Guadalupe. I stand by my concept, that it was a rebellious act and a way of fighting back, on that cultural-religious level, against the oppressive religion of their conquerors. Especially after Mexican independence and the Spanish rule was officially over, the Catholic Church still stood as a dominant and oppressive body." She sipped from the water again and looked in the distance for a moment, turning her head slowly so the whipping wind could move her hair out of her face for her.

"Who was that other goddess you asked them about, Tlazolteotl?" Wind was listening in the same thorough way that he read, and made visual pictures of the words he heard for moments just like this, to come back to things overlooked. He remembered the name from Tia Maite. It was the name of the goddess who ruled the day in the Aztec calendar on which Flora died.

"Tlazolteotl was a darker goddess, far from a virginal or maternal figure, and some say that she was the other side of Tonantzin, making an earlier, more complete goddess figure. She was worshipped elsewhere than the hill of Tepeyac, but the separation of her from Tonantzin was made almost final by the Catholic appropriation of Tonantzin, the mother and virgin only. See, I don't think that the people sold out, I think they preserved what they could, and for the last four hundred plus years they have preserved Tonantzin more successfully than other figures. My work in this area is an act of retrieval. Foucault would think it pretty cute if I called it an archaeology of the self, but it's beyond just myself, and my mother's abandoned traditions, it's happening with others who all want to retrieve and preserve the sacredness of past traditions that are still alive in our being. My work is nothing very new or original. If anything, all I have contributed to the scholarship so far has been just to play up the revolution angle of the preservation. The findings from my fieldwork were sad, but to be expected. People who were clearly of indigenous descent claimed they were not, none of them knew any Nahuatl but one guy, who said his grandmother in the Hidalgo region did, and no one knew the goddess I mentioned. Even though they described the Virgin in ways an Aztec might have described Tonantzin four hundred years ago, they seem to know nothing of their past and claimed to be nothing more than Catholics. I wanted to shake some of them and scream 'what the fuck, look in the mirror, you're darker than I am, and though your culture is mestizo, you're probably not, where the hell do you think you are?' But of course I kept that all inside. If they were doing autoethnographic expression, as Pratt calls it, with the Virgin of Guadalupe, then they have no idea, they were doing it intuitively. And again, I was at the shrine, a catholic shrine. It took me some time, but I learned that there were better places to look for retrieval and the remembering of forgotten Aztec goddesses."

"Do you mean like in D.H. Lawrence's *The Plumed Serpent*, an Aztec god revival cult? That one was to a male god, Quetzalcoatl. But is that what you mean, by better places to look? A cult?" His blood was hot and alive under his skin, which too was hot. The goose bumps on his hands and neck, exposed around the barn jacket, were the product of a nervous system stimulated by the wind and what haze there was between his brain and eyes had blown away. He had listened to her and now the investigator Wind was on the job.

"Cult might be a word you choose to use, but it has such negative connotations. You know your Latin. You know cultus means like culture or education. And that sense is still there, words always carry their true meanings and origins with them, no matter what ignorant people do to them or heap upon them over time. It's just like what happens to religious traditions or land or individuals, actually. So cult is not a word I would use until we strip it back down to its truth, but as I said, I found what I was looking for, though it might not be what you're referring to, or maybe it is? I shouldn't judge, you've impressed me in the past." She was out of her lecturing attitude and initiating a defensive banter with him.

"Thank you. My only inference is that it is a small group or religious sect. The connotation that a cult is just a religion in its infancy. But I'm only trying to figure out what exactly you found. You were only there five days, how much more could you find outside of your time at the shrine? Or did you find what you were looking for here in Atlanta? Is that what you came to tell me about, is that where you took Flora? What you had to check on before we could meet today?" He looked forcefully at her, pushing with his words and eyes, and from his push she pulled back, took in the view and the air again, responding with silence.

"It is lovely, isn't it?" She looked around with a staged smile, an attitude of aloofness. "I don't know why I tease you so much. I guess I just want you to know where I stand, how people, with me as an example, come to the places that they are at. I do respect you, and in trusting Flora, I always have. And we did have such a nice dinner the other night on our own. And now you see what else I have studied. You and I are not just east and west meeting and sparring. A revolutionary squaring off against supporter of state and status quo. And aren't you technically on vacation right now? Breaking some rules I bet, investigating on your own time. Don't you have to have a special license for that?" Her smile softened and sweetened. "Sorry, I'm just busting on you, we're probably more similar than I ever thought. I mean hey, why not? We loved the same woman. She changed both our lives, and so these two lives have been changed in the same way, no matter where they started from."

He returned a sweet smile, allowing her to feel that if this dropping of her guard was nothing more than an act, he was going along with it. On the chance that she was sincere, which she sounded, it was agreeable enough to him in tone and wording for him to hold his own guard just enough at bay to feel the solidarity of their positions and relation. Sutra started to rise and attentive Wind went up with her into the high and exalting air, watching and ready to listen or question, whichever way she went. She stretched and yawned.

"We should go. I have somewhere to be, some people to meet, and it would be great if you can drop me back at the MARTA Station. I checked on what I told you I would. I have done all that I feel I can to help you out and I hope you are sure of what you are doing. I have an address in my bag back in the car that I will give you. Be there at midnight tonight and be punctual. I don't know if you will find what you expect. I don't know what you expect. I trust you will be respectful, that in your search, when you lift a rock to look under it, you don't destroy the rock or what's beneath, that you put it back how you found it. I don't know if all of your questions will be answered, but this is all I can offer." She looked around and surveyed the view, her eyes high. "Today is Xochitl in the Aztec calendar, which means flower, and it is a day for beauty and truth and reflection especially on how fading and temporal life is. The goddess that rules the day is Xochiquetzal, which means 'feather flower' and she is the ruler of music and the arts. It all seems to fit; can't you see that the ancient Aztec knew what they were doing? Today is the eleventh day of the Trecena—that is the term for the thirteen-day week of the Aztec calendar—Itzcuintli," and she smiled with that mixture of impressed and surprised as he nodded knowingly along.

"Yes," Wind puffed between her words. "Itzcuintli, the dog, ruled over by Xipe Totec, the God of Shedding and the releasing of seeds, and it's a time for self-sacrifice, devotion, and duality of illusions and understanding."

"Very good, Detective, you really do catch on quick. I hope if anything ever happens to me, it's you who's on the case. You didn't mention, but also this Trecena is a good time for commemorating the dead and a bad time for holding on to the living. But maybe you are ready for tonight after all. Maybe. It's also a full moon tonight. There is a lot going on at this point in time cosmically, a lot intersecting. Ten, ten, two thousand three in Atlanta, who knew?"

They walked to the nearest trashcan and threw out the water bottles and walked farther on to the edge of the peak, where, before they made their aerobic descent, she spoke one last official-sounding phrase of instruction.

"You'll have to send my regards, I won't be there tonight, I have a date, but they told me to send you and they're expecting you. And actually, they said they have been trying to contact you for some time."

364

17. NIGHT VOYAGE—DESCENT

> Going up that river was like traveling back to the earliest be-
> ginnings of the world, when vegetation rioted on the earth
> and the big trees were kings. An empty stream, a great silence,
> an impenetrable forest. —Joseph Conrad, *Heart of Darkness*

I SHOULD HAVE BROUGHT MY SIDEARM, THOUGHT JONATHAN WIND. I
should have brought my sidearm. But he had not. Nor had he brought
his backup. There was no extra weight or pressure around his waist;
that certain way he could move his hips within his pants, against his
belt, letting the jutting edge of his hip bone control his belt and its free
light movement on his lithe frame. He couldn't wiggle his right foot to
control the shifting of its familiar extra weight either. These throbbing
thoughts in his bludgeoned head were a reflex and even if he could
reach right now for either gun, if even he had one, he couldn't draw it.
Maybe just shift his perception to them through his hipbone, or pat at
his sidearm with his elbow or let his forearm scrape smoothly by it in
a natural movement. Some moments they were an obvious consolation
or assurance. To know they were there, just in case. If there were to be
shots fired he could return fire, and if violence was necessary he could
call upon violence of his own. But they were absent, no emotional or

physical crutch present on his waistline or ankle to assure his fevered, scattered mind with its dependency on security and control. He stood strong, ignoring the pain, and waited, using strength of mind and will, containing all his summoned wind.

His arms were pulled and pinned back, but he kept his chest puffed out and full; he was an inflated solid wall of a man. Even if physically he could go weak or feign weakness, that was not his way, and part of his strength lay in consistency. Pride, strength, and determination were consistent patterns of action for Wind. They all worked together and he would never run blindly into a situation, for pride wouldn't let him and neither would his strength of mind or will. His movements had thoughts behind them, deft and keen. Of course, he *was* presently captive with his arms tightly back behind him to the point where his shoulder blades almost touched, a situation he hadn't quite foreseen.

Even without a firearm there were things he could do, physical tactics with which he could try to navigate this situation. The four-armed grip on his arms and back limited only two of his limbs and supported him upright, but only with the help of his own legs. The bare gray concrete wall was about two feet behind him and only about a foot behind those gripping him. He could go loose at the knees and pushing off he could slam them back against the wall. He could lean to one of them as if to initiate a whisper and when they leaned to meet him he could drop a head-butt and then pull and push the other's weight against him. He could just drop at the knees and pull them off balance with his weight and then take control of both of them. Easily he could stand on one foot and drop a forceful blow with his other foot on one of his detainer's knees. These ideas and more were natural thought reflexes. The buffoon and hunchback didn't seem all that smart and with a little leverage he would be able to overtake them. No, he thought, they were not that smart, but they were definitely very strong.

It was that strength of theirs that held him, that strength and his own awe. He had waited all day distracting himself for this. His focus was so strong within his tired frame that when he left Sutra at the MARTA station and went home, he was able to control his expectations and relax enough to nap. His sleep was strong and heavy and he woke feeling that he had dreamed, but he could not remember anything whole, no narrative threads, but images and fragments he assumed were from the dream of his childhood. Maybe in doubt of dream content his waking self supposed they were from the dream, or maybe he was just hoping that they were from the dream, that even a hungover midday nap on the couch could bring the deep comfort of consistency. The images were basic and the most common of all the times he had had the dream, like flashes of a slide show, old knight, sword, snake, egg, tree, goats, and yellow fire trucks. With the images, from whatever part of his memory they came, he woke alone and resolute. The address Sutra gave him was memorized. He recited it upon sitting up. Three times, slowly and clearly he said it and then exhaled deeply. The sun was beyond the trees beyond his window and in its sinking his living room was flecked with confetti of burning orange embers. Amid the autumnal spatter, he stood and stretched and walked stretching farther with each step to the table that also operated as a desk. He opened his laptop and lying on the keyboard were the five Polaroid pictures of him and Flora. He lifted them and made a neat stack in his hands. Shuffling, he drew to the top the picture he took of her alone, her face gasping in candid pleasure and her breasts lost to her bending position. Closing the laptop, he kissed the top picture and sat the stack down. No one was expected, he had already boxed up all of Monica's possessions that she kept at his place and dropped them at the hospital on Tuesday and it was unlikely that she would stop by, and now he didn't care who saw the pictures and he no longer wanted to hide them.

Though he finally resolved not to bring it, not to bring the element of fear or violence with him to a place where it might not be welcomed, he did take the time that evening to chase away the gloaming dusk light with the living room overhead light and sit down at the table to clean his sidearm. His backup was left discarded on his bedroom dresser where it fell when he undressed the evening before, but he took slow methodical care of his police issue Glock 9mm and followed the routine by taking care of his body. Glasses of water returned the hydration that was stripped away by the alcohol consumption last night, the hike up Stone Mountain earlier today, and the sweaty nap on the couch only moments ago. There were no high-nutrient greens in his refrigerator, which he would have preferred in his thoughtful preparations, but he was sated and energized by the leftover pizza. With controlled mind and movements he chewed slowly and sat in silence without any temptation to put on music or the television. From his jacket hanging on the chair back behind him he drew his notepad and turned to a blank page. On the page he wrote down the Buford Drive address he had been recalling. Then he drew from his back left pants pocket a piece of paper which bore the same Buford Drive address, but in Sutra's hand. He compared the two addresses and confirmed the sameness. A chuckle rose up in his throat at his own anxiety that he might have memorized the address incorrectly, but he applauded his own thoroughness. The address was familiar, not the exact address he recalled but of an inescapably coincidental proximity. The time for which he had been waiting was almost upon him so he brought this stage of his preparations calmly to a close. He changed into a button-down gray shirt and tucked it into brown pants.

Leaving his apartment, he drove north on Highland and cut through scenic Morningside and its expensively pretty and yardless homes to Piedmont, upon which he proceeded again north up to the intersection of gaudily bright sex shops and restaurants at Cheshire Bridge where he turned right along more restaurants, strip bars, and all-girl modeling establishments bearing full parking lots and quiet facades, up into the crowds of cars crossing and turning at Tara Cinema showing the newest art movies, that briefly stymied his progress until he could pass under the bridge of I-85 to finally reach the mouth of Buford Highway before it spilled out into I-85 South and Sidney Marcus Boulevard. Turning right and shooting northeast, he sailed with ease and took in the darkened city on this thickening strip as it grew into the distinct microcosm he expected. He had no idea what the vast and diverse Asian population referred to it as, but to the various inhabitants of Latin descent it was La Buford. Parallel to the interstate he rolled, past the grand glowing neons of Pancho's Mexican Restaurant on his right and the Latin American Association on his left, the new architecture built to shine and esteem even in its night slumber. Uproad he cruised, taking in all the strip malls and freestanding restaurants in parking lots and on corners, with tall signs splashed in tropical colors and radiating neon lights, beckoning with Spanish names festive and descriptive, so familiar to natives and immigrants alike, La Catracha, Restaurant and Nightclub, La Sarosa, Comida China, Havana Restaurant, Marisqueria Mares 7, Brito Supermarket, La Feria Restaurant, El Ocho Billiards, Taqueria de Peso, El Progreso, La Ruleta, El Reye de Todos, Café Mex, Taco Market, La Pastorcita, Taqueria Michoacan, El Porto Mexican Restaurant, La

Tropicanna, Carniceria Durango, Plaza Fiesta, Taqueria Guadalajara. There were names of Vietnamese, Korean, Chinese, and Japanese establishments mixed in, but the first five miles of La Buford were outspokenly Latin. Five miles up, he passed slowly by the turn to which he was heading, almost at the border of the City of Doraville and the "Dekalb International Village," indication that the concentrated Latin population of the previous miles was about to be remixed at a slimmer ratio to the other groupings found in the Buford Highway ethnic cocktail. The turn was the way to double dead-ended Buford Drive, a tributary of the rolling roadway, like a narrow slip of a gully. Carefully, Detective Sergeant Wind looked out the windows at his environment. Through his wavy headlights the asphalt looked like primitive wet rock, worn and smooth by the waters of time. He hung a slick U-turn across three lanes in between the flow of cars and cruised by the familiar destination now on his left. The number was not the same as his last visit, it must be the building next door, he thought. There was time to wait and think.

Detective Wind drove back to Plaza Fiesta and parked behind the north side of the strip mall, behind the Burlington Coat Factory, under one street light where there were no other cars. The address of tonight's event, now clear and confirmed; he sought to organize all of this collected data anew to accommodate the additions. After sitting for some time, at about ten-thirty a Chamblee Police cruiser eased up before him and rolled slowly to the point where their driver's side windows met. As Detective Wind lowered his window, and before the other officer could speak, he flashed his badge and gave a not offensive, but stern, glance and a nod to which the other officer returned a nod and asked if he could be of any assistance, but the detective only gave a head shake and the other officer backed out slowly like rewinding a video image. Experiencing this moment of authority gave Detective Wind encouragement in what he was doing and reconfirmed that what he was doing was correct and correct if not for any other reason than that he was doing it.

A little after eleven o'clock, he forded half of Buford Highway, through minor eddies of traffic, and made his way back up to the parallel stretch off the highway he had scouted before. There were lights on in the long white building next to Tia Maite's and cars parked in both driveways and on the street. He was sure that building would match the address he held; things were coming full circle, which to him was a positive indication. He turned the sharp right onto Buford Drive and made another sharp left driving to the far north end of the street, quiet and dark but for a streetlight. There were no cars on this end of the street and all the little white houses bearing signs of the professional offices they housed looked empty. After determining the numerical pattern of the addresses, he turned around in the last driveway and then turned back out and north on Buford Highway, making a right onto Shallowford Terrace, the street past the grass of Buford Drive's dead-end and into a closed accounting office on the corner. Walking across Shallowford Terrace, he broke from the street behind the first white house and stealthily made his way downhill over grass and around bushes behind the other houses under shelter of shadows. Getting down to that second to last building, next to Tia Maite's, he crept up low against the back wall beneath the windows. It seemed like a dance hall or community meeting space for a local Mexican community, he thought, as he peeked in to see people congregating with cups and conversation in the white rectangular great room; not exactly what he was expecting, but this is where Sutra told him to go, where she said Flora went her last night of life. He was squatting next to a cellar door and seeing that it was unlocked, he thought he could slip down inside and get an idea of what was going on upstairs before going in. He opened the basement door and was instantly overcome by a damp smell of sod and manure followed by a deeper smell and taste infesting the air that he associated with rotting matter, highway death. Into the dark depth, he stepped slowly down the stairs, tightly against the wall, and reached shortly searchingly out into the distance until other hands grabbed his and him and a blow fell against his head.

And that was how he wound up here, detained, arms pinned back, in the basement connecting this building and Tia Maite's office, where beginnings happen for him: his investigation, his confusion, and now—he hoped—his understanding. Part of his tactic in not fighting back was in the knowledge that this is what he wanted, what he imagined all along, and he was more than ready to face what Flora experienced on the night of her death. Held by the buffoon and hunchback, he temporarily abdicated his weight and power to them and allowed his eyes to adjust to the low light in an effort to take in the room. His first thought in surveying was to consider the whereabouts of the albino little person; if the buffoon and hunchback were here he must not be too far away. The pale little messenger not in sight, he squinted through his throbbing head and let the consciousness of his perception yellow with the candlelight, acclimating to the dank and smoky low-lit room. There were shadows in the distant corners, moving shadows. They were just beyond the throw of the little light sources and the scrutiny of his eyes. But other things were becoming clear to him. This room was not just thrown together; it was well worn with layers of dirt and dust covering a rudimentary opulence. Though he couldn't see it all—and even if he could he doubted he could clearly read all they told—the walls gave him a great story in mural, mixing angles and dimensions and sizes; clearly an epic of humanity in a pre-Colombian Aztec style, littered with dozens of little brown people, faces always in profile, journeying, building, settling, and journeying again on all sides of him, all processions leading beyond his line of sight into the dark end of the room and accented by little spots of green spiked maguey cacti, rain clouds, and mountains. He could make out building clusters that must have been Teotihuacán and Tenochtitlan, and others that resembled modern Mexico City and Atlanta's skyline.

Sounds tapped and banged out from above through the ceiling with lighter intonations of scurrying and scraping, while the shadows in the far corners busied themselves faster with rhythmic furtive movements. The two men at his sides held him dumbly, both looking down with the occasional foot tap, ignoring the sounds. Detective Wind didn't even think to speak to them after the initial bump and grab and at this point it felt as if they were all locked in a stubborn silence of waiting. He held his breath and nothing immediate came of the noises above or in the corner shadows so he returned to scanning the room. He was against the back wall facing in the direction that seemed the correct direction for an audience to stand in viewing. To his back right, near the back yard staircase he came down, there was a concrete corridor that led, against a current of journeying mural people, whiter and in contemporary dress, in the direction of Tia Maite's building, and, he guessed, a staircase up to the doorway in her foyer. To his back left was an immediate staircase leading up. The long basement room stretched out away from these entry points into darkness. Beneath the condensed candle light, a high bench chair with crescent moon seat was centered, pedestal tables on each side, and rusting metal slatted drains lining the floor in a square shape around the chair, pedestals, and candles. The fat candles stood free in flanks of four: green, red, yellow, and white, just behind the pedestals on long poles wrapped in corn husks all the way down to their steel claw feet.

Little short flashes of light went off in the dark distant recess and before he could see the fast-moving smoke he could smell the incense; it was being puffed at him and filling the room, mixing its thick burnt tropical wood scent with the biting, fetid smell of rot and sod that greeted him and continued to hover in the room. The olfactory gamut he inhaled ran the space where food and death blended, sour bitterness like vinegar or an aged bacteria-wrought cheese, the eye-watering sharpness of road kill, the enticing fleshiness of grilled meat to the point of salty black ash, and now the dusty floral sweetness of marigolds and copal all growing more potent together. Detective Wind jerked and coughed in the clutching arms and held back from retching, his eyes conducting their own version of purging. Wiping his face feebly against his shoulders he tried to regain sight in the smoke-filled room. The buffoon and the hunchback stood strong, unbothered by the smoke or the odors.

With a bang and a sudden flash of light, the door at the top of the stairs to his left was thrown open. The new air swirled a smoky whirlwind, snuffing the candles and putting the room in darkness past the reach of the staircase. The sound of a rattle shimmered with footsteps down the stairs and a light was switched off above, letting the sound take over the darkness. A second rattle shook out in the same time as the first and many feet were taking the stairs. As the rattlers reached the basement they split up, one of them passing across the middle before the detective. Endless foot to step sounds continued and upon each descending arrival the throngs followed the rattlers' paths. The sweaty smells and shuffling sounds of people filled the space in front of Detective Wind and when the rattle sounds were in the distance on both sides they stopped processing. After a few minutes the door shut at the top of the stairs and the last set of feet came down and joined the dense crowd in the dense basement, raising the stuffy temperature to the feeling of a sauna for the detective and making him want to retch again as he fought to breathe.

There was a silence; then the rattles started again faster, their crazy plinky rhythms beating feverishly. A whooshing sound came from both corners near the rattling and he could feel the crowd start to move and reshuffle to the sides. One at a time, on each side, the candles were lit and Detective Wind searched around him, opening up his vision again to the yellow light now with a greater smoke density. Only one row of people were directly in front of him and the others were against the walls to each side, giving a small amount of room around the metal-grated drains surrounding the chair and pedestals. The source of the whooshing sounds became visible as two men came from around the back of the standing candles working brooms made out of stick and long blades of green, brown, and yellow grass over the concrete floor towards the grating. All the way around the square they worked as Detective Wind watched, noticing their white peasant pants and shirts simply decorated with a woven pattern of blue, red, and yellow, and the fluffy headbands of raw white cotton around their deep brown foreheads; the rattlers dressed the same.

The others watching around him looked like ordinary people of this community that he ran into all the time, a crowd of focused faces varying in shades of brown and cream, salted with the occasional face of pink or peach. There was nothing consistent about the group, many looked clean and tidy of dress, but others wore their poverty and laborious occupations on their clothing. From a few teenagers up, all ages seemed to be covered, encompassing women in nice dresses, casual sun dresses, skirts, pants, t-shirts and tattered shorts and tank tops while men wore everything from tie-less suits to soccer jerseys and cowboy hats, boots, jeans, and studded shirts. All faces, no matter the outfit, were locked on the sweeping, mumbling in a low murmur to themselves, and seemingly oblivious to the presence of one bound by a buffoon and a hunchback in the rear of the room.

The vigorous rattling and sweeping fueled the pungent air, its heated movement, and as the sweepers returned behind the candles, the distant shadows began to stir and the crowd grew anxious and expectant, which he could see on so many faces of taut weathered skin, rich and brown like a jug of earthen clay, beneath the rolling beads of sweat. Little flashes of light went off in the shadows; two on each side, then steady light spreading, revealing moving shapes and still shapes on the back wall. As the outlined forms turned around into people holding candles, they were exposed within their workings and the four new candles per side were placed on tall stands also wrapped in cornhusks with more husks dangling. Light baring the nether halves of the side walls and the back wall completed the mural, sending all of the painted brown and white figures processing along the sides from their settlements on footprint trails past grass, bundles of sticks, rabbits, deer, monkeys, jaguars, vultures, alligators, lizards, snakes, skulls, dogs, and eagles to the Virgin of Guadalupe on a hill and then four large images of Aztec goddesses around the great wide mural centerpiece of the multicolored and intricate Aztec calendar. Detective Wind could tell they were goddesses, and most likely the same one, since they were either birthing or bare-chested, and along with wearing the same headdress, the area around each figures' mouth was black.

Yellow skinned all of them, with black mouths, crescent-shaped rings through their noses, and headdresses of cotton and cactus spines, the two farthest outer ones were squatting and birthing, the one on the left was naked, with face in profile, a white cotton earring, a green, red, and yellow collar above her downward pointing breasts, red and brown braided ropes tied around both calves, and hands with white nails wide by the crack between her legs where a broom-looking object was coming out; the one on the right faced forward with a much bigger headdress and spines pointing left, two fluffy white cotton earrings, a bangled collar of green and white, a bangled chest-plate, arms out and hands up, a small head emerging from the crack between her legs wearing a small version of her headdress, and legs covered from the knees down and feet in sandals. The two closest to the calendar stood, faces in profile, with the left side one in headdress with red wavy tongue out, looped white earring, arms extended straight out in both directions holding in left hand three cacti spines and in the right a dangling cauldron; a braided rope of red and gray was tied to her left forearm, a short mantle of black, gray, and red pointed down from her neck revealing one downward pointing breast, and from her waist hung a red, black, gray, and yellow patterned skirt above sandals. The one on the right side was similar except for slight variations on the same headdress, the mantle in red, gray, and white revealing both breasts, hands holding two spines in the left and cotton and weaving tools in the right, a shorter skirt of red, gray, and white, and red and gray braided bands around the knees. They were terrifying in their size and alien semiotics.

In the new light, as his bleary eyes began to pierce the once mysterious depths, Detective Wind recognized two of the people. With short scurries of movement he saw the albino little person, in a long white peasant shirt and white pants, a glowing blur of grace moving from the back light to the front light laying items on the pedestals next to the chair, always on beat with the terrible swelling drone of the rattles and sweepers, now only sweeping rhythmically in one place. Slowly moving forward from her place by the wall where she lit the last candle with another, he saw her, whom he expected, but she was different from what he remembered or what he could ever imagine. On their first meeting he had not seen Tia Maite standing, but it was more than just that. The fake austerity he scrutinized as charlatanry before in her palm-reading seer act and the sad confused maternal figure she presented as she wept lightly to herself for Flora was so far from the monument of a woman stepping into the light decked in undeniable primal majesty. Her gray hair looked black in an ornate braided pile on her head with spines poking out in a fanning direction. Her face was as flat and wide as he remembered, but its creamy skin had a new tight determined darkness to it around the corners and age lines. He thought he saw her dark eyes flash on him as she clutched a large woven blanket around her shoulders over a long floral skirt and moved her massive mountainous form rigidly up behind the chair. Detective Wind put her actual height at about five foot eight, but from his view now she looked like a giant.

Another woman approached her from the back left corner, flowers in her hair and dozens of beaded necklaces of red and gold around her tan neck covering the tops of her bare black-tipped breasts. She too wore a flowing floral skirt and whispered with Tia Maite in the center of the room as all watched and waited. As they spoke she turned to Tia Maite and exposed her back to the onlookers, tattooed with the head of Frida Kahlo wearing wide slate-blue antlers. They stopped and Tia Maite turned to the crowd; the rattlers and sweepers now silent.

"Penitent sinners, nicniuhuan, vecinos, Eduviges Dyada would like to begin the ritual service by addressing you all, as it is her turn. For any who are here for the first time, we are a people, believers in the Goddess whose home is where we are and where we have been. We die and are reborn with each generation from each past generation. Our home is here, in Atlanta, Georgia, in the United States of America. We speak Nahuatl, our earliest remembered language, we speak Spanish, the language of our conquerors, and we speak English, the language of this land we are conquering. Thank you so very much for being here, muchas gracias, tlazohcamati huel miec." Tia Maite's voice had the thinnest and smoothest of accents, and these first words borne by smoke filled the room so evenly Detective Wind could hear them from behind him.

The other woman passed before Tia Maite and stood directly behind the chair. She took three deep breaths and moved her hands in circles before her swaying breasts as if she was beckoning the smoke into her lungs, candle light glinting off her many ringed fingers. She looked to be in her forties, with long narrow features, and her skin was glowing and radiant with only a light sweat sheen.

"Buenas Noches. I am filthy, as are we all, todos nosotros, en todo. But there is one that is made pure. One that purifies herself with filth and sin. One who is pure enough to take the filth from us all, to call on the power of the cleansing filth goddess. You, Tia Maite, mi Tia, you will be the abuela, you are Toci tonight," said Eduviges Dyada, her accent piercing at every i and rolling at every r.

The rattles went up and rang out hard with the wild whoosh of the brooms following, and the whole crowd, except for the hunchback, the buffoon, and Detective Wind, stamped and clapped low and hard, not in a cheer, but in a beating of their hands together like they beat the concrete floor with their feet. Eduviges Dyada stepped to her right still facing out and Tia Maite walked around the candles and pedestals to stand in front of the chair. Bending slightly at the knee, she bowed her head and the albino little person approached and with his back to the crowd handed Tia Maite something and fastened something around her head. The small white form scurried around behind her as in one great dramatic movement Tia Maite righted herself high and wide and cast back the blanket from around her shoulders, turning her head to her right and extending her arms straight out to each side. The blanket disappeared into the concealed possession of the little person and Tia Maite stood before the room dark and triumphant, tools in her hands, face severe, and wearing a white headband with points that mixed like a thicket with those holding up her hair. Beneath the sharp point of her wide chin, cutting an angle in the flickering room, she wore beads, dozens of beads, tight red ones, looser gold, and the widest of anthracite silver falling over her chest and shoulders, yet still unable to hide her breasts as they rose and fell, disk aureoles of deep coal resting on her stomach, itself barrel-like in shape and color. All the candle light in the long room bent towards her with the push of awe-filled suspirations and to Detective Wind, as it must have been to everyone present, it was as if one of the mural-bound goddesses had stepped down from the wall and traded paint for flesh. In the smoke and greasy candlelight the image bled into reality, and Tia Maite into the goddess.

"So you have come tonight, viajado aquí, to seek purification and confession, for neyolmelahualiztli, to straighten your hearts. Usted ha venido para Ella, so you can serve Her, because you think Ella puede servirle. She serves no one but Herself. If you are here, you are here on bent knee and humbled heart, you are here because she has sent for you, because you are filthy, tlazolli, basura, a sinner, un mero pedazo de soga, una hoja, the shit, cuitlatl, on that leaf. Our earth is a compost heap, rotting filth, timochintin, shitting and eating and rotting from the inside out." She lowered her arms as she spoke, still holding the long spikes and weaving spool, and between each phrase Tia Maite vacillated her tongue far out from her mouth as if she was both lapping at the air and sending forth her words. "Now it's time for purification, purificación, cualtililocayotl. For this purification ritual, como hicieron nuestros antepasados en épocas antiguas, we will draw one penitent to confess and I, as Her priestess, Sere el confesor y escucharé hasta que Ella venga y se coma his sins and purify his body and soul, neyolmelahualiztli. The rest will follow and also be cleansed upon instruction. Now bring the penitent up here, traigamelo, es hora, servants of the Goddess."

Detective Wind knew at once that she was speaking about him and his thoughts were confirmed as the hunchback and the buffoon both kneed him in the back of the knees and dragged him on limp legs up through the crowd directly before the towering Tia Maite. When they stopped they retained their grip on his arms, which were starting to tingle as the move shook them out of their numbness, and the detective was able to retain his own strength of footing. Standing before her, though he was clearly taller, Tia Maite was a greater mass and he still felt that she towered over him.

"Como dicta nuestra tradicion, the penitent must come and ask to be confessed, pedir acercarse a la Diosa, but since you are already here, I will take that action as a request. You have come to the great Mother Goddess, Coatlique, in the form of Tlazolteotl para descargar sus corazones y darle una ofrenda de vida y pecado. Through what we do here, praising Tlazolteotl, restableciendo Yehuatl nelhuiliztli, alimentandola a Ella, giving of ourselves to Her. Nuestra tradicion es una de dualidad, la dualidad vida y muerte, yohualli y tonalli, duality in all things, even our great Mother Goddess. When the conquering Spanish Catholic preserved only Tonantzin en su Maria de Guadalupe, they excluded her other side. Hicieron de Ella una virgen, ocuelichpoctli, untouched, and let us secretly keep our ancient Goddess in Her, but only one aspect of the Goddess. La Madre is more than a virgin, how else would we all be born, como naceriamos todos? They call it a miracle to hide our sexuality, our potency, pero Ella es mas que limpia y casta, She is full and dirty. We came from her womb, the same womb in which She performed the sex act, ahuilneliztli, the same womb inches from where She shits. Amor y lujuria y mierda, it is all there in the same Goddess. Aqui elogiamos Tlazolteotl and reunite Her to Tonantzin, devolviendola a nuestra Madre in all truth and honesty," spoke Tia Maite out to the crowd.

Tia Maite stepped back and brought her weight down into the crescent chair, filling it with piles of her flesh supported by her perfectly erect frame, and laid the tools she carried on the pedestal to her left next to a giant pin cushion of twisted grass out of which black spines stuck. She lifted the tattered cushion of black pins and turned back to the crowd and Detective Wind.

"Mother of the gods, come and hear the confession of this low creature who has lived in filth, en tlazolli. It is he you inspired for filth and it is his filth only you can take away," said Tia Maite to him and everyone else.

Detective Wind's mind and emotions were slowly giving way to the situation in procession behind his body. Since the blow to the head and the following disorientation, he had been straining for control, but the throbbing of his head had been followed by a throbbing in his arms and back and a nausea in the pit of his stomach tearing its way up to his throat and eyes while his senses were dimmed by the lights and the hypnotically flowing crescendos and decrescendos of the rattles and brooms punctuating all of Tia Maite's words and movements. As physical and emotional resistance wore like powder from hard stones of defense, he mentally fought to refresh himself of why he was here, what his investigation entailed, while a fear of vulnerability and truly giving himself over to the ritual at hand and its purpose of confession and purification wore further at his stony defenses.

"Carlito," she called as if out to no one in particular and the albino little person emerged from behind her and stood at attention. "We will begin with a ceremonial blood-letting, el derramamiento de le sangre. Estamos hechosde la sangrede los Dioses and the least we can give back to them is our own blood. This is at once an offering to invoke the Goddess and a first penance for our sins. This is a time of self-sacrifice, the Tracena Itzcuintli, tiempo para tales cosas, para desprender semillas. We cast blood now as a seed of life. Giving of the self is an ancient tradition of our people, from the beginning of time, desde todos los principos del tiempo. After the last destruction of the world it was Quetzalcoatl who drew his penis and from it drew blood, eztli, chalchihuatl, which he then let fall to our ancestors' bones bringing life back to them, to us, to humanity."

In confident practiced movements, the buffoon and the hunchback made their grips on Detective Wind's arms tighter, tilting him backward a little and hooking his legs with their own, allowing him no leverage or control of his support. Before Detective Wind could even ponder their strength, Carlito approached him, laid down a wide strip of corn husk on the ground between them and pulled down the zipper fly of the detective's pants, which was right at arm level of the small man. Struggling, and tossing his head side-to-side were useless actions, and Detective Wind could only watch as the little person reached into his pants and boxer shorts and drew out the shaft of his penis. Bound and exposed Detective Wind stood, gripping at strength with waning determination, as Carlito drew a sharp black spine from the grass ball Tia Maite held and returned to a place of attention in front of the dangling penis.

"This maguey spine will pierce his penis one time for each sin," Tia Maite said, and Carlito held it above his head for all to see. "Its long slender shaft is like a hummingbird's beak, un pico del colibrí, and it draws blood from his penis like the hummingbird, huitzilin, draws life from the flower. Our ancestors, benditas sean sus vistas, did not see the hummingbird like those do today, just a lover of flowers. They saw the hummingbird like he is, a fearless warrior, El Huitzilopochtli, challenger of beasts beyond his size, un cajon de la sangre."

Carlito grabbed Detective Wind's penis with his fingers hooked behind its plum head and stretched its length as far as it would go. Detective Wind tried in vain to shift or struggle and was about to speak before Tia Maite grabbed his attention.

"Filthy penitent!" she spoke loud and harsh directly at him, drawing his eyes to hers, along with those of the whole room. The rattles and brooms stopped.

"Do you have sins of lust and impropriety?" she asked and he could not help but answer yes, hearing the yes and sì echoed from the lips of all those around him.

"Do you have sins of love and deception?" and again he answered yes to her forceful question with the same echo of sì.

"Do you wish to purge, cleanse, and purify?" And as this yes was gasped from his bent body, the rattles and brooms went up beating and whooshing and the echo of yes and sì was like a choral chant rising through the different accompanying timbres around him.

"Carlito!" she snapped in sonorous command.

"He is unclothed and ready to give of himself, to open his heart, to give his secrets and his sins," she said to the crowd as Carlito went to work.

Detective Wind winced and gritted his teeth, the tip of the long black spine artfully tracing across the shaft of his penis by the colorless hand like a surgeon's scalpel looking for the proper cut. In a place with no major visible blood vessels, on the right side of Detective Wind's penis, the little hand drove in the spike through to the other side, pinching only skin and depositing drops onto the husk of corn.

"That is for the impropriety of lust, sex without love, a deception of another," said Tia Maite to Detective Wind, who winced again as Carlito withdrew the spine and milked more blood down from the penis.

"Carlito!" she snapped again.

To the left of the penis he went this time, finding his spot and Detective Wind gritted as the spine went through another pinch of skin dropping blood from its tip to the husk below.

"And that is for the impropriety of love, loving without honesty, a deception of love itself." And as she said this, Carlito took his cue to remove the spine and after the husk was almost fully saturated in the sanguine flow, he whipped a white handkerchief from his pocket with the skill of an illusionist and wrapped it twice around the penis and tied a small knot. Although what she said to him was applicable to anyone, as it was also directed indiscriminately to everyone else in the room, Detective Wind thought through his pain that he had never heard his own inner charges read aloud by anyone else before.

"As we have drawn from this exceptionally filthy penitent tonight, the rest of you can draw from yourselves, extraigan ustedes mismos su propia sangre. It is ancient tradition to draw with spikes from the tongue and I empower you all to bite your own tongues to give your offering, muerdan libremente, pecadores," she said, and as soon as she spoke these words the pensive crowd ground their tongues and leaned in and around those before them to spit blood onto the husk between Detective Wind and Tia Maite. After everyone she followed, biting her own tongue, flicking it in the air like a snake before spitting to the husk on the floor. The rattles and the brooms stopped and everyone was silent with heads bowed and eyes closed and Detective Wind used his last remaining bits of strength to move his sweaty head to and fro, trying to see around the heads of the buffoon and hunchback, trying to see what was going on, what was about to happen. With no notice, and very swift movements, his captors released their grips at once letting him fall to his knees, his arms and legs numb and useless. In the thick hot silence he was slumped on the still cool concrete floor and watched Carlito approach to remove the imbrued husk. He rolled its soggy mass up like he was preparing a tortilla-wrapped meal and then hinged opened the metal grating on the floor where he deposited the wrap. Then the little person drew from the pocket of his short white pants a matchbox from which he delicately extracted a wooden stick match, and striking it, sent it into the drain after the husk. When the short strip of fire burst forth in front of the seated woman the rattles resumed their pounding course and the brooms gave dissonant accompaniment.

"Yo soy Ixcuina, the face of two colors. I am Tiacapan, Teicu, Tlaco, Xocutzin, las cuatro hermanas of the four cosmic trees, y las cuatro fases de la luna. I am Tlaelquani, eater of filth and vanity. Yo soy Tlazolteotl, the eater of shit, la comedora de la mierda, she who sinned before the ever-flooding waters," she roared with slight lisp, sound birthing like wet smoke from her throat and eyes burning red through the haze down to him before she turned slightly to her right and spat twice into a black crusty earthen bowl with tiny sharp cauldron legs that stood on the altar. She stabbed a shining obsidian pestle into the bowl and ground it fiercely down and around, hitting the depth and dragging the edges. Her rows of teeth grit against each other and breath hissed steamily through their enamel dust with each rising and falling eruption of her bosom as her pestle wielding hand continued to fuck the bowl and its thickening pungent contents.

Looking up from his knees he felt her massive bosom, horn-like nipples, and stomach bowl with his eyes and across the distance he could taste the sweat that ran down her neck, smell her teeming folds, hear her big heart beat in time with his own thundering cardio rhythms, and with each grind of her hand his penis jerked slightly with desire and returned again with pain. His mind was clear and following his body now, his agitation contracted to a point of great relaxation, riding sensations as they came to him with strength slowly returning to his body.

Releasing the pestle to the altar, she scooped with her right hand from the bowl a mock bitumen mixture of spit, coal, and blood and wiped it across her face from cheek to cheek around her mouth and chin. Her blacked mouth was the blacked mouth of the images surrounding her on the walls, the last component in her transformation. Still and seated, legs spread wide within her skirt, it was as if she was painted on the walls and the images were alive, and then she would move and she was alive and there was no difference between them.

"I, Tlazolteotl, have heard your words and have taken them in. I inhale your words like the itztli ehecatl, the obsidian wind, de todos usted, I sup on their blackness. This rite is more than one of confession, but a rite of devouring y Me he devorado sus pecados, your shit, and it is mine now, mio para convertirlo en tlazolli y tlalli. You fear me and my power, pero, por favor, continue to purify yourselves. This sin is the most ancient of things, part of the earth itself, beginning with time; it is part of time itself. An ancient word our ancestors have for sexo is tlalticpaccayotl, that which belongs to the surface of the earth. Es cosa sucia y es cosa natural, as are we all. My body is a gorge that does not swell, but will always take in more and more, always demanding, nunca satisfecho. Such is woman; such is the Goddess. When you all go forth from here you will be purified and reborn and will leave this deep place like you once left the wombs of your mothers, como nacido por segunda vez. Purge yourselves through abstinence for four days before I come back to you. Now we drink the drink of the moon and the drink of the earth, for it is said that Ome Tochtli, Conejo Dos, brought back pulque from the moon, but it is also seen pouring forth from the earth's ever swollen breasts and it is the blood of the maguey."

Everyone listened silently as she spoke, even Detective Wind kneeling on the floor, the rhythms of rattles and brooms flowing within her maternal phrasing, both frightening and nurturing, and already her lisp was becoming less noticeable due to the quick healing reflexes of her regularly abused tongue. With her mention of pulque, Carlito scurried to the rear of the room and back, ferrying little white measuring cups as used by dentists out amongst the standing congregation filled with a pungent milky liquid, with such ease that in only a few minutes everyone standing was holding a cup.

"Beban ahora y dejen que la leche de los Dioses repose dentro de sus bocas antes de tragar, letting it sting your wounds in punishment and purification," said Tia Maite, and everyone tipped back their cups and the rattling and sweeping abated.

When all had swallowed and all the dispensed pulque had run down the throats of those once filthy, but now pure, Carlito again scurried about the crowd, which was slowly dispersing towards the stairs, collecting the cups with the assistance of the hunchback and buffoon, more nimble than their size and shapes would indicate. At the top of the stairs a light came on with the ascension of the first to depart and below the rattlers and sweepers blew out each of the many candles in turn. Around the basement room, hunchback, buffoon, little person, two rattlers and two sweepers, all wearing white peasant pants and white shirts with embroidered collars looking gray, dusty, and tired, busied themselves with cleaning, breaking down candleholders, sweeping, and other deft actions more domestic than religious. An electrical stinging sound was followed by quick luminous sparks from the ceiling until full candescence of the room was reached with the reluctant arousal of the overhead fluorescent lights. Eduviges Dyada, having put on a sheer white shirt over her beads, walked up behind Tia Maite and wrapped a blanket over her broad moist shoulders and bosom. Reaching out her right hand daintily over where the pedestal used to be, she let Eduviges Dyada hold it and help her lift her girth up from the tight hold of the crescent moon chair. When she stood, the chair was removed from where it once sat and the room was almost fully emptied out by the routine efforts of the seven workers. The two women leaned in and kissed each other on both cheeks while holding hands loosely like sisters and whispered intimate goodbyes in Spanish and then the smaller one departed.

"Here," Tia Maite offered her hand to Detective Wind who took it and allowed her to help him to his feet where he brushed off his pants, retucked in his shirt, rolled down his sleeves, and wiped off his brow against the back of his forearm and hand.

"Ah, Detective Jonathan Wind, the newest member of my congregation. Wind, viento, it is such a beautiful word in Nahuatl, ehecatl, a strong word. It meant as much to the ancient Aztec as it does to the Europeans, to your people, to all people I would suppose. It is the breath of the gods, the gods themselves moving around invisible. It is the greatest mystery of life, this breath filling our lungs and bodies and then terrifying as it blows down trees and houses and ships at sea. And then it is also nothing, just wind, just air, just the movement of molecules as part of nature, just hot air, nothing," and she sighed and shrugged her shoulders. "So, Detective did you find here tonight what you were looking for?"

"I know Sutra set this up, but it appears you have been expecting me for some time. Would you like to now tell me what's going on?" said Detective Wind, sounding cool and professional like he was back on the job and had just experienced something customary for his line of work; still patting his brow and arranging his appearance of physical composure.

"Yes, you see, I knew who you were right away when you came in and your cards confirmed it. It was an amazing coincidence that you were seeing Flora, for I know your sister. I met her on several occasions. She was dating my grandson, José. It is all quite serendipitous, no? Feels like more than coincidence, the gods letting you know you are never alone, that life is not singular. Anyway, José, you don't know him, but he is a sweet boy, too sweet. Always doing favors for friends and those who are not friends. So sweet, people are drawn to him. He sings, writes poetry, plays the guitar. He is also drawn to all the sweet vices of poets, like drink and drugs. Not too bad with the drugs, but as I said he is always doing favors for those who are his friends and those who are not friends. Your sister and he have been inseparable for months. You would know if you paid her any attention. If you were not only working always, but also deceiving one woman and deceiving love with another woman. She broke down and spoke to me one day about how she felt so alone, from her mother, and from you. She told me a good deal about you and described you like Faust. It was so sweet, such a strong girl, crying like a child and then with such intelligence comparing her big brother to Faust and feeling so sad for him, moving around in his rooms full of books, so sad that he had sold his soul and heart in the pursuit of something or nothing, anything really, always pursuing, never able to rest or live or love, never real. She thought maybe you wouldn't be that way if your father was around, that maybe you were constantly pursuing for his approval that he was never there to give and your mother was oblivious. So strong, so smart. She even said she thought that was Faust's problem, the Enlightenment, if he had God and could accept God's love, he wouldn't have needed the Devil. I was so amused she called you Faust, so intelligent, but it makes sense if she was the little sister of a Faust. Carlito was impressed too," she rubbed the thin white hair of the little person standing next to her before proceeding.

"The Sunday before last, the 28th, when I found out that Astrid was headed with José for trouble I sent Carlito to tell you. 'Go give Faust the message that the sweet girl is in danger' and early that night before the purification ritual he went to find you at the police station, but he saw someone pick you up. He followed you and waited, he is so good. He even missed the ritual. Hearing Astrid talk about you and Faust had him reading the play. So when he went to deliver the message he thought that if you really were Faust then you would understand, and given the context of her trouble, he used the prison scene. It seems you didn't get it the first time so we had to try again in different translations. Little Carlito and my other messengers thought that that was a way to relate to you better, get you thinking, maybe make you think on multiple levels, use more than just your frontal rational mind. Sutra helped us, I saw her after your visit and we figured you would visit her eventually. It was easy to follow you too, a man on a mission but feeling around in the dark. Carlito predicted you would go to the library."

"But what about Flora? What does this have to do with her? What happened to her?" asked Detective Wind.

"You are a poor detective, Jonathan Wind. You do not find what you need to find because you look for what you want to be there, not what is actually there. This never had anything to do with Flora, it was about you, you and your sister," she said and shook her head slowly, condescendingly.

"Flora was here the night she died. She died in a very mysterious way after she left here, naked in her bedroom, burned completely from the inside out, nothing but dust and some teeth left. She saw herself as a sacred prostitute, like the ancient temple prostitutes of Babylon. Your goddess here, Tlazolteotl, is the goddess of sex and lust and purification, things Flora was interested in or otherwise she wouldn't have been here and you are trying to tell me there is no connection," Wind blew at her in hard gusts of breath.

"Do not bark at me Detective. I was Flora's friend, her confidant, her confessor. I had an honest open relationship with her. I have nothing to hide. You have coveted, you have lied, cheated, deceived, and ultimately betrayed. You walled off your dirty wet flesh pleasures in that room where she burned and denied them the light of life and truth.

You have denied your love in deception, it is the same as a blocked artery or colon, life cannot flow when it is denied," she could not help employing her counselor or priestess tone when she said such things.

"But this is not about me," he squinted at her with his head tilted as if questioning her confusion of the situation.

"No it is not about you, nothing is. You are just an observer, not a participant. You watch life, investigate it, but never have any participation or stake in it. She was a woman you loved and fortunately for you she became an investigation you could work on. Instead of working on your life, you can just make work your life. What, do you think what happened to her was some Aztec ritual? Just something poor Flora, needing to be saved by you, got herself into? Do you think we burned her, or she burned herself for something I told her, some ancient practice? There were other gods than Quetzalcoatl that helped out after the last destruction of the world and two of them, Nanahuatzin and Tecuciztecatl both burned themselves to become the new sun and moon. I don't believe that is what happened to Flora. I never told her that story, unless she found it on her own. She was a very fine girl, a lovely girl, but she was not an Aztec goddess. Maybe there is a part of you that is somehow grateful, some angry jealous masculine side, and legally, and in your job, you are even justified in such thoughts. She was a lawbreaker, a criminal, a prostitute, a whore, they spread disease and corrupt your cities. As it says in your Bible, a whore is made the most evil thing and she is slaughtered and burned and you scream Hallelujah and rejoice at her smoke. It is your tradition that has a history of burning whores, not mine. Is that what you imagined, a whore burning for her sins?"

"It's not my Bible, but I'm sure that you know that," he sighed, knowing at this point she was just trying to upset him. "But that is why I am here. I don't imagine anything is going on that I don't have evidence for. I came for answers, you saw her last the night she died, she was here, right? She went home after your purification ritual, a ritual involving cleansing, the purifying of lust and sexual misconduct, liquor and fire. A ritual I am wondering now if she could have tried on her own. So, I look to you for answers. What happened to her?" He was firm and calm, not mean, but with forced, frustrated patience, just imploring and unwavering in his tone and eye-contact.

"What happened, I don't know. She was a seeker, like you, a damned seeker. Always another group or goddess or mystery she pursued, like you with investigations. But I don't know what happened to her. There are many mysteries in this universe, in nature. Do you think you can understand them all? Who do you think you are? Because you love someone, you lost someone, nature will then be laid bare to you in all of her secrets? Things happen and most of the time it is not for you to know. There was a fire, she is dead, gone, it is sad, I will miss her, so will you, and so will others. Her life meant nothing if it didn't mean anything to you. I am sorry, but not everything is explainable. You shouldn't bother with these things, she wouldn't. She left here healthy, purified. It was the same ritual you saw, except, well, we did it a little differently for you," she tried to suppress a smile itching at the corners of her wide mouth. "Normally we allow more individual confessions and do not pierce the genitals, that was just for you. I felt you needed a little more encouragement towards participation. The night she was last here she bit her tongue like the rest and even stayed after to help us clean up. She kissed me on the cheek and left a little after one-thirty to drive herself home. She was not scared and she was scheduled to come to her appointment the next day. She was lovely as ever, glowing in perspiration from the heat and the ritual. As far as I know, it was just something that happened. I do not say accident because there are no accidents, everything fits into the plan of nature, of the gods, but sadly they and their schemes are beyond us. Try as we might, we will never know as much as them.

"What I wonder," she paused and sweetened her tone and deepened her accent. "What I wonder most is, do you search for these answers because you want nature to be neat and tidy, for every question an answer? Or is this some way of holding on to her, knowing she is gone, out of missing her? Maybe you think this is all you have to give her, what you do, your job, an investigation? Maybe that is the only way you know how to love? But I do not know, I am just an old woman. Part of some pagan cult, a fortuneteller, not educated like you," and she ended with a smile and lowered eyes.

"Thank you, I guess I have nothing more to ask you. I believe you, I believe you have told me all that you know," he said flat and evenly, hiding all emotions just beneath the surface of his skin and breath. He turned towards the side stairs to go, but Tia Maite stopped him with a hand on his shoulder.

"Detective," she said softly, and he turned. She kissed him on both cheeks and then let him go.

18. REVELATION

You're an Idiot Wind... it's a wonder that you still know how
to breath...   —"Idiot Wind," Bob Dylan
                                (formerly Robert Zimmerman)

IN THE DARKEST DARK OF THE PRE-DAWN DARK, DETECTIVE SERGEANT
Jonathan Wind finds his way by the distant light he has been walking
towards for what feels like a very long time. The longed for scintillation
is emitted from the plastic crown of a street lamp on top of the hill,
up from the valley out of which he is climbing. It feels to him that it
has taken forever to climb this steep hill and he longs for the glowing
ring at its top and what lies just beyond that limited horizon. That
distant point, just another horizon, not the first, not the last, is enough
to work towards, as he puffs air in and out of his worn and tired body.
He pats reflexively at his pockets but only winds up sending needles
of pain back through his penis; he cannot find a Pez dispenser and
quickly gives up looking. The sound of the occasional car is nothing to
him, a swelling whizzing coming up behind or before, golden headlights on his back or from the front then gone in passing by in their
way. Through red eyes he is fixed on the plastic yellow glow, calm and
cold and reliable in the essence of its construction and lambency. The

empty offices within the empty houses he passes are nothing to him, with no beckoning sound or smell or concern, and as he cuts his boots on the inclining worn asphalt speckled with roughness, his suspirations release ritual-ridden warmth against and into the cool molecules of night air; like a khamsin against a mistral, wind upon more wind, just movement in no shape of all shapes, and energy in all directions.

When he walked out the same cellar door of Tia Maite's by which he entered, he checked his mobile phone, crossing around the back damp dewy lawn, and found a message from his partner. Sonny had found his sister. He said she had been arrested out in Hall County with her boyfriend and some of his friends. They were buying cocaine and got busted. If only Wind had let Astrid be printed other times she was picked up, Sonny said, finding her would have been a lot easier; they would have had her in the system and known who she was. She only had a fake ID on her, a real driver's license she borrowed from a friend and otherwise never told them her real name. Wind could go post bail and pick her up, and he should. Now his job and his life actions could actually help one he loved, but in some ways too late, and so late that he must now help as a police officer, because he didn't help earlier as a loved one. Over the lustrum since he joined the force, his hunger for truth and certainty, when it came to closing any investigation or inquiry, had been implacable. Never doldrums for Wind, in his work he weathered and controlled the elephanta monsoons, scorching harmattans, and blinding siroccos of humanity mid-wretch with the ease of a well-educated and well-armed modern Aeolus. But now he worried whether it was all he was good for and he knew it wasn't enough; not the wholeness of self he once felt it provided; for that too would wash away, an ability for deduction and connection-finding nothing more than a voice in a downdraft, gone.

She was right, Tia Maite was right, he thought. She was right about everything. Everything was right there before him, but that wasn't where he was looking. He wasn't looking where things were, but where he wanted them to be. He was done. The narrative he had created for himself was over. He sought information and then, through that, knowledge. He now had the knowledge he wanted. He knew what Flora had been doing with her time, her last exploration, her last rites. What he was left with, though, was not the certainty he pursued. Where was truth when he had all the facts, the details, and still there was no explanation for her death? He could never get into her bedroom that night, never see how she burned up, see what happened in those last solitary moments. She was lost in all ways, even beyond his understanding, and he was left without, and without truth. She too will blow and wash away as her body and spirit are no more than ash cast to the wind.

He wasted his love, he thought. If he had ever loved. He hoped he had. He hoped it was real. He felt its absence, the space from which it had been removed, from which she had been removed. But he didn't know what else to put in that place now. What else would fit? Work had proved incommodious. He housed this hole, but the depth of the void felt infinite. When he called out into it, bellowed, screamed into it, there was no return. If his pang-sound, his williwaw wail, reached a boundary, it died on its way back to him. His loss couldn't even be qualified by an echo. Totally fearless, tears fell to his cheeks, seeds to turned soil, holy water to cool granite, turning granite gray to brown, with a moist sheen; tears so laden with purpose and past, so heavy and full, that his weight fell with them and his frame was loose and free.

He cried as he walked, but it wasn't as though a dam was breaking, his tears were a slow seep that he would fight if he could, and part of him almost wished he could, but there was no longer the energy or certainty of deed to resist them. Rolling off of him like rain from a porous statue, at the moment they were what was most alive in him, all he had to give. Like that porous statue, their flow would eventually stop, it must, and he knew that; and he knew that those tears would be washed away by time and wind against that statue. He acknowledged the crickets with their pulsing night cries and the distant call of the cicadas fighting to be heard by anyone and those sounds of nature were just another cleansing wash at his wounds of pride, conscience, and consciousness; stimuli like an anemometer judging the amount of life still in him.

He had sense enough not to wipe his eyes on his sleeves or shirt tails for fear that their post-purge fragility had left them open for irritation and irascibility from all the smoke and scent-bearing simooms that had wafted and counterwafted like dust devils about his lithe and wispish form. In the car there was a tissue, he thought, and crossing the grass then street he was at his car. In the car he wiped his eyes, and he controlled the vortex of artificially cool air, a levanter running between the seats, comfort from control and undeniably artificial. Driving added the freedom to move, the wings of passage for his tired feet.

In all his chattering and blathering of wind, the blustery and blubbery cross-currents through his mind and cooling body, decompressing afloat through the empty night, he saw the distant hill over which Tia Maite's office stood in his rearview mirror, like a distant invisible star still emitting, and he promised himself, convinced himself, that he would rather her than truth; he could rest in her as he had before, rest his understanding and certainty on her and her love. But this conviction and promise was moot in the light of the dark night in which he found himself. Northeast he drove, a settling of matters with a new destination, a new destination for a very old love and duty, the oldest he had known; and outside the controlled environment of his car a world raged wildly, clockwise and counterclockwise, anticyclone and cyclone around him, with him, and regardless of him, as it always did and his inner world returned to the keen focus of mind as it always did with pressure neither high nor low.

The great snake stretches and tightens, the old turtle yawns, the leaves on the tree rattle and blow, and the invisible autumn is ever alive. As the white man came as predicted, like a trickster unchained, and snipped each rawhide thread in turn, which suspended the earth from its four corners like a basket, the Weaver Woman, Tlazolteotl, made her move behind, retying in their endless path. In the rolling shift of balance, the stone of Sisyphus lolled up and down, and the waters rose to cover everything but two, and they were naked, rolling into and out of each other, man and woman. The earth dipped, the waters covered, and the two as one rose and multiplied and dipped to die to rise again and multiply. From the four corners suspended by retied threads wind came, coming and becoming, one blow around all directions, four sets of cheeks cracked, swollen, puffed, pursed, and pushing. The flood tide swelled and died, killing and ebbing. Wind continued to blow, and it was breath, it was nothing, and that is all. They play together, eternal forces, rolling, top to bottom, wet to wind, airborne tears, sweat, sperm, and blood, they milk each other to mist and it all washed away.

Over the waters wind carried and in the instant, that eternal instant, when the land was free and the two are one and buildings rose and their towers smoked and burned and pictures hung on walls, of angels and families, loved and loving, and cars rolled on streets that stretch beyond the eye and words of love were attached to things which cannot last and the naked danced in circles and flames burned beyond comprehension and wind will carry on.

And when it all begins to drop, and the thread is snipped before reunion, and it all begins to tilt that way, through the flames, descending, and wind blows within all and around all and all that was and once will be and wind is there behind the way and all is swiftly turning, burning, and the waters rise and all that is not lost is living in the beat of the flame and like the two as one, they are one flame and there is only one flame and wind is fueling the fire burning, yearning, and all that are dying know nothing, now nothing, and hope and then there is the end again and wind will wash away.

ACKNOWLEDGMENTS

THE BULK OF THIS BOOK WAS WRITTEN DURING THE COURSE OF AN MA in Religion at the University of Georgia. Although it was actively begun after the completion of my undergraduate degree at Manhattanville College, the germ of the idea for many of the characters and concepts was planted at that institution; a place where I made great connections and great use of my time. Accordingly, I thank: Dr. Raymond Langley for the mentoring, the philosophy, and the image of a man; Dr. Peter Gardella for the mentoring and all the religions; Carlos Santiago for the Spanish and IT support and for lending his birthday, skepticism, and rationality; Dr. Carolyn Jones Medine for her inspiration in transcending the Academy; Dr. Glenn Wallis for his encouragement and Buddhism. For research in the field, I am indebted to: Scott Medine for the police procedure technical advice and reading; Goddess Freyja for her trust in letting me interview her, the bevy of information, and the character she inspired; and several other unnamed sources across Atlanta.

The bellows that support this flawed and creaky book-producing machine are operated by so many wonderful friends and family, and to them I give my loving appreciation: Ariane and Clint (and John and Catherine) Walden; Dad and Jody; Jonathan and Emily (and Ada) Polk; Matt and Shawn McKinney; Tanya and Andy (and Cecilie) Frazee; Brian and Anna Grace; Gail Polk; Travis and Susie Burch; Michael Petri; Amy and Adrienne Gandolfi; Melissa Leahy; Micheal Karczewski; Daniel and Tiffany (and Elijah) Chameides; Kai Reidl; West Price; Neil Graff; Mark Hewitt; James Treadway; Reg McKnight; William and Crystal (and Quentin and Greyson) Brandon; and my sincerest apologies to anyone I've left out.

Most of all, the book you're holding in your hands couldn't exist without the good people at Deeds Publishing. Thank you to the whole Babcock family, Bob, Jan, and Mark; thank you Matt King for making me look so good; and thank you Mark and Matt for making my cover look so good. David Ingle, you were an essential and insightful editor.

Special thanks to William T. Vollmann for his friendship, his fiction, his advice, and his model of "the writer" (and human) to which I have aspired.

ABOUT THE AUTHOR

JORDAN A. ROTHACKER LIVES IN ATHENS, GA WHERE HE EARNED A Doctorate in Comparative Literature and a Masters in Religion from the University of Georgia. Rothacker majored in Philosophy at Manhattanville College in Purchase, NY, and his life has been split between New York (where he was born) and Georgia. His journalism has appeared in periodicals as diverse as *Vegetarian Times* and *International Wristwatch* while his fiction, poetry, and essays can be found in the likes of *Red River Review*, *Dark Matter*, *Dead Flowers*, *Stone Highway Review*, *Mayday Magazine*, *As It Ought to Be*, and *The Exquisite Corpse*. 2015 saw his first published book-length work, *The Pit, and No Other Stories*, a novella (or "micro-epic" as he calls it) from Black Hill Press. His fiction can also be found in *The Cost of Paper: II* (2015) and *The Cost of Paper: III* (2016), anthologies from Black Hill Press edited by William M. Brandon III. He loves sandwiches (a category in which he classifies pizza and tacos) and debating taxonomy almost as much as much as he loves his wife, his dogs, and his cat, Whiskey.

WWW.JORDANROTHACKER.COM